MISUNDERSTANDINGS & ARDENT LOVE

SUSAN ADRIANI

Quills & Quartos
PUBLISHING

Edited by Kristi Rawley and Katie Jackson

Cover Design by CloudCat Design

ISBN 978-1-951033-89-7 (ebook) and 978-1-951033-90-3 (paperback)

For Uncle Dick, who told us the most interesting stories, and for my mother, who was always there to listen to mine.

I

WHERE MR DARCY IS NOT ENJOYING HIS
EVENING.

November 1812

The stifling temperature of the ballroom was unbearable with the incessant crush of elegantly dressed bodies, the loud thrum of conversation, and several roaring fires, which, despite the crisp autumn weather, were hardly needed. Standing with his back to the richly papered wall, Fitzwilliam Darcy of Pemberley sighed as he slipped his index finger beneath his collar and tugged impatiently at the impeccably tied cravat about his neck. Finding no relief, he hailed a passing servant and accepted a glass of wine. He drank deeply, attempting to quench his irritation as well as his thirst.

Not for the first time that evening an excess of practiced laughter from a gaggle of finely dressed ladies grated on his last nerve, and Darcy wondered why he had ever allowed his aunt, the Countess of Carlisle, to drag him to Lord and Lady Palmers' for such a function. He was in no mood for cards or conversation and felt even less of an inclination to dance.

Darcy absently swirled the contents of his wine glass while his eyes moved with measured deliberation over the fashionable throng. Not one person in attendance sparked a desire to forge a more intimate acquaintance. He stiffened as he noticed too many discerning eyes turned upon him. A disturbing number belonged to those of the female persuasion. Frowning, Darcy fixed his attention upon the burgundy liquid in his glass and allowed his mind to wander.

His thoughts, as always, settled upon the one woman whose admiration he would not consider it a punishment to endure: Miss Elizabeth Bennet. Since that fateful day last April when his declaration of love to her had been met with abhorrence and rejection, Darcy had suffered keenly.

Elizabeth's refusal was a painful reality for him, and a subject he found himself revisiting daily; one that had, even now, remained as permanent and unwavering as his continued attachment to her proved powerful. Never had Darcy been denied something he truly wanted, and he found this lesson in humility far more humbling than he ever could have imagined. His sentiments and his heart were wholly affected, both deeply marred by Elizabeth's reproachful words and refusal of her hand. Whether awake or asleep, her very memory threatened his peace of mind.

Looking back, he realised he had never entertained the slightest possibility that Elizabeth Bennet might reject him. That an unknown, untitled, unconnected country miss with no fortune or prospects to speak of would dare reject his suit was, to a man as wealthy and coveted as Fitzwilliam Darcy of Pemberley, unthinkable; but it was the shock he experienced when Elizabeth had spoken of her dislike of him that dealt the most staggering blow. She did not return his ardent admiration, nor his passionate regard. In fact, she had told him in no uncertain terms that she had never sought his good opinion in the first place, nor had it escaped her notice that Darcy had bestowed it upon her most unwillingly.

Darcy's heart felt heavier and more constricted than it had moments before. How on earth could he have been so unfeeling as to tell her of his struggles—of his failed attempts to overcome his regard for her? What demon ever possessed him to inform the woman he loved that an alliance with her must be considered a reprehensible connexion, a degradation? How could such insults ever cross his mind, let alone leave his mouth? *God in heaven, she was justified in her response!*

Vividly, he recalled the anger that flashed in Elizabeth's eyes as she berated him, not only for his arrogance and his insults, but for a multitude of grievances he had supposedly perpetrated against others for whom she cared, the least of which happened to be his officious interference in separating her eldest sister from his friend Charles Bingley.

Darcy closed his eyes at that recollection. He certainly had been officious in that matter. Again and again, he asked himself what right had he to arrange the lives of two people to suit his own purpose? The answer was as consistent as it was painful: none.

He had since made his confession to Bingley. Though his friend was initially furious with him for his presumption, the information Darcy related regarding Miss Bennet's continued partiality had put Bingley in an extremely forgiving mood; he had hastened to Longbourn and declared himself to the woman he loved within the span of an hour. The smile on Bingley's face when he returned to Netherfield that night had spoken volumes. Not only had Jane Bennet welcomed his addresses, but they were to be married on the twenty-sixth of November in Longbourn Church.

As far as Elizabeth's other accusation, that Darcy had mistreated and wronged his former childhood friend, George

Wickham's true nature and dissolute tendencies had eventually emerged in full force, though far too late and at much too high a cost to allow Darcy to feel any vindication over Elizabeth's enlightenment.

Lydia Bennet and George Wickham were now safely married, thank God, though whether happily Darcy would forever retain a doubt. It had both sickened and infuriated him to stand in church and witness Elizabeth's fifteen-year-old sister pledge her obedience to such a worthless reprobate for the rest of her life, but if there had been another solution to the mess in which Lydia found herself, Darcy had failed to recognise it.

The knowledge that Elizabeth would suffer keenly for the impulsivity and impropriety of her most foolish sister was difficult for Darcy to bear, especially given that he had the means to bring about her relief. And so, he handled it all.

While he had counted on Lydia's marriage to do much for Elizabeth's peace of mind regarding her family's reputation, Darcy was appalled to discover that her mother's enthusiasm for Mrs Wickham's newly married status did nothing but cause further distress. He could not help but wonder whether he had only succeeded in making another grave error in judgment. The more time he spent in Elizabeth's company when last in Hertfordshire, the more deeply he believed that was precisely what he had achieved. There was no longer a sparkle in her eyes, no joy in her step, no laughter bubbling up. For three days Elizabeth barely even looked in his direction. On the few occasions she did meet his eye, it was only to colour deeply and look away in poorly contained distress.

To make matters worse, Bingley and his amiability were received at Longbourn with immense pleasure and much fanfare; Darcy and his reserve were not, as was evident by the cool civility shown to him by Mrs Bennet during his visits. He could not in all honesty say he was surprised. After all, even he must own he had done little to make himself agreeable to the neighbourhood the previous autumn, and no one in residence there—including the Bennets—had any idea it was to him that the principal family of the village was indebted for the restoration of their good name.

After enduring countless days of silence from Elizabeth and varying degrees of incivility from her mother, Darcy arrived at a painful conclusion: there was nothing for him in Hertfordshire. The village, the town, the entire neighbourhood believed both Netherfield gentlemen guilty of caprice; and while the good people of Hertfordshire seemed capable of forgiving Bingley's past transgressions, they were apparently not as willing to oblige Darcy for his.

With a heavy heart Darcy informed Bingley of his intention to leave for London. Though his friend saw him go with regret and had since written to request his company once more at Netherfield, Darcy simply could not bring himself to face Elizabeth again. It was difficult enough seeing her in his dreams—her eyes darkened with passion, tempting him as she whispered words of love and devotion—but to meet her again after all that had taken place, knowing all hope of gaining her regard and her hand was now lost to him forever, proved too painful. Perhaps it was cowardice on his part, perhaps it was shame; Darcy chose to remain in town.

To his dismay, Colonel Fitzwilliam, who appeared less pleased with his evening than Darcy would have expected, joined him then. Unlike his taciturn cousin, the colonel was usually at ease in company, as he did not mind in the least that his status as an earl's son often made him an object of interest for a multitude of eligible ladies.

Darcy quickly schooled his features into a semblance of composure and took a fortifying drink from his glass. His hand was only slightly unsteady as his stoic mask slid back into place. "Are you not dancing?"

Colonel Fitzwilliam snorted as he raised his own glass to his lips and glowered at the assembled crowd. "I believe I am not yet foxed enough. Her ladyship persists in her insistence that I patronise Miss Cromwell and her grandfather Lord Everett this evening. I confess I have not the stomach for it."

Darcy frowned. "Surely there is another lady better suited to your disposition and taste of whom Lady Carlisle approves?"

The colonel scoffed. "I may be sent to the Continent, and my mother is frantic to see me resign my commission. In her desperation to impose her will upon me she has decided that Miss Cromwell, her fifty thousand pounds, ties to the earldom, and seven unsuccessful past Seasons will be the best way to expedite her wishes. I fail to see how such a hasty arrangement of my most intimate concerns shall ever ensure the happiness of either myself or the lady in question. My father, thank God, is attempting to relieve her ladyship of her mistaken notion, although by no means fast enough for my liking."

He gave Darcy a pointed look. "You should know that my mother's machinations encompass your own felicity as well. Lady Harrow is here somewhere with her daughter, Lady Eliza. It is rumoured they have taken a house in Park Street—a little too close for comfort if you ask me, but my mother is certainly pleased. You know she has long considered Lady Eliza an advantageous match for you."

Darcy stiffened. "I have no interest in Lady Eliza. Your mother and hers would do well to abandon their efforts."

"At least *she* is handsome," the colonel grumbled, turning his attention to his wine. "You can hardly say as much for my own prospect this evening. Her ample dowry aside, I suppose even Miss Cromwell must possess at least one winsome quality." He chuckled crudely and drained his glass, grimacing at the finish. "Whatever it is, I shall never discover it, for it is most likely well-concealed beneath one of her chins."

Darcy shot him a disapproving look. While Miss Cromwell was known to possess as hearty an appetite as many gentlemen of their acquaintance, she was from a respectable family. "Take care, Cousin, or you will find yourself on the wrong end of Lord Everett's pistol. You know as well as I that physical beauty often goes no deeper than a cursory level."

"Cursory smursory. Of the two, Lady Eliza is the most preferable prospect, especially if one wants to beget an heir."

Darcy snorted. "You are welcome to her, but *your* heir would be the silliest in England. I have never known a young woman with such ill-formed opinions. Her mother is little better, though I cannot help but find her society even more intolerable than her daughter's."

Smirking, Colonel Fitzwilliam raised his empty glass in a mock toast. "Now who risks facing pistols at dawn? I know you detest the woman, Darcy—and with good reason—but you can hardly fault her for wanting to make an advantageous match for her daughter. After all, what mother does not want to see her daughter well settled? There are many here who would stop at nothing to secure a husband, though I admit I have rarely seen a woman so willing to do *quite* so much to further a match for her daughter as Lady Harrow."

Unbidden, Mrs Bennet came to mind and Darcy frowned. His cousin was correct—there were plenty of mothers who wanted nothing more than to see their daughters advantageously wed, but what a difference he now recognised between Elizabeth's mother and the more resourceful matrons of the *ton* who were, without a doubt, far better acquainted with the intricate workings of the world! When compared to the duplicity and scheming employed by most of the ladies in the first circles of society in their pursuit of a rich husband, Mrs Bennet's machinations appeared almost demure.

Not only was Lady Harrow one of the most cunning of the lot, she was also the most persistent. Even before her husband's death, it was rumoured there was little she was unwilling to do to obtain what she desired, as Darcy well knew from his own past encounters with the woman; but unlike Mrs Bennet, whose manoeuvrings were born of affection and motivated by real concern for her daughters' futures, Lady Harrow was driven by covetousness, greed, and a baser instinct of which Darcy had never approved, especially in a lady.

"I cannot fault any mother for wishing to secure a future for her daughters, but that woman is as base as they come. Her scheming is for herself alone. I cannot abide such singular selfishness. There are other ladies far more deserving of notice from a gentleman of honour, despite their standing in society."

Chuckling, Colonel Fitzwilliam eyed his cousin with a raised brow. "You are feeling charitable I see. That is well and good, but you cannot tell me that when faced with the prospect of marriage to some untitled miss with a meagre dowry or the daughter of an earl, you would choose the untitled miss. I daresay even you would act with more prudence than what your words imply. After all, you can hardly expect an unknown young thing to step into your mother's shoes and act the part of Pemberley's mistress in the manner that would be expected of her. Granted, I suppose she could be taught, but why go through the trouble when there is already an abundance of well-trained young women in town?"

Darcy started at this pronouncement. "Good Lord, Fitzwilliam, you sound like your father. Surely, you believe there exists within our circle a gentleman who craves the companionship and admiration of a sensible lady over the shallow attentions and insincere tittering of the *bon ton*—a man who desires a woman of intelligence and discernment who esteems him for his intellect and his merits rather than his property and the heft of his purse?"

"I imagine most of us would prefer to unite ourselves with a woman of sense and sensitivity as well as beauty," the colonel replied, "but you and I have lived enough in the world to know that finding each of those desirable qualities in one lady is hardly probable, and so I know I must sacrifice certain traits in favour of others. I am afraid my habits shall dictate I marry a handsome woman whose equally handsome income will support me in the style to which I have grown accustomed. You must do the same and you know it. You cannot possibly over-look a woman like Lady Eliza to pay your addresses to, say, a lady with Miss Bennet's situation."

Darcy felt a rush of indignation and, before he could check himself, blurted, "What can you possibly find to object to in Miss Bennet? You appeared to enjoy her company while you were in Kent, with no one else on hand to amuse you except Lady Catherine and our cousin Anne. I vividly recall you admiring Miss Bennet on more than one occasion, a wistful look upon your face and pretty words falling from your lips as you attended her while she played, dined, walked about the grounds—"

"Easy, Darcy. It is true. I cannot deny it. I found nothing wanting in the lady's appearance, manners, or the turn of her mind and did not mean to imply otherwise. No one admitted to the privilege of knowing Miss Bennet would find anything to criticise. I meant only to point out that her situation in life is hardly ideal. One of five daughters—all of them out—with nothing more than five thousand pounds between them, not to mention an entailment hanging over their heads and a high-strung mother? No sane man would do it."

Livid, Darcy shook his head. "So, Miss Bennet was nothing more than sport for you? A pleasant diversion while you whiled away your time at Rosings? You would flirt with her, toy with her, but nothing more! Even if you were a first son and in possession of your brother's fortune, you mean to tell me you would not consider making her an offer of marriage? You would choose to take a girl such as Lady Eliza, with her hefty fortune and empty head, to wife rather than Miss Bennet—a bright, attractive, well-informed young woman who is in every way her superior, save for her woeful dowry and lack of a title!"

His cousin gaped at him. "What the devil has gotten into you?" he asked, indicating a group of matrons across the room whose keen eyes were fixed upon Darcy with eager expectation. "For the love of God, lower your voice, or else half of London shall overhear you."

It was not so much the harshness of Colonel Fitzwilliam's reproach that made Darcy blanch, but the realisation that he had very nearly allowed his temper to get the better of him in front of an audience; an audience for whom his prior perfor-mances had always been carried out with painstaking neutrality and indifference. He exhaled a harsh breath and tugged at his cravat, which felt as tight as a hangman's noose. *This blasted heat must be making me mad. This blasted heat and Elizabeth Bennet!*

With some effort, he composed himself enough to put a rein on his heightened emotions and speak with civility. "Forgive me," he muttered, and drained the last mouthful of wine from his glass. He needed to away, and sooner than later, or else risk saying or doing something truly regrettable.

From the corner of his eye, he could see Fitzwilliam regarding him with a look of grave concern. "Darcy," he said, but Darcy only waved him off, set his empty glass upon a nearby table, and turned on his heel. His long strides were quick as he wove his way through the crowded drawing room and out of the door.

❦ 2 ❦

WHERE ELIZABETH BENNET IS REGRETFUL.

T he hour was late. Shadows danced along the narrow halls of Longbourn House, the walls dappled by the unearthly glow of a full moon. Upstairs a lone candle burned low as Elizabeth Bennet curled her toes beneath her nightshift and settled into one of two upholstered chairs flanking the hearth. A warm fire crackled in the grate, banked for the night by a servant. Its flames lapped at the logs within.

With slender fingers she caressed the well-worn sheets of paper cradled in her hand as though attempting to touch the very soul of the author himself. Despite the warmth of the room, a shiver ran through her body. As her eyes devoured the neatly formed— and by now painfully familiar—lines her mind wandered to the exact moment when he had first placed the letter into her hands in the grove at Rosings Park.

Fitzwilliam Darcy.

Elizabeth traced each letter of his signature with tenderness. She had treated him with such contempt and insolence then, having thrown his proposal of marriage—as arrogant and insulting as his words had been—back in his face with a vengeance, and in the next breath accused him of such wretched wrongdoing against a scoundrel of a man whom she must now call her brother.

While she had not been insensible of the compliment Darcy had paid her with the bestowal of his addresses, it wasn't until many months had passed that Elizabeth came to fully appreciate that which she had so readily scorned: the affection and esteem of a man who, despite his excessive pride and arrogant assumptions, had somehow come to love her well enough to throw off the expectations and wishes of his family and his peers by asking for the hand of an impertinent, penniless daughter of a country gentleman of little consequence.

Four months later she and Darcy happened to meet again in Derbyshire on Pemberley's exalted grounds. Elizabeth was horrified to have him discover her there, of all places—but the Fitzwilliam Darcy who stood before her then was entirely different from the gentleman she had previously known. Gone were his abominable pride, conceit, and hauteur as he not only welcomed her, but sought her opinion of the house and the park and, even more astonishing, her approval. When he turned towards her aunt and uncle and politely requested an introduction, Elizabeth hardly knew what to think.

Never had she seen him so desirous to please, so free from self-consequence or unbending reserve as he was then. She could hardly account for such an alteration in his manners. Could her reproofs at Hunsford have inspired such a transformation in so great and proud a man? Such a possibility filled her with bewilderment and flooded her with unexpected warmth. In half an hour he had shown her a completely different side of himself, and it had come as a most welcome surprise.

But Lydia's thoughtlessness soon put an end to any possibility of intimacy between them. After confiding her family's disgrace to Darcy in a moment of weakness and witnessing his grave countenance and eagerness to be gone, Elizabeth felt certain she would never see him again.

Not a full month later, her wonder continued as Mr Bingley returned to Netherfield Park after a lengthy absence of ten months that had taken on the appearance of permanency. To Elizabeth, it could mean but one thing: Darcy had taken it upon himself to speak to his friend, for what else could have inspired such a drastic turn of events? Such was her shock when three days later Mr Bingley was spotted riding up Longbourn's drive accompanied by another gentleman. Elizabeth stilled in her chair when one of her sisters identified the figure as that belonging to 'the same proud, disagreeable man' who had been with him before: Mr Darcy.

How she had gotten through that visit she knew not, for her mortification had been great and in the form of her mother as Mrs Bennet regaled her guests with the news of Lydia's recent marriage. How Darcy looked Elizabeth hardly knew, for she could not bear to raise her eyes to his face. Why had she not kept Lydia's shame to herself when he had called upon her that wretched day at the inn in Lambton? Whatever possessed her to tell Darcy her family's most shocking news?

Perhaps, if she had held her tongue then, things would now have been very different between them. Perhaps he would have renewed his addresses, though she could hardly imagine that Darcy, who was wronged so unjustly by Wickham in the past, would ever be able to reconcile himself to forming such a connexion to such a man, no matter how ardently he had once proclaimed to love her.

He stayed but a week before quitting Hertfordshire for London, and without taking his leave of his friends at Longbourn. Elizabeth remained in perpetual ignorance of his whereabouts until she finally mustered the courage to enquire of Bingley, who was now to be her brother, whether Darcy remained at Netherfield. Bingley managed to tear his eyes from her sister Jane's fair countenance long enough to inform them all that his friend had gone away to see to some matters of business but would return in ten days' time.

Those ten days came and went with no sign of Darcy. All hope for Elizabeth soon came to an end when she learnt he had written to his friend and informed him his business had yet to be completed and that he did not foresee himself returning to the area as planned. It could mean but one thing: Elizabeth's power over him had sunk.

Elizabeth's thoughts, her hopes, her wishes were every minute turned towards the memory of the tall, reticent man whose penetrating eyes haunted her. Even the colourful leaves and golden hues of the autumn landscape failed to hold her interest and raise her spirits as they had in years past. They served instead as a harsh reminder that winter would soon be upon Longbourn, bringing freezing temperatures that would mean lengthy periods of confinement to the house. Unlike in years past, there would be no beloved Jane to bring her comfort.

In her melancholy, Elizabeth spent many solitary hours roaming the countryside visiting favourite retreats and contemplating the turn her sentiments had taken since that fateful April day in Kent. Why was it, after so many months of reflection, that she now saw with absolute clarity how perfectly suited they were for each other? Darcy's understanding and temper, though unlike her own, would have answered all her wishes. By her ease and liveliness his mind might have been softened, his manners improved; and by his judgment, information, and knowledge of the world Elizabeth would have received benefit of even greater importance. All hope was now in vain; all wishes for another chance for naught. Darcy's present actions—or lack thereof—spoke volumes. Surely, if he loved her still, he would not stay away. The taste of her disappointment was bitter.

In her bedchamber the candle beside her sputtered and flared. Elizabeth pulled her shawl tighter about her shoulders, closed her eyes, and laid her head against the back of her chair. "What a fool I have been," she whispered to herself as she laid the pages of her letter upon her lap. "How could I have been so blind as not to have seen it all before?"

Submersed in her disappointment she silently mourned not only that which she had lost, but that which she now desired more than anything else in the world: the esteem, the admiration, the ardent devotion of the one man who was now lost to her forever.

"Lizzy?"

The sound of Jane's gentle voice drifted into Elizabeth's subconscious and encircled her like a comfortable shroud. Her tone was warm and reassuring, and for just a few moments Elizabeth recalled nothing of Darcy, her disappointment, or her heartache. Her eyelids fluttered open to meet her sister's concerned countenance, illuminated by a glowing wax taper.

"Dearest," Jane said as she tucked a loose strand of hair behind her sister's ear, "come to bed. You cannot spend the entire night in this chair."

Elizabeth exhaled tiredly and looked towards the window, where nothing but darkness was visible through the lace curtains. Her own candle had long since died and the fire was nothing more than hot coals and a few glowing embers. Resigned, she gathered the loose pages scattered upon her lap and folded them neatly, then walked to the bedside table to secret her precious letter within a favourite book of poems before placing both items into the top drawer.

Feeling her sister's steady gaze upon her, Elizabeth forced a half-hearted smile to her lips as she discarded her shawl and loosened the belt of her dressing gown. It did little to mask her sombre mood. "Forgive me. There is so much to be done that I found it difficult to sleep for all the thoughts that are running through my head. I must have drifted off despite it all." She climbed into bed and pulled the counterpane to her chin.

Jane extinguished the candle with a quick breath and the room plunged into darkness. A moment later the bed frame creaked, and the mattress sank a bit lower as Jane joined her.

"Goodnight," Elizabeth murmured, rolling onto her side, purposely turning her back to her sister. She closed her eyes and silently willed a steady, dreamless slumber to descend upon her.

The bed groaned as Jane moved closer and laid her chin upon Elizabeth's shoulder. "Please, Lizzy," she whispered, her voice distressed. "Will you not finally speak of it to me?"

Elizabeth opened her eyes and repressed a sigh of irritation. Long shadows danced upon the wall before her, ethereal and elegant; ghostly images that resembled figures swaying in scandalous proximity—hands, arms, bodies entwined, perhaps in the act of a waltz. Though she had yet to see the fashionable dance performed, Elizabeth knew something of what it entailed and had often wondered what it would feel like to have a gentleman's hand—*his* hand—placed firmly upon her waist, holding her so closely and in so familiar and intimate a fashion for the duration of an entire dance.

Jane shifted her weight upon the bed and Elizabeth quickly recalled herself. "Speak of what?" she asked, her voice subdued, though her complexion was heightened.

"Whatever it is that is making you so unhappy. You cannot deny that you are otherwise, for I see it in you."

"There is nothing the matter with me. I am perfectly well. My spirits may be somewhat out of sorts lately, but it is nothing worth distressing yourself over. I will soon be myself again and all will be as it was."

Jane's fingers stroked Elizabeth's hair. "I am afraid nothing will ever be as it was. Our lives are ever changing, and there has been a great deal of alteration of late. Lydia is a married woman living with Mr Wickham in Newcastle, and I will soon be making my home at Netherfield, wed to my Mr Bingley."

The reality of her beloved Jane living so far from her as three miles made tears prick the corners of Elizabeth's eyes and a lump form in her throat. "I know," she whispered, "and while I cannot rejoice in the situation Lydia has brought upon herself, I am glad for you, Jane. You deserve to be happy. You have suffered much in the past year."

"As have you," Jane replied. "Oh, Lizzy, I know not all of what he has written to you, or what has come to pass between you— nor do I wish to force your confidence—but I beg of you not to read Mr Darcy's letter anymore. It does you no good that I can see. In fact, your spirits are always much worse afterwards. It pains me."

Elizabeth closed her eyes as a few tears spilled down her cheeks and onto her pillow. She wiped them away with the back of her hand and took an unsteady breath, then turned her face towards her sister, whose pale eyes reflected only concern and love in the dim interior of their room. "Very well, then. If it is truly what you wish, I will refrain from looking upon it, if for no reason other than to ease your mind."

Jane's eyes glistened as she reached for Elizabeth's hand. "Tell me," she enquired in earnest, "what might I do to ease *your* mind?"

A pang of sadness swelled within her as she caressed the beautiful sapphire ring upon the third finger of her sister's left hand wistfully, a gift from Bingley. "There is nothing you can do. I must conquer this on my own. I ask only that you continue to have patience with me, for I dread losing you as well. Though Netherfield is but three miles, it will seem like fifty without you here to comfort me as you have all these years. Oh, Jane, how much I shall miss you!"

"And I you! You must promise me you will come often to Netherfield, even if it is only to hide yourself away in the library and immerse yourself in a book. Though the current offerings are somewhat meagre, Charles has told me he plans on adding to it soon with the intention of pleasing you, my dearest sister. You will always be welcome in our home, whenever and for however long you wish to remain with us."

Elizabeth laughed then and smiled with real pleasure. "Then I am afraid your excellent Mr Bingley will grow quite tired of me, for there is nowhere else I would rather be than with my dearest sister."

"Come, Lizzy. Nowhere?"

"Well, perhaps there may be a *few* places I would like to see someday, but I would never wish to be far from you."

"We are to go to London after we are married, and it would give me great pleasure if you were to come as well."

Elizabeth shook her head. "I could not intrude so upon your time with your new husband. Surely, Mr Bingley will want you to himself and I will only be in his way."

"Nonsense. Having you with me will bring me comfort. I confess I am not looking forward to attending dinners and meeting new acquaintances who will no doubt be eager to dissect every aspect of my person, my manners, and my dress. I would feel much easier with you by my side. You shall give me strength."

"Jane," Elizabeth began, but Jane would hear none of her protests.

"Charles and I have already discussed the matter at length, and it is quite settled between us. He would like for you to come as much as I. There is nothing to be done for it except for you to agree, for I refuse to go without you."

Elizabeth laughed. "Very well. I know better than to argue with you once you have made up your mind. And as I have no wish to be the means of disappointing your husband should his bride absolutely refuse to accompany him during his honeymoon, I accept. But only on the condition that you will see to your own pleasure first and leave me to find my own amusement. Poor Mr Bingley will go distracted having to share you so recently after finally earning the privilege of being alone with you."

Jane agreed, and the matter was soon settled between them. Elizabeth would accompany her sister and new brother to London on the day following their wedding, and there she would remain until shortly after Christmas, when the Gardiners were expected to travel to Longbourn for the New Year.

❄ 3 ❄

WHERE COLONEL FITZWILLIAM GIVES MR
DARCY A KICK IN THE BREECHES.

Darcy stood before a large set of French windows in his study, one arm braced against the casement while the hand of his other rested on his hip. Rain was falling in buckets, drenching the manicured front lawn of his Mayfair home. *Would that I was at Pemberley,* he thought resentfully. *Kent, Newcastle, anywhere but London.*

From the centre of the room the Earl of Carlisle's deep, imposing voice injected the easy, comfortable space with a decided chill. "Your aunt informed me she happened upon you last night as you were ordering your carriage, Darcy. I need not tell you she was extremely put out. She had high hopes of you dancing at least once with Lady Eliza. I realise that, for whatever reason, you have decided the girl is not your cup of tea, but she is handsome and in possession of forty thousand pounds. It is ten thousand greater than the sum you will have to recover to retain your current net worth once Georgiana marries. One dance for appearances' sake and to please your aunt would hardly have been a sacrifice. Perhaps upon further acquaintance you would even find the girl suits your tastes, but it appears you are determined not to take the trouble to find out."

Darcy repressed a sigh of annoyance. His uncle was worse than Lady Catherine. Like his overbearing sister, Lord Carlisle was neither used to brooking disappointment nor accustomed to being ignored. Steeling himself, Darcy assumed a well-practiced air of indifference and turned his back on the sodden landscape. "I am as well acquainted with Lady Eliza as I care to be, sir. We have been in company together countless times at balls, card parties, and dinners and I can say with absolute certainty she is one of the last ladies with whom I care to pass my time."

"What could you possibly find to object to in Eliza Harrow? She is a pretty little piece and an heiress to boot, not to mention her mother is a member of the peerage. I see nothing to object to in that, quite the opposite!"

"Lady Eliza is handsome," Darcy allowed, "she is fashionable, and she is rich, but her conversation is inane, her opinions are deferential and rehearsed, and she has not one original thought in her head. We have nothing in common other than the circles in which we move. I do not have to spend any further time with the lady to see how ill-suited we are. Any attention paid to Lady Eliza would only incite speculation and raise hopes I have no intention of fulfilling."

"Opinions!" parroted the earl in astonishment. "Convictions! Surely, you have more than enough intelligent discussions at your club that you would have no need for such conversation in a wife! What the devil does a woman need to understand beyond the urgency of begetting an heir, setting a decent table, and holding her tongue? Original thoughts—bah! That is nothing but a bunch of damned folderol."

Darcy bristled. His eyes locked with those of his cousin, seated beside his father on a broad leather sofa.

Fitzwilliam cleared his throat, then rose from the couch and crossed the room to stand beside Darcy. "Easy does it," he muttered, his voice barely audible as he turned his attention to the window and some concocted amusement or other on Brook Street.

It was sound advice when dealing with the earl. In the past, Darcy had bitten his tongue time and again to avoid agitating his uncle's resentful temper. For the sake of familial harmony, he knew he ought to do so now, but today he felt differently. Perhaps it was the argument he had with Fitzwilliam the night before; perhaps it was the indignance he felt on Elizabeth's behalf; perhaps he had simply had his fill of his uncle's forceful manner and intolerant vitriol. In that moment, Darcy could no more remain silent than he could refuse to breathe. "There is an endless satisfaction to be had in the company of a woman who is well-spoken, well-read, witty, and knowledgeable. A lady who has both the confidence and the ability to offer her opinions freely, readily, and with intelligence and conviction should be recognised and valued by society —not ridiculed and dismissed. It is only with such a woman that a man can achieve a true marital partnership."

"*Marital partnership!*" The earl shook his head with a contemptuous snort. "Marrying such a woman would be the biggest mistake of a man's life, especially a man in your situation, with your fortune and your prospects. Good God, Darcy. If I did not know better, I would think you had taken orders! What a bunch of sermonising! You could do a hell of a lot worse than Lady Harrow's daughter. A pretty, rich, young thing like Lady Eliza is an enticing prospect! Virgins, I grant you, can be tedious to break in, but you need not concern yourself overmuch with that, not where Lady Eliza is concerned." He laughed crudely. "You know Lady Harrow has long admired you. No doubt she would gladly make up for her daughter's shortcomings in the marital bed."

Colonel Fitzwilliam shook his head minutely and uttered a quiet oath, most likely to prevent his cousin from saying something unfortunate in response to his father's remarks.

Darcy was far too livid to heed such a warning. "You may not believe in equality between a man and his wife, but this is a subject on which I hold firm beliefs. I will not be browbeaten into forming an alliance that is less than palatable to myself or any future children that may result from such a union. I will not court the favour of any woman for whom I do not feel an equal affinity and respect, nor will I marry where I feel no affection. And I certainly *never* shall take my wife's mother to my bed! I would rather remain celibate!"

"You want a love match?" Lord Carlisle cried. "What fustian nonsense is this? You cannot afford to be so headstrong and foolish where the business of matrimony is concerned. Pemberley needs an heir!"

"Pemberley shall have one regardless. Once she marries, any children Georgiana bears may easily be named as my heirs. Others have acted in a similar fashion before me. I would not be the first."

The earl glared at Darcy in furious disbelief. "You have completely lost your wits! There is no woman in the entire kingdom who could even begin to fulfil this foolish fantasy of yours. *I* have never encountered a gently bred girl in possession of such an outrageous combination of eccentricities, and I will be damned if you think for one moment I will stand by and watch you marry some vulgar Frenchwoman who is used to being admitted to discussions in which a woman has no place! The most eligible girls in our sphere are not brought up with any of that intellectualism and freethinking nonsense, and rightly so. What man in his right mind wants to come home to a wife who speaks her mind to him after he has been out riding on his estate all day or sequestered with his solicitor? Not a damned one of them!

"In the years since you first reached your majority I have never once seen your fastidious head turned by anything less than a pretty face and pleasing figure. One of those ridiculous blue-stockings with their high ideals and even higher necklines will never satisfy your baser instincts. Mark my words—you will end by revising this farcical list of requirements. The sooner you do so the better!"

"My mind is made up. I will not be moved."

"You damn well will be moved if I have anything to say about it!"

"I will *not*," Darcy insisted coldly, every bit the master of Pemberley as he fixed his uncle with a steely, level look full of barely concealed anger. "I will not yield to convenience, not when doing so will ensure I receive a lifetime of vexation and regret."

Fuming, Lord Carlisle narrowed his eyes. "You would dare to risk all that your beloved father has left to you in trust, to pass the rest of your life on this earth alone without a well-dowered, comely wife to ease your nights and keep your house? You would deprive yourself of the satisfaction of siring a son who would be of your body and your blood, to whom you could pass your wealth, your property—your God-given *legacy*?"

"If by following my convictions I am destined to pass my life unmarried, then so be it. I have Georgiana. I have my family and my friends. An arrangement of convenience, no matter how advantageous for my pocketbook and my social standing, would be nothing short of intolerable to my spirit."

"Intolerable to your spirit!" Lord Carlisle cried, leaping to his feet. His countenance was red with fury. "I find your blasted obstinance and lack of ambition intolerable! You would do well to remember your place in this world! You may be the master of Pemberley, but I am the head of this family! Unless you want to find yourself on the wrong side of my wrath, you will heed my counsel!

"Despite your preposterous notions of equality between the sexes and your ridiculous romantic whims, I have high aspirations for you, Darcy. You have the potential to make a brilliant match for yourself, and by God you should seize the bull by the horns! I should not have to remind you that by marrying the right sort of girl you could double your holdings, gain a title, and obtain a place in Parliament.

"Marriage to an heiress like Eliza Harrow, despite her empty head and insipid opinions, would help you achieve all of this! Your father, God rest his soul, would never have stood for you throwing your life away over some fanciful inclination that is not only unattainable, but irrational and unsound. Richard!" Lord Carlisle barked to his son. "I have had enough of Darcy and his damned idealistic nonsense for one day. We are leaving, else I lose my temper entirely."

"With your permission, sir," Colonel Fitzwilliam replied evenly, "I would prefer to remain. There is a matter of some import I would discuss with Darcy."

Darcy rolled his eyes. His cousin may have been a decorated colonel in His Majesty's army, but he was his father's second son and therefore at the earl's mercy until he made his fortune elsewhere. He would not act without Lord Carlisle's affirmation and risk falling out of favour with his father, at least not over something like this.

The earl uttered an oath, stalked towards the door, and yanked it open. "Do what you must, but by God make your preachy, pig-headed cousin see some measure of sense before he ruins himself!" Having said his piece, he stomped from the room and bellowed for a servant to fetch his carriage.

Fitzwilliam walked to the door and closed it while Darcy curled his hands into fists and resumed his previous post at the window.

"Can I get you a cup of tea?"

"I thank you, no," Darcy replied tersely. He was far too agitated to think, never mind drink tea. How the blazes could Lord Carlisle excuse Fitzwilliam, a second son with a paltry inheritance, from paying his attentions to Miss Cromwell and her fifty thousand pounds, yet persevere in pushing Darcy, who had long been his own lord and master, towards insipid, bird-witted girls like Eliza Harrow?

The answer was as obvious as it was infuriating. Of course, his lordship considered it a hardship for any son of his to be shackled to a woman whose physical attributes he himself considered less than appealing. *Perhaps he should hoist Lady Eliza upon Fitzwilliam then,* Darcy thought bitterly, *especially since Fitzwilliam would gladly choose a similar woman of fortune over a lady whose circumstances resembled those of Elizabeth!*

A pang of longing pierced him as he thought of Elizabeth, and he shut his eyes. "By God, I hate London," he murmured, raking his fingers through his hair. A loud crack of thunder sounded overhead, and Darcy watched his uncle clamber into his carriage and slam the door shut before his harried-looking footman could come around to oblige him. With a lurch, the carriage pulled away from the kerb, but the earl's departure did little to improve Darcy's dark mood.

Across the room, Fitzwilliam sighed. "Darcy, I have known you my entire life. You are dearer to me than my own brother. But while we have always understood each other on a deeper level, there are moments when you baffle me exceedingly. Why on earth do you not simply ask for her hand and be done with it?"

"If you intend to talk me into marrying Lady Eliza, I will caution you to be careful."

The colonel chuckled lowly. "I assure you I am well acquainted with your sentiments on that score. I need no lecture from you."

"I trust, then," Darcy said as he turned from the window, "you will be generous enough to extend the same courtesy to me. I am in no mood for another round of bullying, nor do I feel as though I owe you any further explanation as to my refusal to pay consequence to women who have been slighted by other respectable men."

"Good Lord, you must take me for a simpleton. Between our disagreement of sorts last night at Lord Palmer's and the speech you delivered to my father this morning there is little doubt in my mind you must be in love with Miss Eliza *Bennet*. In truth, I always suspected a partiality on your part, but confess I had no idea it had developed into something so serious. It does, however, explain your beastly mood over the past year, but hardly excuses the unwarranted abuse I have been forced to endure."

If Darcy expected his cousin to say anything, it certainly had not been *that*. He strode across the room to the sideboard, where he braced his hands upon the gleaming mahogany surface and bowed his head. Embarrassment and indecision pressed upon him like a weight. Rarely had Darcy kept secrets from Fitzwilliam, but his dealings with Elizabeth had been different. His feelings for her—his anger and humiliation regarding her refusal and the circumstances surrounding it—were far too painful to share with anyone, even someone he trusted as implicitly as he did his cousin. He took a much-needed moment to compose himself. "It is not," he admitted, "quite so simple."

"It is not?"

"No," said Darcy succinctly, then introduced another topic altogether, or so the colonel most likely thought. "You are aware that my friend Charles Bingley is engaged to be married."

If Fitzwilliam was confused by this sudden change in their conversation, he hid it well. "I had not heard. I do not suppose she is anyone we know?"

Shaking his head, Darcy poured two fingers of scotch into two crystal glasses. "You have not had the pleasure of meeting the lady, but she is not unknown to you. As a matter of fact, she happens to be the very same lady I separated him from last winter. Miss Jane Bennet."

"Miss *Jane* Bennet? Miss Elizabeth Bennet's eldest sister?"

With a rueful turn of his mouth, Darcy offered him one of the glasses. "One and the same."

The colonel accepted it, raised it to his lips, and swallowed half its contents. "That must have come as quite a blow to you, to have gone to such great lengths to separate Miss Bennet from your friend, only to fall in love with her sister. I trust this occurred before you knew your own heart?"

Darcy sank onto the nearest chair and passed a hand tiredly over his eyes. "I hardly know anymore. At the time I told myself it was for Bingley's own good. He is relatively new to society and therefore could not afford to form an imprudent alliance. Upon further reflection, however, I believe I had my own circumstances and standing in society in mind as well.

"To make a long story short, my conscience would no longer allow me to conceal the truth of my involvement in Bingley's affairs, so I made my confession to him when I was last in Hert-fordshire. He was angry, and rightly so, but upon my assurance of the lady's continued affection for him all was forgotten. I received a letter from him last week. He asked me to stand up with him. It escapes me, how Bingley can bestow such an honour upon me after all I have done to wrong him and his betrothed. Tell me, how can I possibly accept?"

The colonel traced the rim of his glass with his index finger. "Quite easily, I imagine. It would no doubt bring Bingley a great deal of pleasure or else he would not have asked it of you. He has always been of a remarkably forgiving nature."

"And his future wife is much the same. In that they are well suited. They will be very happy together. I envy him his good fortune. He has secured the affection, the admiration, the esteem of a worthy woman—a woman he loves and values above all others."

"And you have not?"

"I have not. As a matter of fact, I have been refused."

The colonel, who had raised his glass to his lips a moment before and taken another fortifying sip, choked.

Darcy turned aside his head. He, like Fitzwilliam, was well-aware of the fact that no person in their circle of acquaintance would believe a woman in Elizabeth's situation would dare reject a man such as himself, even if she *did* know the man in question had sought to separate her most beloved sister from his love-struck friend.

"I am surprised to hear that," Fitzwilliam rasped, wiping beads of amber-coloured liquid from the lapels of his tailcoat. "I had thought Miss Bennet was rather friendly towards you in Kent."

Darcy's mouth twisted into a cynical smile as he studied the contents of his own glass, yet untouched. "Then you knew even less of her feelings than did I. It was only with you and her friends, Mrs Collins and Miss Lucas, that she was ever completely friendly and at ease. As for myself, Miss Bennet left me in absolutely no doubt of her feelings."

"She was unkind, then?"

"My behaviour did not merit her kindness," said Darcy, his self-loathing evident in his tone. "After I professed my ardent admiration of her, I went on to insult and demean her family and all her relations, her circumstances, and her prospects. Miss Bennet then accused me of disappointing all her sister's hopes, attacked my character, and proclaimed me to be the last man in the world whom she could ever be prevailed upon to marry. The *very* last man."

Darcy went on to recount the whole of his proposal, Elizabeth's accusations, and her belief in Wickham's claim that Darcy had denied him a living. Finally, he revealed his impulsive need to defend himself and his actions to her in a letter. "I thought she would have at least spoken to her father to warn him of the danger to her sisters and the rest of the neighbourhood, but she did not. In any case, Miss Bennet cannot forgive me for failing to expose Wickham for what he is. She could barely even look at me when we were last in company together. She despises me and I am powerless to change her mind."

"She has admitted as much to you, then? That she holds you responsible for her sister's predicament and her connexion to Wickham?"

Darcy shook his head. "*That* was hardly necessary. Her anger with me was quite evident in the way she avoided nearly every opportunity for discourse between us."

"Do you not think that perhaps Miss Bennet was affected in another way entirely? Could it be possible that she was simply embarrassed by your being there and deeply ashamed? You confessed your dealings with Wickham to her, Georgiana's history—*everything*—yet Miss Bennet's own sister ran off with the blackguard. Now they are married."

"Yes," said Darcy impatiently, "Lydia Bennet did that which Georgiana was planning to do herself. I fail to see your point, Fitzwilliam."

"Darcy," he said exasperatedly, "you berated her family and accused her connexions of being wanting, did you not? I clearly recall you telling me on several occasions what you thought of them, save for the two eldest—that the father is idle in his rule, the mother meddlesome, and the youngest girls silly and wild. How can you believe Miss Bennet does not now feel the full weight of your condemnation? Her family has been disgraced by the act of her sister's impulsive foolishness, her father's neglect, and her mother's indulgence. Is it any wonder she could not meet your eyes? Did it never occur to you that she must view such an enormous failing within her family as proof that your previous censure was justified? That any contempt you felt before is now not only fully deserved but increased by tenfold?"

"I suppose anything could be possible," Darcy admitted, albeit grudgingly. "After my abhorrent behaviour towards her in Kent it would certainly be no stretch of Miss Bennet's imagination to believe me capable of deciding she is unsuitable after everything that has occurred.

"However, if she were at all aware of my involvement in the restoration of her youngest sister's reputation, she would know better than to doubt my devotion to her. But enlightening her is a risk I can ill-afford. Having Miss Bennet feel as though she is under an obligation to me would be far worse than any physical punishment. The bestowal of her gratitude would be intolerable, especially when I desire so much more from her."

"So, you have acted in the same manner you always have regarding that reprobate," Fitzwilliam said darkly as he laid aside his glass. "I suppose he had debts to discharge as well. What did it cost you this time? I would imagine convincing Wickham to marry a girl of little consequence, whose father could do nothing for him beyond a few hundred pounds or so, must have taken some heavy persuasion from your pocketbook."

Darcy discarded his own glass on a nearby table. He had no stomach for it. "I have no complaint about the money. It was not so much as I had originally thought it would cost, though I admit it was far more than either party involved is worth. The bottom line is that I could afford Wickham's price while Mr Bennet could not."

Darcy rested his head against the back of his chair and stared into the fire. "Miss Bennet has relatives here in town, an uncle and aunt on Gracechurch Street whom I had the pleasure of meeting while they were visiting Derbyshire and who have full knowledge of my involvement, as well as my intimate history with Wickham. I could not act without first gaining their approbation."

The colonel appeared incredulous. "And they accepted your explanation as well as your assistance?"

"Not initially, no. In fact, Mr Gardiner refused my assistance, but I eventually managed to convince him that it was owing to my mistaken pride and my failure to lay my own personal dealings open before the world that enabled Wickham to seduce Lydia Bennet in the first place. He relented, but I believe he did so only because he and Mrs Gardiner suspected my partiality for Miss Bennet. I can only imagine what they must now think of me. Though I have since had several interactions with the Gardiners and they have been welcoming and gracious, I have essentially abandoned their niece. God knows it is not what I want to do. I believed Miss Bennet's opinion of me had improved when we met again this summer at Pemberley, but perhaps in that I was mistaken, just as I have been in everything else."

"Then you must do something to remedy the situation," urged the colonel. "Go to Hertfordshire at once. I am sure Bingley will have you."

Darcy laughed darkly. "And I am quite certain he is the only one who will. Aside from Bingley, there is no one in all of Hertfordshire who will welcome me back. On my prior visits I have managed to do nothing but offend the entire neighbourhood. Mrs Bennet was barely civil to me when last I saw her and, believe it or not, many of the single ladies in the neighbourhood went out of their way to spurn my notice. It was sobering, to say the least."

"Well then," the colonel told him matter-of-factly, "you will just have to do as Miss Bennet instructed you to do at Rosings. You must take the trouble of practising. You must assert yourself and improve their opinion of you. There is nothing else to be done."

Darcy groaned, unable to believe this was anything but an impossible task.

"Come now, did you not say that you believed Miss Bennet's own opinion of you had improved over the summer?"

"I did," Darcy muttered, "but it is entirely possible she was so enchanted by Pemberley House and its grounds that she was no longer in possession of her faculties at the time."

"You undervalue yourself. This morose attitude you have worn for so many months hardly suits you. You can be very charming when you decide it to be worth your effort and, in my opinion, Miss Bennet is a woman who is very much worth your effort, despite her unfortunate family connexions and lack of fortune. Judging by the passionate manner by which you defended her to me last evening, it is clearly your own opinion as well."

He squeezed Darcy's shoulder. "I have a confession of my own to make. I am afraid it was I who quite thoughtlessly enlightened Miss Bennet as to your involvement in her sister's affair with Bingley. She immediately claimed a headache and did not come to dine at Rosings later that afternoon. I am heartily sorry for any pain I have caused you by speaking out of turn. It was disloyal of me and poorly done."

For a long moment Darcy stared at his cousin in shock, then shook his head slowly and looked away. *So, that is why Elizabeth had not felt well enough to attend Lady Catherine's dinner.* To his cousin, he said, "Do not distress yourself. Miss Bennet is not stupid. I am certain she suspected my involvement from the moment we all quit Hertfordshire last autumn. You offered nothing but confirmation of that which she had already deduced on her own."

"Even so, I did not make things any easier for you. My indiscretion caused you considerable pain and heartache, and for that I will always feel a deep responsibility and regret. I never should have interfered."

Nor should I have, Darcy thought with rueful irony and more than a little bitterness. He considered it quite fitting that the injustice of his own officious actions had finally come full circle to plague him.

That night, after Darcy completed his nightly ablutions and climbed into bed, he considered all that his cousin had said to him that morning.

If Elizabeth was embarrassed by his being in Hertfordshire, he ought to be thankful. In his experience, being on the receiving end of a woman's embarrassment was undoubtedly better than being the recipient of her anger and scorn. Embarrassment, he could alleviate to some extent. Darcy had done a fair job of it once before when they had met at Pemberley. His prior history with Elizabeth, both in Hertfordshire and in Kent, had been riddled with misrepresentations and misunderstandings, but at Pemberley they were becoming friends; Darcy had been sure of it. Since he was fortunate enough to have earned Elizabeth's friendship before, perhaps he could earn it again.

The people of Hertfordshire were another matter. Gaining their good opinion would require undoing many months' worth of offensive behaviour—nearly an entire year if Darcy included the fact that he had quit the neighbourhood last November without bothering to take his leave of the families who had so graciously invited the Netherfield party into their homes, the Bennets included. Unlike Elizabeth, who had seen him among his dearest relations and in the comfort of his own home, where Darcy was happiest and most at ease, her neighbours had not.

Darcy sighed. While it was far too late to think about making a positive impression—especially in a close-knit country society that he had, very early on, proclaimed to be confined and unvarying—he had little choice in the matter if he wanted to win Elizabeth's heart. He recalled the insulting words he had uttered when Sir William Lucas proclaimed dancing to be one of the first refinements in every polished society and cringed. Without thought or consideration, Darcy had callously observed that it also had the advantage of being in vogue amongst the less polished societies of the world, for 'every savage can dance'.

It was not five minutes later that an impertinent little savage in possession of the finest eyes he had ever seen declined the privilege of dancing with him. It was the beginning of Darcy's undoing. It had been difficult enough to keep himself from seeking her out that evening, but after Elizabeth Bennet had so effectively demonstrated that she was not so easily charmed by his person, his manners, or his address as the ladies of London, it became impossible to tear himself away. Darcy remembered well the colour of her gown and the warm glow of her skin as she refused his request, the sparkle in her eyes as she smiled and laughed with her friends, and the unfamiliar pang of jealousy he had felt when she turned her attention towards any man other than himself.

Darcy ran his hands over his face in frustration. Since meeting Elizabeth Bennet, it had become impossible to find repose for the multitude of thoughts that plagued him and tonight would be no exception.

With an exhalation, he reached across the bed to fumble through a drawer in his bedside table and withdrew a small, elegant-looking bottle. He stared at it for a long moment, then removed the stopper with care and sprinkled a few drops of the liquid contained within upon his pillowcase. As the scent of summer roses freshened the stale air of the room, he returned the bottle to the drawer, lay his head upon his pillow, and closed his eyes.

Elizabeth...

Darcy breathed deeply. It was this scent—*her* scent—that had enveloped him utterly at Netherfield, fed his fantasies, and invaded his thoughts until he barely recalled his own name.

Though deceptively simple, the infusion of rosewater and herbs had been difficult to procure. It had taken a special request at Floris's on Jermyn Street in St James's and some trial and error by the reputed perfumer before Darcy was able to hold a few precious ounces of what he considered a meagre substitution for the woman he wanted but could never have.

Elizabeth's signature fragrance was not the faint, innocuous scent of the dignified, cultivated varieties commonly found in the conservatories and hothouses of London, but the sweet, heady perfume of the wild, rambling blooms of the countryside. A small, private smile tugged at his lips every time he contemplated Elizabeth Bennet in what he had come to think of as her natural environment: the open fields and wooded paths of Hertfordshire. There was nothing of conformation in her and Darcy found it entirely fitting that the scent she favoured mirrored her personality—enchanting, wild, and elusive.

Every awkward exertion on his part would be well worth the effort it would cost him should he become the recipient of Elizabeth's intelligent banter and her laughter and her teasing smile. For the privilege of looking upon her once more, of speaking with her, dancing with her, and hopefully making her his own after so many months of disappointment and uncertainty, Darcy would do as she had once instructed him so many months ago at Rosings: he would take the trouble of practising.

He would take every opportunity to make himself agreeable to the good people of Hertfordshire and pay them every civility in his power. They deserved no less, and, if truth be told, were probably deserving of far more. They were the people Elizabeth had known her entire life. They had helped shape her personality, form her character, and encourage her to be the woman she was today—kind, intelligent, compassionate, and good. It had been obvious to him as long ago as the first assembly he attended in Meryton that she held the people of Hertfordshire in esteem. Perhaps she even loved them, much as Darcy loved and esteemed the people of Pemberley, Kympton, and Darcy House.

Why, then, had he not followed her example or Bingley's? Why had it taken a painful set-down, disappointed hopes, and a broken heart to make Darcy finally see the error of his ways? Why had it taken one impertinent, teasing woman with bright eyes and pert opinions to make him want to change?

Breathing deeply, Darcy willed the tension in his body to dissipate as he settled further into the softness of his pillow. As always, Elizabeth's scent calmed his troubled conscience and offered him solace. Just as he needed air to breathe and food to sustain him, Darcy knew he needed Elizabeth Bennet. Tomorrow he would write to Bingley and hopefully, within a few short days, he would be on his way back to Hertfordshire. He loved her, and Darcy knew without a doubt that he always would.

He hoped it was not too late to make amends.

❧ 4 ❧

WHERE ELIZABETH BENNET MEETS A GENTLEMAN.

lizabeth's skirts billowed in the wind as she wandered the countryside, breathing the fresh air and distinctive scents of late autumn—composting leaves, wood smoke, apples, and hay. The weather was surprisingly mild, enough so to remove her bonnet, which she had done the moment she could no longer be seen from the windows of her father's house. A healthy breeze danced through the fields, and she tilted her face heavenward, inviting the sun's rays to warm her skin as she closed her eyes with a contented sigh. The sky was cloudless, a brilliant, almost impossible shade of blue that presented a striking contrast to the rich golden hues and pale browns of the November landscape.

Beneath her closed eyelids the glow of the sun shone brightly with vivid colours and soft, muted shapes. A familiar pair of eyes appeared, darkening her light-hearted moment. With a jolt, Elizabeth opened her own eyes and extended her arms until her fingertips skimmed the tops of the stalks of dried grass and rye swaying in the wind. It would do her no good to continue to dwell upon a future that could never come to pass. She had lived quite happily for one-and-twenty years of her life without Fitzwilliam Darcy to distract her and make her forget herself with impossible dreams.

It was time to shake off her melancholy. Though the prospect of a future without Darcy was painful to her, Elizabeth knew she needed to embrace her fate wholeheartedly rather than scorn it. The sooner she could master her emotions, the better it would be for her peace of mind; but thus far, exorcising Darcy's ghost proved a task easier said than done. It was a task she sincerely wished she need not do at all. Perhaps she would have more success on the morrow.

With her heart and her head full of him she walked on, but the sound of distant hoof beats interrupted her ruminations. A bevy of partridge took flight and Elizabeth turned, startled to see a lone rider guiding his mount towards her at a rapid pace. The gentleman gained ground quickly and, once upon her, reined in his horse and dismounted with a dramatic flourish.

He sank to one knee and bowed his head. "My lady," he said with a deep, mirthful tenor as he peered at her through his lashes. "I am, as ever, your servant."

Elizabeth found herself staring into a familiar pair of twinkling eyes the colour of thunderclouds. A smile spread across her face as she greeted him with a startled laugh. "Get up! Get up at once, you goose, and let me look at you!"

With a hearty laugh of his own, the gentleman did as he was bid and, with a wide grin that was as familiar to her as her own laughter, touched the brim of his hat. "Do you not think it fortuitous, Miss Elizabeth Bennet, that you are the very first of my neighbours I have the pleasure of meeting this fine day?"

"I do not think it fortuitous at all, Mr Ellis, for I believe you and I have been friends long enough for you to know that I am a creature of habit. You, sir, always seem to know precisely where I can be found. I trust after all this time that you are well?"

"I am," he said as he accepted her proffered hand and pressed it between his own. "It does my eyes good to see you, Lizzy. Cousin Charlotte was correct. The last several years have been very good to you. You look remarkably well."

Elizabeth could not hide the blush that heated her cheeks at his familiar childhood address, nor his compliment. "I can already tell your manners have altered but little, though I can hardly take you to task for them when you pay me such pretty compliments. Are Sir William and Lady Lucas in good health? They must be very pleased to have their favourite nephew back with them at Lucas Lodge after all this time."

"They are indeed! I must confess I am exceedingly glad to be home. My time, both at Oxford and in America, was of infinite value and I would not trade it for the world, but I have sorely missed my family and friends, and this place," he said as he looked about him with a fond, wistful expression.

His countenance, however, soon grew serious. "Did my addressing you as I used to do truly cause you offence? It was certainly not my intent. We have always been easy and informal with one another, you know—you, Charlotte, Jane, and I. But if you desire it, I will address you as Miss Elizabeth from this moment forward. I should warn you, though, no matter how many times the appellation leaves my lips, in my heart you shall remain Lizzy to me."

Elizabeth shook her head, a nostalgic smile upon her lips as she studied the ground. "No, I am hardly offended, only surprised. I have not been so informally addressed by a gentleman other than my father and uncles since I was little more than a girl. I do not object to it in this case, but it will never do should you forget yourself when we are in company together."

"Then I will endeavour to remember myself and respectfully address you as Miss Elizabeth on those occasions. How I have missed our spirited conversations! You were always able to challenge me in ways very few others are capable."

"The same was always true of you. And speaking of challenges, my sisters will be pleased to see you, as will my mother, for your presence here will undoubtedly mean the addition of one more eligible gentleman to the neighbourhood."

Her companion rolled his eyes. "Has your dear mother not yet found suitors enough for all of you that she must now include me in her schemes? She must be desperate, indeed! Given time, I might even be convinced to oblige her, but only provided she pushes me towards her most enchanting daughter."

The corners of Elizabeth's mouth quirked impishly. "I am sorry to inform you, then, that you will have to make do with another. Jane's heart has belonged these many months to Mr Bingley. He let Netherfield Park last Michaelmas and fell madly in love with her. They are to be married at month's end. As you can imagine, we are all ridiculously happy for her."

"And I am nothing but pleased for her as well. I have heard tell of her good fortune from my aunt and cousins but cannot say I am the least bit surprised by the news. I always knew Jane's beauty and infinite goodness would someday capture the notice of an earnest, discerning gentleman.

"You must tell me, though, whether this Mr Bingley truly deserves her. According to Charlotte, he and his party left Hertfordshire rather abruptly last autumn and the gentleman's absence was of some duration. Dare I ask whether it was his admiration of your sister that compelled him to return?"

"Yes, I believe it was," Elizabeth lied, though she told herself it was not a complete untruth, as Bingley's feelings had never faltered, only his confidence in his own judgment. "Both were equally affected by the separation, and I have since come to understand that it was only a lack of courage on the gentleman's part regarding my sister's sentiments that kept him in London for such an extended period. Do not judge him too harshly, for you will be hard-pressed to find a kinder or more amiable gentleman than Mr Bingley. He and Jane are infinitely well suited, and I daresay shall find much happiness together. Indeed, they already have."

"Very well, then. Until I have the honour of making the gentleman's acquaintance, I shall give him the benefit of the doubt, but in return you must now tell me whether Jane's excellent Mr Bingley does not have a friend worthy of you as well."

Elizabeth's smooth countenance faltered, but she recovered her wit quickly. "When compared to Jane's sweetness of temper, my impertinent ways could hardly charm a gentleman of fashion and means. You know it is not in my nature to alter my opinions or curb my spirited tongue simply for the sake of flattery or to garner praise. I am afraid I shall have to content myself with teaching Jane's ten future children to embroider cushions and play their instruments very ill. Now," she declared, "it is your turn to satisfy my curiosity, and I demand to know what news you have of Charlotte."

With a flourish, Mr Ellis produced a thick packet from his great-coat pocket. "My dear cousin is well enough, but she misses your excellent society exceedingly, I am afraid. As a matter of fact, she mentioned several times her hope that you will consent to visit her again in the spring. She shall enter her confinement by then and I believe will be rather desperate for sensible conversation as it seems neither her husband, nor the residents of Rosings Park are reliable enough to perform that particular office with any degree of competency."

Elizabeth smiled knowingly. "I see you have made Lady Catherine's acquaintance, then. Pray, how did you find her?"

Mr Ellis chuckled. "There are simply no words to do her justice. As you can imagine, I by no means share my Uncle Lucas's opinion that she is a woman of true affability, though I will go so far as to indulge the sentiments of our Cousin Collins and agree that no detail is too trifling for that great lady's notice. She has an opinion on every subject, her favourite, of course, being her future son-in-law, his independent fortune, and his fine estate. While I do not know the gentleman myself, I cannot help but pity this Mr Darcy of whom she spoke so intimately, and I daresay constantly."

Elizabeth was taken aback, not only to hear Darcy's name rolling off her friend's tongue, but also to learn that Lady Catherine had spoken so unreservedly of her heart's desire to a perfect stranger; but Elizabeth soon recalled her own past deal-ings with Darcy's cacophonous aunt last April when she had visited Rosings Park. Of course, Lady Catherine would speak of her favourite nephew, his beautiful estate, and their intimacy with him to Charlotte's relations. Elizabeth shook her head in bemusement. Just because the lady desired something did not necessarily mean it would come to pass, especially where Darcy was concerned. With a wry turn of her lips, she said, "Though a union between her daughter and Mr Darcy is undoubtedly her dearest wish, I would not give much credence to Lady Cather-ine's intimations on that score if I were you. I am acquainted with Mr Darcy, and it is my observation that he and Miss de Bourgh would never suit. He paid her no particular attention that I could see when I was in company with them last spring at Rosings, quite the opposite in fact."

But Mr Ellis was quick to disagree. "I do not discount your familiarity with the gentleman, but I have it on authority from Lady Catherine herself that such an arrangement between them does, in fact, exist. My understanding is that it has been a long time coming—the dearest wish of both her and Mr Darcy's late mother. The family has yet to make a formal announcement to their general acquaintance, but the Reverend Collins assures me that will happen shortly. Why, to hear him go on one would think he had a hand in the business! The man talked of nothing but Mr Darcy and his 'excellent fortune of securing dear Miss de Bourgh's delicate hand' for the full week I was under his roof!

"Poor Mr Darcy," Mr Ellis said, and chuckled. "Lady Catherine accused him of spending too much of his time at his estate in Derbyshire and not nearly enough in Kent wooing his betrothed, but that will soon change, as he has plans to travel to Rosings shortly. Apparently, the couple is to become espoused in Hunsford Church at Christmas, honeymoon in the north, and produce an heir by this time next year. As Lady Catherine seems to be a woman who is not in the habit of being denied, I have no doubt she will have her way in the end, despite the persuasive argument the bridegroom has made regarding his preference for the chapel at Pemberley. I sincerely hope for the gentleman's sake that, in addition to his reputed ten-thousand-a-year, he is also in possession of a strong constitution. He will certainly have need of one—that and a very stiff drink!"

Elizabeth stumbled and Mr Ellis reached out and caught her arm, steadying her. "Lizzy, are you quite well?" His concern for her was apparent in his eyes.

"Yes," she stammered. "I am perfectly well. I only caught my foot in a rabbit hole."

It cannot be true, Elizabeth told herself firmly. *Mr Darcy cannot be engaged to a woman who is the exact opposite in spirit, temperament, and appearance as me; a woman whom he had not shown the least inclination for last April.*

That Darcy placed much importance on family connexions she could not refute, but to give way and agree to Lady Catherine's expectations now, after he had already risked her wrath and proposed to Elizabeth, someone so wholly unconnected to him, was confounding. *Whatever would induce him to do it?*

It was the work of a moment before she recalled much to induce Darcy to turn to the bosom of his own family—*her family*. Lydia's scandalous elopement, patched-up marriage, and worthless husband; her mother's enthusiasm for the newly-weds, despite their offences and unrepentant attitudes; Elizabeth's abhorrent connexion to them; and her father's indifference to it all. She held back tears as Mr Ellis whistled shrilly for his horse.

"Perhaps we should proceed on to Longbourn," her friend suggested, seemingly oblivious to her distress. "I would wager you have been gone all morning and, if I recall anything of your dear mother, the moment you set foot in the house she will accuse you of caring nothing for her nerves and scold you incessantly for undoing all your maid's efforts."

His tone took on a conspiratorial lilt. "Tell me, after all these years, does she still instruct you to be mindful of your petticoats? I daresay she does, for every lady knows that any eligible gentleman of consequence would disapprove of a wild girl who roams the countryside for hours on end, especially one who returns with her hem caked with mud!"

Elizabeth felt a flush of heat rise in her cheeks as her friend's teasing words rang all too close to the truth. "Yes," she muttered awkwardly. "No gentleman of consequence, indeed."

A look of concern crossed Mr Ellis's face then and he hastened to offer her his arm. "Do you mind my accompanying you? If you would prefer to continue alone, I can call another day, but confess I am loath to part from you so soon, particularly when you appear to be unwell."

After a brief hesitation she accepted his arm and forced a half-hearted smile to her lips. "I would be grateful to have your company. I am merely a bit fatigued, that is all. I am hardly unwell."

He offered her a rueful turn of his own mouth as he gathered his horse's reins. "You cannot fool me, Elizabeth Bennet, but I shall not press you now for answers you are unwilling to give. We may therefore continue on in silence."

❦

Elizabeth's spirits were in a dismal state by the time she and her companion reached Longbourn. Surely, her own unjust actions and her family's ill-mannered behaviour must have induced Darcy to at least appreciate the benefits of an alliance with his wealthy cousin. Why would he ever return to Hertfordshire and renew his addresses to her when he could easily choose another lady to marry? One who was not only well connected and well dowered, but well-mannered enough to refrain from insulting him when he proposed?

It was with a heavy heart that she entered the house and handed her bonnet and spencer to Mrs Hill. Fleeting thoughts of claiming a headache and escaping to her bedchamber occurred to her, but she dismissed them as quickly as they had come. She took a fortifying breath instead and, assuming an air of congeniality, allowed Mr Ellis to escort her to a cheerful-looking parlour where the windows faced full west. There, they found her mother and sisters seated before a warm fire, chatting amicably with Mr Bingley over tea and biscuits.

"Lord, bless me," cried Mrs Bennet as she rose to greet her new guest with enthusiasm. "Jonathan Ellis, you are very welcome back to Hertfordshire! I do not believe you have met our neighbour, Mr Bingley of Netherfield Park."

"No, ma'am, I have not yet had that pleasure," Mr Ellis replied, smiling as he turned towards Mr Bingley and performed a perfunctory bow. "I believe congratulations are in order, Mr Bingley. I understand from Miss Elizabeth that you are soon to become her brother."

"I am, indeed, sir," Mr Bingley declared with equal cordiality, bowing to Mr Ellis in turn. "I consider myself the most fortunate man in the world to have secured the affections of such a lovely, estimable lady as my Miss Bennet."

Almost immediately Mrs Bennet began to talk of the upcoming wedding and all it entailed. Mr Ellis caught Elizabeth's eye and grinned widely. As previously predicted, this was a topic near and dear to Mrs Bennet's heart and, judging from her friend's poorly contained delight, Elizabeth suspected he had every intention of making the most of her mother's exuberance.

Despite the heaviness of her heart, Elizabeth was delighted to have her childhood friend back in Hertfordshire. While her mother prattled on about wedding clothes, he cast countless amused looks in Elizabeth's direction. Eventually her dark mood lightened, and she responded to his teasing ways by playfully narrowing her eyes at his tomfoolery until the urge to laugh at him for his cheek as he encouraged her mother's enthusiasm to an almost absurd degree became too much. Her lips began to twitch, but any merriment was remarkably short-lived once Mrs Bennet noticed their private exchange. With a smug expression, Longbourn's mistress boldly announced her hopes that all her remaining daughters would soon find husbands.

Elizabeth's mortification was acute and Mr Ellis, properly chagrined himself, hastened to engage Mr Bingley in a discussion about Netherfield. An invitation to stay for supper was issued by Elizabeth's mother and accepted with real pleasure by both men, whose impressions of one another appeared favourable, as did their desire to further their acquaintance.

It was late when the party finally parted company and Mrs Bennet urged Jane and Elizabeth to see their guests to the door. No doubt her thoughts were focused on securing Jonathan Ellis for her second-eldest daughter. Elizabeth reluctantly followed the others out into the vestibule with a frown.

Mr Ellis laughed at her solemnity and, as Bingley took Jane aside for a private farewell, linked Elizabeth's arm with his own and led her from the house, where he ordered a stable boy to fetch his horse.

"Have no fear, Lizzy. I know what is going on inside that pretty head of yours. I am only surprised you would believe me so easily guided by the whims of your mother. You, madam, as you well know, are in no danger of having to suffer any romantic overtures from me." He gave her a playful wink. "Not unless you desire them, of course."

Embarrassed, Elizabeth turned her head aside to avoid his laughing gaze. "Forgive me. Of course, I should have known that you and I would likely be of a similar mind, but my mother has grown more insistent in the years since you have gone away, and I am afraid her single-mindedness has been remarked upon, not only by our general acquaintance, but by others as well. It is a subject that brings me no pleasure and has, in fact, occasioned both Jane and me a significant degree of pain and mortification over the past year. I can no longer find humour in it."

"Hush. I am well acquainted with your mother and her aspirations for you and your sisters. Be not alarmed. I will not fall into her clutches after all these years, though you must realise that no man of any sense would ever consider it a penance to be bound to you in such a way."

Elizabeth withdrew her hand from his arm and pulled her shawl tightly around her shoulders. "And that, I am afraid, is a matter of opinion. Please, let us speak of something else."

"As you wish. My uncle informed me there is to be an assembly, Saturday next. Say you will do me the honour of saving a dance for me, Lizzy, or perhaps two if your father denies me the pleasure of standing up with Kitty."

Elizabeth bit her bottom lip in indecision. One dance would not raise any untoward expectations amongst their neighbours, but her mother was another matter entirely, and one not so easily dissuaded once she set her cap at something. Elizabeth considered refusing Mr Ellis's request but dismissed the idea quickly, for courtesy would then demand that she decline every gentleman who petitioned the same honour. She was by no means willing to forgo the distraction an evening of dancing would afford her, not even to deflect her mother's shameless matchmaking.

"Very well. If you insist upon it, I will dance with you, but I must entreat you to take great care with my toes. I do not enjoy being tread upon by gentlemen who are woefully inattentive to the placement of their feet."

The stable hand arrived then with his horse, and all discourse between them came to an end as Mr Ellis mounted smoothly and tipped his hat to her. He accepted a lantern from the stable hand and urged his horse forward with a quick flick of the reins. Elizabeth's eyes followed him until he passed the pale marking the estate's entrance and turned onto the road. The rhythm of his horse's hooves carried clearly, even as he disappeared from her view.

"Well, that went rather well, I daresay," Mrs Bennet declared once both gentlemen had departed Longbourn and her two eldest daughters had returned to the house. "Jonathan Ellis will be a very fitting match for you, Lizzy. I wonder that I never thought of it before. What should be more natural than to see you as mistress of Lucas Lodge, especially after those odious

Collinses toss us out into the hedgerows when your father is dead?"

Elizabeth sank onto a sofa and exhaled tiredly. "Mamma, as you well know, Sir William has several sons of his own, so there is little chance of Mr Ellis inheriting. In any case, I have no interest in him beyond that of friendship, and his intentions towards me are hardly any different. We have known one another since we were in leading strings. Indeed, no romantic attachment exists between us. We are practically brother and sister."

"Nonsense," Mrs Bennet insisted, wrinkling her nose. "You can be very pretty, Lizzy, when you set your mind to it, and though you are not half so handsome as Jane, your figure is ten times more attractive than those of Mrs Long's nieces. Mark my words. With a little flattery and a few smiles, Jonathan Ellis will very soon be disposed to favour you above every other lady in the neighbour-hood—and you would do well to encourage him! Lady Lucas informed me he inherited a very tidy sum while he was away, and I am sure it is more than enough to live upon—and quite comfort-ably, too! He is young and healthy and so must be in want of a wife. You cannot very well continue to go around refusing perfectly good marriage proposals from every man who conde-scends to ask. You will not retain your bloom forever, you know."

Kitty gave Elizabeth a sly glance. "Mr Ellis is far more hand-some than I remembered, Lizzy. It would not be so bad to be married to him, would it? After all, he is far more agreeable, both in manners and figure, than Mr Collins."

Mr Bennet cleared his throat and gave his fourth daughter a disapproving glare over the top of his newspaper. "Whatever Mr Ellis's physical advantage over your cousin, I absolutely forbid you to speak of it, Kitty! You shall continue to comport yourself with some degree of decency or you will forever remain at home while your other, more decorous sisters enjoy themselves at balls and assemblies. In any case, I doubt Lizzy needs your advice on how to choose her lovers. She is clever enough to manage them on her own."

Blushing, Elizabeth proclaimed with feeling, "I am not interested in forming any attachment with Mr Ellis, and beg you not to speak of such things, especially in front of our neighbours. I could not bear the mortification."

Mr Bennet raised his brows in amusement while her mother huffed her displeasure. "If you continue to take that attitude, then I do not know what will become of you after your father is dead, for I shall not be able to keep you!"

WHERE MR BINGLEY PERSUADES MR DARCY.

Two days after Mr Ellis arrived in Hertfordshire, Darcy returned from a meeting with his solicitor to find Charles Bingley lounging before a blazing fire in his Brook Street home, enjoying a cup of tea.

"Bingley," he said warmly, shaking his friend's hand before claiming the chair opposite him. "I am surprised to find you in London. I imagined you were far too focused on lovemaking to leave Netherfield for any length of time. I am glad for your company, however. Tell me, how much time do you plan on spending in town before you return to the country?"

Bingley grinned. "I cannot deny that I have been most agreeably engaged in Hertfordshire, but after I received your letter, I realised I could not possibly put off meeting with my solicitor any longer. There are some matters of business I should see to and would prefer to take care of them now, so I will not have to attend to them on my honeymoon. With any luck my business here will be concluded in a se'nnight."

Darcy's face fell. "So long?" He had been hoping he could leave for Hertfordshire within the next forty-eight hours.

"I will be the first to admit it is rather longer than I would otherwise wish, but as it happens, I have another reason for being in town." He gave Darcy a look—half laughing, half nervous. "I intend to prevail upon Caroline to return to Netherfield. I have a desire to entertain my neighbours and return the hospitality they have shown me. I also wish to hold a dinner in honour of Miss Bennet before our wedding. I can hardly do so without my sister to help me plan and to act the part of hostess."

Darcy regarded him with some scepticism. "Miss Bingley will hardly be happy. You know she will attempt to dissuade you from your course and, if that fails, will likely refuse to accompany you at all. From what I gathered from your letters, she was by no means pleased with your forming such an intimate alliance with the Bennets."

"No, she certainly will resist, but I do have something up my sleeve. I plan on using your residence at Netherfield for leverage so that I might have her agreement sooner than later, and with far less exertion on my part."

Upon seeing Darcy's look of indignation, Bingley laughed. "Oh, come now, man! You certainly owe me at least this much. Besides, you do not have to stay at home, you know. You can go out shooting and riding from dawn until dusk if you so choose. There is also excellent company to be had, for I have recently made the fortuitous acquaintance of Sir William Lucas's nephew, Mr Ellis."

"You are under no obligation to entertain me while I am in Hertfordshire. I will find my own amusement, at very little inconvenience to you."

Bingley laid his teacup and saucer upon a richly lacquered table and sighed. "I have no doubt of your abilities, Darcy. I ask only that you have faith in my own. Mr Ellis happens to be a dear friend of the Bennets. I like him prodigiously."

Darcy frowned, never having heard the name before in his life.

"I know," Bingley said, holding up his hand, "and because I know *you*, you need not say one word in protest. I am intimately acquainted with your thoughts and opinions regarding the Bennets and the society they keep, and Mr and Mrs Wickham particularly. Believe me when I assure you that Mr Ellis is one gentleman whose manners and credentials will garner even your staunch approval."

"Bingley," Darcy began, embarrassed as he recalled his previous poor behaviour and ill opinions of his friend's soon-to-be relations, but Bingley ignored him in favour of promoting Mr Ellis.

"He has spent the last fourteen months in America, and the three years preceding those at Oxford. For so young a gentleman, his experience and knowledge of the world is impressive. He is also rich, having inherited a sizeable sum of money from a distant relative on his father's side, which he then invested quite wisely. He is a very industrious gentleman, not to mention extremely good-natured and agreeable."

Darcy rubbed his chin thoughtfully, suitably impressed. "America, you say. In addition to being industrious, your Mr Ellis must be quite an adventuresome gentleman as well. How did he find America? Was it to his liking?"

"You can ask him yourself, but I believe he liked it very well. He is but four-and-twenty, yet he has not only forged the Atlantic, but has plans to go all the way to Constantinople someday, perhaps even to the Orient. Now *that* is what I call an adventure."

"Indeed," Darcy agreed, his interest piqued by the prospect of conversing with such an interesting, well-educated, and well-travelled gentleman. "I look forward to an introduction, if you would be so kind as to arrange one."

"Nothing would give me greater pleasure than to introduce my newest friend to my oldest," Bingley replied, rubbing his hands together with a pleased smile. "Good. Good." He reached for his cup with an expression of undisguised congeniality and took a sip of tea. "I should probably forewarn you. Not only is Mr Ellis an excellent conversationalist, but he also happens to be a champion of my future sister and her pert opinions. I understand from Miss Bennet that he and Miss Elizabeth were nearly inseparable when they were children. In fact, they have managed to entertain the rest of us with the most amusing stories of their youthful adventures. As you can imagine, it causes Mrs Bennet no insignificant degree of vexation to see one of her daughters carry on so with any gentleman who could be the answer to all her hopes, but I find Miss Elizabeth's attitude refreshing. I daresay so does Mr Ellis."

Darcy started at the inclusion of Elizabeth's name. While he had hoped to glean some intelligence of her from his friend, he was ill-prepared to hear such a disturbing recitation. Gone was the picture he had formed in his mind of an amiable, well-read, industrious gentleman with whom he could possibly forge an equal friendship. Instead, Darcy imagined a clever young man whose wit, intelligence, and easy manners might not only gain Elizabeth's interest, but perhaps even secure her heart.

Oblivious to his friend's distress, Bingley prattled on about his new neighbour's abilities and achievements. Jonathan Ellis was an expert horseman and a first-rate scholar; he was eligible, handsome, and rich. Darcy's jealous mind revolted as all sorts of unsavoury scenarios formed: Elizabeth, laughing at something Ellis had said. Elizabeth, completely smitten. Elizabeth in love.

The idea of Elizabeth being in love with any man other than himself made Darcy feel ill.

Eventually, the rational portion of his brain began to prevail over the fantastical. Mr Ellis had only just returned to the area after many years away; therefore, it was impossible that such a deep romantic attachment had formed in so little time as two days. On the other hand, this was a young man whom Elizabeth had apparently known her entire life. What if an attraction between them had existed before Mr Ellis had gone away? What if their attraction had been of long standing? What if their admiration of one another had been rekindled? What if...

Unable to sit still a moment longer, Darcy abandoned his chair and strode to the window. He ran one hand across his mouth in an agitated manner before placing both upon his hips. Like a child who wanted his own way, he was suddenly impatient to go to Hertfordshire; but Bingley had only just arrived in town and had yet to conduct his business. What Darcy wanted was futile.

"Whatever is the matter with you?" Bingley enquired with much apparent puzzlement. "Are you feeling unwell?"

"Not at all," Darcy replied crisply, standing with his back to his friend as he glared at the street below. "I am well, thank you."

"Good. Then I trust you will be in fine form come Saturday next. There is to be an assembly in Meryton, and I sincerely hope you will dance at least a few dances. I cannot countenance your standing around in your usual stupid manner. The people of Hertfordshire have been very gracious to me, despite the inconsistency in my behaviour to them over the past year. I am determined to give them no further reason to think poorly of me, or of any member of my household. I will brook no opposition, Darcy. I will have you dance."

"I shall endeavour not to disappoint you."

"See that you do not, for I will not take kindly to anyone slighting my future sisters, and that includes you. Perhaps you might even consider humbling yourself enough to ask Miss Elizabeth for a set. I daresay you owe her as much. You slighted her at the first assembly, you know, though I doubt you even recall it now. In any case, it would be a wonderful opportunity to make it up to her."

Master of himself once more, Darcy faced his friend. "You are quite right. Throughout our acquaintance, I have done nothing but occasion pain to Miss Elizabeth Bennet. Perhaps I will ask her for the honour of the first set."

Bingley chuckled. "You do not have to go that far. Besides, I am quite certain she is already engaged for those dances or will be very soon. You would do better to ask Caroline to stand up with you for the first two and be done with it, so that you might enjoy the rest of your evening in peace. Miss Elizabeth can wait."

But Darcy could not. He frowned, and while Bingley likely misinterpreted his churlish demeanour as an aversion to dancing with his sister, the hard set of his friend's jaw should have been a telling indication of far more.

The week passed with a painful degree of slowness for Darcy, as his thoughts centred upon Elizabeth and her activities in his absence. He was in a perpetual state of agitation. To distract himself, he spent countless hours at his fencing club. In addition to honing his skill with a foil and promoting an outlet for his pent-up frustration, fencing required concentration, which prevented his jealous mind from constantly dwelling upon a certain Hertfordshire beauty and the charming gentleman who was, according to Bingley, a possible rival for her affections.

He dined with his friend in Grosvenor Street on several occasions. While Bingley's request that his sister accompany him to Hertfordshire was initially received with abhorrence, once she understood Darcy was to return as well, her consent was rapidly attained; but Caroline Bingley was hardly eager to leave London. A trip to Bond Street was arranged so she could visit her modiste. There were also evenings to be passed with friends at the theatre, the opera, previous invitations to dinners and card parties, to say nothing of the mornings devoted to leave-taking, for Miss Bingley's acquaintance in town was by no means insignificant.

By the end of the seventh day, Darcy's nerves were frayed and his patience worn thin. Knowing there would be no reprieve from more of the same attentions once they arrived in Hertford-shire, Darcy declined a third invitation to dine at the Hurst residence, opting instead to pass his final evening in London quietly at home.

All hope for a solitary evening was dashed when Colonel Fitzwilliam called and demanded Darcy's company at the theatre. Though he did not wish to go, Darcy's fondness for his cousin persuaded him to acquiesce. If all went well in Hertford-shire, he had no idea when they might meet again, especially if Lady Carlisle's worst fears were realised and Fitzwilliam was sent to the Continent to face Bonaparte and his army.

The two gentlemen proceeded to Covent Garden in Darcy's coach. London was a little thin this time of year, but the reticent master of Pemberley could find nothing to repine on that score. He was happy to forgo conversing with people whom he felt so little a desire to impress.

Colonel Fitzwilliam, however, took his time in the theatre's lobby admiring the ladies who peered coyly at both gentlemen from behind their silk fans. Eventually, they reached the sanctuary of Darcy's private box. Darcy wasted no time stepping inside. The rich fabric of the curtain fell soundlessly across the entrance like a protective shield and his stoic demeanour relaxed.

The two impeccably attired gentlemen painted a very agreeable picture. While one of them was clearly gratified by the attention they drew, the other exuded an air of practiced indifference. As the final bell sounded, indicating the performance would soon begin, the colonel nudged his pensive cousin in the ribs and directed his notice to a box situated across the theatre from their own. Darcy stiffened as his eyes locked with those of Lady Harrow and her daughter, Lady Eliza, whose lips turned upward in a coy smile of recognition. Unwilling to risk Lady Carlisle's displeasure should she learn of their attendance from her friends, both gentlemen rose from their chairs and bowed gallantly. The two ladies barely had time enough to incline their heads in acknowledgement before the orchestra began to play.

During the performance, Darcy was careful not to allow his gaze to wander. He focused his attention solely upon the actors on stage. Halfway through the first act Fitzwilliam leaned towards him, tilted his chin in the direction of Lady Harrow's box, and whispered, "I do not suppose you would care to pay your respects?"

"Not if it can be avoided," Darcy murmured. "I will not have half of London believing I intend to pay my addresses to Eliza Harrow. It is not widely known, but I leave for Hertfordshire tomorrow. You are a clever man. I trust you can deduce my intent on your own, if not the outcome."

Colonel Fitzwilliam clapped his cousin on the shoulder. "I am proud of you. It is about damned time."

The two gentlemen chose to forgo refreshment during the first intermission, and so it was that the colonel happened to catch a glimpse of two familiar figures entering the box across the way. "Dash it all," he muttered. Darcy's attention was caught, and Fitzwilliam nodded towards the Harrows, who were engaged in a flutter of activity. "My parents have joined their party."

It was at that moment the earl happened to catch sight of his son and nephew across the way. Darcy cursed under his breath as his uncle inclined his head to them. Lord Carlisle's gaze was pointed and steady. "I suppose we cannot escape paying our respects now. Why did you have to insist on the theatre tonight, of all nights? Had you no idea of your parents' intentions for the evening?"

The colonel offered his perturbed cousin an apologetic look. Darcy sighed irritably as he rose from his seat and followed him out of the box. It was slow going as both gentlemen made their way through the fashionable crowd milling about the theatre. They encountered countless acquaintances who wished to extend their greetings, though most seemed satisfied with a cordial nod or a quick bow as they passed, for which Darcy was thankful.

When at last they entered Lady Harrow's box, it was nearly time for the second act to begin. Darcy's countenance had become stiff and unyielding, while Colonel Fitzwilliam wore a friendly, open look full of ease and good humour, despite any feelings he had to the contrary. They were welcomed with much enthusiasm by the ladies. Small talk ensued until the ringing of the second bell. Darcy, anxious to extract himself from the sharp eyes of Lady Harrow and her eager daughter, began to make his excuses.

Lady Harrow, unwilling to see her guests depart so soon, offered Darcy a languorous smile. "There is no reason why you and Colonel Fitzwilliam should not join us for the remainder of the play. I daresay there is more than enough room for all of us."

Darcy glanced at his uncle, whose dour expression foretold the lecture that would follow should his nephew decline. Resisting the urge to roll his eyes, he extended his gratitude to Lady Harrow.

The earl nodded his approval while Lady Carlisle rose with alacrity. With the aplomb of a woman used to having her way, she neatly manoeuvred her nephew into a vacant seat beside Lady Eliza, who regarded him with a smile that bordered on provocative. It was an arrangement that afforded Darcy no pleasure. He felt the heavy gaze of the young lady upon him through the rest of the performance and, even more disconcerting, the brazen and repeated brush of her mother's leg against his own from her place to his right. When the curtain fell for the last time, signalling the end of the performance, he was the first to take his leave.

❦ 6 ❧

WHERE DARCY ALMOST LOSES HIS TEMPER.

Darcy awoke just before dawn to the steady tempo of a relentless, icy rain pelting the windows of his Mayfair home. Struggling to swallow his disappointment, he glared at the canopy overhead. As he was not in the habit of torturing his servants by forcing them to sit atop a carriage in weather unfit for his horses, he would remain in town another day. As the wind picked up, driving a thick sheet of freezing rain against the side of the house, Darcy muttered an oath and yanked the counterpane over his head.

He did not stir from the warm cocoon of his bed until many hours later. Though the weather had improved, there was still no chance of travelling any great distance that day. A cold, steady rain ensured the roads outside of town would not be serviceable.

As he sat down to a late morning meal, Lord and Lady Carlisle were announced and shown into the breakfast parlour. Considering the haste in which he had taken his leave the previous night, Darcy was unsurprised. He laid aside his newspaper, ordered a fresh pot of coffee, and waited for the browbeating to begin. His wait was not long.

Lady Carlisle began without preamble as she accepted a cup of tea from a footman with a peevish countenance. "Lady Harrow and I were quite put out last night when you and Richard went away so abruptly and, I daresay, so was dear Eliza! I am appalled by all the rushing about you have been doing lately. It is extremely unbecoming."

Darcy dismissed the servants. "My apologies, Lady Carlisle. I had fixed plans early this morning that have since been delayed due to the weather. I assure you it was not my design to offend."

The earl harrumphed, but the countess inclined her head, seemingly placated. "In that case, I trust you will endeavour to arrive in Park Street this evening in excellent time and remain there for the duration of her ladyship's party. I also expect to see you smile more. You are a handsome young man with the entire world laid out at your feet, yet you rarely smile when in company, particularly in the company of ladies. I cannot imagine why you would not."

A feeling of foreboding settled in Darcy's stomach. "Lady Harrow is hosting an evening party?"

"Fear not, Nephew," said the earl with a sardonic smirk. "Only the most eligible ladies have been issued invitations. You need not concern yourself with their suitability, only the size of their dowries."

Rolling his eyes, Darcy helped himself to some toast. "I fear you are mistaken. I cannot recall receiving any such invitation from her ladyship. It is likely she does not mean to include me in her scheme."

"But of course she does," his aunt insisted. "Really, Darcy! You know Lady Harrow is fond of you, and Lady Eliza admires you exceedingly! All our closest friends will be there, and Richard as well." She levelled a stern look at him. "I am warning you now —do not so much as attempt to monopolise his attention for your personal amusement. This evening Richard shall spend his time more productively by applying himself to Miss Veronica Morrison's entertainment. You would do well to emulate his efforts by devoting yourself to Lady Eliza in a similar fashion."

"Begging your pardon, Aunt, but this is the first intelligence I have received of any such obligation for this evening. Are you *quite* certain my attendance is expected?"

"For heaven's sake, do not be obtuse," said the countess with an irritated huff. "Lady Harrow informed me herself of her intention to include you in the party. The invitation is most likely adrift amongst that unsightly mountain of correspondence you have piled in your study."

"There are currently no unopened letters on my desk other than what may have arrived this morning. Therefore, I cannot share your confidence, madam."

"The invitations were only sent *out* this morning," said Lady Carlisle exasperatedly. "It is an impromptu affair, intimate, to be sure, but the epitome of elegance. It is not an occasion to be missed. I understand Eliza is to play her harp."

Darcy stared at her. "Not only must Lady Harrow's household be in utter chaos, but the weather is undeniably wretched as well. I doubt it will suitably improve by this evening, at least not so much as to label her party the success she wishes."

Lord Carlisle snorted as he reached for a muffin. "Not all of us are as soft with our staff as you are, Nephew. Servants are servants. They are paid to do what they are bid, not what is agreeable to them. Lady Harrow's minions always manage to rise to whatever occasion is at hand. If they did not, she would never keep them on, and they damn well know it. As far as the weather, none of the ladies included in the party will allow this insignificant drizzle to keep them at home, not when there are eligible young men to receive them. Surely you are not afraid of a little rain?"

Darcy bit back a bitter retort. "Hardly, but I must decline. I am engaged to spend this evening with friends. I trust you will convey my regret to Lady Harrow when you see her."

Though he abhorred disguise, Darcy saw no harm in employing a bit of deception in this case. He would call upon Bingley later to discuss the delay in their plans, but beyond that he had little to do that day and no fixed engagements for the evening. Dining with Lady Eliza, her mother, and their insipid friends would be a punishment, especially after being denied the bittersweet pleasure of calling upon Elizabeth. God willing, Darcy would be in Hertfordshire by mid-afternoon tomorrow and dancing with Elizabeth Bennet by eight o'clock tomorrow night.

"What do you mean you are already engaged?" his aunt demanded with some distress. "We have been invited to dine at Chadwick House! Certainly, you can put these other people off until another time."

"I am afraid that will be impossible," said Darcy, spreading jam on his toast. "I am travelling to Hertfordshire tomorrow, presumably at first light."

Lord Carlisle frowned. "You mentioned nothing to me about having any business in that part of the country. How long do you expect to be gone?"

"I am not yet certain. My friend Bingley is to marry a local lady within a fortnight, but I hope to remain in the area until Christmas, when I join Georgiana at Pemberley."

The countess frowned with distaste. "Really, Darcy, I thought you would have given up that acquaintance by now. I must admit I never understood your desire to associate with such a family. There is absolutely no advantage to be gained by your knowing them. Any benefit from the connexion is all on their side."

"Bingley and I have been friends since Eton. I could not ask for a better one. He is now well-established in society and has taken possession of a fine estate, Netherfield Park. He is in every facet of his conduct a gentleman and I am proud to know him."

Lady Carlisle laughed sardonically. "What of his sisters? Do they conduct themselves as gentlewomen? The eldest, married off to that drunken dandy when she was barely of age? And do not get me started on the youngest! There cannot be too little said on that subject, for it is hardly friendship she seeks from you, or any other gentleman of means for that matter. The whole family is interested only in what they can get. Their nature is entirely mercenary, and you are woefully naïve if you believe otherwise."

"My parents never saw anything to object to in my friendship with Charles Bingley," said Darcy with mounting annoyance. "My mother was fond of him."

"And in that respect your dear parents were fools. Of course, they could not possibly issue any objection to your so-called friendship with the upstart son of a rich tradesman when the son of Old Wickham, your father's steward, was forever with you at Pemberley." Lady Carlisle wore a mocking expression as she raised her teacup to her lips. "I believe we all know how well *that* boy turned out."

"There can be no comparison between the two," Darcy charged as he tossed his napkin aside and drove the tip of his index finger onto the table for emphasis. "While one man is wholly respectable, honourable, and good in everything he does, the other has chosen to pursue the path of a debauched reprobate. You do my friend a gross injustice."

"That is enough," said the earl sternly. "However much we disapprove of such connexions, it is done. I shall not begrudge you your friendship with the man. Bingley has stood by you for many years. He saw you through the loss of your parents, and your loyalty to him does you credit. But I digress—there is a matter of significant import I came to address today and address it I shall, once and for all."

Of course, Darcy thought resentfully, bristling under his uncle's reprimand. *Of course, there is some other purpose for this morning's inconvenience.*

Though Darcy was a grown man and master of a vast estate, the earl believed neither age, nor means alone gave any man the right to make his own choices, not so long as certain familial obligations remained unfulfilled. Only after he had secured his future—taken a wife and sired an heir or two to ensure the continuation of his bloodline—did a man earn the right to follow his own course.

As for the institution of marriage, Lord Carlisle may have been be a proponent of it, but he by no means held it sacred. He considered fidelity to be something a man owed to other men and to God; not a solemn vow made in earnest at the altar and kept for the sake of a wife.

"No doubt," Lord Carlisle began sourly, *"no doubt,* you recall my dissatisfaction with the preferences you professed last week when Richard and I called upon you. I have no idea what has gotten into you over the last several months but, God Almighty, I intend to find out.

"You used to be a reasonable, level-headed young man—not unlike your father at your age—but my brother-in-law was far too practical a man to have ever entertained such notions of vagary with any degree of seriousness, nor would he have encouraged his only son in such a direction. No, sir! George Darcy knew what he was about, understood the seriousness of his obligations, and fulfilled his duty to his family and secured a successful future for himself with a woman with affluence and wealth."

"As we established yesterday, sir, your opinions on matrimony and society's estimation of a lady's worth versus my own are very different," said Darcy, attempting to tamp down his annoyance with the turn the conversation had taken. "I see no reason to pursue this argument."

The countess stared blankly at him, but the earl glared.

Darcy affected not to notice. "As for my father, his decision to marry my mother was ultimately his own. It certainly could not be said their marriage came at the cost of any personal sacrifice to himself. He forfeited nothing of his own happiness when their union was formed. Not only did my father love my mother, but he held her in the highest esteem."

"Perhaps," the earl allowed, "but you cannot be so naïve as to believe their marriage began as such. That George Darcy thought himself in love when he was first introduced to my sister is ludicrous! Her opinions meant nothing compared to her title and her fifty thousand pounds. Your parents were both practical people who recognised and embraced the full potential of their union for what it was—a brilliant alliance of two ancient, respectable families, vast property, and extensive wealth.

"I will not pretend that your mother did not have other inducements at her disposal beyond those of our family's material riches to entice your father—she was, after all, a handsome woman and greatly admired in her day. But let there be no mistake about it—your father's devotion to her came later, as did her affection for him—several years later, after she had done her duty and given birth to you. I had thought your father, as fastidious as he was about upholding familial responsibility and honour, would have explained to you the reality of their union long ago. I now see such a task must fall to me, as does the matter of reacquainting you with the way the land lies in this family."

"You can have nothing further to say—" Darcy began, but the earl held up a hand to silence him and forged onward in his usual forceful manner.

"Be silent until I have done! I am patriarch of this family and as such I cannot, nor will I ever, condone the flippant attitude with which you have chosen to address the urgent business of providing your estate with an heir! Your obligation to your father's memory, your sworn duty in this life, and your top priority is to make an advantageous marriage and sire an heir to continue the legacy you have inherited, and the fulfilment of your duty is overdue!"

Lord Carlisle slapped his hand heavily upon the table. "I should not have to remind you that the manner which you choose to go about fulfilling your obligations will not only affect your future, but that of Pemberley and Georgiana as well. You are not some inexperienced young buck who has only recently reached his majority, but a seasoned lord and master of a great ancestral estate in possession of an income and various other holdings worth nearly fifteen thousand pounds per annum!"

"I am capable," said Darcy in a clipped voice, "of finding my own wife in my own time."

"Given the preposterous convictions you are currently courting, you will be a bachelor forever! By God, it is not healthy! A man needs a wife! A man needs heirs, plain and simple! It is the order of the world, and I expect you to rise to the occasion and do as you are bid to preserve your rightful place in it. You *will* choose a wife. You *will* marry. You *will* sire an heir, and you will do so before Georgiana makes her debut next year so that you can provide your sister with the proper guidance required to one day assume her own place among London's elite!"

Silence fell upon the room and Lord Carlisle turned his attention to his discarded muffin. Through a red haze of fury and indignation, Darcy glared at him. Earl or not, family patriarch or not, he had no right to lecture Darcy as though he was an adolescent schoolboy! Darcy's outrage was such that he did not trust himself to speak.

His uncle appeared none the wiser, but Lady Carlisle, who had been soberly sitting across the table, gave Darcy a staunch look of disapproval and clucked her tongue. "I suggest you calm yourself, Nephew. What your uncle says is true. You may not believe so at this juncture, but one day you shall awaken from this daze of perpetual bachelorhood in want of something more substantial and satisfying. Then, and only then, will you appreciate all your uncle has said."

She sniffed disdainfully and cast a narrowed glance at her husband. "Of course, you will never find what you seek in one of your clubs, Darcy, and certainly not in the arms of some cheap courtesan! You must think of Georgiana and of Pemberley. You must think of yourself and of your respectability. With the appropriate woman as your wife, you will increase your wealth, property, and position in society. The woman a man chooses is responsible for the making of that man."

In her words and her tone and her countenance, Darcy recognised the tension and resentfulness present in his aunt's own union. Though still furious with his uncle for his officiousness, Darcy soon felt that fury begin to dissipate. Their marriage, like so many marriages among those of London's *bon ton,* had not been forged from affection, but born of convenience. *How ironic that a match of convenience inevitably becomes an inconvenience without a true admiration and respect for one's spouse.*

Knowing there was nothing to be gained by pursuing a topic none of them would ever agree upon, Darcy swallowed his ire and reached for his coffee cup. His relations and their antiquated opinions would be gone soon enough. He could feign civility for another half an hour and think of pleasanter things in the meantime.

Across the table, Lord Carlisle appeared perfectly content to enjoy the rest of his repast in silence, despite the lingering hostility in the air. He claimed another muffin and took a hearty bite. A shower of crumbs landed on his waistcoat, and he absently brushed them away.

Lady Carlisle turned her nose up at him and rose from her chair with an abruptness that made both men turn their heads with a start. "Your uncle and I have given you much to contemplate this morning," she said stiffly, "but we must be going before the hour grows later. I have other calls to make. I will, of course, convey your deepest regret to Lady Harrow and Lady Eliza when I have the pleasure of seeing them this evening. They will be extremely disappointed to forfeit your society. They had their hearts set on your attendance, as did I, but I suppose that is of little consequence to *you.*"

Rather than reply with a sardonic retort, Darcy inclined his head. "I thank you, Lady Carlisle."

"It is of little matter," she replied with a dismissive wave of her hand. "Since you seem to be so busy running after your friends, however undeserving they are, I will host an intimate dinner with our own dear friends upon your return to town next month, before you travel to Pemberley. Do make sure you attend, Nephew. You are a member of this family and it would be most unseemly if you were to twice fail to make an appearance." With that, the countess took her leave.

The earl tossed the remainder of his muffin onto his plate with an oath and glared at the back of his wife's head.

Exhausted by their antics and eager to have them gone, Darcy rose from his chair to see her out, but his stubborn uncle remained seated and placed a firm hand upon Darcy's arm to restrain him. Lady Carlisle noticed not. She had already bustled out of the room with her nose in the air as the train on her gown trailed gracefully behind her.

"Despite your high-handedness," said his lordship, "you are smart enough to know you cannot possibly entertain mixed company without a wife on hand. Georgiana can act as hostess for a time, but certainly cannot continue once she makes her own match. You will need a woman in your home, Darcy—one who understands the art of pleasing your guests, as well as the art of pleasing a man."

The earl gave his nephew a crass, meaningful look impossible to misinterpret.

Darcy struggled to repress a fresh wave of disgust. "Georgiana is not out and is therefore unprepared to leave my protection. As for myself, let me make one thing perfectly clear—I shall never abide any woman, especially one I have no interest in, being foisted upon my notice or paraded before me as though she were a piece of horseflesh! I will choose my own wife in my own time and will brook no opposition to my choice or permit any attitude of disrespect towards her should the future Mrs Darcy fail to meet with the approval of any member of society, including those of this family."

His uncle, however, merely smirked and waved him off with a bark of coarse laughter. "Go to the country and sow your oats at your friend's estate for a fortnight or two. I daresay you will find a fair bit o' muslin to keep you well enough occupied until your return. But once you are back in London, I expect you to go out more, mix with society, and find some pretty, young heiress who strikes your fancy. It need not be Eliza Harrow if you are truly set against her. I will handle your aunt.

"If you do not wish to be shackled to your cousin Anne, however, I suggest you get to it before Catherine mistakes your bachelorhood for confirmation that you plan to appease her. God help you, Darcy, if she does! Lord knows you will find no earthly pleasure in that quarter. What a prissy, sickly thing that girl is! I would rather gouge my eyes out with a spoon than dip my quill in that inkwell."

Though he had never found Anne de Bourgh appealing, Darcy muttered a retort on behalf of her honour and walked briskly towards the front hall where he could see his aunt standing before a gilded looking glass adjusting her pelisse. Darcy's butler attended her.

Before he could set foot in the hall, however, the earl took hold of his nephew's arm once more and yanked him to a halt. "You had better take care in that blasted country shire. Be discreet about your pursuits, whatever they are, or you will feel the full weight of my temper when you return. I will not abide your name being linked with a scandal!"

Darcy could not remember a time in his life when he had ever looked forward to travelling any distance in a carriage with Caroline Bingley, but come the following morning, he settled into the seat opposite her in his own conveyance gratefully. The last week had tried his patience severely. His uncle's expectations were the least of his problems. The most worrisome was Elizabeth's reception of him once he reached Hertfordshire. Added to that was the presence of one Mr Ellis. How that gentleman might affect Darcy's plan to engage her heart was anyone's guess. Darcy found he was no more prepared to face a rival for Elizabeth on this day than he had been eight days prior, when he first learnt of the man's cursed existence from Bingley.

As the well-sprung coach-and-four rocked and swayed over the bumpy London road, jostling its three occupants while the driver negotiated deep, frozen ruts, Darcy made a half-hearted attempt to attend to the conversation at hand. If Bingley noticed his friend's distraction, he did not remark upon it, and Miss Bingley, Darcy had long ago discovered, was often gratified to receive nothing from him beyond an occasional monosyllable.

They travelled until midday before stopping at an inn, where they broke their journey and spent a comfortable hour before a blazing fire partaking of a repast of cold meat and other such fare before setting out once more. Shortly after their carriage turned back upon the main road, both Bingleys succumbed to the effects of the rich meal they had consumed and the idle state of travel. Darcy watched their eyelids droop and their heads loll against the back of their seat and sighed with relief. At last, he was left to his own devices and in blessed silence.

It was not long afterwards that the rhythmic swaying of the conveyance forced Darcy's own eyelids to grow heavy. He laid aside the book he had been attempting to read, stretched his tall frame as best he could upon the seat, and arranged a thick rug on his lap. Soon, he was asleep.

❦ 7 ❦

WHERE MR ELLIS AND MR BINGLEY BOTH LOSE THEIR PATIENCE.

Rubbing the last vestiges of sleep from her eyes, Elizabeth peered through the curtains of her bedchamber window and smiled. The entire lawn was blanketed by a thick layer of frost. Even the branches and tree trunks were robed in a shimmering sheen of rime, giving the landscape a magical transformation. Careful not to disturb Jane's slumber, Elizabeth dressed in near darkness, struggling with the buttons at the back of her gown. Donning her outerwear, she descended the stairs and hurried from the house.

Though the temperature was cold, the appearance of the sun slowly ascending the distant hills was a vast improvement over the dark, angry sky the previous day. She made her way to the stables, where one of the boys saddled a horse for her and held the reins as she mounted from the block with practiced ease.

With a flick of her wrist Elizabeth urged her mount, an even-tempered chestnut mare named Abacus, towards an open expanse of fields on the far side of her father's estate. Clouds of steam from their quickened breaths rose in quick succession as Elizabeth increased their pace. She smiled with pleasure as the wind whipped back her bonnet, wreaking havoc with the simple hairstyle she wore. Before long, her hair flowed free as each pin was cast off—a metaphoric trail of breadcrumbs through Longbourn's frost-covered fields.

Elizabeth Bennet was often called a great walker, but she was also an equally competent horsewoman. Her only regret was that she was not able to ride more than one season during the year with any regularity—and the coldest one at that; but there was nothing to be done. The horses were needed in the fields or to pull the family's carriage. At Longbourn the crops and the harvest were first and foremost, and riding—unless one conceded to the geriatric pace of Old Nellie, the brood mare—was a rare indulgence the Bennet ladies were seldom able to afford.

After nearly reaching Meryton, Elizabeth doubled back until she found herself upon Netherfield's land. Solemnly, she sat astride her horse and watched as the great chimneys emitted a steady stream of smoke, an indication that the servants within were busy preparing for their master's homecoming. Jane had been distressed by the unexpected delay in Bingley's return, but Elizabeth had reminded her that Miss Bingley was to accompany him. There was little chance Netherfield's master would risk travelling with his sister in such weather as they experienced the previous day. The assembly would be held that night. For her sister's sake, Elizabeth hoped her future brother would arrive in good time to attend it.

Several minutes passed in quietude before Abacus, not usually prone to skittish behaviour, sidestepped towards the open field and tossed her head. Elizabeth smoothed her gloved hand over the mare's thick neck and murmured comforting words while she scanned her surroundings, searching for the cause of her horse's distress.

A short distance away she spied Jonathan Ellis riding his own mount.

"Good morning to you, Mr Ellis," she called to him. "Save for the starlings, I did not expect to meet with anyone so early on such a cold morning."

He tipped his hat to her as he approached and guided his horse alongside her own. His cheeks were bright from the cold. "Good morning, Lizzy. What brings you to Netherfield on this chilly morning?"

"I could not sleep. The property needs a little liveliness, I think. It appears quite empty without our amiable neighbour."

"Certainly, you are not fretting over Mr Bingley's return?"

"Jane misses him, but her impatience for his return is nothing to my mother's anxiety. Had Mr Bingley failed to inform her of his determination to return with his sister, I am convinced that Mamma would have gone to London herself to fetch him by now. You know today is the day of the assembly, and it would never do for any of her daughters to be without a partner for the first set."

Mr Ellis chuckled. "From what I have seen, Jane and her Mr Bingley not only appear well matched, but very much in love."

"They are, and I must say my future brother's adoring looks and saccharine speeches could not be more welcome after the dejection Jane suffered last winter. She deserves this happiness. They both deserve it."

"And what of your own happiness?"

A flock of blackbirds landed on Netherfield's front lawn, their calls amplified in the crispness and quiet of the early morning hour. Elizabeth turned her head aside to watch them. "I rejoice in Jane's good fortune. Her happiness cannot possibly be equalled."

Mr Ellis looked meaningfully at her. "Come now, this show of indifference has gone on long enough. I am not so easily put aside as the rest of the world, nor so effortlessly distracted by a book or talk of your sister's impending wedding. You are suffering—anyone with half a brain can see it. You can no more deny it than I can ignore the looks of concern Jane casts in your direction."

"Jane worries a great deal too much. It is her nature, nothing more."

"It is not in Jane's nature to fret over you so much, Lizzy. At least not without just cause. She is your most trusted confidant —the one person in the world whose counsel you most value— yet it is clear to me, by her actions and your own, that you have not shared with her the cause of your disheartened spirits. You must know your continued reluctance to do so will only further alarm her."

Elizabeth bowed her head, and with great gravity pretended to examine her horse's reins. She was in no humour to indulge her friend's curiosity, but his observations were astute enough that she could not easily dismiss his concern. Past experiences reminded her she could not simply brush Mr Ellis off and be done with it. He was far too persistent and too little swayed. "I refuse to mar this joyous time by relating to my dearest sister that which will afford her little pleasure. It would be selfish of me and unfair to her."

"Confide in me, then. Permit me to share your burden, to bear some of the weight that presses so heavily upon your heart. It pains me to see you thus."

Elizabeth fell silent.

"Lizzy," her friend chided. "Something transpired during the time I have been away. What was it, pray? Surely, enough time has passed that Lydia's marriage to Lieutenant Wickham is no longer of any concern?"

Though Elizabeth bristled at Mr Ellis's intimation of her sister's disgrace, she could not fault him for his solicitation, especially when sincere worry for her well-being was evident in the crease of his brow. His desire to alleviate her concern reminded her of the closeness they had shared in their youth. Together, they had raced across the countryside, waded through murky ponds, and kept each other's confidences, however trivial they now seemed.

Elizabeth longed for that simpler, less complicated time of her life—a time when a certain gentleman from Derbyshire had not existed to her, a time when she was not plagued by heartache and mortification or pained by regret.

She bit her lip in indecision. *I have kept my own counsel for so long. Perhaps sharing my burden might do me some good. Perhaps it may even begin to loosen the hold Mr Darcy has upon my heart and allow me to move on once and for all.*

At length, she said, "There was a gentleman I grew to care for, but he left for town some months ago and has not returned. It seems unlikely he ever will."

Mr Ellis appeared startled by the news, but quickly regained his composure. "You have received word from him, then?"

A flush of heat warmed her countenance and Elizabeth looked away. "No understanding exists between us. I have learnt from a mutual friend that he does not plan to return to Hertfordshire in the foreseeable future. More recently, there has been some speculation of an engagement to another lady, though I have yet to receive confirmation of it from another source. Being acquainted with some of the particulars, I am inclined to discredit it as a rumour and nothing more, but the idea of him pledging himself to another—either now or in the future —pains me."

"Were only your own affections engaged, or do you believe him attached to you as well?"

"He was by no means unaffected, though his admiration was not generally known. I do not know for certain whether he still holds me in a tender regard. For many reasons, ours has not been an easy history. We move in very different circles and, in the eyes of his most intimate acquaintance, my family and I must be considered beneath him, especially now that Lydia—" Elizabeth's words caught in her throat. She glanced at her friend and saw his countenance resembled a storm cloud.

Despite his agitation, Mr Ellis allowed her a moment to compose herself and held his tongue.

Elizabeth knew him well, though. He would speak his mind soon enough. Training her eyes heavenward, she laughed without humour. "I hardly know what I am about anymore. I have no idea what to think after all that has transpired. I know only that it is over and done. Perhaps it is for the best."

"Codswallop," he said tersely. "I know precisely what to think and I assure you it is nothing so generous as the explanation you recited to me just now. Such a heartless scoundrel does not, cannot deserve you. How any man could dismiss an intelligent, discerning, lovely young woman such as yourself astounds me! He is not worthy of your regret, never mind the title of gentleman. I demand to know his name."

Though his loyalty moved her, Elizabeth had no intention of revealing Darcy's identity to anyone, most especially her over-protective friend. "You do not know him, so it makes little difference. Despite what you believe of him, he is a good man, a gentleman in every respect, and it pains me to hear you refer to him in such disgraceful terms. I beg you would not."

Her friend only scoffed.

"Mr Ellis," she said, "I do not wish him any ill will and certainly no harm. No one else knows or even suspects such an attachment exists on my part other than you. Even the gentleman himself is likely ignorant of my affection for him. No damage has been done beyond my disappointment, which is no one's fault but my own for failing to better guard my heart."

Mr Ellis shook his head at her, looking as though he had tasted something sour.

A heavy, charged silence settled upon them and Elizabeth soon felt herself bowing under the weight of it. In desperate need of a distraction, she looked upon Netherfield—the house, the fields, the countryside, anywhere but at her disapproving friend.

At last, she could bear no more. "Enough! This disappointment has dampened my spirits long enough and it distresses me to no end to imagine you and I are now at odds with one another because of it. To further dwell upon my predicament will do neither of us any good. I insist you cease your resentfulness. Now that I have spoken of it—now that I have confided in you—I am more determined than ever to put the entire business behind me. All will soon be well. Indeed, it must."

"By all means," Mr Ellis decried, "let us pretend the entire business never happened. Let us pretend that your heart remains whole and that you and this scoundrel parted as the best of friends. Yes, all is extremely well!"

Elizabeth's temper flared. She had been foolish to think that baring her soul would bring her any measure of solace. She should have told him nothing of her disappointment, nothing of her regret, nothing of her broken heart. "Enough has now been said on the subject, sir. We ought to speak of something else."

"Enough has not been said, in my opinion, but if you wish to simply sweep your heartache under the drawing room carpet as though it is of no consequence then by all means, madam, go right ahead." He made a broad sweeping motion with his arm and pretended to dust off his hands. "There," he said sardonically. "Now everything is simply magnificent!"

"That is not what I meant at all," Elizabeth said heatedly. "Stop being obtuse!"

"*I* am being obtuse? That is rich indeed!" Yanking his hat from his head, he raked his gloved fingers through his hair in frustration. The abruptness of his movements startled his horse and Mr Ellis took several moments to soothe him with gentle strokes and quiet murmurs.

Elizabeth observed him as she stroked her own horse, drawing what comfort she could from the warm steadiness of the animal, and wondered whether she and her friend would part amicably or whether their argument would leave a lasting tear in the tapestry of what had always been a strong, easy friendship. She sincerely hoped for the former.

It soon became apparent her friend felt the same. "Damnation," he muttered as his horse had begun to graze. "It gives me no pleasure to argue with you, nor to occasion you pain...unlike another gentleman so wholly unworthy of your time, affection, and clemency—"

"Mr Ellis," Elizabeth warned. "I beg of you—*stop*. Do not make me regret confiding in you. Do not make my heartache worse."

He looked at her then, and in his eyes, Elizabeth saw more than righteous anger for what she had suffered in his absence. She saw pain and regret. He passed his hand over his eyes and donned his hat. "In such cases as these, I suppose it is wise for a man to concede defeat while he still has his head attached to his neck."

"Your sensibility regarding such matters is indeed commendable."

Mr Ellis exhaled heavily. "Forgive me. It was not my intent to upset you or to add to your distress. As for my concern for your well-being, I am afraid that is a topic upon which I can never capitulate. I will, however, endeavour to refrain from raising the subject of your heartache between us in the future. If you are amenable, I shall agree to disagree, but only on the condition that you do me the honour of dancing the first set with me this evening. It is not every day I have an opportunity to open an assembly with one of Hertfordshire's brightest jewels."

After their argument, his teasing was most welcome. "Your apology is accepted, as are your terms. The first two dances are yours, even though you do sound alarmingly like your well-meaning uncle when you say such ridiculous things."

He tipped his hat to her, and Elizabeth was relieved to see him smile.

The occasion called for some levity. "I have no doubt you will keep me well entertained this evening, Mr Ellis, but do take care to remember my new slippers. They are much lovelier than the pair Mr Collins ruined at Mr Bingley's ball last autumn. But on that subject, I shall not importune you. We have had enough disquiet for one morning, I fear."

"Your dear father would likely be of a different mind, at least regarding Mr Collins. What is it he says? 'For what do we live for, but to provide sport for our neighbours and laugh at them in our turn'?"

Elizabeth found she could not laugh, not at present. "Believe me when I say such advice is not nearly so amusing when it is your turn to be laughed at, sir."

"No, I would imagine it is not." His countenance grew serious once more. "I *am* sorry, exceedingly sorry, that we have quarrelled. Knowing I was absent when you and your sisters needed a brother to protect you pains me beyond words. All of you are dear to me, but you must know it is your friendship that has been one of the most important of my life."

She could not help being touched by his words, and the genuine sincerity and sentiment behind them. "There is nothing to be done now except to move forward. In Jane's case, hers is the happiest of endings, so there is no cause to repine in that quarter. Even Lydia appears satisfied with her situation. I know you wish to erase the ache in my heart and restore my spirit to its former happy state, but I am afraid that is not within your power. I am yet uncertain whether it is even within mine. We shall see what the future holds. Perhaps, if I am *very* lucky, in time I may meet with another Mr Collins."

Mr Ellis eyed her sceptically, likely knowing Elizabeth could never accept any man so obsequious and void of good sense as their cousin's husband. "What say you to a gallop across your father's fields? We could both do with some good-natured exercise after such a serious discussion. Such gravity hardly becomes us."

"No," Elizabeth agreed, "it does not." Eager to put their disagreement behind them, she spurred Abacus to a gallop.

With an exclamation, Mr Ellis roused his own mount into action, and soon both friends were racing across the fields bordering Netherfield as they urged their horses back towards Longbourn. Elizabeth was in the lead, her dark hair streaming behind her in the wind, while Mr Ellis followed closely in pursuit. The sound of his encouraging cries and the relentless pounding of his horse's hooves served as a constant reminder that her lead was not likely to last long.

☙❧

A quarter hour later, Elizabeth tumbled through the front door of Longbourn House with a smile on her lips. Her hair was unbound and wild, the hem of her skirts and even her petticoat was damp and caked with dirt, and her boots were a muddy mess. As she ascended the stairs and made her way down the hall to the bedchamber she shared with Jane, Elizabeth could hear her mother shrieking about the state of the bonnet she had discarded on the table. A warm fire crackled within, and Elizabeth shut the door behind her with a contented sigh.

Across the room, Jane stood before a large looking glass in nothing but her stockings, stays, and chemise as she held a white gown accented with pale blue embroidery and a matching sash against her figure.

She turned when Elizabeth entered and laughed as she took in her sister's dishevelled appearance. "Goodness, Lizzy! You look as though you took a tumble through the fields. I hope for your sake Mamma has not seen you."

Elizabeth wrinkled her nose as she attempted to tame her tangled curls with her fingers. Abandoning her hair, she busied herself with her half-boots instead. The ties were thoroughly caked with mud.

With care, Jane laid her gown upon the bed. "Here, allow me to help you."

"Absolutely not," Elizabeth cried, twisting away from her pristine sister as she tugged the remaining boot from her foot and flung it onto the floor. "I will not have Mamma blaming me for any flaws in your appearance. You shall remain as you are—a vision of angelic perfection." She crossed the room and stood before the looking glass, where she scrutinised her appearance with a critical eye. Her hair looked as though birds had nested in it. Her gown had fared little better. Elizabeth bit her bottom lip and sighed once more, this time resignedly. "On second thought, I would appreciate your assistance with the buttons on my gown. I can never seem to unfasten them myself." She swept her mass of unruly hair over her shoulder and presented her back to her sister.

Jane kissed Elizabeth's cheek as she began to work the covered buttons free. "Nor can you fasten them properly on your own. How I love you and your impulsive nature, Lizzy! You make me forget myself and any vexation I may harbour towards the rest of the world."

"I am happy to be of service," Elizabeth replied dryly as Jane released the last button and eased the garment from her sister's shoulders. "Since when, though, has it ever been in your nature to be as judgmental as that statement implies? Tell me, when have you ever looked unfavourably upon any person, or thought even one ill thought regarding any of our acquaintance?"

"It is true. I cannot help but feel everyone deserves the benefit of the doubt. For the moment, however, I am disappointed with Mr Darcy."

"Mr Darcy?" she enquired anxiously. "Whatever for?"

"For a great many things. Not only has he brought much melancholy to you by writing that letter of his, but I have lately realised how much pain he occasions Charles as well by refusing to return to Netherfield these past months. Charles asked him to stand up with him, you know, yet to my knowledge Mr Darcy has not even bothered to send him a reply. I begin to suspect he does not intend to continue their acquaintance. It is shameful! He is Charles's oldest friend! It angers me, Lizzy. I cannot help it."

Elizabeth was surprised. Jane had always staunchly defended Darcy and his actions to *her* in the past; she could not help feeling disconcerted by this sudden shift in their balance. She clasped her sister's hands as they sat upon the bed, taking care to avoid Jane's discarded ball gown.

"You must not blame Mr Darcy for failing to return to Hertford-shire. We know nothing of his business. We are hardly qualified to determine whether he is presently free to leave London or not. As far as severing his ties with Mr Bingley, I do not believe he would ever abandon his friend. I know Mr Darcy values their relationship very much. Our own family, though, you must own, is another matter entirely."

Jane looked at her askance.

"You cannot honestly blame Mr Darcy for wishing to distance himself as much as possible from us now that Mr Wickham is our brother. Though he may not be often in company with us in the future, Mr Darcy has no way of knowing that for certain. He is only aware that we are joined forever to an unscrupulous man who has wronged him repeatedly, as well as his beloved sister. The idea of meeting with him, even in passing, must be intolerable."

"Lizzy, if Mr Darcy had only divulged some of the truth of his dealings with Mr Wickham in the beginning, when we first formed the acquaintance, perhaps Lydia might have been spared such a fate as she must now endure. He kept all knowledge of Mr Wickham's behaviour and dissolute tendencies to himself. Mr Darcy need not have disclosed his private affairs, only a few details of Mr Wickham's character and general habits. His refusal to act has led to our family's suffering, and now Mr Darcy chooses to shun us! Please do not ask me to acquit him of his accountability for that, for I simply cannot do it, at least not at present. Not when he persists in treating my Charles so shabbily."

"Jane—" Elizabeth began, but Jane had not done.

"No Lizzy," she said firmly. "Perhaps if Mr Darcy were to oblige Charles and come to Netherfield, I could find it within my heart to forgive his failings as I have in the past, but I cannot do so now. I do not like to see my future husband slighted, especially by one of his dearest friends. His pain is my own and I feel it acutely! Forgive me for speaking so plainly. I do not wish to upset you as well."

Elizabeth turned her head aside as she squeezed her sister's hand. It pained her to have Jane think so ill of Darcy, but there was nothing Elizabeth could do about it. It was unlikely he would be returning to Hertfordshire, at least not until the wedding if at all. She certainly could not imagine him staying for any length of time if he did come.

Of course, there was always a chance they could be thrown into company together if his connexion with Bingley remained intact, as Elizabeth was sure it would, but she felt that Darcy would probably take every opportunity to distance himself from Mr Wickham and, therefore, from her. She suspected his sense of pride and familial duty was perhaps still too great to allow Miss Darcy to be in company with a woman who could claim the title of sister to George Wickham.

It was cruel, it was unfair, but it was the way of the world, and Elizabeth found that while she was gravely disappointed herself with Darcy for failing to fulfil all her hopes, she could by no means hold him accountable for Lydia's foolishness, nor for his fervent desire to protect his own sister from exposure and censure. As for the news of his purported marriage to his cousin, that was a subject upon which Elizabeth chose not to dwell, else she become submersed in a perpetual state of disconsolation. For the loss of Darcy's affections, she had mourned long enough.

❧

The clock in the drawing room at Netherfield Park struck nine times. Darcy exhaled in frustration as he paced the length of the room. Across from him Bingley sat slumped in an armchair by the fire, his fingers drumming an impatient staccato on the upholstered arms as he glared at the floor.

Darcy's own impatience swelled. "Good Lord, Bingley, we have missed the first set! By the time we arrive, the assembly will be over!"

Bingley shot him a look of equal exasperation. "What would you have me do? It is not as though we can leave without Caroline."

"It is not as though your sister wants to attend the assembly in the first place. She made that much clear this afternoon. We would be paying her a kindness by leaving her at home."

Bingley's expression grew thoughtful for a moment. "I suppose there is some merit to that plan," he conceded, "but you know we cannot possibly act upon it. She would be furious."

"Who would be furious, Charles?" Miss Bingley enquired as she entered the room. She came to stand before Darcy, a self-satisfied smile upon her face as she extended her hand to him.

Darcy accepted it, executed a quick, perfunctory bow, then released her. He felt his temper flaring and, to put some distance between himself and the source of his agitation, he crossed the room to retrieve his hat and gloves from the writing desk. "Why, Miss Jane Bennet, of course," he responded coolly. "I understand your brother engaged her for the first two dances, which we have long since missed. She is no doubt wondering what has become of him."

Miss Bingley waved her hand dismissively as she examined her reflection in a gilded looking glass upon the wall. She adjusted an ostrich feather on her turban. "Oh, that is nothing. She has likely found some other partner to amuse her by now. I daresay she has hardly even noticed your absence, Charles."

"Shall we go?" Bingley asked in a tight voice. His patience with his sister had apparently reached its end.

❧ 8 ❧

WHERE MR DARCY DOES NOT DANCE.

The second floor of the Grey Goose, where the Meryton Assembly Hall was located, was filled to bursting. The music was lively, as one would expect at a country dance, and there was a great amount of revelry between the single gentlemen assembled as they vied for the opportunity to claim the most desirable partners. Darcy blanched when he heard Elizabeth's name mentioned in concert with that of Mr Ellis. It seemed that gentleman had received the honour of opening the dance with her, as Bingley predicted.

His progress was as tedious as it was slow, and some effort was required to push his way through the crowd, particularly with Miss Bingley clinging to his arm. Bingley had hurried ahead to search for Miss Bennet, leaving Darcy to escort his sour sister.

Other than a few deferential bows of recognition, the people of Hertfordshire seemed inclined to let him be, and for that he was grateful. At present, he was focused on one task: locating Elizabeth Bennet. Even the advantage of his tall frame did little to aid him in such a crush. After an indeterminable amount of time, he caught sight of Bingley on the opposite side of the room. Mrs Bennet was speaking animatedly while Bingley watched Miss Bennet dance with one of her neighbours. Shaking his head, Darcy dragged Miss Bingley in their direction to pay his respects to Elizabeth's mother.

"How do you do, Mrs Bennet?"

Mrs Bennet ignored him and welcomed Miss Bingley with a great show of cordiality and much fanfare. When Darcy was finally acknowledged by her, it was with an air of one who had been slighted herself.

"Mr Darcy," she said, "you are welcome, too. It is a great surprise to see you here tonight. We had begun to think your business would keep you from Hertfordshire indefinitely."

Despite her rudeness, Darcy made an effort to appear affable. "I regret it has been so, but I assure you, madam, I have completed my business and hope to spend some weeks here with my Hertfordshire friends before I must return to Pemberley for Christmas. If I am late, my sister, who is currently in Derbyshire, will never forgive me."

Both Bingleys stared at him, as did Mrs Bennet.

Darcy ignored their astonished expressions and cleared his throat. "I trust your family is in good health?"

"Oh, yes," Mrs Bennet stammered. "We are all in excellent health, sir. But I must say it is hard, very hard indeed, having my youngest daughter settled so far from me. I do not know how poor Lydia shall get on living at such a distance as Newcastle, where she knows no one, save for her dear Wickham. I thank goodness it will not be so with Jane and Elizabeth."

Darcy, far from gratified to hear any mention of Wickham's name, was even less pleased to hear such a reference made to Elizabeth. "Is that so?"

"Why, of course, it is so! Netherfield is but three miles from Longbourn you know, and Lucas Lodge is not half that distance. There is no guarantee, I suppose, Lizzy will be able to settle there after the wedding—but what a fine thing it would be if she did!"

Alarmed by such a proclamation, Darcy could do no more than stare.

After what seemed to him a small eternity, Mrs Bennet comprehended his confusion and said, "Oh! But you have not heard, Mr Darcy, that Sir William's nephew, Mr Ellis, greatly admires my Lizzy. And a more agreeable, clever gentleman you will not find anywhere. I daresay he considers her to be the prettiest girl in the world, despite what some *other* gentlemen might think of her looks. He opened the dance with her this evening. What a handsome couple they made, too!"

Though an entire year had passed, Mrs Bennet's reference to what had been Darcy's initial opinion of her second-eldest daughter was perfectly clear, as was the smug, satisfied look she cast in his direction. Darcy's mouth felt as dry as a desert.

In contrast, Miss Bingley smiled widely. "How comforting for you, Mrs Bennet. It must indeed be a relief to know that dear Miss Eliza and her *fine eyes* may soon be so advantageously married and settled within such an easy distance of Longbourn. Tell me, has a date been set for the happy occasion?"

In no humour to endure Miss Bingley's jealous allusions in addition to such distressing talk, Darcy withdrew his arm from her grasp and moved to stand on the other side of his friend. His head reeled as Mrs Bennet tittered satisfactorily.

Surely, Elizabeth cannot possibly be engaged to this man—not in so little time as ten miserable days, even if she has known him practically her entire life!

"Not of yet, Miss Bingley, but I expect we will not have to wait long before he makes Lizzy an offer. Oh!" she cried. "Here comes Jane!"

Bingley had already departed and was hurrying across the room to intercept his betrothed, who was at that moment being led from the set by her partner. He kissed Miss Bennet's proffered hand, then greeted a man Darcy vaguely recognised as Robert Goulding with a good-natured smile and a cordial bow.

As she gazed at Bingley, Darcy observed Jane Bennet's serene countenance brighten and silently prayed there was any chance that Elizabeth would dare to look upon him with pleasure. Bingley placed Miss Bennet's hand upon his arm and covered it with his own, then led her to where Darcy stood with her mother and Miss Bingley. Further pleasantries were exchanged and Darcy, no longer able to restrain himself, enquired after Elizabeth.

Miss Bennet studied him for a long moment before she said, "My sister is well, Mr Darcy. She was lately dancing with one of our neighbours, Mr Crowell, whose family owns an estate not ten miles from Longbourn. Are you acquainted with him?"

Before he could answer that he did not, in fact, know Mr Crowell, Mrs Bennet said, "As you can see, sir, there are plenty of eligible gentlemen in want of a pretty partner this evening. Of course, that was not the case at the last assembly you attended in Meryton. Now that Jane is to be married, my Elizabeth is quite the favourite here tonight, and she is in excellent looks, if I do say so myself. Ask anyone in attendance and they will tell you it is so, especially dear Mr Crowell."

She turned to Miss Bennet. "What a fitting match he would be for your sister, Jane, if this business with Mr Ellis comes to nothing. But that is hardly likely, is it? Mr Ellis has been most attentive since his return!"

Miss Bennet offered her mother a tight smile and, to Darcy's relief, the music resumed before any more could be said of Elizabeth's suitors.

Eagerly did Bingley lead Miss Bennet to the centre of the room, where countless other couples were forming a new set. Having yet to see any sign of the object of his desire—or her admirers—Darcy excused himself and made his way to the other side of the room, where he took up a post near the bottom of the formation against the far wall.

Before long, his hopes were answered.

Elizabeth moved with the same grace and lightness of foot she always employed whenever Darcy had the pleasure of seeing her dance. Her flushed countenance and bright eyes were a telling indication she had likely not been without a partner all evening. Her gown, the colour of fresh cream with accents of deep burgundy and gold embroidery, fit her to perfection. Darcy was enthralled by her beauty, which only appeared to have increased since he had last seen her. An all-too-familiar ache of longing swelled to a powerful proportion within his chest.

Elizabeth was engaged in a lively conversation with her partner, a handsome gentleman who answered her remarks with an alarming ease that indicated a familiarity between them Darcy did not want to consider. Contrary to the last time he had been in company with her, Elizabeth appeared self-assured and happy. Her current, carefree demeanour was a far cry from the despondent state and decidedly low spirits he had last witnessed in her. Though he was pleased to see her spirits so well recovered, Darcy could not help but feel some degree of pain; the restoration of Elizabeth's exuberance was obviously not owed to him.

The dance forced her to separate from her partner and, as Elizabeth crossed in front of another gentleman, Darcy admired the graceful curve of her neck and the enticing manner that a few wayward curls caressed her skin. Swallowing his desire, he wished more than ever he had the right to step forward and tear her away from her partner, especially as the two reunited a moment later, resulting in a mischievous curve of her lips. As the gentleman took her hand in his own, Darcy could not control the jealousy that seared through him, nor the decidedly pained expression that crossed his face. His stoic mask began to slip.

In the next moment, Elizabeth circled around her partner, her eyes met Darcy's, and her teasing smile was transformed to an expression of shock as she came to a sudden halt in front of him, the steps of the dance all but forgotten.

❧

Elizabeth could hardly credit that he, of all people, could be standing directly in front of her; but as she stared into his eyes, as dark and piercing as ever, and observed the strong line of his jaw, which was clenched so tightly his temples throbbed, she could not deny that it was indeed Fitzwilliam Darcy and no other.

What on earth is he doing here? she wondered in astonishment. *He is far too early for Jane's wedding to Mr Bingley if that is his purpose in coming. Oh! Confusing man! Why can I not be free of him, even for the span of one night?*

Mr Ellis touched her arm, a fleeting brush of his fingertips against the sleeve of her glove, and enquired as to her well-being. His voice, as he spoke her name, held a note of puzzlement as well as concern and prompted Elizabeth to remember herself. She quickly tore her eyes from Darcy and fixed them on her friend instead.

The host of distasteful expressions that had crossed Darcy's face mortified her, but Elizabeth's manners prevented her from repaying his show of disdain with her own incivility. She acknowledged him more formally with a brief curtsey and swiftly re-joined the dance. Within seconds she and Mr Ellis were enveloped by the energetic mass of swirling ivory skirts and dark-coloured tailcoats as they moved about the set. Forcing a smile to her face, Elizabeth reminded herself to breathe.

As soon as the dance ended, she excused herself and made her way with alacrity through the back hall to one of the dressing rooms, where she stepped inside and locked the door. Her breathing was as rapid as her heartbeat.

He had come! But why had he chosen to return on this night of all nights, when she was finally enjoying herself for the first time in many months? Why tonight, when she was finally, finally able to put him from her mind without her traitorous heart wishing for his presence or mourning his absence?

Elizabeth glimpsed her reflection in the looking glass upon the wall and expelled a shaky, rueful laugh at the sight of the elegant young woman who stared back at her. She could not deny that tonight she was in excellent looks, an observation reinforced again and again by the countless compliments and admiring glances she had received, as well as her full dance card. Though Elizabeth had been invited to dance on countless other occasions, her popularity on this night was such that she would not have to sit out during any of the sets unless she required rest or refreshment. It was a delightful novelty for her, and the reality of it had brought a smile to her face. For the first time in her life, Elizabeth had been given a taste of what it was like to be Jane.

At Mrs Bennet's insistence, Longbourn's upstairs maid had gone to great lengths to transform Elizabeth into the graceful beauty reflected in the mirror. In honour of the occasion, her mother had presented her with a lovely gold and ruby necklace that perfectly matched her new gown. It was a precious family heirloom passed down through many generations of Bennets. The expensive piece of jewellery not only completed her rich ensemble but gave Elizabeth the appearance of a well-dowered young lady of some consequence and restored a good deal of the confident sparkle she had lacked for so many months.

But Elizabeth was not fooled. She knew that her mother's sudden focus on her appearance was only a ruse, done with the hope that her least favourite of her five daughters might soon secure Mr Ellis for a husband, or perhaps some other eligible gentleman. Despite her mother's intent, Elizabeth found such attentions oddly edifying. Though she had no interest in securing Mr Ellis for anything beyond a few dances—and certainly no intent to encourage a romantic attachment—she determined to enjoy the advantages to be reaped from her newly acquired elegance. She had succeeded in doing so—and with great amusement and satisfaction—until the moment she had come face to face with Darcy.

With some effort, Elizabeth willed her racing heart to calm. Absolutely nothing had changed. She was still the same person she had always been. For the moment, she was dressed in jewels and satin, her hair was arranged with more sophistication than she was used to wearing it, and her lips were painted with just a touch of rouge; but she knew that none of her accoutrements altered her circumstances. She would forever be sister to George Wickham, a man who deserved no distinction or recognition from any of them, least of all Darcy. If she were to believe Mr Ellis's intelligence—that Darcy had finally acquiesced to Lady Catherine's demands to marry Miss de Bourgh—it mattered little in any case.

Elizabeth expelled a short, humourless laugh. Did it honestly matter who or when Darcy eventually married? With a scoundrel for a brother, a man of Darcy's notoriety and consequence in the world could never afford to sink so low as to offer a second time for her. It was a testament to the strength of his friendship with Mr Bingley that he had come back to Hertfordshire at all.

Struggling to keep her composure, Elizabeth bit her bottom lip and removed her gloves so she could splash some water from a porcelain basin upon her flushed cheeks. She could not stay within the dressing room for the rest of the evening, nor could she claim a headache and escape to Longbourn. Her mother would never permit it. There was nothing to do but return to the assembly and hope that Darcy's presence in Hertfordshire would not succeed in discomposing her for long.

Ten more minutes passed before Elizabeth felt mistress of herself enough to return. Despite her lingering trepidation, she donned her gloves, straightened her skirts, and opened the door. She had advanced no more than a few feet when she discerned a familiar figure moving towards her in the dimly lit hall.

Elizabeth hesitated, unsure whether she ought to continue, remain where she was, or retreat as Darcy's long, deliberate strides closed the distance between them. Her hands went immediately to her skirts, where she nervously twisted the expensive fabric with her fingers before she caught herself and hurriedly smoothed any offensive creases. Surely, her mother would be displeased were she to catch Elizabeth fidgeting with her new finery in such an appalling manner.

Finally, he came to stand before her, his mien serious, and Elizabeth's courage, as it often did in the face of such intimidation, rose. Knowing there was no way to avoid speaking to him at this point, she curtseyed and forced herself to address him with far more composure than she felt. "Mr Darcy, you are welcome back to Hertfordshire."

He executed a perfunctory bow but remained silent. His steady, steely look did nothing to put her at ease. Elizabeth's discomfort increased.

Why on earth does he not speak? she wondered with mounting agitation as she fought the urge to fidget with her gown. She glanced towards the door at the far end of the hall that led to the ballroom, then back again, just in time to catch his eyes darting from her heated cheeks to her daring décolleté.

Elizabeth felt her colour heighten, followed closely by a surge of indignance. The deserted back hall of the public assembly rooms, where anyone could happen upon them and misinterpret their awkward meeting as something far more clandestine in nature, was far from a respectable place to linger. "Good evening to you," she said, and stepped forward with the intent to go around him and return to her family.

"Miss Bennet," he said in a rush. "Please forgive my appalling ineptitude and allow me to say that you have never looked more—"

"Tolerable?" The word had barely left her tongue when Elizabeth regretted it, almost as much as she regretted the awkwardness and estrangement that existed between them.

For one awful, excruciating moment Darcy looked exactly as Elizabeth felt: as though he could hardly believe her gall. However, instead of anger and indignation, Elizabeth recognised a very different emotion as it crossed his countenance: a look of shame so complete and deeply felt it made her wish she could disappear into thin air.

"Sir," she stammered, horrified and ashamed of her rudeness. "I have no idea what has come over me. I did not mean to—"

"No," said Darcy succinctly. "I am sure you did not."

Unnerved by the severity of his address and at a loss as to what she ought to say to him at this juncture, Elizabeth fell silent.

It was Darcy who spoke. "You are well within your right to chastise me. Not only have I been inexplicably rude to you this evening, but I was woefully out of line last autumn as well. Regrettably, I can offer no justification for my conduct towards you then, other than to say I was in a very disagreeable humour that evening. Georgiana, as you know—" Here he stopped, cleared his throat, and said with great solemnity, "Forgive me. Of course, the events at Ramsgate were no justification for the way I spoke of you."

"Sir, you need say nothing to me on that score—"

"I must, Miss Bennet. Of course, I must. My behaviour throughout the course of our acquaintance was not what it ought to have been. If I could take it back I would do so in a trice, but I do not, unfortunately, possess that power. Instead, I can only express my deepest regret for having offended you, and my sincere intent to refrain from doing so in the future."

With an audible swallow he gestured to her gown. "You are incredibly beautiful this evening. I have never seen you look more so. Your gown, your hair...you are utterly enchanting."

If Elizabeth thought the air between them had been thick with tension before, it was nothing to what she felt after Darcy bestowed such an astonishing and unexpected compliment upon her. After the deplorable way she had spoken to him, Elizabeth found it impossible to credit that he would wish to gratify her vanity now, especially after all that had taken place during the summer. Her quiet but startled, "Thank you, sir," was barely audible.

Darcy inclined his head and almost shyly cast his eyes to the floor. He was gloveless, and his fingers toyed with the signet ring Elizabeth had always known him to wear. She marvelled at his conduct, uncertain as to what action she ought to take for she had only ever seen him behave in a similar manner once before—last April before he had declared himself to her at Rosings.

With her heart in her throat, Elizabeth raised her eyes. She observed his fidgeting fingers, noted the expensive fabric and gleaming gold buttons of his tailcoat and the fine linen of his artfully tied cravat. At last, her gaze settled upon his face. His eyes, she realised with a start, were no longer downcast, but fixed upon her with the same inscrutable intensity with which he had watched her throughout most of their acquaintance. It was a look Elizabeth remembered well from Kent, from Derbyshire, and more lately from her dreams.

An extraordinary, all-consuming heat coiled from the base of her spine outward, warming her body from within, and with it came a wave of panic so acute she was almost crippled by the implications of it. In danger of losing the last fragments of her fragile equanimity, Elizabeth suddenly wanted nothing more than to be away from him.

Before she could so much as look towards the door to the ball-room, Darcy reached out and boldly captured one of her hands between his own, preventing her escape. Elizabeth inhaled sharply at the contact.

"Miss Bennet," he rasped, then paused to clear his throat. "My dear Miss Bennet. Will you do me the honour of dancing with me?"

Elizabeth could do nothing but stare at his hand, which held her own so firmly she could not think beyond the wondrous impropriety of it. The exquisite warmth of his touch rapidly suffused her gloved fingertips, the length of her arm—her entire body. Tantalised and tempted in ways she had always been forbidden to consider, she dared not raise her eyes to look upon his face, nor into the depths of his own eyes; his piercing gaze would only serve to discompose her completely. She parted her lips, but words failed her utterly.

Since Lydia's shameful elopement, Elizabeth had endeavoured to forget him but without success. She had endured months of continued disappointment and regret, and it was only very recently—the matter of no more than a few short hours—that she felt she had finally begun to make some sort of progress, however slight, in tempering her longing for this impossible man.

Slowly, deliberately, Darcy's thumb stroked the back of her gloved hand. The inexplicable intimacy of the gesture sent another jolt of heat through her body and Elizabeth found herself growing furious, not only with Darcy for the liberties he was taking, but also with herself for her body's traitorous reaction to his brazen ministrations. A burning indignation, not only for his presumptive forwardness and impropriety, but also his lengthy absence and previous disregard, simmered in her veins. Why had he sought her now, alone in a darkened hall, after he had deserted her months ago without so much as a parting word? Elizabeth was no more equal to solving that mystery than she was remaining in his company. She was flustered, bewildered, and in danger of losing her composure. She needed time to think, and to do that she required distance.

She attempted to retract her hand from Darcy's grasp, but he appeared disinclined to permit it.

"Mr Darcy," she admonished in a tremulous voice. "We are in public. I do not wish to be the subject of a scandal, nor provide fodder for any of the gossips in attendance. I regret to inform you all my dances have already been claimed."

Acute disappointment flooded every bone in Darcy's body as he released Elizabeth's hand at once. "Of course," he said. "Perhaps another time. Pray forgive me for my presumption." With a heavy heart, he watched her gather her skirts and flee from him, slowing her pace to one of sedate respectability only as she neared the entrance to the ballroom. Not once did she look back.

Darcy did not attempt to approach Elizabeth again that night. He was far too affected by the bittersweet memory of her hand in his, her intoxicating scent, the wide mix of varying emotions upon her face, and the indignation in her voice before she had run from him. Why did he ever think it would be simple with her? He had planned to take things slowly—to ask her to dance with him and take his cues from her, to see where the rest of the evening led them—yet he had reacted badly from the first moment he had seen her with another man.

Many hours later, Darcy ran his hands over his face, groaning as he recalled the enthusiasm with which Bingley had introduced him to Mr Jonathan Ellis. He had been struggling for some time to master his emotions and was not at his best when he finally returned to the ballroom to see none other than Elizabeth's solicitous partner speaking companionably with his friend.

Though Bingley performed the introduction with much apparent pleasure, Darcy and Ellis exchanged only polite civilities. Their conversation was stilted and insipid as each took the other's measure. It was impossible for Darcy not to wonder what Ellis meant to Elizabeth, and what she in turn meant to Ellis. Was it merely the protective concern of a childhood friend that drove the younger man to watch her for the rest of the night, or was it something deeper, more like a lover would feel? It had alarmed Darcy to see the overly familiar manner with which Bingley's new friend had touched Elizabeth's arm earlier, and the way his mouth had formed the intimate syllables of her name. It was a painful scene Darcy knew would not soon fade from his memory, one he had already replayed repeatedly in his mind.

Darcy yanked his cravat from his neck in the dim interior of his bedchamber at Netherfield. After tossing the long strip of linen onto a chair with his previously discarded coats, he strode to a window that gave him a bird's eye view of the darkened landscape illuminated by the stark glow of the full moon. The long, skeletal shadows of barren trees stretched across the park lawn.

Darcy's shoulders slumped. The full weight of his disappointment in his meeting with Elizabeth felt like a crushing blow.

Would he never do anything correctly regarding her? Would his lovesick brain ever be able to find the right words with which to convey his tender feelings? Even more importantly, would Elizabeth ever be able to forgive him his past offences and come to care for him, if only a little? He closed his eyes, rested his forehead against the window, and welcomed the sharp chill of the glass as it seeped through his skin, into his bones, and wrapped itself around his aching heart.

At Longbourn, safe within the walls of her own bedchamber, Elizabeth's thoughts were of a similar bent. She closed her eyes against the eerie canvas outside her window and sighed. Her breath left a filmy cloud upon the pane. She removed her fingertips from the glass and pressed them to her cheeks as the curtains fluttered closed, willing the chill to soothe the agitation she had felt since the assembly.

After she left Darcy so abruptly in the hall, Elizabeth feared he would not respect her desire to put some distance between them, but her fear had been unfounded. Though his eyes had sought her continuously throughout the evening—more so, it seemed, than ever before—he had kept his distance. Rather than remain in the background, as he had done during his previous visits to Hertfordshire, he had stunned her by exerting himself and conversing with her neighbours.

True to her word, Elizabeth was not without a partner for the remainder of the night. She danced every dance. Her sore feet and a slight hole in the toe of her new slippers were testaments to her popularity as a partner. She was grateful that Mr Ellis had not, in his concern for her, arranged to dance with her a third time. Such a pointed attention would have incited certain expectations, not only with her mother but with the rest of the neighbourhood as well.

As was his custom, Mr Bennet chose to remain at home and, not for the first time that evening, Elizabeth was glad for his aversion to such a gathering. She would have dreaded hearing her father's opinion of her encounter with Darcy on the dance floor, as well as his observation of Mr Ellis's attentions to her.

Across the room the bed creaked as Jane shifted in her sleep. Though she knew she ought to be abed herself, Elizabeth felt more agitated than tired. She desperately wished it was morning, so she might escape the restriction of the house and feel the freedom that being out of doors afforded her. She longed for time alone to decipher her current emotions, to better contemplate Darcy's boldness, his piercing looks, their strained conversation in the darkened hallway, and what it all meant. That he had purposely sought her out was not something Elizabeth could easily dismiss, nor was the reality that he had chosen to do so while she was alone.

But why? she wondered. What could possibly result from such a clandestine meeting? Nothing, she knew, other than more pain and mortification for both had they been discovered. Darcy, no matter what he might have to say to her father in his defence, would have been reviled by the neighbourhood and trapped—honour-bound without recourse in the event of their discovery. As for Elizabeth, her reputation, much like her heart, would have been in tatters. Such uncharacteristic, almost desperate behaviour on his part made Elizabeth question whether he honestly regretted her, or whether he simply desired to make peace with her away from the prying eyes and untoward expectations of an audience.

With a quick, frustrated breath, she extinguished the flickering candle upon the mantel. Darcy had been in Hertfordshire for no more than a few hours yet had already succeeded in discomposing and confusing her more than ever. Should he remain in the country until the wedding, the next few weeks would be difficult at best. Elizabeth would have to find a way to steel herself against the effects of his presence until after her sister and Bingley married. Only then would he leave the country and return to London, or to Derbyshire, or to Kent.

Mr Ellis's pronouncement flickered in the back of her mind, and Elizabeth struggled to extinguish it. Though every rational sentiment she possessed rejected the idea of Darcy settling for his dour cousin, she could not find peace. Perhaps he did not intend to remain in Hertfordshire until his friend's wedding at all but was merely passing through on his way to Kent. The very idea of Miss de Bourgh—or any lady other than herself—becoming his wife left an ache in her heart that could not be ignored.

It was at that moment, with her head full of past regrets, that the painful reality of her situation carried its point with finality. Forgetting Fitzwilliam Darcy would be impossible; but equally impossible was the prospect of being at ease with him. There was no doubt in Elizabeth's mind she would be unequal to meeting him with the appearance of indifference any time soon.

So long as he remained in Hertfordshire, Elizabeth resolved to avoid being alone with him as much as possible. It would do her no good to subject herself unnecessarily to his magnetic presence any more than it would to subject Darcy to her society. For the sake of her sanity, she would do what she could to ensure both their reputations and their respectability remained intact.

❧ 9 ❧

WHERE MR BINGLEY EATS PASTRY AND TALKS
A VAST DEAL.

While Bingley was in very good spirits the following morning, the same could not be said for Darcy. When he summoned his valet, the hour was closer to noon than nine and his disposition was far from pleasant.

He performed his morning ablutions, dressed, and half an hour later entered the breakfast parlour, where he made his way to the sideboard. The fare he found there did little to tempt him. Bingley's penchant for sweets bordered on obsession. It was an obsession Darcy did not share, at least not at the breakfast table.

He shook his head, distastefully eyeing a gleaming silver platter piled high with assorted pastries. Resigned to the fact there would be no bacon or eggs that morning, he selected a poached pear and some toast instead, poured himself a cup of coffee, and claimed a chair beside his friend at the table. Miss Bingley, Darcy noted, was blessedly absent. His grim mood improved.

"Are you planning on eating anything besides that pile of toast?" Bingley asked as he spread an inordinate amount of butter on a sticky-looking pastry and took a hearty bite.

Darcy observed him with equal parts fascination and revulsion. "Bingley, you do realise that pastry must be made almost entirely of butter. Surely, you will make yourself ill by adding more."

"Codswallop," Bingley proclaimed around a mouthful of pastry. "Cook has outdone herself. You have no idea what you are missing."

"Most likely a stomach ache and apoplexy," Darcy muttered as he took a bite of his toast and reached for the London newspaper.

Bingley clucked his tongue in disapproval. "I was not going to say anything but since you seem to be in a critical frame of mind this morning, I believe I shall follow your example and confess that I am disappointed in you."

"Are you?" Darcy remarked dryly. He raised his coffee cup to his lips and turned his attention to an article about the war.

"Indeed, I am. You promised most faithfully that you would dance at the assembly last night, yet you did nothing to honour your word. It was most unseemly."

Darcy set his cup upon the table and made a show of straightening his newspaper. If he ignored Bingley, perhaps he would simply stop speaking and leave him in peace.

"Darcy," said his friend exasperatedly. "You promised you would dance!"

With a long-suffering exhalation, Darcy folded his newspaper in half and tossed it onto the table, where it landed with a muffled slap. "After spending more than half the day confined to a coach, then waiting countless hours while your sister readied herself, I was no longer in the mood, Bingley. Fault me for it if you like, but you cannot deny I did an admirable job of exerting myself with your neighbours, despite my deficiency. I spoke with Mr Goulding of husbandry, to Mr Pruitt and Mr Wiley of politics, to Mr Thatcher regarding the state of the roads and the likelihood of a harsh winter and, to my detriment, I indulged old Mrs Long and her sister for a quarter hour while she complained of her rheumatism. It was only afterwards that she recalled I was single and rich and summoned her nieces, who, owing to an insufficient number of ladies in attendance, were engaged for the rest of the night. I was hardly idle."

Shaking his head, Bingley reached for his teacup. "It was an assembly, for heaven's sake. Conversation is well and good, but one is expected to dance at an assembly. But did you? The answer to that question is a resounding *no*. Not. Even. Once."

Darcy rolled his eyes.

"While I applaud your efforts with my neighbours, you essentially ignored Miss Elizabeth Bennet! Glaring at her from across the room while she danced hardly counts. It was not terribly gallant of you, especially after you told me in London you would make a point of asking her to stand up with you. Now you have slighted her twice."

"I did no such thing," Darcy replied irritably. "Had Miss Elizabeth shown any inclination for my society at any point during the evening, I can assure you things would have turned out differently. As it was, she appeared to be much in demand, particularly with your new friend."

At the mention of Ellis, Bingley's countenance brightened considerably. He plucked another pastry from his plate. "I noticed that as well. I cannot blame the chap one bit, you know.

Miss Elizabeth was in excellent looks last evening, even you cannot deny it. I daresay she looked very pretty indeed."

"She looked extremely well," Darcy allowed, hoping his friend would soon tire of the topic.

Bingley did not. "I confess I find the idea of an attachment between my future sister and my new friend delightful! In fact, I am hard-pressed to think of a more deserving gentleman to call my brother should a certain happy event take place. Well, except for you, of course, but many years have passed since I have entertained any hope of that possibility. After all, if you have not paid your addresses to Caroline by now, there is little chance of so intimate a connexion between us ever coming to fruition, eh?"

"Not unless I make an offer to another of your sisters," Darcy muttered darkly.

Bingley choked on a mouthful of pastry.

Darcy felt the colour drain from his face.

For eight-and-twenty years he had been the soul of discretion, yet suddenly he had an appalling lack of it. He reached for his coffee cup and downed the contents simply to have something to do. Perhaps Bingley would leave well-enough alone, or at the very least have the decency to continue to choke on his croissant.

Bingley did neither.

"*Another* of my sisters!" Errant bits of pastry decorated his waistcoat and the lapels of his jacket. "Have you completely taken leave of your senses? Hurst may very well like his port, but even he has not fallen so far off the wagon that he would fail to notice another man engaged in a dalliance with his wife! In fact, I would wager a good deal of my fortune that my brother-in-law would call you out over it—and I cannot say that

I would blame him one bit! *Make Louisa an offer!* Why, I am of a mind to call you out myself!"

"Louisa?" That Bingley could think for one moment he was interested in Louisa Hurst was as incredible as it was appalling. Despite the fact she was married, the turn of her mind made Eliza Harrow seem brilliant in comparison. "For the love of God, Bingley," he said indignantly, "in all the years you have known me, when have I ever shown the slightest inclination to entangle myself with a married woman, let alone either of your sisters!"

Bingley stared at him. His facial expressions ran a gambit of emotions—stupefied, furious, and indignant.

A full minute passed.

Darcy glared at him.

Suddenly, Bingley erupted into laughter. "Darcy!" he exclaimed. "You trickster! You very nearly had me going with that bag of moonshine."

Darcy blinked at him, utterly perplexed.

Wiping tears of laughter from his eyes, Bingley shook his head and reached for his teacup. Upon finding it empty, he discarded it. He glanced at Darcy and nearly started laughing again. "Oh, come now, man. How thick do you think I am?"

Darcy had no idea how to answer him and so remained silent.

Chuckling, Bingley rolled his eyes. "Obviously, you cannot expect me to believe you intend to pay court to one of the Bennets."

"What the deuce is that supposed to mean?"

"Oh, they are *tolerable* I suppose," Bingley drawled, his tone reminiscent of Darcy's haughty baritone, "but not handsome enough to tempt *me.*"

Darcy felt a flush of heat spread from the back of his neck to the tips of his ears. "I had not thought you capable of holding such a low opinion of anyone, Bingley, let alone your future sisters, especially Miss Elizabeth Bennet, who has long been the particular favourite of your future wife."

"I have always had nothing but the highest opinion of the Bennets—Miss Bennet and Miss Elizabeth in particular, as *you* well know. You, on the other hand…"

Darcy became angry. "I hardly think—"

"No, you do *not* think, and therein lies the root of the problem. Tell me, who knows better than I your opinions on the matter? Who knows better than I your initial disapproval regarding my attachment to Miss Bennet last year? Given the callous manner with which you have dismissed the entire family in the past, I would wager no person within fifty miles of Hertfordshire would believe you would consider courting one of Mrs Bennet's daughters, especially now that her youngest is wed to a man you despise."

"George Wickham," said Darcy darkly, "has absolutely no—"

Again, Bingley interrupted him. "I know. I know. You, more than anyone, have just cause to hate Wickham, but that is beside the point. The entire village has long known how fervently you dislike the blackguard, so you can hardly hold me —or anyone else—accountable for disbelieving it is within your power to see past *that* offence, my friend."

Darcy turned aside his head, though whether he did so mostly in umbrage or shame he could not say. Bingley's chastisement of his past behaviour brought back countless unpleasant memories of how Darcy had once conducted himself, not only in the company of Elizabeth and the Bennets, but in Hertfordshire society in general. He was as disappointed in himself as he was disgusted. "Forgive me." He said no more. He did not trust his voice not to falter.

"No," said Bingley contritely, "no." He laid his hand upon Darcy's shoulder. "Pray forgive me. I meant no offence, nor was it my intent to cause you distress. But knowing the Bennets as intimately as I do and, given your initial opinion of them and their situation in life, I find it difficult to credit you would alter your views in so complete a fashion as to make an offer to one of them. As Miss Bennet's sisters are well-aware of your senti-ments, not even the remotest possibility exists that they would be willing to overlook your former treatment of them and welcome your suit if you honestly felt an inclination to present one.

"That aside, while they are all extremely pretty, there is no denying Miss Catherine is too immature for your tastes, Miss Mary too severe, and Miss Elizabeth...Well, you have been at odds with her for nearly the entirety of your acquaintance. For God's sake, you once proclaimed her *'not tolerable enough to tempt you,'* in public! And no matter what you might think of Mrs Bennet, she would never force her daughters to accept any man who does not sincerely admire them, nor any man they cannot esteem."

"Of course, not," Darcy muttered repentantly. "I meant no offence."

Bingley scratched his head but made no reply. He appeared to be deep in thought. "Come to think of it," he muttered distract-edly, "do you remember that clergyman who stayed with the family last year? As I understand it, he made Miss Elizabeth an offer, which she refused with her father's support. Miss Catherine mentioned her mother was furious, as he is cousin to

Mr Bennet and set to inherit Longbourn after his passing. I believe Mrs Bennet still holds it against Miss Elizabeth. He married the former Miss Lucas instead."

"Mr Collins?"

"I feel a bit sorry for the poor sod to be honest. He was absolutely convinced he could change her mind and actually refused to accept her refusal." Bingley chuckled. "He would have had better luck trying to change the weather. Miss Elizabeth declared she would not have him and would not allow herself to be persuaded otherwise. In my opinion, it was for the best."

Darcy could not disagree. He was hard-pressed to imagine anyone more ill-suited to be husband to the witty and clever Elizabeth Bennet than the sycophantic, weak-minded Mr Collins. Having been refused by Elizabeth himself, Darcy could well imagine what her rejection of Mr Collins's proposal entailed.

Too soon, the ridiculous, awkward proposal Darcy imagined Mr Collins had issued transformed into a proposal of a more disturbing nature, where the agreeable Jonathan Ellis solicited her hand. Darcy felt physically ill. Swallowing his trepidation, he sent up a silent, fervent prayer: should that gentleman ever feel the urge to propose marriage to Elizabeth, may she refuse him as well.

Over the course of the next se'nnight Elizabeth allotted little time in her daily routine for any activity beyond the preparations required of her for Jane's wedding and her subsequent trip to London. To her immense relief, her busy-ness not only worked to her advantage but aided in upholding her resolve.

Though she had never looked upon a visit to the modiste with quite the same enthusiasm as her sisters, save for Mary, who preferred books to satin and bows, Elizabeth accompanied her mother and Jane to Meryton without argument. Darcy, it seemed, was in no hurry to leave the country now that he had returned. Elizabeth's presence in the village shops spared her the heartache and pain of sitting with him in her mother's parlour should he happen to accompany Bingley to Longbourn while her sister and mother were out.

Of course, some interaction with Darcy could not be avoided—church services and dinner parties, for example. But Elizabeth felt the likelihood of a far more familiar exchange between them in such a public venue was slim. By nature, Darcy was a private man and, although he had sought her out while she was alone in the deserted back hall of the Grey Goose the night of the assembly, she could not imagine he would dare to behave in a similar fashion in a crowded drawing room under the scrutiny of her family and countless curious neighbours, nor was Elizabeth inclined to permit it.

Their mutual connexion to Bingley had already thrown them together on several occasions. Though Elizabeth noticed Darcy's gaze often turned upon her, he had not spoken to her of anything more consequential than the weather since the night of his return, and always in the presence of others. Rather than become immune to his presence, or even used to it, Elizabeth was disturbed to discover her feelings for him only intensified.

To make matters worse, Mrs Bennet had taken to singing Elizabeth's praises to anyone so good as to provide her with a willing audience, particularly within earshot of Mr Ellis, Mr Crowell, and, to complete Elizabeth's mortification, Darcy, whom Elizabeth suspected had only returned to her mother's good graces because his ten thousand a year and connexions in town proved too powerful a lure to spurn. Darcy may not have shown an inclination to marry any of her daughters, but it was just like Mrs Bennet to assume it was entirely probable he knew other rich gentlemen who would.

Constantly did Elizabeth and Jane attempt to curb their mother's effusiveness, but as usual there was no deterring Longbourn's mistress from her designated course. As Mr Bennet offered no help reining in his wife, there was little for Elizabeth to do but suffer in silence and bear it as best she could.

Upon returning from a particularly trying day at the dress maker's in Meryton, Elizabeth, her sisters, and mother entered the house to find the two gentlemen from Netherfield awaiting them in the front parlour. Though this pattern of behaviour was familiar and even expected from Mr Bingley, Elizabeth could not help being surprised at Darcy's coming, as the weather that day was extremely cold, icy, and wet.

The promise of a warm fire in the quiet solitude of her room, a thick rug draped upon her lap, a hot cup of tea, and a book in hand had buoyed her spirits through most of the harrowing ride from the village; the addition of Darcy to their party now made retreating upstairs impossible. Her mother, she knew, would be anything but pleased by her going away and was likely to cause a scene if Elizabeth attempted it. Resigning herself to her fate, she readjusted her shawl and stood passively behind her sisters as her mother greeted their guests.

"How very good it is of you, Mr Bingley, to call upon us in such wretched weather. And you, too, Mr Darcy. I hope you have not been waiting long."

In the distance the low rumble of thunder could be heard, a dramatic accompaniment to the heavy deluge currently soaking half of Hertfordshire. Elizabeth smiled politely at Bingley while carefully avoiding eye contact with his friend. If nothing else, she was grateful to be safely indoors as opposed to her father's draughty carriage. Surely, she could sit for half an hour in her mother's parlour and maintain a pleasant, unaffected air. Surely, Darcy would keep a respectable distance from her in front of her family. She stood taller and stepped forward. She would face him. She would not hide.

"We have only just arrived ourselves," Bingley assured them as he accepted his future mother's customary kiss upon the cheek and escorted Jane to the smaller of two sofas by the fire. "Knowing that your mornings have been devoted exclusively to wedding preparations of late and that we were therefore likely to miss your delightful company once again, Darcy suggested that we call in the afternoon instead."

"How very thoughtful of you, sir," said Mrs Bennet, gracing Darcy with a wide smile. "We would have hated to miss you, would we not, girls?"

"You are too kind, madam," Darcy replied. "I hope our presence here is not an imposition. I have no desire to add to any fatigue you might feel after spending your morning in the village."

"Nonsense," said Mrs Bennet with a dismissive wave of her handkerchief. "It is nothing that a bit of pleasant company will not soon remedy. You must stay for supper, Mr Darcy, as I am certain this dreadful weather will not let up anytime soon. Mr Bingley, you know, has a standing invitation to dine with us and, as you are his dearest friend and therefore nearly family yourself, you must stay as well. There! It is settled. Ring the bell for tea, Kitty."

"I appreciate your generosity, Mrs Bennet," Darcy replied. His eyes darted to Elizabeth, then away. "But I do not wish to impose upon your hospitality, especially on such short notice."

"Nonsense, sir. It is no imposition at all. In fact, if this rain continues beyond the supper hour, you and Mr Bingley are most welcome to stay the night with us as well. We are always a very merry party here at Longbourn. After all, where else can you find such stimulating conversation, or such pretty companions?"

Elizabeth shut her eyes. Her mortification was acute.

❧ 10 ❧

WHERE ELIZABETH IS MORTIFIED BY HER FAMILY.

Dinner that night was an uncomfortable affair for Elizabeth with Mrs Bennet and Kitty supplying a freshet of neighbourhood gossip, Mary interjecting words of moral turpitude, and Mr Bennet presiding over them all with a detached sort of amusement until he had enough of their foolishness and abandoned his table, his family, and his guests to sequester himself in his library. There he would dwell for the rest of the night while the Netherfield gentlemen remained with the ladies.

Mortified beyond measure by her father's rudeness and her mother's constant, nonsensical chatter, Elizabeth hastened to the window seat on the far side of the parlour to fetch her embroidery. She had planned to retrieve her fine work and claim the only chair beside the fire. Her sister Mary claimed it instead.

She watched as Bingley, Jane, and Kitty settled themselves upon one sofa and her mother and Darcy upon the other. The prospect of joining them—of being in such proximity to Darcy while her mother went on about Jane's wedding clothes and Elizabeth's own eligibility—was horrifying. Elizabeth found herself returning to the only other available option: the window seat. She did not possess the energy to steer her mother's conversation to more suitable topics for the rest of the evening, nor did she feel equal to sitting beside Darcy on the same small couch.

The tea things were brought in, coffee poured, and dessert served but Elizabeth declined all. As could be expected, the conversation on the other side of the room was a lively one, and quite one-sided. Despite her increasing mortification, Elizabeth could not bring herself to check her mother's enthusiasm any more than she could bear to look upon the figure of the one person in the room who most commanded her interest. Trusting Darcy must be sitting stiffly upon the couch staring into his teacup while her mother rambled inappropriately about stockings and petticoats, Elizabeth was startled to glimpse a pair of black riding boots slowly making their way towards her from across the room.

As Darcy stood gazing out of the window at the sodden park, Elizabeth doubled her efforts and attempted to concentrate on her task, but the wretchedness of the evening combined with the awkwardness such a history as theirs afforded felt suffocating. She knew she ought to acknowledge him and introduce some subject or other, but she hardly knew where to begin. At present, the only topic that came to mind was their clandestine encounter in the back hall of the assembly rooms and the way her traitorous body had reacted to his touch. It was a subject most unfit for a drawing room—or any room for that matter—and Elizabeth could not prevent the heated blush she felt rise in her cheeks.

Several minutes passed in uncomfortable silence before she finally worked up the nerve to steal a glance at him from beneath her lashes. She watched, transfixed as Darcy picked up a discarded book and settled himself beside her. There was an abruptness to his movements she could not account for, but soon attributed it to the irritation he must feel after passing such a tedious evening with her family. He opened the book, scanned several pages, and cleared his throat. When he did not speak, Elizabeth returned her attention to her embroidery.

As she worked, she could not help but feel ashamed. By avoiding the seat beside Darcy on the sofa earlier and essentially ignoring him now, she was slighting him, much as her father had at dinner. She was showing him in no uncertain terms her manners were not only as poor as her father's, but worse. Elizabeth's throat felt conspicuously tight. To have him think of her in any way that was less than complimentary pained her exceedingly.

Had Darcy treated her with such disregard at Pemberley she knew precisely what her opinion of him would have been. She marvelled at the courage he had shown then; at the way he had recovered from his shock when he first saw her, and the way his long, eager strides closed the distance between them as he crossed the lawn to welcome her. He had walked with her, talked with her, and attended her with sincere interest. Elizabeth coloured deeply. Is this how she was to repay his kindness to her then? Is this how she was to repay his solicitation and hospitality—with muteness and avoidance?

She could not, would not allow Darcy to think any worse of her than he surely did. Strengthened by her resolve, Elizabeth turned towards him, and said with as much assertion as she could muster, "Do you mean to frighten me, Mr Darcy, by coming in all this state to observe my paltry attempts?"

Though he appeared startled, the hint of a smile soon tugged at the corners of his mouth. He closed his book and cast it aside. "Not at all. If I am not mistaken, Miss Elizabeth, I believe we have already had this conversation once before. As you know, it is neither my intent, nor my design to frighten you, but quite the opposite." He indicated her fine work with his hand. "Your attempts in any case are far from paltry. No one can fault you. In fact, I see much before me to admire."

His tone was warm, his gaze intense, and both, when combined with his nearness, were enough to cause Elizabeth's breath to catch. It was by no means what she had expected him to say. The expression in Darcy's eyes at that moment burned as brightly as any flame and it unnerved her. His look was entirely familiar.

Her traitorous heart quickened. Only by expending a tremendous amount of effort did Elizabeth manage to keep her wits about her. Before she could think of an appropriate response to Darcy's comment, he said, "I hope the preparations for your sister's wedding have not kept you from enjoying your customary rambles through the countryside. When I was first in Hertfordshire you favoured a path that I have since come to understand spans a lovely stretch of woods upon your father's estate."

Here he paused, bowed his head, and readjusted the cuffs of his shirt sleeves. "I also recall that you rose quite early to walk out in the mornings while you stayed with Mrs Collins in Kent."

Elizabeth's blush intensified at his reference to her time there, for she could not help but feel all the shame of her abominable behaviour towards him then. She lowered her eyes, acutely conscious of the long overdue apology she owed him for the unjust accusations she had made against his character so many months ago. With Mr Bingley, her mother, and sisters just across the room it was neither the ideal time, nor place to broach such a sensitive and deeply personal topic. "I am afraid I have had no opportunity of late to indulge many of my usual pursuits. There is much to be done for Jane's wedding and little time, it seems, in which to accomplish it all."

He leaned forward and regarded her in earnest. "I am very sorry to hear it. I know how much you enjoy being out of doors. Perhaps once your sister is married to my friend you will be at leisure to resume your daily exercise, that is if the weather is not too disagreeable?"

Elizabeth could not be certain, but it almost sounded to her as though Darcy was issuing an invitation rather than merely posing a simple question for the sake of polite conversation. Such fanciful thoughts, she knew, were dangerous. For the preservation of her already frayed equanimity, Elizabeth quickly changed the subject. "Are you enjoying your stay with Mr Bingley?" she asked as composedly as possible while she coaxed her needle through the linen in her hand. To her relief, both her stitches and her hand continued steady and precise.

"I am, though my visit thus far has been rather less productive than I had initially hoped."

His ambiguous remark was followed by silence. Against her better judgment, Elizabeth raised her eyes to his face.

❦

"Miss Elizabeth," Darcy murmured, boldly drawing closer to her, "there is so much I wish to—"

His voice faltered as Mrs Bennet's shrill laughter overwhelmed the room. He saw Elizabeth startle and shook his head, irritated with himself for his eagerness. Now was hardly the time to declare himself—not with Bingley and her mother and sisters within earshot.

A glance in their direction, however, revealed that none of them appeared to be paying them any mind, not even Mrs Bennet. This prompted a sigh of relief from Darcy, who proceeded to mentally chastise himself for his impatience. If he did not slow down, he would surely scare Elizabeth off again before he managed to improve her opinion of him.

He straightened, cleared his throat, and began anew with a safer topic. "Since my arrival, Bingley has been much engaged with preparations for his wedding to your sister. As a result, I have been left to my own devices. It is nothing I did not expect, of course, especially under the circumstances."

To his relief, the tense set to Elizabeth's shoulders relaxed. "I am sorry to hear that you are so often without the companionship of your friend, especially since you are here in Hertfordshire to support him."

"It is not so bad as that. Though I had hoped to pass my days in a very different manner, I am not entirely alone. Miss Bingley, as you might imagine, has been a most attentive hostess in her brother's absence, and the Hursts are due to arrive by week's end."

"Ah. *Those* are happy circumstances indeed. Miss Bingley, I recall, is a very conscientious hostess and particularly aware of her guests. I do believe she must be quite content with the arrangement, and no doubt takes every opportunity to dote upon you while her brother is away from home."

There was no mistaking the archness in her tone and Darcy was delighted. His speech had yielded the desired effect. He said, *"Quite* is a bit of an understatement, I fear. As much as I wish to hold Bingley accountable for abandoning me to such indulgent solicitation, I can hardly blame my besotted friend for preferring the company of your sister to that of myself." He inclined his head towards the two lovers. "I am happy for them. They are much in love and make a charming couple."

The sincerity in his tone coaxed a gentle smile from Elizabeth. "I cannot argue with you, and though I am sorry for your sake, their obvious devotion to one another thoroughly warms my heart. Whenever they are together the strength of their attachment renders them completely lost to everyone and everything around them. I imagine theirs will be a blessed marriage and one of great joy, although my curiosity demands to know how they will fare amongst the society of strangers when they appear so oblivious to all else in the company of their dearest friends."

Darcy found her smile both bewitching and contagious. "Yes. I can well imagine encountering them at Haymarket Square or Almack's on a Wednesday evening, the height of the London Season in full swing around them while they are absolutely oblivious to the splendour of the place, or the puffed-up self-importance of its patrons."

"I was unaware the esteemed Lady Patronesses of Almack's issued vouchers to gentlemen whose fortunes were acquired through trade, no matter how significant their yearly income or beautiful and genteel their wives. But on this I shall defer to your superior knowledge of the subject."

Darcy's smile slipped from his face. Mortified, he inwardly chastised himself for such a thoughtless remark. Of course, neither Bingley, nor his Miss Bennet, nor any of their relations would be granted admittance to such an exclusive venue as Almack's, where even the privileged second sons of those who moved in the first circles of London society were excluded—a penance for the order of their births. He frantically tried to think of something to say to make his blunder less but found himself at a loss for words.

It was Elizabeth who filled the silence, but despite her teasing words, Darcy thought he detected a note of contrition. "I believe you are correct, sir. Mr Bingley and my sister would undoubtedly become so absorbed in their own society they would entirely forget themselves in such a glorious setting as London, and everyone else for that matter. In fact, I shall likely be left to shift for myself during the coming month—and this after I have foolishly agreed to reside with them in the same house!"

"You are for London as well?" He was shocked but by no means displeased by such an unexpected turn of events. "I had not heard."

"I cannot imagine that you had," Elizabeth replied with a cryptic turn of her mouth. "Rather than stay with the Hursts in their home, Mr Bingley has taken a house for us. I will be at their disposal."

Darcy could hardly believe his good fortune. Elizabeth residing in London was a most promising prospect. Though it cost him considerable effort, he resisted the urge to grin like a fool. "And how long will you remain in town?"

"A little more than a month, I believe."

"I see," said Darcy as he endeavoured to conceal his growing excitement.

Though he had hoped Bingley would grant him leave to remain at Netherfield once he and Jane removed to London for their honeymoon, Darcy had no idea that his heart's desire was to accompany them to town as well. There was no denying that having Elizabeth in London was a far more effective way to carry out a courtship, as it would afford him an opportunity to call on her and to improve her opinion of him away from the interfering eyes of her family and friends. This included the accursedly agreeable Mr Ellis, whose relationship with Elizabeth not only gave every indication of being one of long standing, but also one of mutual pleasure. When coupled with Mrs Bennet's unchecked enthusiasm for the match, the possibility that a deeper attachment existed between them was becoming increasingly difficult for Darcy to ignore.

Darcy had been in Hertfordshire for a week, but not until that moment in her mother's drawing room had he been granted any real opportunity to converse with Elizabeth for more than a few brief moments since the assembly. Any prior conversation was brief and always under the watchful eyes of others. Aware of her fondness for walking out, Darcy had made a point of riding within the vicinity of her father's estate each morning with the hope of encountering her alone. Luck, however, was never with him. He had not been given so much as a fleeting glimpse of Elizabeth among the barren fields and wooded paths of Hertfordshire—not even a flash of her skirts among the trees.

They had dined together several times since the assembly, but the parties had been so large and boisterous that very little private discourse was had by anyone beyond the most basic of civilities or mundane discussions. Darcy also had the misfortune of being seated so far from Elizabeth on each occasion that he had found himself struggling against the constant, almost overpowering urge to crane his neck to better see the curve of her cheek as she conversed with her neighbours at the other end of the table, usually with Mr Ellis, who appeared more than happy to be her constant dinner companion.

At one point, Darcy wondered whether Elizabeth might have had a hand in the orchestration of the seating, though he soon realised that could not possibly have been the case, as not all the dinners were held at Longbourn. Though there were times when Darcy had noticed her eyes upon him, the way Elizabeth avoided conversing with him only served to make him acutely aware of the fact that she was still far from being at ease in his company. Whether Colonel Fitzwilliam's conjectures were correct, and she was merely so mortified by her family's connexion to Wickham and dreaded Darcy's opinion on the subject, or whether Darcy's own fears were closer to the truth, that Elizabeth's opinion of *him* was still so very low, the master of Pemberley honestly could not say. He only knew that things could not continue as they were between them, not if he hoped to win her heart.

Now that Darcy was armed with intelligence of Elizabeth's plans, he was presented with another option, one he determined to make the most of. He resolved to quit Netherfield the moment the Bingleys did and follow them to town without delay. He would not waste such a precious opportunity to spend time with Elizabeth in London.

As newlyweds, he knew the Bingleys would likely sequester themselves at home for a good portion of their stay. Darcy's head filled with countless delightful images: escorting Elizabeth to the theatre, to the opera, to museums and exhibitions, to tea rooms and coffee houses, to book shops, and, of course, to Hyde Park. The possibilities were endless.

There was, however, still the issue of propriety. As he was a single gentleman and Elizabeth an unmarried lady, they would never be allowed to be entirely alone together. Darcy also knew that Jane, no matter how preoccupied she might become with Bingley on her honeymoon, would never be so careless with her favourite sister as to consign Elizabeth unto Darcy's care without the supervision of a chaperon. Despite the fact he had followed her into the back hall of the Grey Goose to speak with her, he had no wish to jeopardise Elizabeth's reputation.

Then there was the matter of a hostess. As his uncle had pointed out before Darcy had left London, the fact that he did not presently have one would keep him from entertaining Elizabeth in his London residence. These issues would certainly have to be addressed, but for the time being Darcy was content to sit quietly beside the woman he loved in her mother's parlour and formulate his plans for the hours he hoped to pass in her company while in town.

💐 II 🦋

WHERE MR DARCY AND MR BINGLEY ENGAGE
IN GENTLEMANLY PURSUITS, AND JANE SAYS
HER PIECE.

Several days later, the Netherfield gentlemen set out two hours after sunrise to spend a cold but pleasant morning fowling for pheasants. Bingley's estate, though not nearly as vast as Pemberley's grounds, was home to countless species of game birds, deer, and wild boar.

As it often did, engaging in sport provided Darcy with an excellent distraction. He had begun the morning with a headache, but after shooting six brace he felt much improved, despite the fact his friend had bested him and bagged eight. They entered the manor house in high spirits, surrendered their fowling pieces, and shed their coats as the clock in the drawing room struck half past two in the afternoon.

Then and only then did Bingley realise he had not only failed to pay his daily call upon Miss Bennet but had forgotten her existence entirely. Cursing, he ran up the stairs and called for his valet.

An hour later, after freshening up and eating a cold lunch before a warm fire, both gentlemen set out for Longbourn. Guiding their horses swiftly along the Meryton road, they arrived at the pale that marked Mr Bennet's estate in very good time. They turned onto the lane, entered the drive, and were greeted with a flurry of activity. A cart loaded with band boxes and parcels, some quite sizeable, was in the process of being unloaded by Longbourn's servants.

Beyond that, directly in front of the house, a smart-looking conveyance with a matched pair was parked. Save for the driver and footman who were seeing to the removal of the luggage, the carriage appeared devoid of occupants. As the Netherfield gentlemen approached the hustle and bustle, Darcy was afforded a better view of the trunks and valises stacked beside the equipage and realised the Gardiners had come from town for Miss Bennet's wedding.

Doubtful that paying a call upon the family at this juncture was wise, he tugged on his horse's reins, intent upon turning back. While he did not doubt that Mrs Bennet would always be happy to see Bingley, especially now that his boots were polished and free of mud, he was certain the Bennets would be more inconvenienced by their coming at such a moment than they would be pleased.

Bingley appeared to be of a different mind; he bounded up the front steps with his usual exuberance and entered the house. Hoping his presence would not cause any vexation, Darcy consigned his horse to a groom and followed his friend.

They were shown to a small sitting room at the back of the house that Darcy had not previously seen and left to wait for Miss Bennet and her mother before a cheerful-looking fire. Five minutes later the door opened, and Darcy saw it was not Mrs Bennet who accompanied Bingley's betrothed, but her sister-in-law, Mrs Gardiner. His delight upon seeing her again was considerable.

Mrs Gardiner greeted them warmly. "Mr Darcy. Mr Bingley. What a pleasure it is to see you both again."

"The pleasure is entirely ours, Mrs Gardiner," said Darcy with a sincere smile as he stepped forward to take her hand. "You are looking extremely well. I trust you have suffered no ill-effects from your recent journey from town."

"None whatsoever, and may I say that you also appear to be in excellent health, sir?"

"Thank you. I have found the fresh country air of Hertfordshire agrees with me far more so than the stale atmosphere of London. How are Mr Gardiner and the children? I trust they have accompanied you for the wedding as well and are also in good health?"

"They are all extremely healthy as well, though we were wondering whether my husband's business would allow him to make the journey with us today. My children are currently being entertained by two of my nieces in the nursery, and I believe my husband is settled at last in my brother's library, enjoying the benefit of a warm fire and a well-deserved dose of quietude."

"Ah, yes," said Bingley with a winsome grin. "There is nothing I like better after passing many cold and tiresome hours in a carriage than sitting before a fire in the company of good friends. But I am afraid you must be exhausted, Mrs Gardiner. Here, come and take a seat by the fire. I insist."

"Thank you, sir," she said, and allowed Bingley to lead her to an upholstered chair situated close to the hearth.

While Bingley was occupied with Mrs Gardiner, Darcy greeted Miss Bennet. "You are looking very well this afternoon, Miss Bennet."

"I thank you, sir," she said, stepping neatly around him. She settled herself upon a small velvet sofa located to the left of her aunt's chair and arranged her skirts over her lap. Bingley claimed the vacant seat beside her.

Darcy settled into the chair opposite Mrs Gardiner's as the flustered housekeeper entered the room bearing a large tray laden with an assortment of biscuits and cakes and a steaming pot of tea. She arranged it all upon a low table before the fire, curtseyed, and bustled out of the room.

Jane proceeded to pour the tea.

"I hope," Darcy said to Mrs Gardiner, "you have arrived at Longbourn to find all of your family in residence here in good health."

"I did, sir," she replied. "They are all very well, though perhaps a little harried today."

"Yes. It has not escaped my notice. I believe I have never seen so many band boxes in my life, not even on Bond Street before a ball."

Mrs Gardiner laughed good-naturedly while Bingley turned to Jane with a twinkle in his eyes. "If I had not already been privy to the vast amount of frippery my sisters absolutely insist is necessary for a lady of fashion, I confess I might have become downright alarmed upon seeing the number of items paraded through Longbourn over the last several days. You may rest easy, Miss Bennet. Netherfield has more than enough closets and wardrobes to hold your new acquisitions. If I show any cause for concern, I swear it is born solely out of the possibility that Caroline may feel a sudden inclination to buy more, so as not to appear to disadvantage when you are seen together in town next Season."

"I would not wish for my future sister to suffer from such a misapprehension. You must put Miss Bingley's mind at ease and inform her at once that the remainder of my trousseau was delivered yesterday. Most of the items you have seen come through today are not mine. They are Lizzy's."

Jane handed her future husband a delicately painted cup and saucer while Bingley chuckled. "Well, that is very good news indeed, especially for my pocketbook!"

After handing her aunt an identical cup and saucer, she turned to Darcy. "Tea, Mr Darcy?"

It took him a moment to answer her, so startled was he to hear the various parcels and new finery coming into the house at that moment were intended for Elizabeth and not the future Mrs Bingley. "Pray forgive my curiosity, but is there a particular reason Miss Elizabeth has purchased so many new gowns?"

"Of course," she said sweetly as she handed him a cup of tea. "As a favour to me, Elizabeth will join us in London after the wedding. My mother was adamant that she has new things as well. But I do not believe you were privy to our plan, Mr Darcy, for it is not generally known."

"As it happens, I do know of it," Darcy replied, accepting the proffered teacup and saucer. "Miss Elizabeth informed me herself the other evening after we had dined together."

"I confess I am surprised to hear it."

Darcy's lips lifted infinitesimally. "No more surprised than I, Miss Bennet, I assure you."

"My mother," she continued with a shrug of her shoulders, "is determined Elizabeth shall be presented to her very best advantage. As you once observed yourself, sir, society in town is far more varied than one often finds here in the country. Far be it from us to forget your remarks on the subject. None of us would ever wish to appear so terribly out of place in so grand a locale as someone of your consequence is used to frequenting."

Darcy blinked at her in astonishment, then looked to Bingley and Mrs Gardiner. If Miss Bennet had not insulted him, he would have found their identical expressions almost comical. Both appeared incredulous, as incredulous as he. "I believe you are mistaken, madam. I cannot think of any reason why you and Miss Elizabeth would appear out of place in any setting. Certainly, wherever you are known you must be respected and valued and, if I may be so bold as to say so, much admired."

"I thank you for saying so, Mr Darcy, but such pretty sentiments are precisely that—sentiments and little else. You may have lived in the world, but you have never met with us in any other setting, only here in Hertfordshire among our own small sphere of acquaintance, where we are known and have been welcome our entire lives."

"I must disagree," Darcy replied in earnest. "You forget I encountered Miss Elizabeth at my home in Derbyshire over the summer and in Kent last April. In Kent, I spent some weeks in her company and could not help but admire her natural way with people. I found Miss Elizabeth even more charming and lovely than she was in Hertfordshire and her manners just as easy and unassuming in my aunt's drawing room, where she could claim a prior acquaintance with no one except myself and Mrs Collins."

"Yes," Bingley said. "Yes indeed." His eyes darted uneasily between his friend and future wife much like a pendulum on a clock. "I have rarely met with any lady who has a pleasanter disposition than Miss Elizabeth." He cast a hasty glance at Miss Bennet and Mrs Gardiner and cleared his throat. "Present company excluded, of course."

Grateful for Bingley's intervention, Darcy looked to his friend with an appreciative smile and took a sip of tea, hoping to put his thinly veiled argument with Miss Bennet behind him.

Miss Bennet had other plans. "I am aware of a great many things that occurred in Kent, Mr Darcy, and while I cannot disagree that my sister may have appeared easy in your company, only one who is privileged enough to know her intimately would fully comprehend her innermost feelings and wishes with any degree of accuracy." She held Darcy's astonished gaze with a wilful determination few had likely witnessed in her. "As a matter of fact, after passing several weeks in Elizabeth's company I would wager a great deal that you, sir, more than anyone else, can imagine how my sister might react should someone dare to treat her with an air of arrogance and presumption and so wholly misinterpret her cordial sentiments as something more than what they are, especially when her preference has always been perfectly clear to those of us for whom she cares."

"Jane," Mrs Gardiner admonished sternly. "You have said quite enough!"

Darcy paled, then coloured deeply. Knowing that Elizabeth and her eldest sister were close, he was not altogether surprised to learn that Elizabeth had told her of his proposal. Despite his love for her, he had deeply upset Elizabeth with his insensitive description of her situation in life and his unsolicited opinion of her family. Who else would it have been more natural for Elizabeth to turn to for solace than Miss Bennet? With a sinking heart, Darcy wondered whether Miss Bennet also knew of his interference in her own affairs with Bingley. For the sake of any future relationship with Elizabeth, he silently prayed that she did not.

That Jane Bennet would not only bait him but dare to expose him in such a manner was as cruel as it was inappropriate. Darcy hardly knew how he would contain his anger and embarrassment and, without quite knowing what he was about, abandoned his chair.

Miss Bennet stiffened, coloured, and quickly lowered her gaze to her lap as Darcy stood before her in furious indecision. His eyes alighted on the other occupants of the room, both of whom were openly staring at him in shock, and he sobered.

With as much civility as he could muster, Darcy addressed Miss Bennet. "Pray, excuse me, madam. I have recalled a pressing matter of business that requires my immediate attention."

Without raising her eyes, Miss Bennet solemnly proclaimed, "I would not dream of keeping you from your important matter of business, Mr Darcy. My mother, however, will no doubt be disappointed to hear of your leaving us so suddenly."

"It is not my intent to cause offence. I thank you for your hospitality." He performed a stiff, perfunctory bow before turning his attention to Mrs Gardiner, who appeared horrified by their exchange.

Darcy's mien softened considerably, as did his tone. "I hope we will meet again soon, Mrs Gardiner. Please convey my warmest regards to all your family, and my sincerest regrets. Indeed, I am...I am very sorry. Pray excuse me."

Bingley stood at once, his expression a mixture of distress and confusion. He opened his mouth, clearly intending to speak, but Darcy spoke first.

"There is no need to trouble yourself, Bingley. Enjoy your visit with your betrothed and her family. If you would be so generous as to make my excuses to Mrs Bennet, I would be most appreciative."

He performed a perfunctory bow and strode from the room into the hall, livid, as much with himself for his inability to rein in his temper as he was with Jane Bennet for her ill-contrived effort to take him to task and humiliate him publicly for a matter that was certainly no concern of hers.

As he entered the main foyer, the Bennets' butler spied him and quickly retrieved his greatcoat and hat. "I shall have your horse saddled directly, sir. It will be the work of a moment."

"There is no need, Hill. I believe a long walk will be preferable. Good day to you." With that, Darcy threw open the door and quit the house.

❧ 12 ❧

WHERE ELIZABETH AND MRS GARDINER BOTH TELL STORIES.

Though it had been many years since Mr Bennet's daughters had need of a nursery, Longbourn's was in excellent condition. Over the past several weeks the floors were scrubbed spotless by servants, the carpets beaten, the walls painted, the curtains mended, and the beds made up with fresh linens and goose down pillows.

Presently, the door to the apartment stood ajar. Just inside, the incandescent glow of flickering candlelight cast long, animated shadows on the walls.

Seated upon one of the beds with the littlest Gardiner nestled on her lap, sat Elizabeth. A blazing fire had been lit in the grate hours before to chase away the night-time chill. Its crackling flames were gay and pleasant, creating a cosiness that had invited the Gardiners' two eldest children to climb onto the bed and settle themselves at their cousin's feet.

"What happens next, Cousin Lizzy?" the eldest girl asked. Her dark eyes sparkled with excitement as she leaned forward in anticipation of what Elizabeth would next relate. Long chestnut curls tumbled past her shoulders in charming disarray. Impatient, the girl pushed them aside. Emily Gardiner, at seven years old, looked much like Elizabeth had at that age, an observation often remarked upon by their parents.

The toddler on Elizabeth's lap twisted in her embrace so she could better see her cousin. Her eyes were dark like her sister's, but where Emily's gaze was open and expectant, Rosalie's was sleepy and serious. "Pease, Issy?" she said as she twirled a lock of Elizabeth's hair between her plump little fingers.

"Very well, then," Elizabeth continued with an affectionate smile. "Without so much as another word, the prince placed the maiden upon his great white steed and whisked her away to his magnificent castle in the far north, where they lived happily ever after."

Ten-year-old Robert frowned. "That was an exciting story," he proclaimed, "but hardly likely, I think."

Emily nodded, then bit her lip. "Cousin Lizzy, why would the maiden ever agree to marry the prince after he was so rude to her? How could she ever have come to love him?"

Elizabeth extended her hand, grasped Emily's, and gave it a gentle squeeze. "Dearest," she said kindly, "the maiden was as wrong about the prince as the prince had been about her. She had grossly misjudged his character because of one thoughtless comment he had made at the beginning of their acquaintance, and she believed the tale of untruth told by the charming Black Knight. She did not take the trouble to get to know the prince herself, and so in the end the maiden suffered for her prejudice just as much as the prince."

Emily took a moment to consider her cousin's words. "So, the maiden would have liked the prince to begin with if he had not been rude to her. She should never have listened to the Black Knight, for he was full of gossip and lies about the prince and turned out to be a wicked ogre." She wrinkled her nose in disgust.

"And the prince," said Robert to his sister, "was not mean-spirited at heart, only irritable because he bore the burden of so many responsibilities on his shoulders."

"I believe you both have the right of it," said Elizabeth.

"And I believe it is now well past your bedtimes," said Mrs Gardiner as she entered the room.

"Mamma!" the children sang, their faces bright; all except for little Rosalie, who was asleep in Elizabeth's arms.

"Hello, my darlings. Did you enjoy your story?"

"Oh, yes," Emily said, grinning happily. "Cousin Lizzy tells us the most wonderful stories."

"She does," Robert agreed, "even though they could never, ever happen. A maiden could never really slay a dragon, you know, Mamma."

Laughing, Mrs Gardiner glanced at her niece with a raised brow. "I believe it would depend upon the type of dragon in question, Robert. How often has your father told you it is never wise to underestimate anyone's abilities based upon what society in general tells us? You must consider all the facts before forming your own opinion, no matter how fanciful the situation at hand may seem. Now, thank Elizabeth for sharing such an exciting story with you."

They thanked her enthusiastically and settled into their beds, arranging their counterpanes snugly around them.

Elizabeth handed the sleeping babe to her aunt and kissed Robert and Emily goodnight. "Perhaps after breakfast I might be able to tell you another story, if your Aunt Bennet allows it. There are still a great many things to do for Jane's wedding, but we shall see what the day brings. Goodnight now. May you have only the sweetest dreams."

"Goodnight, Cousin Lizzy," they said in unison, stifling their yawns. "Goodnight, Mamma."

"Goodnight, my loves," Mrs Gardiner replied as she tucked her youngest into bed and pulled the counterpane to her chin. "Sleep well."

They slipped from the room and Mrs Gardiner closed the door. "You have a natural way with children, Lizzy, and mine are so attached to you. They have talked of nothing else for the past fortnight, you know, but seeing you and Jane."

Elizabeth smiled as they made their way down the hall, their arms linked companionably. "I assure you the feeling is mutual. I am equally attached to them."

"You have always possessed a talent for spinning interesting tales. I very much enjoyed what I heard tonight. It carried an important lesson, which the children were able to grasp with minimal encouragement, I might add."

"Each time I see my young cousins I am further impressed by their powers of perception. They go about solving problems and analysing facts in such a rational, insightful manner, especially Robert. Though Emily is equally bright, her temperament is far more passionate. She does not hesitate to speak her mind, but neither does she appear to fully consider the consequences of her words. I do not mean to imply that she is rash or unfeeling, only that she has very decided opinions for one so young, and no qualms whatsoever about expressing them wholeheartedly."

The corners of Mrs Gardiner's mouth lifted with a smile. "Indeed. In this, as in so many ways, she is much like you were at her age. However, I suspect that Emily will learn to curb her enthusiasm in due time before much harm can come of it. She has a wonderful example by you, Lizzy, and if you were to guide her, I am sure she would do all in her power to emulate your restraint."

Though she ought to have been gratified by her aunt's words, Elizabeth felt anything but pride. "I thank you, Aunt, but I hardly deserve such praise, especially considering the story I shared with the children this evening. You, more than anyone, must know how ashamed and regretful I am for what I have done."

Her aunt steered her towards a small, curtained alcove at the end of the corridor that would afford them some privacy. "I am afraid I do not understand you, my dear. What have you done that would cause you to feel shame? I can think of nothing. The tale you told was captivating, not to mention it brought to the fore a wonderful lesson in humility. There is no shame in that."

"I was not referring to the tale itself, but to the circumstances that brought about such a story in the first place. The awful accusations I made...even as I thought them, I knew I should have kept my remarks to myself, but I did no such thing. I was so angry that I ended up saying such terrible, hateful things! I was very wrong and can never take any of it back."

"Elizabeth," said Mrs Gardiner in confusion and alarm, "whatever are you talking about?"

"Surely, you of all people, cannot possibly claim ignorance of the matter—not when you are acquainted with so many of the particulars."

But it soon became evident by the puzzled expression upon Mrs Gardiner's face that she did not, in fact, have any understanding of the matter. She repeated the sentiment to her niece, who stared at her in disbelief.

"Aunt, you must recall how I wrongfully misjudged two very different men in the span of only a handful of months. My behaviour towards Mr Darcy was particularly shameful and it distresses me, now more than ever. I cannot think of my prejudice against him or my unjust actions without experiencing the acutest mortification, nor can I consider the value of what I have truly lost without feeling the deepest regret and remorse."

"Lizzy, do you mean to say the tale you wove for the children is an account of your history with Mr Darcy and Mr Wickham?"

Elizabeth's cheeks flamed. "I ought not to have done it, I know, but it is too late at this point to take it back. Indeed, it is too late to take back any of my past actions."

"I had no idea," Mrs Gardiner admitted. "But how can this be? I was under the impression that you and Mr Darcy had since put your differences of opinion behind you. I thought you were friends."

"To an extent I suppose we are. On several occasions, Mr Darcy has not only graciously overlooked my impudent behaviour but treated me with more kindness and consideration than I deserve. While I have since forgiven him his offences, I cannot so easily forgive myself my own. There is nothing in my conduct during the entire course of our acquaintance of which I can approve. I was naïve and foolish to ever believe Mr Wickham and his gross misrepresentation, not only of himself, but of Mr Darcy's character."

"That is indeed most unfortunate," Mrs Gardiner agreed, "but not entirely your fault. You knew nothing of the actual particulars, only what Mr Wickham claimed and what Mr Darcy would not refute. You knew nothing of either man's true nature—"

"But I should have known!" Elizabeth said with emotion. "I should have known better, but I was so determined to dislike Mr Darcy because he refused to dance with me that I wrote him off as being haughty and proud, rather than circumspect and reserved. I tried to laugh at his slight, but his comment about my inferior beauty wounded my vanity, so you can well imagine how little it took for me to find further fault with him, especially after Mr Wickham came to Hertfordshire and ingratiated himself with the entire village. Undeserving, hateful man..."

Wiping tears from her eyes, Elizabeth swept the panel of rich, brocade drapery aside and looked out the window. With a rueful laugh, she lowered herself onto a settee upholstered in green velvet and sagged against its softness.

Mrs Gardiner claimed a place beside her and offered her a lace handkerchief. "Dry your eyes, my dear. Take a moment to calm yourself. It will do you no good to upset yourself now. Both gentlemen misrepresented themselves in their own way, and quite consciously I might add. It is unfortunate, but that does not make it any less true."

"Perhaps," Elizabeth agreed, drying her tears, "but it was Mr Wickham, a scoundrel of the highest order, who managed to cast his spell and charm me as effortlessly as he did everyone else. I held Mr Darcy's reserve against him, while I embraced Mr Wickham for his very lack of reserve. My behaviour towards both men was not at all what it ought to have been."

"You were wrong," said Mrs Gardiner gently, "to have behaved as you did, but given the intelligence at the time, and taking the manners of both gentlemen into account, it is not difficult to understand why you felt inclined to do so."

Elizabeth's recollection of the ferocity of her resentment towards Darcy at that time was too mortifying and too deep-seated to be shaken free by her aunt's rationality. "While I appreciate your faith in me, it was childish and beneath me to punish Mr Darcy for his remarks when I ought not to have overheard them in the first place. It mattered little to me whether we were in the company of our neighbours, his friends, or even his nearest relations—it brought me satisfaction to see Mr Darcy discomposed by my sharp tongue."

She exhaled harshly. "My only defence—and I know it is by no means an excuse for my poor behaviour—is that I believed he intended to discompose me as well. Of course, I learned soon enough how mistaken I was on that score. How Mr Darcy has since found it within himself to look beyond my trespasses I will never know, especially as I have yet to offer him an apology for my unjust accusations and insolent treatment of him. He has since proven himself to be unfailingly gracious and fair, while Mr Wickham has done nothing but behave far from respectably, towards all of us."

"Mr Darcy is truly the best of men," Mrs Gardiner stated with quiet conviction. "Since we first had the pleasure of meeting him at Pemberley, he has been nothing but kind and generous to us—all ease and friendliness. We are fond of him, and it is obvious to your uncle and me that Mr Darcy is extremely fond of you."

"I cannot imagine why," Elizabeth said feelingly. "Except for Jane, Uncle Gardiner, and you, my entire family and I have done nothing but behave poorly at every turn—not to mention I am now sister to a man Mr Darcy despises above all others. I am the last person in the world who deserves his notice. I certainly do not deserve his esteem."

"I believe Mr Darcy considers you worthy of both and that, my dear, is all that truly matters. The rest will come in time, of this I am certain." Mrs Gardiner clasped Elizabeth's hands between her own and applied a gentle pressure. "As for Jane," she said peevishly, "I would not be so quick to nominate *her* for sainthood."

"No one," Elizabeth insisted, "is so good, nor so kind as our dear Jane. If she is not worthy of sainthood, I do not know who would be worthy in this world of ours."

"I have often thought much the same, but after witnessing her behaviour this afternoon I must disagree. I saw no kindness in your sister today—only petty meanness."

Astonished, Elizabeth looked at her aunt askance, but Mrs Gardiner offered nothing by way of an explanation. "Jane did appear less animated than usual at dinner, but I noticed nothing amiss in her manners or address. Mr Bingley also appeared distracted and out of sorts. Perhaps they have quarrelled."

"I would wager a great deal they probably have," said Mrs Gardiner.

"But surely, if that is the case, the entirety of the blame for their disagreement cannot be laid at Jane's feet, Aunt. It is not in her nature to intentionally wound Mr Bingley any more than I believe it is in his to knowingly inflict distress upon her. Whatever has occurred must be the result of a simple misunderstanding between them and nothing more."

"I am afraid there is more to it than that, my dear—much more. Though it has never been Jane's way to knowingly occasion pain to anyone in the past, in this case her words appeared contrived to achieve precisely that end."

Again, Elizabeth was all astonishment. "To Mr Bingley? I cannot believe that she would ever—"

"No, Lizzy," said Mrs Gardiner, and in her tone, Elizabeth detected a note of irritability not often present in her aunt's voice. "Not to Mr Bingley, although he was by no means unaffected by her poor performance. I am sorry to say the object of Jane's scorn was none other than Mr Darcy."

"Mr Darcy!" Elizabeth cried. "That is impossible. He is Mr Bingley's dearest friend." However, Elizabeth had no sooner spoken the words than she recalled that Jane had been angry with Darcy for some time. *But surely, Jane would never give voice to her resentment...*

"It is my belief your sister did not intend to quarrel with Mr Darcy," Mrs Gardiner admitted, "at least not from the onset, but I would not describe her mood as congenial when the gentlemen called. She was displeased Mr Bingley had arrived so late in the afternoon after shooting all day with Mr Darcy. She was even more displeased that Mr Bingley had not come to Longbourn alone. She confessed as much to me when I enquired, and I could not help myself. I gave her such a set-down as I have ever delivered!"

Elizabeth felt the colour drain from her face.

Her aunt had not done. "From the moment we entered the room, Mr Darcy was nothing but amiable and polite. Jane's provocation of him was entirely unmerited, her insinuations unfeeling and cruel! The entire scene was perpetrated in front of both Mr Bingley and me. Honestly, Lizzy, the disregard with which she treated Mr Darcy was positively shocking! I did not blame him one bit for wanting to go away in the manner he did. I confess I wanted to go away myself."

"There must be some mistake," Elizabeth stammered. She could hardly credit all her aunt had related and was desperate to exonerate Jane of any wrongdoing. To believe her most beloved sister would stoop so low as to abuse the very man Elizabeth herself had treated so unjustly was beyond the pale! "It is not sound," she said, her stomach knotted with worry. "It is unlike Jane to behave deplorably to anyone. Perhaps she was feeling unwell this afternoon. Perhaps she was overly tired. Did she give any indication she was not herself? Did Mr Darcy say something to upset her? This makes absolutely no sense."

"It certainly does not," Mrs Gardiner agreed, shaking her head sadly. "Not everything was clear to me, you understand, but your sister's actions and demeanour up until that point gave me no cause for concern. Not once did I fear she would act upon her contention and torment Mr Darcy in such a manner.

"Elizabeth," she continued, lowering her voice, "I want you to know I heard enough of her speech—more than enough, in fact —to deduce that an exchange of a very personal and private nature must have transpired between you and Mr Darcy while you were visiting Kent. I can only assume that you confided the details of that exchange to Jane. Not only did she allude to it, but she was quite angry when she did. She appears to hold him accountable for whatever discord occurred between you there. Tell me, is there any truth to this?"

Though Elizabeth knew she ought to answer her aunt, she found herself powerless to do more than stare in stunned disbelief. She would have expected such behaviour from Lydia and their mother—even Kitty—but never from Jane! Darcy's insulting proposal and Elizabeth's furious response to it were topics far too painful and mortifying to broach when the sisters were alone, never mind mention in company! But according to her aunt that was precisely what had happened!

Elizabeth was devastated. Never had she believed her favourite sister, who had always been nothing but solicitous and kindhearted, capable of such unfaithfulness! Never had she considered her equal to such coldness and cruelty! Jane may have been ignorant of the true extent of Elizabeth's feelings for Darcy, but she was by no means ignorant of Elizabeth's improved opinion of him.

Though she suspected Jane's original motive must have been to protect *her*, Elizabeth could neither find it within her heart to appreciate the gesture as she ought, nor dismiss her sister's interference in such an acutely personal matter. She could imagine how furious Darcy must be with her for sharing such painful and mortifying details with her sister, only to have them thrown back in his face—and in public no less!

Elizabeth's distress was acute.

Mrs Gardiner embraced her. "Lizzy," she said kindly. "You care for him. I know you do. There is no sense denying it."

"Yes," Elizabeth confessed on a breath, dissolving into tears. "How will I ever make this right? I know very well that nothing can be done to make this right! Mr Darcy will take every opportunity to avoid an acquaintance with us now."

"Be sensible, my dear. I very much doubt that your sister's tongue has managed to undo Mr Darcy's admiration for you. His sentiments run much deeper than that and you do him a disservice by implying otherwise."

Swiping angrily at the wetness on her cheeks, Elizabeth disagreed. "I thank you for your assurance, but you cannot possibly know such a thing, not for certain."

"Do not underestimate the power of a gentleman's devotion, my dear. Fear not. We will get to the bottom of this. I will do all in my power to help you make things right between you and your Mr Darcy, but you must have faith. You will see. Such happiness is not beyond your reach, despite having two very selfish sisters."

❦ 13 ❦

WHERE MR BINGLEY IS ANGRY WITH MR DARCY. AGAIN.

"For the love of God," Bingley grumbled as he paced the length of Netherfield's library. "Do not apologise, Darcy. Simply explain to me why Miss Bennet said what she did to you in her mother's parlour today and be done with it! If I am forced to abide another second of cryptic nonsense, I swear my head will explode."

"You mean to say Miss Bennet did not enlighten you?" Darcy asked in disbelief. After the set-down he received from her that afternoon, he was stunned to learn Jane Bennet had not confided all to Bingley. He supposed he ought to be grateful she still possessed some discretion, but her affront against him stung. He could feel no charity towards her, not presently.

"No, she did not." Bingley yanked his cravat from his neck with a churlish huff and tossed it onto a chair. He strode to the hearth, grabbed a brass poker, and stabbed the logs in the grate until the low-burning fire roared to life. "After you quit Longbourn, Mrs Gardiner was good enough to grant me a private interview with Miss Bennet. I demanded an explanation from her, and do you know what she said? That she was not at liberty to explain anything of the situation to me, that her conscience would not permit her to elaborate upon so much as one word that was spoken without the consent of her sister, Miss Elizabeth."

Bingley tossed the poker aside with an oath, only to have it land upon the hearth with an angry clang. "I found Miss Bennet's response not only inadequate, but her attitude unacceptable! In two days, I am to become her husband, Darcy—*her husband*—at which time she and all her sisters will become my responsibility in some manner or other. I believe *that* entitles me to know something of their affairs, no matter how private and confidential in nature."

Darcy ran his hand over his face and swallowed an oath of his own. While he had by no means forgiven Jane Bennet for treating him so contemptuously, neither had he been so blinded by his anger that he failed to see he had no one to blame but himself for her hostility in the first place. True, she should have never alluded to such an indelicate and painfully private topic in front of others, or at all for that matter. But if Darcy himself had not made such a prideful, arrogant speech to Elizabeth seven months prior—if he had only exercised some measure of restraint over his opinion of the Bennets and held his tongue and his temper after she refused him—this mortifying exchange with Elizabeth's eldest sister would have never occurred.

The painful reality of the matter, Darcy knew, was that Jane Bennet was correct. If he had invested any time at all in becoming better acquainted with Elizabeth and her preferences, if he had taken the trouble to discover who she was beneath that mask of archness and sweetness she always wore and peeled away the layers of her wilful impertinence, if he had courted her properly and recognised, not only the merit, but also the reward to be found in pleasing a woman worthy of being pleased, *then* perhaps a very different outcome than the wretched end he had met with and suffered from these many months might have been realised.

That aside, Darcy saw as clear as day his past actions once again driving a wedge between Bingley and Miss Bennet. He was disgusted by it. "I would be lying if I were to tell you what transpired today in your future mother's parlour did not anger and offend me. I cannot, however, hold Miss Bennet accountable for her enmity towards me, only her lack of discretion. Though her behaviour was...uncharacteristic, to say the least, I can assure you she is justified in her reproofs. The instance to which she alluded occurred some months ago and is a private matter between Miss Elizabeth and me."

"And this is all the answer I am to expect?"

Darcy remained silent.

Bingley's incredulity quickly gave way to anger. "Until today, my Jane was the sweetest woman in the world! She was obedient and respectful, almost to a fault! Never would the demure angel I fell in love with last autumn dare to speak disrespectfully to either of us. For the life of me, I cannot imagine what could have transpired between you and Miss Elizabeth to affect my future wife in such a way, but I am determined to find out! You will tell me or, so help me, with the foul mood I am in I may just hold this offence against you indefinitely!"

"Quite a bit can happen between two people over the course of a year," Darcy muttered darkly. "Whether you approve of Miss Bennet's recent behaviour or not, her actions present a perfect example of exactly how much a person is capable of alteration. It appears your intended is neither so simple, nor uncomplicated as you believed her to be when you first encountered her. For that, my friend, you should consider yourself fortunate."

"Fortunate!" Bingley cried. "How can you possibly consider this recent turn of events in any way fortunate?"

"Surely, you do not desire an insipid wife?"

Bingley glared at him. "I know Miss Bennet is not as clever or philosophical as her sister Miss Elizabeth, but neither is she lacking in intelligence. The point I am trying to make is this— had I wanted a complicated, outspoken woman for my wife, I would have set my sights in another direction entirely. How on earth am I to have a harmonious marriage if my future wife is not the modest, complaisant lady I believed her to be?"

"You cannot possibly be considering breaking your engagement!"

"What? Of course, I am not!" Bingley replied heatedly. "What do you take me for? At this point it is too late to withdraw my suit even if I wished it, which I certainly do not! You need not concern yourself, Darcy. I am no longer so fickle with my affections, nor so quick to fall in and out of love as I once was." He fixed his friend with a look that perfectly communicated his disgust and shook his head. "Apparently, though, I am still susceptible to distraction." Swearing under his breath, he sank onto a nearby couch and cradled his head in his hands. "Why in the world cannot the subject of women be a simple, straightforward business?"

With a bitter, rueful laugh, Darcy laid his head against the back of his chair and stared at the ceiling. Its wide, pale surface was bathed in the soft, flickering glow of the fire. "Because women, and Bennet women particularly, are neither simple, nor straightforward, as I have discovered for myself over the course of the past year in spades."

"Is that so?" Bingley enquired dryly.

"Precisely so." Darcy drew a fortifying breath, then proceeded to recount to his friend the bulk of his whole, sordid history with Elizabeth Bennet.

Though Bingley remained close-mouthed during the entire narrative, his dissatisfied expression turned to astonishment, then indignance, and finally fury. When Darcy had done, he leapt from the couch. "Devil be hanged! I had not the slightest idea you even admired Miss Elizabeth! To think you wanted her even as you and my sisters insisted that I abandon Miss Bennet last winter! Tell me what gave you the right to meddle in my relationship with Miss Bennet when you wanted nothing more than to marry her sister! Why, I ought to draw your claret!"

Never had Darcy seen his friend so angry, not even after he had confessed his role in Bingley's separation from Miss Bennet. He braced himself for the inevitable. Any second now he fully expected Bingley to clock him in the jaw and order him from Netherfield. Aside from Colonel Fitzwilliam—who was a blood relation—it was Charles Bingley who had always been at Darcy's side, his oldest and truest friend since their formative years. It pained him to imagine a future where Bingley no longer deigned to acknowledge him. The prospect sickened him, and Darcy knew, once again, he had absolutely no one to blame but himself for any of it.

He watched as Bingley paced the length of the room uttering curse after curse, and realised it was not only the loss of their friendship he feared, but the consequences associated with that loss. His thoughts drifted to his tenuous relationship with Elizabeth, who would be bound forever to Bingley through her sister. How would he ever manage to see her in London if she were there under her sister's and brother's supervision? How would he be able to properly court her if Bingley wanted nothing more to do with him and refused Darcy access to her?

Darcy felt like a selfish fool! Here he was, about to lose Bingley's friendship, yet his thoughts were turned as they always were, to Elizabeth. Disgusted with himself, he dropped his head into his hands. Severing his ties with Elizabeth had probably been Jane Bennet's chief motivation when she had called him onto the carpet earlier, and from what Darcy could see her contrivance may have worked. *By God, how the tables have turned!*

"It has become apparent," Bingley said to him shortly, "that I have spent far too much time over the last few months listening to you confess your sins against me. Frankly, I am sick of it. Since the day we were fortunate enough to be blessed with their acquaintance, we have both conducted ourselves beyond poorly with the Miss Bennets, but you, my friend, are in a class by yourself.

"I cannot speak for you, but I for one will never be able to forgive myself for the way I treated Miss Bennet last winter. As disappointed and furious as I am with you for your offences against Miss Bennet and her family, I believe I may yet possess the power to pardon you one last time."

Darcy raised his head.

Bingley's expression was uncharacteristically hard. "You are my dearest friend. In the future, I urge you to remember what that means." Without breaking his gaze, he extended his hand to Darcy.

Awed by his friend's seemingly endless supply of generosity and immeasurably grateful for his forbearance, Darcy stood at once and clasped Bingley's outstretched hand tightly. "Thank you," he said soberly. "I am aware I do not deserve your forgiveness any more than I do your friendship, but once again I find myself exceedingly thankful for both."

Bingley withdrew his hand and clasped Darcy's shoulder firmly —perhaps a bit too firmly—before sinking onto the couch and resting his head against the back of it. "Unless you do something that will infuriate me anew," he muttered, "you shall always have it."

৩৯৩

Though her night had yielded little rest, the following morning Elizabeth slipped from the house before her family members made an appearance downstairs. The hour was much later than her regular rising time and she was tired, but her mind and emotions remained in constant upheaval as she meditated, again and again, upon Jane's betrayal of her trust. When coupled with the very real indignation and pain she knew Darcy must have suffered in the wake of it, Elizabeth did not know if she wanted to scream at the top of her lungs in anger and frustration, or simply break down and cry. She was standing beside her mother's hermitage, dangerously close to doing the latter, when a hack chaise made its way down the drive and drew to a stop in front of the house. While the prospect of facing her family that morning had not appealed to her, the prospect of entertaining company at such an hour appealed to her even less. Elizabeth hastened towards the woods that bordered her father's property, where there happened to be a narrow footpath that would aid in her escape.

"Lizzy!"

The familiar, shrill, entirely unexpected voice of her youngest sister carried from the gravel drive all the way across the lawn to where Elizabeth was about to set foot upon the path. She stopped mid-stride, turned, and gaped as Lydia Wickham, who was headed straight towards her, broke into a spirited run.

"Lydia!" *What on earth is she doing here?* Elizabeth wondered, mystified. The possibility that Mr Wickham was able to obtain leave for Jane's wedding was almost laughable. He had only joined the regulars a few short months ago. It was impossible he had been granted time away from his new post so soon.

"Lord, Lizzy!" Lydia laughed once she reached her, bright-eyed and breathless. "Judging by the look on your face, you could not have suspected a thing, I daresay! What a good joke! How do I look?" she demanded as she spun around, her colourful skirts swirling about her ankles.

Lydia's enthusiasm was much the same as it ever was and, despite her initial shock at her youngest sister's arrival, Elizabeth felt a sentimental little smile tug at the corners of her mouth. She moved to embrace her. "You look lovely."

"I do, do I not?" Lydia answered, pecking her elder sister primly on the cheek. "It is not quite the fashion in London, but it is well enough for Newcastle. Though there are oceans of officers as far as the eye can see, there are hardly ever any parties or assemblies, so it does not signify what one wears most of the time. I was hoping to order some new gowns while we were in town in any case, but Wickham insists we do not have the funds for it. I shall ask Papa for some pin money while I am here, so I can visit a modiste when we return. Surely, he can spare a few hundred pounds. It has been an age since I have had any new things."

Marriage had apparently done little to curb Lydia's spendthrift ways. Rather than remark upon it, Elizabeth said, "I take it, then, Mr Wickham is here as well?"

"Of course, he is here! We are husband and wife, you know, and do nearly everything together. Even though he is on important business for Colonel Whittaker, my dear Wickham insisted I accompany him. Is not that sweet? Since we were headed all the way to London anyway, it was practically nothing to travel to Hertfordshire as well, and so here we are!"

Elizabeth frowned. "If Mr Wickham was sent by his colonel on business, is he not expected to complete his assignment and return immediately to his post?"

Lydia waved her hand dismissively. "Oh, la, Lizzy. A few extra days will hardly matter. The journey between Newcastle and London is so long and tedious that no one in the entire regiment will be any the wiser. Besides, I told Wickham I should break my heart if I missed Jane's wedding. I could not bear the idea of all of you having such a merry time without me, so of course, we came to Longbourn. He is the best husband, is he not?"

"Has Mamma seen you yet, Lydia?"

"Lord, no, for we have only just arrived. Wickham spotted you as soon as we turned into the drive, and I was determined to catch you before you disappeared into the woods, or else we would have never laid eyes on you again until supper."

Lydia linked her arm with Elizabeth's as they began to walk towards the house. "Wickham can hardly wait to see all of you. Out of all my sisters, I believe you are his favourite. By the by, do not think that means anything. Even though he did pay you a bit of attention in the beginning, in the end he wanted to marry me above everyone."

Elizabeth pursed her lips. "Of course," she replied tersely. "How could any of us possibly forget?"

George Wickham was as charming and eager to please as Elizabeth remembered him. She said as much to her Aunt Gardiner, who shook her head in wonderment as she claimed a seat beside her niece in Mrs Bennet's front parlour and took up her embroidery.

Though his appearance was little altered, and his regimentals flattered his figure, Elizabeth no longer thought Mr Wickham handsome. Perhaps it was the way he pandered incessantly to her mother, or gratified Kitty's vanity, or sought to ingratiate himself with her aunt that made Elizabeth see him as less. Or perhaps it was simply the fact that no matter how outwardly attractive a person appeared to the world, an ugly character once revealed would ultimately render its possessor ugly as well.

"I say, Miss Elizabeth," said Mr Ellis as he commandeered the vacant chair beside her. "Your brother-in-law gives all the appearance of being a respectable gentleman." He had arrived with his cousin Maria as the breakfast table was being cleared, and though Mr Bennet had extended an invitation to join Mr Gardiner and himself in Longbourn's library, Mr Ellis had declined. Instead, he chose to join the ladies and Mr Wickham, upon whom Elizabeth's father had not bestowed such a pointed mark of favouritism.

Elizabeth looked up from her fine work to observe her brother-in-law laughing pleasantly with her mother, sisters, and Maria Lucas on the other side of the parlour. He was all ease and friendliness, compliments, and smiles, and all the ladies, save for Mary, appeared enthralled. Elizabeth could not imagine why. Mr Wickham's very presence only served to vex her. She was desperate for a distraction but more than that, desperate to get away.

"You are a man of the world," she replied. "You ought to know that appearances can oftentimes be deceiving."

He regarded her with a raised brow but said nothing in response.

Across the room, the ladies tittered amusedly while Lydia erupted into laughter. "La, Wickham!" she cried. "You are too entertaining by half! I daresay all my sisters must envy me—even you, Jane. Though your Mr Bingley does have five thousand a year, he is not half so much fun, nor so handsome as *my* husband.

"How grand it would be if someone were to give *me* five thousand pounds! What pin money and gowns I would have, and what jewels! Mr Bingley will likely buy you half of London, Jane. You are too lucky by far."

Mrs Gardiner glanced at Elizabeth. "I would have thought," she remarked, "that Lydia would have learnt restraint once she settled into married life. I am very sorry to see that is not the case." There was no mistaking the disapproval in her tone.

"You deceive yourself, Aunt," Elizabeth replied coolly. "Lydia, you see, employs restraint to the same effect that her husband employs candour and economy."

Mr Ellis's lips twitched. "You do not like him," he said, folding his arms across his chest. "That much is obvious to me, though I cannot say that I blame you. He is as smooth as butter. I suppose he will be dining with us at Netherfield this evening, for your mother will undoubtedly want to show him off."

Mr Ellis had no sooner mentioned Netherfield than Elizabeth felt the colour drain from her face. She was horrified to think of Darcy meeting with Mr Wickham; moreover, she was horrified by what Darcy would likely *feel* during such a meeting. Being in the same room would be painful enough, but to have such a wretched association thrust upon him without warning would undoubtedly be worse.

"Oh, Mr Wickham!" Mrs Bennet declared. "You are charity itself for coming all this way! You must stay for a fortnight at least. I could not bear to part with you and Lydia sooner."

Mrs Bennet's pleasure at their coming was undeniable. Mr Ellis was correct. Elizabeth's mother would want to show Mr Wickham off to their neighbours every bit as much as she would Lydia in all her newly married glory. A son-in-law, especially one so dashing as Mr Wickham, was worth the price of gold to Mrs Bennet, and Lydia had always been her favourite child, second only to Jane. It was ridiculous to expect Longbourn's mistress to observe politesse and leave the Wickhams at home; nor would she consider penning a note to Netherfield, informing the Bingleys of the unexpectedness of her married daughter's arrival.

Elizabeth's agitation increased, and with it, her inattention to her current task. She felt a headache coming on and laid aside her embroidery. A moment later, she rose from her chair, intent upon quitting the room in quest of some fresh air.

"Whatever are you doing?" Mr Ellis asked, rising politely in acknowledgement.

Elizabeth startled, hesitated, and finally spoke. "The air in the room has grown stagnant. I am merely going for a walk."

His eyes shifted from Elizabeth to the other side of the room, where Elizabeth's mother fussed over Lydia with unabashed enthusiasm. He pursed his lips. "A bit of fresh air would do me a world of good as well. I will escort you, Miss Elizabeth."

"There is no need, sir," she insisted at once. "I am perfectly capable of finding my own way through my father's park."

"I have no doubts regarding your capabilities. Banish me to a remote corner of the woods if you like, but do not abandon me to the whims of your mother and Mrs Wickham. I have not Mr Wickham's fortitude." With a debonair smile he extended his arm, indicating she should lead the way.

Elizabeth looked to her aunt, but her aunt looked far too amused to be of service to her.

"Go on, Lizzy," she said. "Take a turn about the garden with Mr Ellis. The change of venue will do you a world of good. As for myself, I will check on the children, else they get themselves into mischief."

Exasperated, Elizabeth ignored Mr Ellis's proffered arm, turned on her heel, and strode towards the door. Under different circumstances she would have appreciated her friend's gallantry and welcomed his society, but she was by no means pleased to have his companionship thrust upon her, not when she desired solitude.

"Where are you going with Mr Ellis, Lizzy?" her mother demanded when she spied Elizabeth making her way across the room. "It is not every day that your sister is come back, and with Mr Wickham, too!"

"I am going for a walk, Mamma. I cannot speak for Mr Ellis. Perhaps he would like to see the hermitage. If so, he can find his own way." She addressed her friend. "Do go and see the hermitage, Mr Ellis."

"Oh!" Mrs Bennet exclaimed, brightening. "But of course, you must show Mr Ellis the hermitage, my dear!" She turned her attention to Mr Ellis, her excitement barely contained, and declared, "How wonderful this is, sir, and so spontaneous, too! Take all the time in the world, but do not keep us in suspense forever! I want to hear all about it once you are come back!"

Elizabeth was mortified to see her mother winking at her—much in the same manner she had at Jane before Mr Bingley had proposed marriage—and felt a flush of violent heat. Surely, her mother did not think Mr Ellis meant to propose to her! But one look at the gratified smile on Mrs Bennet's face made Elizabeth's heart sink. She dared not look at Mr Ellis but walked swiftly to the door and threw it open.

"Yes," Mrs Bennet sang, "be off with you now, and do not forget to speak to your father once everything is settled between you! He will want to know every particular!"

Elizabeth quickened her pace.

❧

"Mr and Mrs Thomas Bennet, Miss Bennet, Miss Elizabeth Bennet, Miss Mary Bennet, Miss Catherine Bennet, Mr and Mrs Edward Gardiner, and Lieutenant and Mrs George Wickham, sir."

If Mr Bingley was taken aback to see the Wickhams being presented to him in his finest drawing room, he hid his surprise extremely well. "Of course. How wonderful," he proclaimed with a smile as he greeted everyone and made the proper introductions between his future family and several of his own relations who had arrived two days prior from Scarborough. After everyone was comfortably situated, wine was procured from Netherfield's cellars and offered to his guests.

Unlike his friend, Darcy could barely conceal his astonishment. As he watched George Wickham engage in pleasantries with Bingley as though the blackguard was perfectly entitled to receive his notice, Darcy's consternation turned to anger. He rose from his chair with his wine glass in hand, walked to the other side of the room, and stationed himself before a large window that overlooked the park. It was dark as pitch.

How the devil has that man come to be in this house! How is it possible that he is not with his regiment? It was not without difficulty that Darcy refrained from quitting the room altogether to send an express to Colonel Fitzwilliam. *Surely, Wickham would not have been granted leave to travel such a distance for a wedding in the south when there are duties he must be expected to perform in the north!*

As though she had the ability to read his mind, Mrs Bennet chose that moment to declare to the room, "It was the most wonderful surprise when I saw my darling Lydia and her dear Wickham walk into the house with Lizzy this morning, Mr Bingley! Upon my word, he is the most considerate husband in the world to bring her all the way from Newcastle for her sister's wedding tomorrow, is he not?"

"Yes," Bingley replied. "Very considerate indeed."

Darcy may have imagined it, but he thought he detected a note of terseness in his friend's tone. Perhaps Bingley was not as amenable to seeing the Wickhams as he first thought.

"I thank you," said Wickham equitably. "Of late, my dear wife has been desolate being so far from Hertfordshire, and so I found that I could not possibly deny her the pleasure of being within the bosom of her family a moment longer. After all, it is not every day one of my dear sisters is to marry such a kind-hearted, benevolent gentleman. It would be unpardonable to miss paying our respects on such a happy occasion."

Via the reflections in the windowpanes, Darcy's eyes sought Elizabeth. She was seated upon one of Bingley's couches. Her posture appeared rigid. Despite her serious, almost angry mien, he could not deny that she looked extremely lovely wearing what he supposed was one of many new gowns that would soon be travelling with her to London. She reached for her wine glass and took a slow, measured sip.

"Do you hear that, girls?" Mrs Bennet cried. "Now *that* is thoughtfulness for you! *That* is generosity for you! Indeed, Mr Wickham is the very best of men, is he not? Should you happen to visit your sister in Newcastle, I am certain he would be able to introduce the rest of you to some equally dashing and solicitous officers. What say you, sir?"

"I say amen to that, ma'am. It would be my pleasure to have my sisters to stay with us. As a matter of fact, I can think of several gentlemen off the top of my head who would be extremely gratified to make their acquaintance. None of my sisters would go unadmired in the north."

"Oh, yes! You must all come to Newcastle," Lydia cried, "even you, Mary, for it is as good a place as any to get you a husband, I daresay."

"I thank you for my share," Mary answered curtly, "but I do not particularly like your way of getting husbands. I would rather remain respectable than behave like a common—"

"Hush, you foolish girl," said Mrs Bennet. "You shall become a spinster at this rate! You ought to be grateful your sister is willing to take you under her wing at all. Lord knows you do nothing to attract any notice here, not like your other sisters. Why, in the last month Lizzy has managed to catch the eye of several promising young men who are more than capable of providing her with a very comfortable situation. She will soon follow your sisters' example and have a doting husband of her own. Indeed, she could very well receive an offer this evening if only she would wipe that sour expression from her face." She turned towards Bingley's aunt with a wide smile and said, "Mr Ellis is a charming young man, and quite wealthy, too! I was certain he intended to propose to Lizzy this morning, but it turned out he had to go away on some errand or other and did not get around to it."

The sound of breaking glass was heard across the room. It took Darcy a moment to realise it was not the wine glass he clutched in his own hand that had shattered, but Elizabeth's.

In haste she had risen from her seat. A heated blush deeply coloured her complexion, not dissimilar to the liquid presently soaking her gloves. What was left of her wine glass lay discarded upon the table—several large shards of crystal amidst a dark puddle of cabernet. "I am so sorry," she cried, frantically dabbing the soiled silk of her gloves with her handkerchief. "I do not know what has come over me!"

Bingley leapt from his place beside Jane to offer his own hand-kerchief and to ring the bell pull for a servant. "Think nothing of it, Miss Elizabeth. It is only a bit of wine, after all. It is quite all right. I am exceedingly sorry about your gloves."

"As am I!" Mrs Bennet exclaimed. "What a careless girl you are! I ought to have known you would do something to ruin your appearance this evening, and before Mr Ellis is able to see you, too! I do not know why I even bother to buy you any new things when all you do is treat them with such ill-care!"

"If I were to have new gloves, Mamma," said Lydia, "I certainly would not treat them so carelessly, especially gloves as grand as Lizzy's."

"Nor would I," echoed Kitty.

"If Lizzy treats all her new things in such a manner," Lydia continued, "perhaps I ought to have them instead. As a married woman, I will know how to take proper care of them."

"Why should you have Lizzy's new things?" Kitty cried indignantly. "You have a husband to buy you gowns and gloves—and besides, I am two years older!"

Horrified, Darcy watched Elizabeth blanch. She clutched the soiled handkerchiefs in her hands, which appeared to shake slightly, and addressed the mistress of the house with as much composure as she could likely muster. "Pray, excuse me, Miss

Bingley. I have no desire to leave a mark upon your furniture."
She did not wait to hear Miss Bingley's reply.

Darcy was at a loss as he watched Elizabeth all but run from the room. Her departure was accompanied by sympathetic murmurs from Bingley's relations. His first instinct, to damn propriety and go after her to provide what little comfort he could, was currently at war with that of his second: taking Mrs Bennet to task for humiliating her daughter—two of her daughters—in such a callous manner in public. As he had no claim on Elizabeth, neither impulse was viable, nor appropriate. He turned his attention instead to the few rational members of Elizabeth's family and was at once relieved to see that Mrs Gardiner had begun to stand.

It was Jane, however, who would follow Elizabeth from the room. Darcy watched her lay her hand upon her aunt's arm, and the two women engaged in a short, but earnest conversation.

When Miss Bennet had gone, Mr Bennet's voice rose over the din of his two youngest daughters who, to Darcy's astonishment, continued to argue. "Kitty, Lydia, that is quite enough! No one will have Lizzy's new things besides Lizzy. They are hers to do with as she pleases. I do not care if she wears them in the fields after a rainstorm or while wading knee-deep in the brook, so long as I do not hear another word on the subject."

"The brook," his wife cried. "Mr Bennet, you cannot possibly—"

But her husband fixed her with a stern look that brooked no opposition. "I suggest you introduce another topic, Mrs Bennet, for this one is closed." With a nod to his future son-in-law, Mr Bennet lifted his wine glass and proceeded to drink the entirety of its contents.

Bingley plastered a tight, congenial smile upon his face and enquired after the health of Mrs Bennet's sister, Mrs Philips, who was also to be a guest at Netherfield that evening. Within seconds, Mrs Bennet took charge of the conversation much as she usually did, speaking animatedly to all those who would listen about the various other families residing in the neighbourhood, including their situations and prospects, as though nothing untoward had just occurred.

When the topic turned to Mr Ellis and the Lucases, who were expected to arrive at any moment, Darcy had borne more than he felt he could possibly be expected to tolerate. He discarded his wine glass and made his way to a secondary door located at the back of the room, bent on seeking relief from the exposition taking place using whatever means were within his reach.

❧ 14 ❧

WHERE ELIZABETH CONFRONTS JANE.

"To sit there and be subjected to such a spectacle! I cannot do it, Jane! And Mr Wickham!" Elizabeth proclaimed, the anger in her voice irrefutable evidence of her dislike of him. "We all know what he is, yet our mother continues to flatter and flirt with him as though he has never done anything to wrong our family, to say nothing of the way she spoke to poor Mary, as though Mary is of no consequence whatsoever and Lydia, everything that is respectable and good!"

Blinking back tears of frustration, Elizabeth sank onto a small couch fashioned in the French style, elegantly upholstered in blue and grey silk. The stains upon her new gloves were unsightly. No amount of washing would ever restore them. They would have to be dyed. She expelled an agitated breath at the thought of what her mother would have to say on the matter, then shook her head, too disgusted by all that had transpired throughout the day—nay, the entire week—to care. She pulled them off and tossed them onto a table.

With a quiet exhalation, Jane claimed a seat beside her. "It was very wrong of Mamma to speak so callously to Mary, and to you as well. She should not have done it. As for our brother, as disturbing as the situation between Lydia and Mr Wickham was in the beginning, they are married now, Lizzy, and all is well. There is nothing anyone can do to change what came before. It is time to move on. Lydia appears healthy and happy, and Mr Wickham is doting and attentive. Perhaps he really does care for her."

Elizabeth laughed ruefully. "He has never cared for her, Jane, nor is he likely to start now. Do not allow his insincere smiles and false flattery to fool you a second time. He is capable of caring for none but himself."

"I cannot believe he is as bad as he once was, not now. He brought Lydia all the way from Newcastle to see us, after all. If that does not speak well of him, I do not know what does."

"Nothing does!" Elizabeth cried. "Jane, how can you still fail to see him for what he is? His actions today are exactly why I am determined to think of him as I have before. Lydia told me he had important business in London for his colonel—business that cannot be delayed—yet here he is attending your wedding. It is not sound!

"I refuse to believe Lydia's claim that Mr Wickham has authorisation to bring her along on official military business, nor do I believe he has been awarded leave to go so far as Hertfordshire. Their accounts of their circumstances differ greatly, not only regarding his business and the time he is permitted for leisure, but other details as well. Why, just this morning Mr Wickham boasted to our mother that he is prospering in his profession, yet, according to Lydia, they are sufficiently low on funds."

"Perhaps he is practising economy. Perhaps he is merely concealing the extent of his good fortune from our sister so that he can purchase a house for them. Some day they will start a family, and you know as well as I how careless Lydia is with money."

"Oh, yes," Elizabeth muttered resentfully, "but in that, I am afraid they are much the same."

"I see you are determined to think the very worst of him."

"And, as usual, you are determined to think the very best, even though it is far from plausible, not to mention more than Mr Wickham deserves. How soon you have forgotten Mr Darcy's letter! How soon you have forgotten what Mr Darcy's own sister suffered at Mr Wickham's hand!"

Jane's fingers fidgeted with the ribbons that decorated the sleeve of her gown. "It is no more than Lydia has suffered," she replied, "or any of us."

"No," Elizabeth agreed, "it is not, but that does not mean that Mr and Miss Darcy are not entitled to the same empathy and understanding to which we are entitled. You spoke of forgiveness and moving forward just now, but I understand you did not heed your own counsel when Mr Darcy and Mr Bingley came to call yesterday."

Jane's eyes widened and, though the moment was fleeting, Elizabeth felt vindicated for having called her sister's behaviour to the fore. Too soon, however, more painful feelings encroached, and the full weight of her sister's betrayal settled upon her shoulders like a shroud.

"Lizzy," said Jane soberly, "it is hardly the same thing."

Elizabeth could hardly believe her ears. "How could you?" she said to her, finding it increasingly difficult to keep her emotions in check. "How could you be so callous? Nay, so spiteful! You had no right, no right at all to speak of my personal business to anyone, especially in public, and especially to Mr Darcy, of all people."

"I am sorry, exceedingly sorry, you feel injured by what I have done."

While Elizabeth recognised contrition in her sister's tone, she detected a note of resentment as well, as though Jane had been the wounded party in this instance and not Elizabeth and Darcy. Elizabeth shook her head in disbelief.

Jane forged onward. "You, more than anyone, ought to understand why I could no longer hold my tongue. To be in the same room with him and listen to him speak of you in such glowing terms yesterday, all the while knowing how he treated you in Kent—without thought, regard, or consideration for your feelings! My feelings on the subject were simply too much to contain any longer. His superior attitude injures people, Elizabeth! He injured you—I know he did—from the very first moment of his acquaintance with us when he dismissed you as being only tolerable. He injured Charles by refusing to return to Netherfield for months on end, and because I love you both so very dearly, his actions injured me as well. You know this! You know this because it is what I confided to you just the other morning. Can you not comprehend why it was finally too much for me to overlook? Why I was tired of simply doing nothing?"

Elizabeth stared at her. While she perfectly comprehended the resentment that Jane harboured towards Darcy for wounding a most beloved sister, at present she found herself far more sympathetic towards Darcy for what he had likely felt in the wake of Jane's vitriol than what Jane had ever felt on Elizabeth's behalf in the wake of his.

"Just as you said earlier regarding Mr Wickham and his behaviour, that is in the past and there it ought to remain. Mr Darcy offended me on many prior occasions, but I no longer believe it was consciously done on his part. Since we met last summer, he has been unfailingly gracious and kind despite my poor treatment of *him*. He does not deserve your disapproval, your censure, or your scorn. He is a good man. In fact, it has been many months now I have considered him one of the best men of my acquaintance. He deserves to be treated as such, by all of us."

A long moment of charged silence followed.

"Perhaps I was too harsh," Jane allowed, albeit grudgingly. "I am sorry that I could not control my temper yesterday. I am sorry I betrayed your confidence. I am sorry for so many things, but God forgive me I cannot be sorry for the way I feel. Perhaps in time I shall be able to overlook all Mr Darcy's transgressions, but at present they are still too great. My disappointment with him runs too deep. My irritation is still too fresh to allow me to fully forget all he is responsible for. I have no proof, but I believe he played as prominent a role in Charles's absence last winter as either of my future sisters. Every time I contemplate it, it makes more sense to me. Every time I contemplate it, it makes me angrier with him."

Elizabeth struggled to formulate a response. She knew if she told Jane the truth, that Darcy was indeed guilty of such a crime, her sister might very well hate him forever; but neither could Elizabeth lie to her. "You have accused Mr Darcy of keeping Mr Bingley from Hertfordshire, but Mr Bingley is a grown man and master of all he says and does. If what you say of Mr Darcy is true, then Mr Bingley's failure to trust his own judgment speaks just as badly, if not worse, of him—yet you welcomed him back as soon as he reappeared upon our doorstep. Without uttering so much as one word in reprimand, you allowed him to renew his acquaintance with us and his attentions to you. You forgave him for abandoning you last year and for breaking your heart."

"You believe I forgave Charles too easily?"

"The decision to forgive Mr Bingley was yours alone to make. No one knows your heart better than you do but considering the circumstances, you cannot possibly accuse one man of such a crime without also holding the other accountable for his actions in the matter. It is not just."

"Charles returned to me."

"Yes, but he returned ten months later, with Mr Darcy at his side. Does that not strike you as more than a mere coincidence? If it were Mr Darcy who prevented Mr Bingley from returning, do you not think it incredible that Mr Darcy would then choose to accompany his friend when he paid a call upon you at Long-bourn, effectively offering his support and sanction of Mr Bingley's attentions?"

Jane said nothing in response.

Elizabeth said, "I understand how you can feel the way you do but having such an outlook can change nothing of any consequence now. A resentful nature fosters more resentment. It is a lesson I learned only too well in the past year, and I now have nothing but regret to show for it. For the sake of a harmonious future with Mr Bingley, you must let your prejudice against Mr Darcy go. He is Mr Bingley's oldest friend, and he is honourable and good."

"Do you truly think so well of him now?" Jane asked. "Do you honestly believe Mr Darcy deserves your good opinion? That he has earned both it and your forgiveness?"

"I do," Elizabeth told her feelingly. "He does, and he deserves yours as well."

Jane bowed her head. "My behaviour yesterday has distressed you. The last thing I intended by taking such action was to cause you unhappiness. As for the rest, I will try to open my heart to forgiveness, but it will take time, Lizzy. I ask for your patience."

"So long as you extend the same courtesy to Mr Darcy, I shall have all the patience in the world. His good opinion is important to me, Jane. I cannot put it any plainer than that."

With trembling hands, Jane busied herself smoothing non-existent creases on her gown. "After what has come to pass, I will understand if you have changed your mind and wish to remain at Longbourn while Charles and I travel to London on our honeymoon. I will hold nothing against you, nor shall Charles."

"That will not be necessary," said Elizabeth gently as she covered Jane's hands with her own. "If you still wish for me to accompany you to town then, of course, I will join you as planned. I have no desire to punish you or cause you any heartache or discomfort by refusing you something that would please you. I would never do that to you, Jane, especially during the most joyful time of your life. Despite what has transpired, despite the injury your actions and words have caused, both to me and to Mr Darcy, you are still my dearest sister. It may be a while yet until I can forgive you entirely, but I could never love you less."

"Dear Lizzy!" There were unshed tears in Jane's eyes as she clutched her sister's hands. "I am relieved to hear it!"

"Come now," Elizabeth chided, blinking back her own tears as she embraced her tightly. "Do not cry. It will never do should Mamma and Mr Bingley see you with red eyes."

"No, I suppose it would not," Jane agreed as she released her, reached for her handkerchief, and dabbed at her eyes with a tearful smile. "We ought to return now. There is only so much that my poor Charles and his relations can endure at the hands of our mother and sisters. Not to mention there are surely others who are anxious to see that you are well."

Though she could not argue with Jane's logic, Elizabeth was in no hurry to return to a place where she had suffered so much mortification in so little time, and all in the presence of Darcy! She could well imagine what he must think of her now. Her family's conduct, and her own for that matter, was irrefutable proof that none of them had altered their ways.

Darcy would stay for the wedding, then leave. While he would likely continue his friendship with Mr Bingley, Elizabeth knew he would do all within his power to avoid contact with her in the future. Though she could not imagine Darcy marrying his cousin, he could have no designs upon her either, not after her family had exposed themselves so deplorably. He was lost to her forever, and the ache in Elizabeth's heart was made all the worse.

Her throat felt painfully tight. A lump had formed there, and she swallowed thickly to dislodge it. "I will be along in a moment," she managed to say. "I am afraid I still require a few minutes to myself if I am to face our mother and the rest of Mr Bingley's guests with any degree of fortitude."

Jane hesitated, but Elizabeth forced a half-hearted smile to her lips. It was the most she could offer. She was dangerously close to losing her composure. "I will be fine and shall return before long. Please, go without me."

Jane kissed her cheek. "Do not linger too long."

Elizabeth watched her walk towards the door with a mixture of relief and regret, knowing that while they had made their peace with one another in a sense, a thick ribbon of tension remained. As though Jane sensed it, too, she paused just before the threshold and said, "I will do my utmost to distract our mother, but should she fail to notice the length of your absence, you know very well that our father and Aunt and Uncle Gardiner will not, nor shall Mr Ellis once he arrives." Then her sister quit the room.

❧ 15 ❧

WHERE MR DARCY SPEAKS TO ELIZABETH OF A
MATTER MOST URGENT.

"Thank you," Darcy muttered from the shadows of the dimly lit hall as Miss Bennet pulled the door closed behind her. He had felt Ellis's name like a slap yet ignored the slight and executed a perfunctory bow, which Miss Bennet deigned to acknowledge with a barely discernible nod of her head. Her entire person appeared stiff and unyielding. Her pale blue eyes held his in a silent battle of wills.

"If you truly esteem my sister as you claim," she warned in a low voice, "do not place her in a situation she would not desire. She has suffered enough, as have we all."

Miss Bennet left, and Darcy expelled the breath he had been holding.

It had not been his intention to eavesdrop. He had been on his way to his bedchamber to pen a letter to his cousin regarding Wickham. Then Darcy heard Elizabeth's voice, rigid with anger, from beyond a partially closed door, and froze. Her tone was all too familiar. To say he was surprised to hear her displeasure directed at her dearest sister was an understatement. He was shocked, especially when Elizabeth confronted Miss Bennet about the exchange that took place between them in Longbourn's drawing room.

That was nothing compared to the astonishment Darcy then felt as Elizabeth claimed she not only considered Darcy's conduct to be honourable, but that she counted him among the best men of her acquaintance.

Never had Darcy felt such elation!

Before such a triumphant moment could be savoured, Miss Bennet laid the blame for Bingley's ten-month hiatus upon his shoulders. Any buoyancy he experienced from Elizabeth's commendation of his character sank as quickly as it had risen.

For what felt like an eternity, Elizabeth was silent. Darcy feared she would confess his involvement—she had, after all, confided in Jane regarding everything else. But she surprised him yet again. Not only did she keep his hand in their separation a secret but pointed out Bingley's fault in the business as well.

And then, without any warning, Elizabeth spoke eight words that made Darcy feel as though he could fly: 'Mr Darcy's good opinion is important to me'.

By God, hearing those words had thrilled him! For the first time in many long, bleak months his heart swelled with real hope.

Then Miss Bennet pulled the sitting room door open and discovered him lurking outside in the hall. Instead of announcing his presence and berating him soundly for his audacity, Elizabeth's sister did the very last thing he had anticipated. She schooled her shocked expression into one of cold politeness, addressed him civilly, and allowed him to remain where he was.

Now Darcy was alone, free to approach Elizabeth as he had wanted to for weeks. He had bided his time and hoped for a chance exactly like this one: an opportunity to speak with her without being scrutinised under her family's watchful eyes or overheard by her neighbours.

If there was a time for Darcy to act, it was now.

He placed his hand on the door handle, but the soft rustling of fabric, likely the rich satin of Elizabeth's gown as she moved about the room, made him pause. There was no guarantee his intrusion upon her privacy would be met with any degree of pleasure, or even tolerance. Darcy laid his forehead against the door, listening to the muffled swish of her skirts. It was strangely hypnotic. He closed his eyes and wondered what in the world he would ever say to her. He knew what he wanted to say, but also realised it was imprudent on his part. Elizabeth had been upset with her sister only moments before. The possibility that any residual anger could be turned upon him in a moment of ill-timed rashness was great.

When he heard Elizabeth begin to weep Darcy knew he must act, if only to offer what consolation was within his power. He pushed the door open and entered. The interior was dimly lit, but he could make out Elizabeth's figure in the centre of the room, perched on a small sofa. His long strides brought him quickly to her side.

She did not react or even appear to notice his approach, not even when he knelt before her on the carpet. With his heart in his throat, he watched her as she wept. Her head was bowed, her face cradled by her hands. He did not want to add to her distress but knew he must speak, if only to let her know she was no longer alone. "Miss Elizabeth," he said gently.

Elizabeth raised her head with a startled gasp. A moment later she appeared to recall herself and self-consciously swiped at her tear-stained cheeks with her fingers. She had removed her soiled gloves and Darcy noticed her hands trembled. As if she had discerned his thoughts, Elizabeth quickly folded them upon her lap and linked her fingers so tightly her knuckles turned white.

The acuteness of her wretchedness pierced him. "Miss Elizabeth," he said again, and covered her hands with his own in a gesture meant to express his commiseration and offer comfort. "What can I do to bring you relief? Shall I send for your sister? Or for Mrs Gardiner? I can go directly. Or would you prefer a glass of wine? May I fetch one for you?"

Elizabeth stared at him with wide, startled eyes. One lone curl clung to the apple of her cheek. Darcy was enthralled by it. Despite her suffering, she looked achingly lovely. He lifted a hand to brush the errant curl aside, but that tender action suddenly proved too much for Elizabeth. She yanked her hands from Darcy's, leapt from her seat, and hastened to the window. After a full minute of excruciating silence, she raised one shaking hand to her forehead.

"Pray forgive me," said Darcy with far more composure than he felt. "Clearly, you are in distress, and I have no right whatsoever—"

"My God," she replied, nearly choking on her words. "How can you stand it? How can you possibly stand it!"

Darcy was on his feet at once, moving purposefully to the window to stand just behind her. He was close enough to feel the warmth of her body. Coupled with the heady scent of her perfume, he felt dizzy. "Stand what?" he asked, his voice uncharacteristically hoarse as he forced his feet several steps in the opposite direction, effectively increasing the distance between them to one infinitely more proper.

"All of it," she cried, her voice catching as she turned to face him. "My mother, my sisters, that scoundrel I must call my brother...*me, sir!* How can you bear to be in our company after the way we have conducted ourselves and continue to conduct ourselves, even now? After everything that has transpired in the past year to bring shame and scandal upon my family, why do you still surround yourself with us? What could you possibly gain but censure and dissatisfaction for your sacrifice? It would have been better for you to stay away!"

Darcy slowly shook his head. "It is no sacrifice to be able to spend time with you. As for staying away...you must know that is a prospect that has long been distasteful to me."

Elizabeth closed her eyes as though pained. "I find that difficult to believe. My family—"

"Your family loves you. Despite anything you may have to say to the contrary, that much has been made obvious to me in many ways, at many times. You are not your mother. Neither are you your sisters or your father. You govern yourself, and your comportment has always been exemplary."

"You are blind, sir. I am no different."

"You are *entirely* different."

"And you, Mr Darcy, are entirely mistaken! Can you deny that I have treated you poorly in the past? Do you recall no instance when my behaviour was no better than what you witnessed this evening? I can think of one occasion particularly when my manners and address were, in every respect, reprehensible, unfeeling, and unjust."

"No," he said, knowing she referred to the afternoon of his ill-fated proposal. "Not even then. You said nothing to me that day, nor any other, that I did not deserve."

"I believe we both know that is not the case," Elizabeth replied. Her fingertips swiped angrily at a fresh set of tears.

Darcy produced a handkerchief from his waistcoat pocket and offered it to her. "Your eldest sister is correct, you know. From the very beginning I gave you little incentive to like me. Your words and your anger at Hunsford were justified. As painful as your reproofs were for me to hear, you did me a service."

"A service," Elizabeth repeated bitterly as she accepted his handkerchief and dried her tears. "I did not realise I was providing a service when I accused you of wronging a lying reprobate who aspired to make his way in the world by gambling and seducing young women, all the while masquerading as an officer and a gentleman."

"Perhaps not," Darcy replied gravely, "but you did not know then what Mr Wickham was. I did nothing to enlighten you, your family, or your neighbours. It was wrong of me, nay, irresponsible and selfish of me, to fail to act."

Elizabeth turned aside her head. "You are generous with your absolution, but completely in the wrong on this matter. There is nothing dishonourable in shielding a loved one from society's scorn. You were right to protect your sister from scandal."

"I was wrong when I did nothing to protect yours from suffering a similar fate."

"We are at an impasse." Elizabeth bowed her head. She appeared to be studying his handkerchief. With great care, her fingertips traced the stitching of Darcy's initials.

Darcy felt his heart swell, moved and hopeful beyond measure by the intimacy of her gesture. His hand closed firmly, completely around hers. "I have *always* enjoyed your company," he quietly confessed. "That is something that will never change. Your family may do what they will, but there is nothing that shall deter me or cause me to waver from my course. I am no longer insensible of the debt I owe your parents, your eldest sister, and the Gardiners especially. Without their guidance, you would not have become the caring, intelligent, utterly enchanting woman I have the honour of knowing. For that, I will always be grateful."

Elizabeth coloured deeply, and Darcy feared she would withdraw her hand. He need not have worried.

"And what of my impertinence?" Her words may have rung with challenge, but her tone contained far less fire than he had come to expect from her. She sounded endearingly uncertain.

"Your impertinence," he replied, "is unequalled."

Her lips quirked.

Darcy's thumb began to stroke the back of her hand—a slow, even caress that sent a discernible shiver through her entire body. "I have long considered your impertinence charming and have been desolate without it these many months. I have *missed* you. I hope you do not think me too forward."

Elizabeth's gaze remained steadfast upon the movement of his hand as he continued his tender ministrations. "In such cases as this," she said feelingly, "it is, I believe, the established mode to express one's gratitude for the sentiments avowed, and to return them if one is able." She raised her eyes to his. "You are too good, Mr Darcy, and too forgiving by far—"

"Please. I do not wish to quarrel with you over which of us possesses the more forgiving soul, not tonight. With your permission I would like to put aside our difference of opinion until another day. Perhaps you would be so generous as to receive me during your stay in London and we may revisit it then. After all, I cannot imagine you will have anything better to do while the newlyweds stare at one another with adoring calf eyes for an entire month."

"Are you teasing me?"

Though he detected only a hint of her usual archness in her tone, the corners of Darcy's mouth turned upward in satisfaction. "I am. Despite what you believe, both your kindness and your impertinence have had a most positive and lasting effect on me."

Elizabeth shook her head. "I would not go so far as to say the effect has always been positive, sir, but it is certainly something to behold. As to whether it is lasting or not, I suppose I shall have to wait and see for myself."

It was Darcy's turn to flush with warmth; the gratification and the unadulterated pleasure he derived from the implications of her admission were irrepressible. "It is owing to you," he said with absolute certainty. "Whether or not you realise it, whether or not you accept the credit for it, knowing you has changed me and changed me for the better."

Elizabeth bowed her head. "You are too generous. As it so happens, I can very easily recall a time when that was not the case."

"And once again," he insisted, though not unkindly, "you are mistaken. No one familiar with the matter can deny it was I who inspired *your* ire, *your* dissatisfaction, *your* disapproval, and *your* repugnance. From nearly the first moment we met I managed to injure you with my thoughtless remarks, but it did not end there. Throughout our acquaintance, unconscious and ignorant though most of my actions were, I continued to inflict upon you pain of the acutest kind. It was inexcusable, especially when your beauty, tenacity, wit, and inherent sweetness incited nothing in me but confusion, admiration, and ultimately a deep and all-encompassing adoration and regard."

He averted his eyes. "It has been many months since I first acquainted you with my feelings on this subject, and while I am certainly altered, my feelings are not. Much has passed between us since then—much that I regret. I cannot possibly begin to right all the wrongs I have committed against you and your family. There are so many that I honestly have no idea where to begin."

He was startled when Elizabeth's grip upon his hand tightened almost painfully. "You already have," she whispered fervently. Her eyes met his with a sincerity that made his pulse quicken. "Mr Darcy, I *must* apologise to you. You cannot know how much I have come to regret my past actions. For months I have dwelt upon nothing but my injudicious treatment of you. My behaviour at the time was unpardonable. I cannot think of it without abhorrence."

Her apology, though unnecessary in his eyes, moved him. He took a tentative step forward, then another, until the physical distance between them was entirely improper, nothing more than a hairsbreadth. "You must think upon it no longer, I beg of you."

Elizabeth made to speak, or, more likely, Darcy thought, to argue with him, but he was impatient to move beyond their current conversation. He would have no more of her apology, not when he felt so strongly the fault was his and his alone. He shook his head minutely, his countenance earnest as he silently implored her to utter nothing further on the subject.

By some miracle, she obeyed him.

In that moment, the expression upon Elizabeth's face so closely resembled the stuff of Darcy's dreams that his heart stuttered in his chest. Her gaze was so intense and her expression so tender and full of affection that he felt the effects all the way to the recesses of his soul.

It was this realisation that caused his careful reserve to unravel completely. Raising their joined hands to his lips, he pressed a sensual, lingering kiss to Elizabeth's palm. When she uttered no protest, he drew her into his arms. Her soft, tremulous sigh as her body melted fully, completely against his own was the sweetest sound he had ever heard. Overcome, Darcy touched his forehead to hers; their clasped hands rested between them upon the lapel of his coat, warm and vital over his pounding heart.

He was intoxicated by the feel of her—her presence, her warmth, her scent. The reality of Elizabeth in his arms was more heavenly, more exhilarating, more soothing than anything he had imagined, and what was more, it felt right. Now that he knew what it was to hold her, Darcy was more determined than ever not only to endeavour to deserve her regard, but to secure her love; to court her relentlessly for as long as it would take, until she agreed to spend her life with him. He closed his eyes and expelled a ragged breath, for the moment, content to simply hold her in his arms.

❧ 16 ❧

WHERE ELIZABETH SPEAKS TO MR DARCY, MR ELLIS SPEAKS TO ELIZABETH, AND ALL ARE CONFUSED.

After learning of his argument with Jane the day before, after the appearance of Mr Wickham, and after bearing witness to her family's mortifying performance that evening, Elizabeth had been certain Darcy would no longer want anything to do with her; but how wrong she had been!

Her heart was filled to bursting, full of the man before her, and full of gratitude for his generous nature and forgiving heart. Could she honestly have understood him correctly? After all this time, had he truly intimated he still loved her?

"Were you in earnest when you said you would call upon me in London, sir?"

Darcy tightened his grasp upon her hand, pressing it more firmly against his chest as his other moved from her waist to gently cradle the back of her head. "I will call upon you every day if you will allow it."

Elizabeth smiled. "Not only will I allow it, I shall welcome it."

"Then it is settled," he told her as his fingers toyed with a curl at the nape of her neck. Though he treated her with care, she was excruciatingly aware of his touch, especially when one of his fingertips lightly grazed the skin of her neck.

Elizabeth heard as well as felt Darcy's breath hitch in time with her own. His ministrations ceased and he removed the hand that had been playing with her hair, placing it gingerly upon the small of her back instead. A slight tremble in his fingers and quickening of his heart were the only outward indications that he was as deeply affected by Elizabeth as she was by him.

His voice sounded achingly tender when he said, "I fear you will grow heartily sick of me. By now you must know my heart is yours. I cannot pretend to sentiments I do not feel. I cannot feign indifference, not with you. I must know. I must know the depth of *your* feelings else I go distracted."

"My feelings?" she said in wonderment. She was firmly within the circle of his arms, his body warmed her like a fire, and their breaths mingled with each exhalation. Surely, he did not doubt her heart belonged to him, that she was entirely, solely, irrevocably his? "Cannot you tell?"

"I have misread you so many times I fear I can no longer rely on my own judgment. I must defer to your honesty."

"Let there be no doubt," she told him feelingly, "I am forever altered. My feelings are very different. In fact, they are quite the opposite of what they once were."

His breath escaped him in a rush, and he released her hand to enfold her completely in his arms. "Elizabeth," he said on a breath, pressing his lips first to her hair, then her cheek, and her shoulder. "May I speak to your father?"

Elizabeth's heart skipped a beat, though whether it was the result of the words he uttered, the use of her Christian name, or the exquisite sensation of his lips as they caressed the bare skin of her shoulder with bold intent, she could not discern. Her mind struggled to form a coherent response. "What will you tell him?"

"I will tell him whatever you wish."

Through the finely spun wool of his tailcoat, Elizabeth felt the virile strength of Darcy's heart, its furious tempo in perfect rhythm with her own. She turned her head and brazenly brushed her lips against his cheek, a featherlight gesture that Elizabeth did not bestow lightly. "What is it that *you* wish, Mr Darcy?"

"For you to be mine," he said hoarsely.

The earnest simplicity of his statement moved her beyond words. Overcome with emotion, Elizabeth struggled against the impulse to weep. What she must have put him through! The heartache and indignity he had surely suffered because of her must have been considerable, yet after all this time he not only loved her, but wished to marry her—she, Elizabeth Bennet of Longbourn—not Anne de Bourgh of Rosings Park or Miss So-and-So of London. She said, "Then you may tell him that I am."

"Dearest Elizabeth," he whispered. The reverence and adoration in Darcy's voice as he pronounced her name was irrefutable. Gradually, his hold upon her loosened, but only so much as to enable him to better see her face. Elizabeth could not deny the expression he wore as he gazed upon her was that of a man wholly, unabashedly in love.

She marvelled at Darcy's devotion to her. Even after her vehement refusal of his first proposal and Lydia's scandalous elopement and patched-up marriage to a man he rightly hated, Darcy continued to love her. Overwhelmed, Elizabeth did not dare trust herself to speak, but instead gave him what she desperately hoped was a warm, encouraging smile full of adoration and love.

To her immense joy, Darcy returned it. He soon grew serious, however, and ever so slowly inclined his head towards hers. Elizabeth's heart beat so rapidly she feared it would take flight. Her eyelids fluttered closed, and she felt his breath upon her face, the tip of his nose as it grazed her cheek, and at last his lips, soft and sure as he pressed a gentle kiss to her mouth.

"Mr Darcy," she said on a breath. She felt his smile against her lips as he kissed her again.

"Fitzwilliam," he said softly.

"Fitzwilliam," she repeated tenderly, raising her hand to cradle his jaw.

Darcy drew her closer, deepening their kiss, and Elizabeth was lost.

❧

"Elizabeth Bennet!"

In her present blissful state, encircled in Darcy's arms, it took Elizabeth a moment to realise it was not Darcy who had addressed her with such fierce urgency, but Mr Ellis.

Gasping, she came to her senses quickly, but not as expediently as Darcy, who had not only released her, but now stood a respectable distance away. The damage, however, had been done.

Mortified to have been caught in a passionate embrace that likely gave every impression of an orchestrated liaison, Elizabeth felt a flush of heat spread from the top of her head to the tips of her toes. She supposed she ought to be thankful it was her friend and not her mother or Caroline Bingley who had discovered them, else the entire neighbourhood would know of her wantonness.

Nervously, she smoothed her hands over her skirts and desperately tried to calm her racing heart. Her breaths came quickly. Her lips felt swollen from Darcy's many kisses, and a wayward curl clung to her face. She brushed it aside with slightly shaking fingers and looked hesitantly at Darcy. As was often the case, Elizabeth found his steady gaze fixed upon her. His countenance was grave, but in his eyes, she recognised his steadfast concern for her well-being. She attempted to give him a small, reassuring smile, but feared it was more of a grimace. His lips were kiss-swollen as well.

The door closed with a resounding slam that caused Elizabeth to flinch.

Mr Ellis gave the lock a savage twist. "Are you out of your senses to be accepting this man's attentions?" he demanded in a low, furious voice.

Elizabeth felt her already heightened complexion deepen. "Mr Ellis," she stammered. "I—"

"What in the world are you *thinking?* Mr Darcy is engaged to be married!"

Elizabeth stared at him in shock. She could not account for the violence of her friend's objection to their marrying and was about to tell him as much when she suddenly realised it was not Darcy's engagement to *her* to which he referred, but Lady Catherine's vehement assertion that Darcy was to marry her daughter. Elizabeth paled. "Mr Ellis," she said, "Mr Darcy is *not* engaged."

Mr Ellis gaped at her as though she had lost her mind.

"Yes," she amended, "I suppose he is to marry, but—"

"How could you be so careless as to put yourself in such an untenable situation! Your mother will take to her bed, but not before she informs all of England of the sordid details surrounding your ruin!"

Before Elizabeth could form a reply, Darcy moved to stand beside her. He appeared livid. "I will remind you, Mr Ellis, that you are speaking to a lady whose family holds you in esteem, though at this moment I cannot begin to fathom why. As for my being engaged, it is a highly personal matter that I intend to keep private until my betrothed and I see fit to announce it. I ask for your discretion."

"My discretion?" he cried indignantly. "Tell me, Mr Darcy, where is *your* discretion in this business? Where is your *honour!*"

"Do not question my honour, sir!" Darcy replied angrily. "I must yet speak to her father."

"Is this supposed to be some sort of joke?"

"No," Elizabeth said, "Mr Darcy is—"

"A joke!" Darcy demanded heatedly. "I am no trickster, Mr Ellis. I find little humour in such tactics."

"Oh, come, sir! *'You must yet speak to the lady's father?'* It is my understanding the lady's father has been dead above ten years now."

"*Dead?*" Darcy parroted. "Mr Bennet was alive and well not half an hour ago. I demand to know what you are playing at!"

"What *I* am playing at! What are *you* playing at, Mr Darcy? You are an engaged man! You have no business carrying on in the licentious manner you have with my friend!"

Darcy strode angrily across the room. "Miss Elizabeth may be your friend, Mr Ellis," he coldly replied, "but she will soon become my wife. Our engagement is no concern of yours. I have had enough of your interference and insinuations. I would advise you to mind your own affairs and leave me to manage mine!"

In the next moment Mr Ellis's countenance turned from incensed to incredulous. "Engaged to *Lizzy!* That is impossible! The engagement to which I refer is your engagement to your cousin, Miss Anne de Bourgh!"

In any other circumstance the dumbfounded look that appeared on Darcy's face at that moment would have made Elizabeth laugh if she did not already feel as though she might cry.

"You believe me engaged to my cousin?" Darcy cried in wonderment. "Where on earth would you have come by such a notion!"

Mr Ellis tugged succinctly at his tailcoat. "Your aunt, Lady Catherine de Bourgh, announced the news some weeks ago while I attended her with my family in Hunsford. She was most enthusiastic about your proposal."

Darcy opened his mouth to speak, but before he could so much as utter a monosyllable Elizabeth laid her hand upon his arm and said to her friend, "Mr Ellis, you are mistaken if you believe that Mr Darcy would ever declare himself to me after reaching an understanding with another lady—*any* other lady. He is the most honourable man I know. It is not in his nature to employ disguise of any sort. It is true Mr Darcy is engaged, but not to Miss de Bourgh. He has just become engaged to *me.*"

"My aunt has long suffered under a misapprehension of her own design. Much as I respect my cousin, she and I would never suit." Darcy turned to Elizabeth and his voice softened considerably. "You must know the only proposal I have ever uttered is to you." His sincerity and adoration were evident, not only in his expression as he looked upon her, but in the affectionate way he reached for her hand.

Elizabeth surrendered it willingly with a smile, warm and loving.

Darcy returned it with equal emotion.

Mr Ellis stared at them. "Mr Darcy is the gentleman you have regretted these many months. Mr Darcy is the man for whom you have pined." He exhaled heavily and proceeded to rub his forehead.

"Of course," Elizabeth said feelingly. "Of course, it is Mr Darcy."

Mr Ellis slowly shook his head. "I am happy for you, Lizzy, sincerely happy. But while I would like nothing better than to wish you both joy you are much mistaken if you believe Lady Catherine will stand for Mr Darcy marrying you. I may not know her intimately, but I have seen enough to know she is used to having her way in all matters. She was emphatic in her assertion Miss de Bourgh was to have him and expounded upon every detail surrounding the business. Mr Collins conceded every particular."

Darcy rolled his eyes. "Mr Collins," he muttered sardonically. "Of course, such a report must be true if *Mr Collins* claims it is so." He fixed Mr Ellis with a look that fully communicated his displeasure with the business. "Mr Collins does not speak for me, Mr Ellis, nor does my aunt, nor any person so wholly connected to me. I do not take kindly to interference from any quarter, especially as pertains to my domestic felicity. I will speak to my aunt but make no mistake—I will marry Miss Elizabeth. She will be my wife."

"I am glad to hear it. Though Miss Elizabeth is undoubtedly capable of speaking on her own behalf, I am gratified to know she has found a champion in you. Allow me to be the first to offer my heartfelt congratulations." He extended his hand, and after a slight hesitation Darcy shook it. "I apologise for my assumptions, as well as my harsh words. Miss Elizabeth is my dearest friend. I meant no offence."

Mr Ellis looked to Elizabeth and his gaze softened. "I take it back, Lizzy," he said, and in his tone, she could hear his fondness for her. "Every word. I could not have parted with you to anyone less worthy. I will say nothing more of the matter, either to you, your Mr Darcy, or anyone else."

Elizabeth withdrew her hand from Darcy's and extended it to her friend, who clasped it tightly. "I do not wish to take any attention from Jane and Mr Bingley," she told him. "They will marry tomorrow. There is time yet to make our announcement once they are settled."

"But I shall speak to your father," said Darcy. "I would not wish to keep our engagement from him. I would imagine you desire his blessing."

Elizabeth inclined her head with a small, pleased smile. It was precisely what she wished.

Mr Ellis relinquished her hand and pulled his watch from his waistcoat pocket. He studied it with a critical eye and replaced it with an exasperated exhalation. "I was sent by your mother, a duty that could not be avoided. Perhaps we all ought to return together, so no one thinks that you and I have been alone all this time. They have surely gone into dinner by now."

"Perhaps that would be best," Darcy agreed as he extended his arm to Elizabeth. "Shall we return to the rest of the party, and see if there is supper enough for the three of us?"

Elizabeth linked her right arm with Darcy's and her left with her friend's, overjoyed to have Darcy's love, Mr Ellis's friendship, and the steadfast devotion of both.

How she got through dinner without alerting her mother to her engagement Elizabeth knew not. She could barely contain her happiness and every minute feared she would give herself away, stealing Jane's spotlight on her last evening as an unmarried lady. She need not have worried. Once Mrs Bennet saw her second-eldest daughter escorted into the dining room by both Mr Ellis and Darcy, she appeared quite content to direct her attention to Jane and Bingley for the remainder of the evening.

To Elizabeth's delight, Darcy stayed close to her, as did her friend, who seemed intent upon knowing Darcy better. Though she suspected Darcy would have preferred to be alone with her in a quiet corner of the room once the gentlemen had re-joined the ladies for coffee, he was open and agreeable towards Mr Ellis, whose intelligent discourse showed him to be a well-informed, well-educated man of the world.

The Gardiners joined them, and Elizabeth listened to her friend's account of America and its industry with great interest, contributing her own observations and remarks freely, as did her aunt. Elizabeth found their opinions and insights were not only welcomed by Darcy and Mr Ellis, but frequently solicited. It pleased her immensely to be included in such a discussion with the gentlemen, and to be treated as their equals regarding topics that were widely considered beyond women's capabilities and therefore always relegated to men.

The church service the following day was everything Darcy had anticipated—respectable and intimate, with none but the two families and Darcy in attendance. Though Jane Bennet made a lovely bride, Darcy had eyes for none but Elizabeth. So captivated was he by her beauty in the morning light as it streamed through the windows, he had nearly missed hearing the parson's request that he present the ring.

The breakfast was held at Longbourn, a short walk from the church made all the shorter due to the chill in the air and frost upon the ground. Though they had not been admitted to the church, many of the Bennets' neighbours and close friends attended the breakfast. Once the wedding cake had been distributed, the ladies abandoned the dining table in favour of the comfort of Mrs Bennet's drawing room. The gentlemen remained and, after the dishes were cleared away, cigars and a bottle of French brandy—nearly impossible to obtain in England since the start of the war—were offered to the gentlemen by Mr Bennet to further celebrate the occasion. Such generosity was met with much enthusiasm and approving smiles.

Now that the ladies were no longer present, the men were free to indulge in far more interesting conversations than society deemed suitable for those in possession of more delicate sensibilities, and soon the room was filled with the sound of satisfied, well-entertained gentlemen enjoying themselves as they could not otherwise in the company of the ladies. Darcy studied the amber liquid in his glass before raising it to his lips. The fine brandy slid down his throat with ease.

"You are very introspective this morning, Mr Darcy," Mr Gardiner observed as he settled into a vacant chair beside Pemberley's master. "I trust you are well?"

Darcy offered Elizabeth's uncle a sincere smile, albeit a fleeting one. "I am very well, only distracted. It is good to see you."

"And you as well, sir." Mr Gardiner appeared to study him for a moment, taking a slow sip from his glass. "My niece," he said matter-of-factly, "looks extremely lovely this morning, would you not agree?"

Darcy's lips twitched with amusement as he averted his gaze. He had always suspected Mr Gardiner could see right through him, and here was his proof. "I daresay all of your nieces look lovely this morning," he responded lightly, tracing his finger along the edge of his glass. "Did you, perhaps, have a particular one in mind?"

The elder gentleman chuckled. "I imagine she is the one who has been on yours since we had the pleasure of meeting at Pemberley this summer."

"You have gotten to know me quite well since then," said Darcy with a small, secretive smile, "but not well enough, it seems. She has occupied nearly every thought I have had far longer than a few mere months."

"I would wager you have occupied hers as well. She and my wife are very close. Far closer, I would say, than she has ever been to her mother." Mr Gardiner laid his hand on Darcy's arm. "I would not," he said quietly, "put stock in anything my sister utters about my niece and a certain gentleman from Hertford-shire. She has many opinions and ideas that her daughters do not share, especially the two eldest. If anything comes of it, I will stand with you both, as will my wife. It is the least we can do after all you have done for us."

Darcy felt a sudden flush of heat spread from the back of his neck to the tips of his ears. "I am grateful to have your support, but you and your family owe me nothing. I did only what I ought to have done—what I should have done far sooner."

He glanced down the length of the table at Wickham, who was laughing almost raucously with a young man he understood to be none other than Mr Crowell, and frowned. Mr Ellis and Robert Goulding, who were conversing with several other gentlemen, turned towards the pair. Darcy was not surprised to see both wore nearly identical expressions of disapproval.

Darcy shook his head, irritated with himself as much as he was with Wickham. He had been so caught up in making love to Elizabeth the night before and so overwhelmed by the reality of their engagement this morning, that he had forgotten to write to his cousin to apprise him of Wickham being in Hertfordshire. Darcy's frown deepened as he watched the reprobate reach for the decanter and refill his empty glass somewhat sloppily. He appeared to be enjoying his brandy more than was considered prudent.

"I cannot account for him being here," Mr Gardiner murmured, inclining his head in Wickham's direction, "but I do know that Lizzy is very upset by it. She is convinced he is here under some false pretence or other, and I confess myself inclined to agree with her." He took a sip from his glass. "Do you believe he intends to stay beyond the wedding?"

Darcy swirled the contents of his own glass and shrugged. "I do not know, but I intend to send an express to my cousin in London as soon as may be. He is a colonel in His Majesty's army and will know how to make the proper enquiries with Wickham's commanding officer in the north. As soon as he is in possession of the information we seek, Colonel Fitzwilliam will advise me on what ought to be done."

Mr Gardiner nodded in understanding, then nudged Darcy's shoulder and inclined his head towards Mr Bennet. "I can think of one thing you can do in the meantime."

Darcy looked towards Elizabeth's father, only to find the man himself staring back at him from across the table with the same impertinent look in his eyes that Darcy had often seen in Elizabeth's. He drummed his fingertips against the side of his glass as he returned Mr Bennet's enquiring gaze with what he hoped was his usual mask of composure.

Mr Bennet raised one brow at him, and Darcy repressed an urge to smile at the feeling of familiarity that one, simple gesture produced. At that moment, Mr Bennet reminded Darcy much of his second daughter.

"Is there something you wish to speak to me about, Mr Darcy?" Longbourn's master calmly enquired.

Raising his glass to his lips, Darcy swallowed the rest of his brandy and placed the empty glass upon the table. "As a matter of fact, there is something I wish to discuss with you, Mr Bennet, if you would be so generous as to indulge me."

Mr Bennet finished his brandy and leaned back in his chair, linked his fingers across his stomach, and waited for Darcy to enlighten him.

"Perhaps we might convene elsewhere," Darcy suggested. "What I have to relate is regarding a personal matter."

The elder man frowned but pushed his chair away from the table without comment. "Lead the way, then, sir," he said as he stood, gesturing for Darcy to precede him.

As Darcy rose from his chair, he noticed Wickham's eyes were turned upon him, his expression inscrutable and his complexion flushed from the effects of alcohol. If his former friend was anything, he was astute. Would he suspect that Darcy's desire to speak with Mr Bennet privately was due to his sudden appearance in Hertfordshire, or had he discerned the truth?

Darcy straightened to his full height and regarded Wickham coldly, inclined his head to Mr Gardiner, and quit the room. *First things first,* he told himself. He would deal with George Wickham later.

❧ 17 ❧

WHERE ELIZABETH FINDS RELIEF FROM HER
MOTHER.

As the morning of Jane's wedding wore on, so did Elizabeth's equanimity wear thin. Having now married off two of her five daughters, Mrs Bennet seemed more determined than ever to see the other three settled as well. After enduring countless comments and hints about Mr Ellis's attentiveness to her second daughter and her expectation that another wedding would likely follow on the heels of Jane's, Elizabeth could bear no more. With a tight smile, she excused herself from the circle of well-intentioned matrons gathered around her mother and made her way to where the tea things were placed. She was in the midst of refilling her teacup when she was joined by Mr Bingley's aunt.

Unlike her two married sons and their wives, Mrs Lawrence had not left the country for a relative's house in Essex from the church steps but was bent on going to London with Miss Bingley and the Hursts instead. Elizabeth well recalled her words to her eldest, and the twinkle in her eyes as she had pronounced them:

"I may be old, but I am not yet dead, and I should like to go to the theatre again before it happens. I shall write to you, but only if I have nothing better to do."

Elizabeth liked her prodigiously.

"Goodness," she said to Elizabeth as she selected several marzipan sweets sculpted to resemble asparagus and placed them upon a painted china plate. "If I am ever of the mind to take another husband, I do believe I will impose upon your dear mother to arrange the entire affair, including the office of finding the bridegroom."

Though it was far from her favourite topic, her companion's words inspired Elizabeth to imagine her mother throwing herself wholeheartedly into the business of finding Mr Bingley's aunt, a woman at least twenty years Mrs Bennet's senior, an eligible husband. She was excessively diverted by the prospect. "How are you enjoying Hertfordshire, Mrs Lawrence?" she asked, pursing her lips so she would not laugh.

Mrs Lawrence saw what she was about and gave Elizabeth a conspiratorial wink. "I daresay I would enjoy it better if I had a touch of brandy in my tea."

Elizabeth smiled. "I believe my father has some brandy in his library if you would like some. It will be the work of a moment. No one need know."

Mrs Lawrence regarded her thoughtfully for a moment, but then sighed and shook her head. "I shall wait until teatime. I am a patient woman, Miss Bennet. You must have patience, you know, when you have a household to run, six lusty boys to manage, and an incorrigible husband bent on behaving like one."

"You are a widow, are you not?"

"A rich widow," she replied, and grinned. "Let us sit." She linked her arm with Elizabeth's and led her towards a cushioned window seat on the far side of the room. She rearranged several pillows and settled herself in the centre, taking care to balance her plate upon her lap. "This will do nicely. It is bright and comfortable, and out of earshot of the gossips."

"Indeed," Elizabeth agreed. Her lips twitched as she claimed a seat beside her.

"Oh, to be young again," Mrs Lawrence said pleasantly, regarding Elizabeth with what could only be described as a mischievous look. "I well remember being desirable, pretty, and in love. You seem to be in quite a pickle."

"Whatever makes you think so?"

"Because it is true."

Elizabeth raised her brow archly and took a sip of tea.

Her companion laughed and patted Elizabeth's hand affectionately. "I like you very well, Miss Bennet. It is no wonder you have two handsome young men who pay you every attention. It is a pity your mother is so determined to see you married to the one you do not want. A fool could see it is the other gentleman who has captured your heart, and rightly so, for he is besotted with you. Your poor mother, bless her, is oblivious to the entire business. She will see you married to the other one or die trying. I must admire her tenacity, if not her discernment." She dropped her voice and said conspiratorially, "Fear not. Your lover will never allow it. Still waters run deep you know. I have never been to the sea, but I imagine it to be much like your Mr Darcy—calm and even-tempered at the shoreline, but intense and passionate the farther one ventures from the coast. You are a lucky woman to have captured the heart of such a man."

Elizabeth could only stare at her. That Mr Bingley's aunt would speak so unreservedly of such topics was extraordinary, but even more extraordinary was the lady's pronouncement that Darcy was Elizabeth's lover, and an ardent one at that!

Mrs Lawrence clucked her tongue. "I did not mean to discompose you, my dear. I am old and therefore have adopted the habit of speaking my mind whenever I see fit. I have lived enough in the world to recognise a love match when I see one. I wish you much joy, and hope you are not offended by my boorishness."

"I am not offended, Mrs Lawrence," Elizabeth stammered, "but I am surprised. No one in my family, save for my Aunt Gardiner, has discerned our regard for one another. Not even my sister, Mrs Bingley, is aware of the depth of our attachment."

"Mrs Bingley seems a very pretty, sweet-tempered, pleasant girl but, as is often the case with those in love, she is likely oblivious to its existence in others. Your aunt, Mrs Gardiner, strikes me as an astute, genteel lady, and she seems to be well acquainted with your Mr Darcy. Have they known one another long?"

"They met in the summer when we were visiting Derbyshire. It is where Mr Darcy makes his home."

"And since then, they have been in company together many times I daresay."

"They were in company together but three days," Elizabeth replied, "and have not met again until this week, when my aunt and uncle arrived from town."

Rather than offer further comment on the topic, Mrs Lawrence inclined her head towards the door. "The gentlemen are come to join us. Your young man will be by to claim you in a moment. I shall not leave you, however, for I should like to know him better. I imagine he is as stimulating a conversationalist as he must be a kisser."

Elizabeth nearly choked on her tea.

In the privacy and quietude of Mr Bennet's library, Darcy penned an express to Colonel Fitzwilliam while his future father-in-law stared pensively out of the window. Their interview had gone well, Darcy thought, all things considered. Mr Bennet, though surprised to learn of his desire to marry Elizabeth, did not deny his permission. His chief interest, he claimed, was to see his favourite daughter respectable and happy, and if she insisted marrying Darcy was the way to do it, Mr Bennet would give the couple his blessing.

Wickham was another matter. Darcy had no idea whether Mr Gardiner had divulged any of Darcy's personal dealings with Wickham to Elizabeth's father, and since Mr Bennet did not know it was Darcy who had brought about Wickham's marriage to Lydia, he was reluctant to bring them up. The fewer people who knew of his involvement the better; but in the end Darcy decided a little enlightenment would benefit Mr Bennet far more than keeping the man in the dark.

He revealed only the most necessary particulars of his history with his former friend: Wickham's penchant for gambling and carousing, his lack of ambition, his refusal of the living Darcy's father had left to him, and the squandering of the three thousand pounds he had received from Darcy in lieu of that living. Darcy said nothing of Wickham's attempt to seduce Georgiana to gain her fortune; neither did he mention arranging Mrs Wickham's marriage, purchasing Wickham's commission, or paying the blackguard's debtors.

When he had done, Mr Bennet had been subdued, but not angry. In fact, he had shown very little emotion at all. He had simply risen from his chair and walked to the window, answering in the affirmative when Darcy had requested paper and pen to write to Colonel Fitzwilliam. At the window he remained.

Darcy finished addressing his letter, then laid aside his pen. He had used his signet ring with his own coat of arms upon it to seal the missive; it was imperative his cousin recognise the letter not only originated with Darcy, but that there was likely urgency attached to it.

"Mr Bennet."

Mr Bennet turned from the window. "Have you finished your letter, Mr Darcy?"

"I have, sir."

"Then I will call for a servant." Longbourn's master gave the bell pull a firm tug. "You may rest assured it will reach London by nightfall, well before the departure of my most worthless son-in-law."

Darcy rose from his chair at the desk, crossed the room, and handed his letter to Elizabeth's father.

He took it and bowed his head, giving the impression of reading the address. "He is a true scoundrel. The very worst of men," said Mr Bennet gravely. "It appears I have been remiss with my daughters, even my favourite. Elizabeth warned me of the dangers of sending Lydia to Brighton. She begged me to curb her wild animal spirits and to keep her at home, and do you know what I did, Mr Darcy?"

Though he had a good idea what her father had done, Darcy answered in the negative.

"I laughed at her. I laughed at her, then asked if her younger sisters' silliness had scared off any of her lovers. I told her no squeamish youths were worth her time and sent her on her way."

Darcy trained his eyes upon the carpet beneath his feet as he struggled to maintain a respectful silence. If asked, he would have confessed to feeling equal portions anger and sorrow—anger that Mr Bennet had not only discredited but dismissed and ignored Elizabeth's counsel on such a matter, and sorrow over the pain she must surely have felt when he had.

"I was very wrong to have done it." He looked to Darcy. "You are a man of the world. Do you have nothing to say on the subject?"

"I will always have much to say on the subject of Miss Bennet, but I doubt I can say anything at this juncture you have not already said to yourself."

A knock sounded upon the door then and Mr Bennet bade the person enter. It was his butler. Mr Bennet handed him Darcy's letter. "Make sure this express is sent to London at once, Hill."

Not wishing to remain any longer in Mr Bennet's company when he longed to be in Elizabeth's, Darcy excused himself and made his way to the drawing room where the ladies were gathered. Though he knew he would likely have no time alone with her, he felt a pressing urge to let her know, by whatever means were within his power, that she was not only loved, but valued.

He entered the crowded room and spied her sitting on the other side of it, nestled in a cushioned alcove with Bingley's aunt. The pale, winter sun shone through the window behind her, bathing her profile in soft, muted light. Mrs Lawrence tilted her head towards Elizabeth's and spoke to her, making her laugh. Darcy could not repress his smile. He had always loved her laughter. It was rich and dulcet, genuine; nothing like the insincere tittering of so many of the young ladies he knew in town.

"Good afternoon, Mrs Lawrence, Miss Bennet," he said as he stood before them. "I was hoping you would permit me to join you."

He could not help but notice Elizabeth's blush as she inclined her head to him with a small, private turn of her lips. "Of course, sir. We would be honoured."

As there was not room enough for him beside Elizabeth, Darcy claimed a seat beside Bingley's aunt. "The honour is mine, Miss Bennet."

"Mr Darcy," Mrs Lawrence said without preamble. "You failed to return with the rest of the gentlemen, and I was wondering what had become of you. According to Miss Bennet, you are far too clever to have become lost."

Darcy raised a brow at her statement and watched as Elizabeth turned aside her head, her lips lifting in a smile as she took a sip of her tea. "I should hope not," he said to her. "I was speaking with Mr Bennet. Our conversation was of some duration."

"Of a matter most urgent, I suppose?" Mrs Lawrence grinned. "You appear to be a man not prone to procrastination, I see. Good. Very good. Have you ever been sea bathing, Mr Darcy?"

Elizabeth choked on a mouthful of tea.

"I hear it is a wonderful experience and most vigorous," Mrs Lawrence continued, ignoring her friend's distress. "The rush of the tide, the rolling waves, the zealous exertion in the bathing machines—it is all so exciting, do not you think?" She raised her teacup to her mouth and looked at Darcy, who noticed her eyes sparkled with something akin to mischief.

"I would imagine it is most invigorating," he agreed, then cast a concerned glance at Elizabeth. "Are you well, Miss Bennet?"

"Perfectly well," Elizabeth answered. She dabbed her lips with her handkerchief and looked pointedly at Bingley's aunt, who smiled serenely back at her.

"That is a lovely handkerchief, Mr Darcy," said Mrs Lawrence conversationally. "The embroidery is a credit to the lady who made it, but I cannot for the life of me figure out what the 'G' stands for, sir. I do hope it is not Gregor. My sister's second husband was named Gregor and I detested him."

It was then Darcy noticed the handkerchief in Elizabeth's possession was not hers, but one of his own. His initials, FGD, were prominently stitched in the corner. He recalled when Georgiana had given it to him as easily as he recalled pressing it into Elizabeth's hand the previous evening. He looked to Elizabeth to see how she fared and saw her cover her face with her hands. Darcy was alarmed to see her shoulders shook. "Miss Bennet," he said to her.

She would not answer him and as they were in company, he dared not offer her the comfort he had the evening before. He looked to Mrs Lawrence for assistance, but the elder lady only appeared diverted by her friend's behaviour. Confounded, Darcy returned his attention to Elizabeth and gently touched the back of her hand. It was then he realised she was not in fact weeping but making a concerted effort to hold in laughter.

After several moments Elizabeth's laughter waned and she appeared mistress of herself once more. Wiping her eyes, she turned to Mrs Lawrence and fixed her with a look of mock indignation. "You, Mrs Lawrence, are incorrigible."

"My husband, Lord bless him, said much the same to me throughout our forty years of marriage. I believe it is my constant teasing of him that kept things lively. What say you,

Mr Darcy? Surely, a man such as you would not want a dull wife?" She raised one brow as though issuing a challenge.

Darcy glanced at Elizabeth. Her bottom lip was caught between her teeth as she regarded him expectantly. A slow grin spread across his face. "Certainly not, madam. There is something to be said of impertinence. Miss Bennet's has been my dear companion for many months."

At this, Mrs Lawrence laughed merrily. She extended her hand towards Darcy and patted his arm. "You will do nicely for my friend, sir. Quite nicely indeed."

❧ 18 ❦

WHERE NEARLY EVERYONE FAVOURS LONDON
EXCEPT MRS BENNET.

There was a bite in the air the morning after the wedding that made Darcy think twice before leaving the warmth of his bed. He was downstairs and out of the house at his usual hour, however, galloping across the park towards an expanse of frosty fields by the time the day had barely dawned. Overhead, the sky appeared crowded, full to bursting with a mass of leaden clouds that rolled over the hills of Hertfordshire with the unrest of an advancing army. Their presence, coupled with the scent of snow on the air, made Darcy anxious to be gone from the country.

By the time he returned to the house, Darcy found the rest of Netherfield's party at the breakfast table. Even Miss Bingley and Mrs Hurst, who were habitually late risers, were present, sedately sipping their tea beside the newlyweds, their aunt, and Mr Hurst. After bidding them good morning, Darcy walked to the sideboard, filled a plate with bacon and eggs, and joined them.

"How was your ride, Darcy?" Hurst asked as he shovelled a forkful of egg into his mouth. Bingley was engaged with his bride, Mrs Lawrence with her bacon, and Miss Bingley and Mrs Hurst, for once, appeared more interested in the temperature of their tea than in Darcy's comings and goings.

"There is snow on the air. I recommend we depart as soon as may be else we get stuck. The roads are dreadful even in pleasant weather."

Bingley looked away from his wife. "Will it be bad, do you think?"

Darcy swallowed a mouthful of coffee. "If you would like to gain London by this afternoon we ought to leave soon. The wind is blowing from the south, so there is a good chance we can get ahead of it if we make haste."

Bingley laid his napkin aside and pushed his chair away from the table. "I will order our carriages readied and have the servants prepare for our departure." He rose and extended his hand to his wife with an affectionate smile. Placing her hand in his, Mrs Bingley accepted her husband's assistance with a warm look and a blushing countenance. Miss Bingley and the Hursts followed their example with alacrity, claiming they did not wish to be stranded in Hertfordshire if they could avoid the inconvenience.

Darcy, having barely touched his breakfast, rose as well, and offered his hand to Mrs Lawrence. "No doubt you are anxious to go to London, ma'am."

"I certainly am, Mr Darcy, but not, I think, so anxious as you." She gave him a conspiratorial wink and called to her nephew. "I do not think there will be room enough for Miss Bennet and me both in your carriage, Charles. I have a great number of reticules and I insist on their remaining within my view."

"I assure you, Aunt," Bingley replied cheerfully, "you have no cause for worry. There will be more than enough room for everyone, even Caroline."

"Oh, I daresay Caroline will ride with Louisa and Mr Hurst, as they are all for Grosvenor Street. Miss Bennet and I shall ride with Mr Darcy, for he will be all by himself in that great coach of his. Surely, you would prefer to be alone with Mrs Bingley now that you are married to her."

Darcy repressed the urge to smile at her machinations and shook his head. The lady was nothing if not resolute; but rather than being irritated with Mrs Lawrence for arranging his affairs as she saw fit, he felt grateful to her. She would no doubt make an excellent ally once they reached town, and most likely a lack-adaisical chaperon.

"Darcy will be fine on his own," Bingley replied, waving her off. "As you are also for Grosvenor Street, I think it wise that you accompany Louisa and Hurst as well. Jane and I will take Lizzy with us as planned. If the weather is unpleasant, Darcy will want to go home directly. I would not wish to inconvenience him."

Mrs Lawrence gave Darcy a look that clearly communicated her frustration with Bingley's congeniality and rolled her eyes at the ceiling.

By the time that all three coaches had departed Netherfield and arrived at Longbourn the temperature had dropped several degrees. Heated bricks warmed the feet of the travellers, and heavy rugs draped their laps. Miss Bingley, the Hursts, and Mrs Lawrence were settled snuggly within the Hursts' conveyance and there they chose to remain while Bingley and Jane alighted from theirs to collect Elizabeth and take their leave of the family. Darcy followed them, avoiding the servants bustling about with trunks and valises, reticules, and bandboxes, all waiting to be loaded onto the waiting carriages.

The moment he entered the parlour, his eyes sought Elizabeth. He noticed her at once, standing in the centre of the room wearing a nostalgic smile as she embraced Miss Mary and Miss Catherine. It was a lovely show of affection between the sisters and Darcy did not wish to intrude upon it, not when a full month would pass until they were reunited.

He turned his attention to Mrs Gardiner instead. She stood just behind Elizabeth, conversing with Jane and Bingley. Her two daughters accompanied her. Emily, the eldest girl, held Mrs Bingley's hand, admiring her wedding ring. Darcy left them to their conversation.

Mrs Bennet was conspicuously absent, as was her husband, but Darcy soon discovered Mr Gardiner and his son Robert standing beside the window in the far corner of the room. The elder gentleman's expression as he observed the displays of domestic felicity was indulgent, while Robert looked positively bored. Darcy crossed the room and joined them.

"I see you and your family are for London this morning as well, Mr Gardiner."

"That we are, sir. We are only waiting on my wife and daughters to say their goodbyes and we will be off. The weather looks as though it might become tricky, and we are anxious to away."

"We are of the same mind it seems. The temperature has dropped since dawn, and I fear we shall see snow before long if we do not make haste." Darcy turned his attention to the tall, smartly dressed young man who stood sedately beside his father. "How do you do, Master Gardiner?"

Robert offered him a polite bow. "I am well, thank you, Mr Darcy. I hope you are also well?"

"I am very well today, thank you. Have you enjoyed your visit at Longbourn?"

"Yes, sir, very much."

"And what did you most enjoy?"

Robert grinned at him, looking much like his father when he smiled. "We were here for Cousin Jane's wedding," he said, his voice taking on a conspiratorial tone, "but Cousin Lizzy is my favourite. She is great fun and tells the most exciting stories."

Darcy raised his brows. "Does she? And what was your favourite?"

"The story about the prideful prince and the prejudiced maiden, without a doubt. There was an ogre in it, but also a moral lesson."

Darcy's brows shot to his hairline. "I believe I would like to hear it someday. Do you think your Cousin Lizzy would agree to tell the story to me as well?"

Robert was about to answer him when a great commotion was heard in the hall.

"No!" Lydia cried as she entered the room, stomping her foot upon the floor for emphasis. "I want to go to London! There is nothing for me here, Wickham."

"Lydia," Wickham said as he pursued her, "I will be much occupied by business. You will have nothing to do in town while I am engaged. You had better stay at Longbourn."

"La, Wickham! I shall go to the shops and to the theatre. I need not sit at home, for I am a married woman and can therefore venture out alone!"

Wickham would not be moved. "You shall remain at Longbourn, Lydia, with your mother and sisters and that is final."

She turned her back upon her husband with a sour expression, but her countenance brightened when she spied Darcy standing with Mr Gardiner and Robert. "I will not remain at Longbourn," she told her husband defiantly, "and you cannot make me!"

To Darcy's horror, she crossed the room and addressed him directly. "Mr Darcy, you must tell Wickham to take me to London at once!"

Darcy stared at her in shock. He could not believe Lydia Wickham had the gall to approach him in such a fashion, never mind make such a demand of him.

"Lydia," Wickham said sternly as he glanced at Darcy, "be silent."

Lydia, however, continued to demand that Darcy speak to her husband. "Tell him, Mr Darcy! Tell him I ought to go to London, for I know Wickham will listen to you above everyone, much as he did when we were all there the last time."

Darcy could only stare at her as he felt the colour drain from his face.

"Mrs Wickham," said her uncle, "you have said quite enough." There was no mistaking the disapprobation in his tone. With a pointed glance at his wife, he took Lydia firmly by the arm and escorted her from the room.

After consigning her daughters to Jane and Bingley's care, Mrs Gardiner bade Wickham accompany her and, with a look that clearly expressed her displeasure with Lydia's behaviour, hastened after her husband.

Lydia's protests could be heard from the hall.

With a grim countenance, Wickham quit the room.

Darcy could barely believe such a scene had occurred, and was not only incredulous, but livid. Though Mrs Wickham's comportment had been poor when they had dined at Nether-field the evening before Bingley's wedding, it was nothing compared to the conduct she exhibited today. Darcy attempted to swallow his ire. If he incurred Elizabeth's wrath or that of her father because of Lydia's wagging tongue and unrepentant ways, he could not be held responsible for his actions!

After all that had been done to discover her in London—the expense of bringing about her sham of a marriage to an unscrupulous man, the Gardiners' efforts to impress upon her the necessity of strict secrecy regarding Darcy's involvement on her behalf—the ungrateful, undeserving, spoilt brat dared to allude to the business anyhow!

Mrs Bennet, likely hearing the ruckus her youngest daughter had made, chose that moment to join them. "What in the world was all that commotion about?" she demanded, looking to each of her daughters for an explanation. "Where is your Uncle Gardiner? And where is my dear Lydia?"

While Bingley answered her to the best of his ability, Elizabeth looked to Darcy. That she was disconcerted as well as embarrassed was evident. She opened her mouth to speak, appeared to think better of it, and started towards him instead.

After being accosted by Mrs Wickham only moments before, Darcy was in no mood for Elizabeth to make demands of him. Informing her that he had acted on her family's behalf and paid Wickham an exorbitant price to marry her foolish chit of a sister was out of the question. He shook his head minutely and hardened his gaze, silently warning her to stay away.

He could tell at once, by the flash of disappointment that appeared upon her countenance and in the expression of her eyes, that Elizabeth had not expected him to look upon her so harshly. Her eyes held his, her gaze lengthy and searching, before she quit the room.

The acuteness of her disappointment distressed him, but Darcy could not follow her, not when she would surely demand answers from him that he was by no means willing to reveal to her, especially in her father's house.

"I do not understand," said Mrs Bennet. "Why would my dear Lydia want to go away again so soon? She has only just arrived!"

Exasperated, Bingley looked to Jane, who shifted the youngest Gardiner upon her hip. "They are husband and wife, Mamma," Jane reminded her. "Surely, you must agree a woman's place is with her husband."

Mrs Bennet threw her hands into the air. "Mr Bennet!" she shrieked. "Oh, Mr Bennet! Come quickly! You must make Lydia stay at home for the next fortnight at least, for she is determined to go to town with Mr Wickham!"

Darcy turned on his heel and strode from the room, through the foyer, and out the front door. He did not stop at his carriage but continued up the drive and onward towards the pale that marked it.

It was there that Mr Gardiner found him ten minutes later, solemnly pacing the width of the drive. "Mr Darcy," he said, "I am grieved by Lydia's abhorrent behaviour towards you. Please allow me to apologise on behalf of my wife and myself."

"You are not responsible for Mrs Wickham. As ever, she appears to have no qualms about speaking for herself. You and Mrs Gardiner owe me no apology."

Mr Gardiner's expression darkened. "You are benevolent, sir. Constantly, my wife and I lectured Lydia on the necessity of maintaining strict secrecy regarding your involvement in her marriage last summer! Not ten minutes ago we repeated the urgency of keeping her mouth firmly shut on the subject but believe she cannot be trusted to remain silent, especially when she is denied her way. The last thing we want is to indulge her, but fear if left at Longbourn while her husband goes to London, she will reveal all. We have therefore proposed to take them both to town but will pay them no courtesy or acknowledgement beyond that gesture."

"That is generous of you, Mr Gardiner, but you are already five in total. Travelling with two more will surely be a burden. Though I cannot—*will not*—offer the Wickhams passage to town, I would like to be of assistance to you and Mrs Gardiner. Please allow me to see her and the children safely to Gracechurch Street."

"That is kind of you, sir, but Madeleine and I think it best if we both travel with the Wickhams. Perhaps you might consider conveying Elizabeth and our two eldest instead. Robert and Emily would view it as an adventure, and their accompanying you and Elizabeth would be looked upon as entirely proper by her father, I am sure." Mr Gardiner looked meaningfully at Darcy and extended his hand. "Elizabeth informed us of your engagement. I believe congratulations are in order, Mr Darcy. Madeleine and I were hoping, praying for you to find your way to each other. We are sincerely happy for you both."

"I thank you," Darcy replied warmly as he shook hands with Elizabeth's uncle. "She did not want the occasion of Mrs Bingley's marriage to be eclipsed by news of our own engagement, and so we are waiting to make our announcement to the rest of her family. Mr Bennet has given his consent."

Mr Gardiner regarded Darcy thoughtfully. "I hope you will not wait long to announce your intent to marry. An engagement is a time of great joy and discovery for a young couple, especially if they are fortunate enough to love each other. If I may offer you a few words of advice—do not allow anyone to dictate your course with Elizabeth, not even Elizabeth, else you will find yourself ever yielding for the sake of others' enjoyment and rarely satisfied yourself."

There was truth in Mr Gardiner's words, and it occurred to Darcy that much of his life had been spent doing exactly that: denying or delaying his own wishes and desires to spare his loved ones the pain of having disappointed theirs. His father, Lady Catherine, Anne, Lord and Lady Carlisle, Georgiana, Fitzwilliam—even Elizabeth. He recalled each sacrifice he had made to either ensure their pleasure or ease their pain with startling clarity. Bowing his head, Darcy adjusted his gloves. His mouth twisted ruefully. "I fear I have grown used to it."

"And that is precisely why you should think of your own felicity now. You are engaged to be married. It has been a very long and difficult road. Do not add to the distance you have travelled to reach this juncture but forge a new path full of promise and joy. You owe yourself that much, and what is more, you deserve it." Mr Gardiner laid a firm hand upon Darcy's shoulder, inclined his head, and made to leave.

"She does not know," Darcy uttered softly.

Mr Gardiner paused and regarded him with a quizzical expression. "I beg your pardon. Who does not know of what, sir?"

"Elizabeth." Darcy exhaled harshly, rubbing his mouth with his gloved hand. "She knows nothing of my involvement in bringing about her sister's marriage. We were not engaged then. No understanding existed between us. I acted without her approbation, without her knowledge, without having any claim upon her whatsoever.

"I had no right to offer the assistance I did, never mind provide it. I knew you and Mrs Gardiner suspected my attachment to your niece, but that was all it was at the time. Not an engagement, not an understanding, but an attachment felt so deeply, so sincerely that I could not bear to sit idly by and do nothing, not when I had the means to prevent Elizabeth's suffering. I acted with the sole purpose of bringing her relief, and in doing so I deceived you."

"The only person you have really deceived, Mr Darcy, is yourself." He laid his hand upon Darcy's shoulder. "Come, sir, or we will surely find ourselves stuck in Hertfordshire for the remainder of the week. Talk to my niece. You are to be married, after all, and it will not do to begin your life together with secrets and misunderstandings between you."

❦

It was slow going upon the London road. After stopping at a posting inn to water the horses and partake of a light repast, the four carriages with their fifteen occupants were once again on their way to town, albeit at a more cautious pace than had previously been assumed.

Elizabeth directed her cousins' attention to the thick, white flakes of snow falling steadily outside the window of Darcy's coach.

"They are lovely, Cousin Lizzy," Emily cried with pleasure, pressing her nose to the glass. "They look like Mamma's lace doilies, only much smaller. I wish I could catch one and keep it in my box of treasures."

"And what would you do with it?" Elizabeth asked.

Emily grinned. "I would take it out in the summer when it is very disagreeable and hot, and it would feel cool in my hands."

"Would it not melt?" Darcy enquired from the seat opposite, where he sat beside Robert.

"No, Mr Darcy," Emily said patiently, "for my snowflake would be made of magic."

Darcy raised his brow. "Is that so?"

"Yes," she insisted.

Robert rolled his eyes. "There is no such thing as magic, Emily. I am sure Mr Darcy must be laughing at you."

"Much the contrary, Miss Gardiner, I assure you," Darcy insisted. "Is not the very idea of magic the foundation of dreams?"

Upon hearing Darcy's pronouncement, Emily's eyes sparkled with delight.

Robert, as sceptical as ever, frowned. "There cannot be magic *snow,* for it does not exist. It is not logical."

"Must *you* always be logical, Robert?" Emily asked irritably.

Robert shrugged his shoulders. "It is far better to be logical than illogical."

"That is your opinion," Emily said with a huff. "I believe being logical all the time must be incredibly boring. Do you not agree, Mr Darcy, that being forever logical must be incredibly dull?"

Darcy appeared not to know how to answer such a question from such a quarter. He looked to Elizabeth with an expression of helplessness, but his intended only pursed her lips, attempting to conceal her amusement.

He started to speak, then stopped and shook his head.

Elizabeth, seeing the depth of his struggle, took pity on him. "You enjoy arithmetic, do you not, Emily?"

"Of course," Emily replied. "It is my favourite subject besides reading."

"Well, the subject of arithmetic is very logical, would you not agree? There are many different methods one may employ when solving an equation, but there is only one correct answer. It is nothing if not logical."

Emily pondered that for a moment, then grinned. "You are terribly clever, Cousin Lizzy. You must know everything there is to know in the world."

"Believe me when I say I do not. In fact," Elizabeth said, looking meaningfully at Darcy, "there is much I have yet to learn."

Darcy held her steady gaze briefly before turning his attention to Robert and enquiring whether he also enjoyed arithmetic. Though he appeared composed, the way he pointedly avoided looking at Elizabeth gave her the distinct impression he felt anything but easy. Though they could not speak unreservedly in front of her young cousins, Elizabeth was hopeful her uncle would allow them to speak privately once they reached Gracechurch Street. There was much she wished to ask regarding Lydia's behaviour that morning. It was likely her aunt would invite Darcy to stay for supper in any case, and Elizabeth determined she would do all in her power to persuade him to accept.

✣ 19 ✣

WHERE ELIZABETH IS DETERMINED, AND MR DARCY IS RELUCTANT.

"That was wonderful, my dear," said Mr Gardiner, following his wife's lead as she rose from the dining table. He turned to Darcy with a good-natured grin. "We are an intimate family party this evening, sir. Shall we forgo a separation?"

Darcy, who had also risen, inclined his head. He had developed a genuine affection for Mr and Mrs Gardiner, and it pleased him to be counted among the members of their family. "I am most amenable."

He offered his hand to Elizabeth, who was beside him on his right. As she placed her hand in his, wrapped the other around the sleeve of his coat, and settled her fingers in the crook of his arm, Darcy's smile softened. The weight of her hand, however slight, felt significant, as significant as the lightness in his heart.

"I was wondering if Mr Darcy and I might speak privately, Uncle?"

There was a quality to Elizabeth's tone—a certain strength to her voice—that foretold a purpose Darcy suspected would bring no enjoyment. His smile faltered, then faded altogether when Mr Gardiner not only agreed without question but offered the use of his study.

"Lizzy," said her aunt, "the children have been sent to the nursery for the night and the servants will not bother you in that part of the house. Leave the door open if you please. Your uncle and I will be in the parlour should you need us."

The Gardiners left them, and Darcy escorted Elizabeth from the dining room in a haze of weighted silence reminiscent of their earlier days at Longbourn. Too soon, they entered Mr Gardiner's study. Elizabeth removed her hand from his arm and Darcy crossed the room to stand before a large set of windows draped in rich, crimson velvet that overlooked the street. The neighbourhood outside the Gardiners' home in Cheapside, though different from that of his Brook Street residence in Mayfair, was not unfamiliar to him. He had spent many evenings gazing out of these very windows last summer when he had been arranging Lydia's marriage to Wickham.

Darcy linked his fingers behind his back and sighed as he watched the silhouette of a lone cat wrap itself around the foot of a lamppost. There was something about being in the Gardiners' home that soothed him. Even through the stressful ordeal of negotiating with Wickham and all that entailed, Darcy had been able to come to this house at the end of each day and find peace. Now, as he stood within the walls of Mr Gardiner's study once more, he decided perhaps it was not the house that brought him comfort, but the people who resided in it.

The Gardiners, though Darcy considered them perfectly entitled to do so, were not the sort of people who made demands of him. From the moment he appeared on their doorstep, through his painful recitation of his dealings with Wickham, to his insistence they allow him to have his way in their family's most wretched affair, Mr and Mrs Gardiner were welcoming, agreeable, and even affectionate towards him.

"Mr Darcy."

Darcy shifted his focus from the snow-covered street to the window's reflection and sighed once more, this time in resignation. Elizabeth stood with her hands behind her back, pressed against the door to the room. Despite her aunt's instructions to leave it open, Darcy noticed she had chosen to close it instead.

"Are you avoiding me, sir?"

He rubbed his brow as he perceived a distinct note of archness in her tone, then turned to face her. "Indeed, Miss Bennet, I do not dare."

"I am relieved to hear it. It would be a most unpropitious start if my future husband were suddenly intent upon avoidance."

Unsure of the correct response in such a situation, Darcy made no reply.

Elizabeth bit her lip. "Will you not tell me how Lydia has come to petition you, of all people, to persuade her husband to bring her to town?"

Of course, Elizabeth would not mince her words. It was a trait Darcy had always valued in her but on this subject, he found himself wishing she were not so direct. Explaining the matter, to her or to anyone, was not only distasteful to him, but out of the question. He said simply, "I cannot."

She raised one impertinent brow. "You cannot or you will not?"

When he failed to offer clarification, Elizabeth straightened and crossed the room to stand before him. "Come, Mr Darcy, we are to be husband and wife. Let there be no secrets between us. Certainly, none that concern my sister and Mr Wickham."

"I cannot speak of this, not with you. Not ever."

"Why?" she asked, her frustration apparent in her voice. "What is so terrible, so unspeakable that you cannot confide in me? The Gardiners are privy to whatever has taken place. I know that much from the scene that unfolded this morning at Longbourn, though neither my aunt nor uncle would utter a word. You have nothing to fear in that quarter. But Lydia is a poor secret keeper, sir. Shall I apply to her instead? Or perhaps I should bypass her altogether and enquire of Mr Wickham? Surely, he will have something to say on the subject."

Darcy imagined Elizabeth confronting his former friend, and worse still, the embellishments and falsehoods Wickham would likely add to the tale to make Darcy's life a misery. He grew livid. "Absolutely not. I forbid it. No good will ever come of your applying to *him*."

"No good indeed," she replied in annoyance. Lifting her chin, she turned on her heel and strode to the fireplace, where a fire flickered brightly in the grate. Her shoulders slumped, and Darcy watched her wrap her arms around herself, more likely to draw comfort than to ward off a chill. He shut his eyes, understanding too late she was disappointed and injured as well as angry.

They stood in silence, the crackling of the fire the only sound in the room. *Is this how it is to be between us?* he wondered with mounting unease. At Netherfield Elizabeth had agreed to marry him and the moments that followed had been blissful. Now they were in London, and she was mad at him. Was their newly acquired joy to be so fleeting? Was keeping his part in her sister's marriage from Elizabeth worth sacrificing their own contentment?

When Darcy considered it in those terms he could not answer in the affirmative. Nothing was worth such a sacrifice. But how could he ever confess what he had done? He had assumed a role he had no business assuming in the first place. He had acted when he had no right, no claim to Elizabeth. Though Darcy had determined to restore Lydia Bennet's respectability, his true purpose was to preserve *Elizabeth's* respectability; to protect *Elizabeth's* reputation; to restore *Elizabeth's* happiness. Everything he did he did for Elizabeth. Everything he did he did out of love for her.

In his preoccupation, he failed to notice Elizabeth had abandoned her station at the hearth and returned to him. Her head was bowed, and her hands were clasped tightly.

She spoke. "I was wrong to threaten to press Mr Wickham for answers you clearly do not want me to seek. I am well acquainted with his character and know he is unlikely to be truthful in any case, especially where your good name is concerned. Please forgive my disloyalty, Mr Darcy. My remarks were not only undeserved, but inappropriate. You are the last man in the world I wish to injure. If you feel such secrecy is necessary, that is your prerogative. I am only sorry you feel I cannot be trusted to maintain it."

In her voice and in her expression, Darcy not only recognised contrition, but genuine distress. "You believe I do not trust you?" he asked, truly surprised by her statement. "Elizabeth, I trusted you to keep Georgiana's secret after you refused me. I trust you implicitly in all things."

She stared at him, her eyes wide and troubled, and slowly shook her head. "I cannot account for your reasoning. It makes no sense. If you still trust me to keep your sister's secret, then why can you not apprise me of whatever secret encompasses my own sister? If it is as you say, you would share your burden with me and you would do it willingly, knowing I would gladly bear the weight of it with you. There must be something you do not trust me with in this case."

My heart, a voice in Darcy's head whispered in reply. He swallowed thickly and averted his eyes. As much as revealing his role in her sister's marriage disturbed him, it pained him far more that Elizabeth believed he did not trust her. There was nothing else to do but speak. There was nothing else to do but confess all. With great difficulty, he began.

"When I saw you that day in Lambton—when I came upon you after you had read Mrs Bingley's letter..." But Darcy found there was too much sentimentality, too much raw emotion attached to seeing Elizabeth alone and weeping at the inn to continue in that vein. She had been heartbreakingly beautiful, even in her distress, and he feared he would reveal more about his feelings for her in that moment than his purpose during the moments that had followed.

He extended his hand to her, his palm facing upward to show he had nothing he wished to hide. Elizabeth stepped forward, closing the distance between them metaphorically as well as physically, and accepted it. Darcy relaxed, if only slightly. He began again.

"You were supposed to dine at Pemberley that afternoon, but instead you departed for Hertfordshire with your aunt and uncle. The fault was mine, and I resolved to go to London at once. It would be difficult, but not impossible to find them. I knew Wickham well, whereas your father and uncle did not. His habits, his vices, his contacts, his haunts—I knew all.

"At last, I discovered them and was able to meet privately with your sister. I begged her to return to her friends at once, but she would not be persuaded. Neither would Wickham agree to make her his wife. He told me he intended to make his fortune by marrying an heiress and laughed at the prospect of tying himself to your sister, who was practically penniless."

Darcy shook his head as he recalled the utter futility he had felt when faced with Wickham's disregard for Lydia, and Lydia's staunch determination to continue living with him. "Your sister would not listen to reason. She insisted they were to marry, and it did not signify when. Despite her stubbornness, despite her foolhardiness, I could not abide abandoning her to reap what she had sown. I negotiated with Wickham. I met with your uncle. They were married the following month."

"You paid him," Elizabeth said on a breath, tightening her grip upon his hand. "You, and not my uncle, paid Wickham to marry Lydia. Thoughtless, selfish Lydia, who never spared one thought, one concern for what her recklessness would cost any of us! Your generosity to her, your unexampled kindness, was more than she deserved."

Darcy's mouth twisted as he stared at their joined hands. "It was not kindness or even empathy towards Mrs Wickham that prompted my interference. I did not bring about their marriage for her sake. You called her selfish, but I, too, am a selfish being. Elizabeth," he said, raising his head so he could look into her eyes, "I thought only of you."

"And I, sir," she replied in earnest, "am exceedingly grateful. On behalf of all my family, please allow me to thank you for what you have done."

As though her words had burned him, Darcy retracted his hand from hers. "Your family owes me nothing, nor do I require your thanks. I do not want it." He ran his hand over his mouth in agitation and silently cursed himself for being curt and disagreeable when he ought to have been gracious. "Forgive me. This is precisely the reason I did not tell you about my involvement. This is precisely the reason I never wanted you to know what I have done. I do not want your gratitude, Elizabeth. I do not want the foundation of our life together to be formed from *gratitude.*"

"Our life together will always owe something to gratitude, sir. Whether you like it or not, I will always be grateful to you, not only for finding Lydia, but for finding *me*—for loving me enough to humble yourself not once, but twice. You put aside my injudicious treatment of you, my unjust accusations. You confided in me, opened your heart to me, and allowed me to know you as you truly are in every facet of your conduct—an honourable man, a doting brother, and a devoted friend. Your generous nature and your forgiving heart taught me humility."

She reached for Darcy's hand and squeezed it, tightening her hold when he attempted to withdraw from her once more. "I agreed to become your wife—to bind myself to you for as long as I live—not because I am grateful to you, Fitzwilliam. Not because you are handsome, or because you have ten thousand a year, or because Pemberley has the most beautiful park I have ever seen, but because I love you and cannot bear the thought of living my life without you."

"You love me?"

Elizabeth nodded. "I do, with all my heart. I thought I confessed as much two nights ago when we were alone at Netherfield. I thought you understood as much when you asked to speak to my father."

Darcy reached for her, and she came willingly into the circle of his arms. "It was implied, but not spoken. Your esteem, your affection was enough. I was hopeful your love would follow in time."

"When?" she asked as she laid her chin upon the lapel of his coat and tilted her face to his. Her eyes were deceptively deep, framed by long, thick lashes the colour of ink. "If I did not already love you now, when would I begin, do you think?"

Darcy raised one hand and gently traced a line from her temple along the curve of her cheek with his fingertip. He was inordinately pleased when her eyelids fluttered closed. "When we were married and settled at Pemberley, perhaps in the summer or the following winter. You once told me you have never seen a house more happily situated than Pemberley. If there was any chance of making you love me, I was convinced it would happen there."

Elizabeth opened her eyes, but rather than the teasing look he had expected from her, Darcy was surprised to see a distinct flicker of sadness. She raised one hand to his cheek, then the other, and cradled his face in her palms. "Pemberley is lovely," she told him with uncharacteristic seriousness. "There is much of you in the house, in the grounds, and in all aspects of its history and prosperity. But you are *so much more* than Pemberley, Fitzwilliam." She drew his head towards hers and without warning, pressed a tender, enduring kiss to his mouth.

The moment their lips touched Darcy could barely think. He had not expected Elizabeth to initiate any such intimacy so soon —most assuredly not in her uncle's house. That she had done so thrilled him beyond measure and sparked a desire he dared not consider. She ended the kiss slowly—reluctantly, Darcy thought—with a barely audible gasp that did nothing to restore his equanimity.

Elizabeth stared at him from beneath her lashes. Her lips were parted, and a heated blush coloured her cheeks. She appeared astonished, as though she had shocked herself with her own daring.

Darcy could not be more pleased. "Promise me you will kiss me often when we are married," he said to her. "Promise me you will never stop." He caught her hands and brought them to his lips, kissing first one, then the other before positioning both over his heart.

Elizabeth shook her head at him and coloured more deeply, but the corners of her mouth were upturned, and the hint of a bashful smile played upon her lips. "I promise to make sure you know how much you mean to me, whatever that might entail."

"There is something you might do now, and I would be indebted to you." Mr Gardiner's words from that morning had resurfaced in the back of his mind, urging Darcy to give voice to his desire.

"I will do whatever you wish, so long as it is within my power."

Darcy kissed her fingertips, then each blushing cheek, and finally her mouth—a featherlight press of lips that, despite being gentle, made both their hearts quicken. "Mrs Bingley is married. She and Bingley are on their honeymoon, and you will reside with them in Park Street for some time. Elizabeth," he whispered, closing his eyes as he slowly dragged his lips along the column of her neck, where he placed a lingering kiss.

Her breath caught and Darcy inhaled the heady fragrance of her skin: summer and roses—*Elizabeth*. He found the pulse just beneath her ear and sucked lightly, taking care not to leave a mark. He grazed her skin with the tip of his tongue. "I want to tell Georgiana you will be her sister," he murmured. "I want Colonel Fitzwilliam to know you have accepted me. I want to inform Bingley, and your sisters, and all our relations without delay. I want to call upon you each day and be free to spoil you every minute we are in London."

He returned his attention to her neck, where he laid a trail of sensual, open-mouthed kisses from her ear to her shoulder. "I want to marry as soon as we may," he said against her skin as his voice grew unsteady. "I want to take you to Pemberley for Christmas. I want to marry you in the chapel there and make you mine in body as soon as you say 'I do' to the minister."

"I am sure the minister is delightful," Elizabeth said breathlessly as her fingertips brushed the edge of his cravat, then his collar, "but I would prefer to say 'I do' to you." She grazed his jaw, then the hidden flesh of his throat and Darcy was lost.

Whether her touch had been innocent or purposeful he could not discern; he felt only the insistent rush of desire. Before he could check himself, he claimed Elizabeth's lips in an ardent kiss and wrapped her tightly in his arms. "Please," he said hoarsely. "Say yes. Say you will marry me at Pemberley."

"At Christmas?"

"At Christmas," he told her, peppering her face with kisses. "Or before, but not a day later. Georgiana would be so pleased. The Gardiners will join us. I will send for your family—your parents and sisters. You will want your father to give you away."

Elizabeth, who Darcy was certain had been smiling a moment before, suddenly stiffened in his arms.

Fearing he had gone too far—that he had demanded too much of her too soon—he ceased his ministrations at once. "Forgive me," he said as he released her and increased the distance between them. "Forgive me. I should not have taken such liberties. I should not have pressed you so urgently." Agitated and embarrassed, he silently cursed himself for his zealousness. "Of course, you would rather wait. You must think me a barbarian."

Elizabeth smoothed her gown and trained her eyes upon the floor. "I do not. Do you think me wanton?"

Darcy could hardly believe she had asked such a thing. Surely, of the two of them, she was the respectable party. "Never. Your conduct is far from wanton. As surely as I prayed you would eventually come to love me, so did I also pray our union would be one of mutual ardency. We are to be married. You are receptive to my touch and responsive to my kisses. I consider myself most fortunate. I am only sorry the fervency of my attentions has upset you."

"It has not," she insisted, blushing furiously. "You mentioned my family and I immediately thought of...My parents are not affectionate people. My father does not hold my mother in esteem. He desires neither conversation nor companionship from her. He spends his days in avoidance while she passes her time with gossip and matchmaking. Forgive me, but she spoke to Jane of duty on the eve of her wedding—not affection, not love, not...ardency. We were told, in no uncertain terms, that a husband would not welcome any such response from his wife."

Darcy reached for her hands. "And what sort of response," he quietly enquired, "is a husband supposed to desire from his wife?"

Elizabeth placed her hands in his. She would not, however, meet his eyes. "A husband neither expects, nor requires, a response from his wife in their marriage bed. According to my mother, I am impudent, stubborn, unfeeling, and selfish. If she knew how I have behaved with you, sir, she would add lustful to my list of accomplishments and refuse to acknowledge me altogether."

Darcy frowned as he imagined Mrs Bennet berating her daughter for desiring him. In his opinion, Elizabeth had nothing to repine, except perhaps the misfortune of having a mother who lacked discernment and a father prone to neglecting his wife.

"I have said as much before but will gladly say so again—you are very different from your mother. In fact, you are very different from every lady I know. You are intelligent and insightful, kind-hearted, and spirited. You are curious and passionate. I would not trade a life with you for anything in the world, especially a life with an insipid girl who professes opinions that are not her own."

He was startled to hear her laugh.

"Is that not what you once accused me of doing, Mr Darcy? Professing opinions that are not my own?"

Darcy recalled not only his words to her, but the arch look that appeared in her eyes as he had pronounced them, and grinned. "That was only when I first knew you, Miss Bennet. I have long accepted the opinions you profess are entirely your own."

Her smile warmed him, and Darcy drew closer to her. Rather than claim her lips, he placed a tender kiss upon her temple and another on her brow. "Come," he told her, tucking her hand into the crook of his arm. "Let us find the Gardiners before they come in search of us."

❦ 20 ❧

WHERE ELIZABETH SPEAKS OF A SUBJECT
MOST INAPPROPRIATE.

T he following morning, Elizabeth opened her eyes to sunlight dappling the walls of the cosy bedchamber she usually shared with Jane whenever they stayed with their aunt and uncle Gardiner. She stretched like a cat beneath the counterpane and sighed contentedly, admiring the elegant pattern of silver and sage leaves upon the walls. Darcy had offered to see her to Park Street the night before, but her uncle insisted Elizabeth remain in Gracechurch Street instead. The weather had grown colder and more unpleasant as the evening wore on, and her aunt was concerned about the state of the roads. It would have been improper for Darcy to have escorted her all the way to Park Street in any case, as neither Bingley nor Jane had thought to send a maid to act as her chaperon, and Mrs Gardiner's could not be spared.

Though an invitation to stay the night was extended to Darcy as well, he declined, assuring Mrs Gardiner his coachman was an excellent driver. The snowflakes sifting down upon the frozen streets would pose no problem for him, the horses, or the equipage. Darcy had some business in the morning but would call upon them in the afternoon.

A knock upon the door of her room convinced Elizabeth she had stayed abed long enough. "Come in," she said. She had expected her aunt but was pleasantly surprised by Emily instead.

"Cousin Lizzy!" she cried, skipping across the room with a wide smile. "Mamma said you spent the night with us. Will you spend the day as well?"

Elizabeth threw off the counterpane and laughed. "I believe I will, but I must go to Jane and Mr Bingley at some point, else they think I have changed my mind and run away."

"Can you not change your mind?" Emily enquired, sitting beside her on the bed. "Surely, you can stay with us for as long as you like. We shall take excellent care of you, and Mr Bingley and Cousin Jane will be happy for they are married and will want to be alone. If you stay with them, you will only be in their way."

Elizabeth regarded her young cousin with raised brows. "Wherever did you hear such a thing?"

"From Aunt Bennet."

Of course, Emily would happen to overhear her mother's uncensored commentary. Elizabeth pursed her lips disapprovingly. "Well, Aunt Bennet is quite mistaken. Jane invited me to stay with her in Park Street, and Mr Bingley is very pleased about it. We will be a merry party. Rest assured, I will not be in anybody's way."

Emily regarded her sceptically. "Aunt Bennet was insistent. I would not wish for you to displease her, Cousin Lizzy. She is most frightful when she is vexed!"

Frightful indeed, Elizabeth thought wryly. She decided a change of topic was in order and patted Emily's knee reassuringly. "My mother can be quite insistent when it comes to having her way, but as she is in Hertfordshire and we are in London there is no need to give it another thought. Now," she told her, "I will be exceedingly grateful to you if you will help me decide which gown to wear this morning. I can never seem to make up my mind."

⚜

Half an hour later, after Emily was consigned to her governess, Elizabeth found Mrs Gardiner at the breakfast table enjoying a cup of tea. "Good morning, Aunt," she said warmly, claiming a seat beside her.

"Good morning, my dear. I trust you slept well?"

"Very well, despite Jane's absence."

"I can imagine," her aunt replied with a sympathetic smile, "it must be difficult for you to be without her, and for her to be without you. I remember when my eldest sister married her husband. I missed her terribly, but it was not long after that I met your uncle, and we were married. I still missed her, of course, but I loved Edward with all my heart. We are most fortunate. Ours has been a blessed union, and our love for each other has only grown stronger with time."

Even from a young age, Elizabeth recognised the Gardiners' marriage was very different from her parents'. Her aunt and uncle possessed a true affection for one another. They enjoyed each other's company, sought the other's counsel, and valued their spouse's opinions. Theirs was precisely the sort of union Elizabeth hoped to achieve with Darcy: a true partnership where familiarity and time would not lessen their affection and respect for one another but nurture and cultivate both, allowing their love to mature and their marriage to thrive.

Elizabeth recalled the half an hour she had passed with Darcy in her uncle's study the previous night. Yes, they had argued, but they had listened to each other as well. Both had confessed secrets, professed feelings, and shared moments steeped in intimacy that made Elizabeth blush. She remembered well the way Darcy's arms encircled her waist, the way his breath heated her skin, the way his lips tasted, and the way his words, honest though they were, warmed her in places his hands had never touched. Even now, Elizabeth could feel the ghost of his caress upon her skin, his lips upon her neck. She wondered if he could feel hers as well.

"Lizzy?" Mrs Gardiner prompted with a laugh. "Where did you go, my dear?"

Elizabeth was startled to see she was still seated at the breakfast table with her aunt and felt a flush of embarrassment. "Forgive me. You were speaking of your marriage to my uncle, of the affection you share, and I could not help but think of Mr Darcy and what our own marriage might entail."

"You love him, and Mr Darcy loves you. I daresay so long as you are honest with one another and treat each other with consideration and respect you shall be very happy."

"I cannot imagine treating him any other way, nor can I imagine Mr Darcy mistreating me in any manner." She bowed her head as her fingers toyed with the embroidered edge of her aunt's tablecloth. "We quarrelled last night about Lydia and Mr Wickham. He did not want to tell me what he had done for her. I was angry and hurt and felt he did not trust me to keep whatever secret he was determined to conceal from the world."

"I see. And did you resolve your differences? It certainly appeared that way when you joined us in the parlour before Mr Darcy took his leave."

"We did. I apologised for making demands of him, we spoke at length, and he confessed all. He is unlike any gentleman I have ever known. His expectations and desires are not at all what I anticipated from a man such as he."

Mrs Gardiner raised her brows. "Expectations and desires, Lizzy?"

Elizabeth felt a flush of heat, uncertain what she ought to reveal. Not only had she allowed Darcy's ardent advances, but she enjoyed them. Her mother, who had advised Jane to do nothing to either encourage or prolong Bingley's presence in her bed, would have been scandalised, but Madeleine Gardiner shared little in common with Elizabeth's mother. She was intuitive, patient, steady, and possessed an innate and intimate knowledge of the world Mrs Bennet did not. The two women could not be more different; but perhaps their views were not so varied regarding amorous behaviour between an unmarried lady and her betrothed. While Elizabeth could imagine her aunt's reaction would by no means be as severe as her mother's, she doubted Mrs Gardiner would appreciate such wantonness taking place in her home.

"Lizzy," her aunt chided. "I believe there is much you are not telling me. Unless it is something truly alarming, you can be assured of my secrecy."

Elizabeth knew as much already, but admitting she desired her future husband was easier said than done. After some hesitation, she said, "Mr Darcy and I shared much last night, but I fear not all we discussed or did is considered proper. I am sorry. I hope I do not shock you. My mother would probably take to her bed."

"Did Mr Darcy do something that offended you?" Mrs Gardiner asked, her brows creased with concern. "Did he make you uncomfortable or coerce you to do something you did not like?"

Elizabeth shook her head, blushing profusely. "No," she confessed. "Quite the opposite."

"Ah," Mrs Gardiner replied knowingly. "I take it you have been kissed, but is that all?"

"That is not all," Elizabeth admitted. "Mr Darcy held me. We spoke of our feelings for one another in great depth. At one point, it was I who brazenly kissed him. My mother would be appalled."

"I see. It sounds to me as though you are conflicted. Exactly what is it that is bothering you? Is it what you and he have done, that you enjoyed it, or is it more your mother's professed disapprobation of such affection between a man and his wife?"

"It is not so much what Mr Darcy and I have shared as it is my mother's notion of how a lady should behave in such circumstances, whether she is married or not. Mr Darcy enjoyed when I responded favourably to his affectionate gestures. He was moved when I kissed him. I do not believe I will ever be capable of passivity in the marriage bed, not when I feel so much."

To Elizabeth's surprise, Mrs Gardiner gave her a sympathetic smile. "Your poor mother does not share your passionate nature, and though I do not doubt she cares for your father, theirs is hardly an equal marriage. It pains me to say it, but they neither esteem nor respect each other as a husband and his wife ought to do. Your father does not desire your mother's opinions or her society, certainly not the way Mr Darcy desires yours.

"Despite what your mother has led you to believe, there is no shame in desiring the man you marry, nor in expressing that desire, especially where there is a real and abiding affection. Mr

Darcy appears to love you deeply. He is a quiet man, a serious man, but the way he looks at you is indicative of his strong attachment. He is a man of the world. That he feels passionately for you is not surprising, nor is your own response to his ardency. It is natural to want to return his kisses and caresses, and it is perfectly acceptable to do so once you are safely married. Until then, you both must take care. Mr Darcy spent much time and money to preserve your respectability. It would not do for either of you to forget yourselves. Your reputation is at stake, as is Mr Darcy's honour. I would hate for the sacrifices he made for you—for all of us—to have been made in vain."

When her aunt excused herself to meet with her cook, Elizabeth adjourned to the drawing room where she took up her embroidery and contemplated all her aunt had told her.

According to Mrs Gardiner, it was perfectly natural, not only for Darcy to desire her, but for Elizabeth to desire him as much. It had been a relief when her aunt had neither chastised her nor accused her of wantonness; but that sense of relief was short-lived when her aunt alluded to all Mr Darcy had done to preserve her reputation when Lydia not only allowed but encouraged the attentions of a scoundrel.

Though she did not doubt Lydia had flirted with and encouraged Mr Wickham to an outrageous degree, Elizabeth had only to feel Darcy's nearness—his hand on hers, his lips upon her skin, the heat of his body as he held her—before she was lost to sensation. Like her most foolish sister, there was no thought, no question of whether surrendering to Darcy's tender ministrations was right or wrong; there was only the undeniable draw Elizabeth experienced when she was close to him—the delicious, pleasurable ache from his touch.

She reminded herself that she and Darcy were deeply in love, where her sister had only believed herself to be—and Mr Wickham had admitted he was most assuredly not. Her sister had been in public—in Brighton with friends—while she and Darcy had been in the privacy of her uncle's house, safely ensconced behind a closed door. There was little chance of the children or any of the servants seeing them. But how would she have felt had her aunt or uncle witnessed their amorous exchange?

When Mr Ellis discovered them at Netherfield Elizabeth had been mortified, but having the Gardiners come upon such a scene would have been infinitely worse. There was no doubt in her mind she would have been severely chastised by her uncle for her lack of restraint; Darcy would have suffered harsher treatment and would have been forced to bear the weight of disappointing a man he held in the highest regard.

Elizabeth turned her head aside and looked out the window, where the sun cast its weak winter rays upon the snow-covered street. She could not imagine making Darcy suffer such an indignity, not when he had gone to so much trouble for her by bringing about her sister's marriage to a man he could barely tolerate, never mind respect. And he had done it—not for Lydia —but for her.

He loved her, and though Elizabeth returned his love in equal measure, she knew being alone with him and allowing his romantic overtures—however much she craved his society and his touch—posed a certain danger, not only to her reputation, but to his. After all she had put him through, the last thing she wanted was to deny Darcy something that pleased him; but the consequences of ceding to their desire before they were wed were, to Elizabeth, not worth the risk of discovery. She resolved to be stronger.

WHERE MR DARCY INFORMS HIS LORDSHIP OF
HIS NEWS, AND HIS LORDSHIP IS SERIOUSLY
DISPLEASED.

"Mr Darcy, my lord."

Lord Carlisle raised his eyes from his breakfast plate and dismissed his butler with a brusque wave of his hand. "Nephew," he said gruffly, wiping his mouth with a linen napkin. "I see you have come back. I thought you were staying with your friends in Exeter until Christmas."

Darcy greeted his uncle and kissed Lady Carlisle's proffered hand. "I have been in Hertfordshire, not Exeter. My plans have since changed. Bingley and his bride have removed to town with their family, and I decided to follow them."

Lord Carlisle grunted. "Sit down, Darcy. Have a scone."

"I am glad you are come back, Darcy," said Lady Carlisle brightly as she handed him a cup of tea. "Now I can plan my dinner with our friends sooner than later. Lady Eliza will be overjoyed to see you. She was desolate when she heard you had left town, and I daresay so was Lady Harrow. If I did not know better, I would think the countess fancied you herself! She barely batted an eye when Lord Townsend failed to make an appearance the other night."

The earl snorted derisively. "Townsend is twice Darcy's age. Of course, she would prefer a young stallion to an old goat."

"You know nothing of the sort," the countess replied haughtily. "Lady Harrow is nearly twenty years Darcy's senior. She is old enough to be his mother."

"His mother!" Lord Carlisle laughed coarsely. "Mothering is the last thing on that woman's mind, especially when she looks at Darcy."

"Henry!" Her face was pinched with anger.

Her husband rolled his eyes and waved her off. "What brings you here this morning, Nephew? Surely, it is not to indulge your aunt's folly by speaking of the Harrows."

In his mind, Darcy was asking himself that same question. He had been in his uncle's house for less than five minutes and already he had been provoked and mortified. He took a fortifying sip of tea and lamented the fact there was no hope of acquiring anything stronger. Where the earl was concerned, getting to the point as expediently as possible was his best form of recourse. The sooner he disclosed his purpose, the sooner he could take his leave.

He set his teacup upon the table and looked his uncle in the eye. "I am engaged to be married."

Her ladyship gasped with delight. "How wonderful! I knew you would come to your senses and make dear Eliza an offer!"

"I am not engaged to Lady Eliza," Darcy told her firmly.

"Of course, you are not," the earl said sardonically, giving his wife an exasperated look. "Eliza Harrow is not Darcy's cup of tea. He wants a girl with a brain. With opinions, and convictions." He looked pointedly at his nephew. "You are stubborn, but not so foolish you would dare to choose unwisely. Who is she?"

"Miss Elizabeth Bennet of Hertfordshire."

"Eliza Bennet?" said his aunt in confusion. "I do not know any Bennets."

Lord Carlisle frowned. "I have never heard of her either. Who is her father?"

"Miss Bennet's father owns a modest but thriving estate called Longbourn. The Bennets are the principal family of the village there."

"What is she worth?"

Darcy bristled. He knew his uncle would ask about Elizabeth's dowry, but the earl's manner of enquiry, much like his manner in general, was offensive. He was tempted to say that Elizabeth Bennet was worth more than money or a title but knew such romantic notions would never satisfy his practical uncle. It would only try his patience. "Miss Bennet will receive one thousand pounds upon her mother's death."

The earl choked on his bacon. "A thousand pounds!" he sputtered once his coughing fit had waned. "That is nothing! That is pin money!"

"Miss Bennet is not chattel," Darcy replied sternly. "She is lovely, intelligent, and witty. I hold her in the highest regard. She makes me happy."

"She will make you a laughingstock!" Lord Carlisle said disgustedly, shoving his plate aside. "I cannot believe what I am hearing. She has drawn you in! You, Fitzwilliam Darcy of Pemberley, one of the most eligible men in England, trapped into marriage by a penniless chit! A fortune hunter!"

"Miss Bennet is no fortune hunter," Darcy said coldly.

Lord Carlisle swore under his breath. "You had to go to the country. You had to stand up with your damned friend. You would have been better off staying in London and sowing your oats in King's Place or Drury Lane like the rest of society!"

"I have no desire to pass my time with bit actresses and courtesans. I want a wife."

"So, you picked the first piece of muslin you saw in that blasted shire, dipped your pen, and succumbed to her charms!"

Darcy was furious. "I did nothing of the sort! Miss Bennet is a gentleman's daughter! I have known her for more than a year and have admired her for nearly as long. This was not the first time I proposed marriage to her, but it *is* the first time Miss Bennet has done me the honour of accepting me."

Lord Carlisle stared at Darcy as though his nephew was a stranger. "Let me rightly understand you," he said lowly. "You proposed marriage to this girl—this, this *upstart*—only to be refused, and yet you returned to her with your tail tucked between your legs to beg like a dog?" He slapped his hand heavily upon the table. "You are George Darcy's son! You are the grandson of an earl! You are the master of Pemberley!"

Darcy stood so abruptly his chair tipped over and made a resounding bang as it hit the floor. "I am more than Pemberley!" he informed his uncle, livid. He struck the table with his fist, rattling the china.

Lady Carlisle flinched.

"I am more than a piece of property! I am more than an annual income, or an exclusive address in town, or a private box at Covent Garden!"

"You are the sum of the parts that make up the whole!" Lord Carlisle spat, seething as he leapt from his own chair. "Pemberley is a part of that whole! It is a damned big part!"

"There is also honour," Darcy reminded him, tugging impatiently at his coat as he struggled to regain control of his temper. "There is conviction. There is benevolence and self-respect."

"And what of duty! What of sacrifice!"

"My entire life I have done nothing *but* my duty—to Pemberley, to my parents, to my sister, and to you. I have made sacrifices. I have made concessions. I will make no more."

"You are making a grave mistake," his uncle warned in a cold, hard voice. "Such a girl will be your ruin! I cannot abide this. Georgiana needs a woman who knows her stuff! This country nobody cannot help her become a member of good standing in London society! What does this girl have to recommend her? Nothing! What does she have to offer you? Nothing! She has no right to such an honour!"

"She has every right! She has my respect! She has my esteem! She has my admiration and my regard! Miss Bennet is not a simpering, disingenuous girl, but a warm-hearted, clever woman who somehow, despite my poor behaviour to her in the past, has seen past my offences and decided *I* am worthy of *her*. I will marry Miss Bennet. You may attend us or not, but, by God, you will not disrespect her, or I will sever my ties with this house."

Disappointed and furious, Darcy looked to his aunt, who stared at him with her mouth hanging open. He bowed curtly, turned on his heel, and quit the house.

"I hear it did not go well," said Colonel Fitzwilliam as he claimed a chair in Darcy's study. He settled into the soft, burnished leather, crossed his ankles, and linked his fingers behind his head.

Darcy glared at him from behind his desk, though it was not his cousin who had angered him, but Fitzwilliam's father. "I would be lying if I said I expected it to go smoothly. The man is a misery. There is no pleasing him. He actually suggested I take a mistress in front of your mother."

The colonel grimaced. "Yes. I understand the subject was revisited after you departed. My father has frequented Drury Lane with great regularity over the course of their marriage. Until this morning, my mother was under the impression he had an insatiable appetite for the theatre, not a rapacious passion for several of its actresses. There was much screaming and flailing about. She locked herself in her apartment, but not before hurling half the china at my father's head and threatening to divorce him."

Darcy raised his brows. "Divorce? Surely, her ladyship would not dare."

Fitzwilliam shook his head. "My mother is angry and humiliated, but I doubt she will actually sever ties with him, nor would my father allow it. He would view it as a scandal from which the honourable House of Fitzwilliam will never recover. He will take pains to make amends, though by the look of things I am not so sure my mother is of a mind to forgive him any time soon."

"Nor am I," Darcy muttered, running a hand over his face. "But it is done. I paid the call, and I informed him of my intent."

Fitzwilliam grinned. "Congratulations, Cousin. Her meagre dowry aside, Miss Bennet is everything you deserve. I daresay she will make you very happy."

"I could not care less about her dowry but yes, Elizabeth is wonderful. She returns my regard. She loves me."

"Of course, she does," his cousin said matter-of-factly. "I envy you. You swallowed your pride and followed your heart and won Miss Bennet's in the process. If I could have but half your good fortune in my choice of wife, I will consider myself a lucky man."

"When I was last in town, Lady Carlisle informed me you were to entertain Miss Morrison. Dare I ask how you got on?"

Fitzwilliam shrugged. "Miss Morrison was not awful. Neither was she exceptional. Have you seen her?"

"I have not had that pleasure."

"I would not necessarily refer to the experience as a pleasure. It was crowded and hot and Miss Morrison was pretentious and cold. She has blonde hair, forty thousand pounds, a large bosom, and absolutely no sense of humour. My father liked her prodigiously."

"And do you like her?"

"I have given her no thought whatsoever. She is not unattractive, but she is uncommonly dull." Frowning, he scratched his chin. "According to my mother she sings and plays the harp, but I have seen nothing of it. She did not exhibit that evening, nor any other evening I have been in company with her. In fact, she spends an inordinate amount of time devouring cucumber sandwiches and cake, followed by trips to the water closet. She is a terrible conversationalist. Truly, I do not think the lady knows any words above two syllables."

"Miss Morrison sounds rather…"

"Lacking," said Colonel Fitzwilliam with a theatrical sigh. "She is merely another lady—indistinguishable from the rest—who has been endorsed for the marriage market by the *bon ton*. She is tolerable I suppose, but she is no Miss Bennet."

Darcy threw a piece of sealing wax at him. "Miss Bennet is mine. You must find your own wife. If I recall, you wanted a simpering lady with a large dowry, not a woman of sense with only a thousand pounds."

"As the son of an earl it is my prerogative to change my mind," Fitzwilliam said, smiling widely as he shifted his weight in his chair. "Let us speak no more of wives. It is all my mother talks of lately and I am beginning to detest the subject."

"Very well. I trust you received my express?"

"I did, and I took the liberty of sending my own on to Newcastle. If anything is amiss with Wickham, my friend Colonel Whittaker will inform me, though it will take a few days for his reply to reach London. I never thought I would say this, but what Wickham claimed may likely be true—he could very well be on an errand for his colonel. It is a bit odd he thought to drag his wife with him all the way to Hertfordshire and attend Bingley's wedding, especially if he is not overly fond of her society."

Darcy's mouth twisted with distaste as he recalled the way Mrs Wickham accosted him in her mother's drawing room yesterday morning, completely lacking in propriety and determined to have her way like a spoilt child. "He is not the only one."

"I am sorry you were forced to see either of them while you were in Hertfordshire. I would have been tempted to run him through."

"Believe me, I was sorely tempted, but my focus cannot always be directed towards Wickham. I had better things to do with my time."

Colonel Fitzwilliam smirked. "I imagine you did. What are your plans for the day?"

"My only matter of business," Darcy replied, reclining in his chair, "was to inform your father of my engagement. Other than that, I will pay a call to Miss Bennet in Gracechurch Street this afternoon and then see her to Park Street after tea."

"Park Street?"

"Yes. Bingley has taken a house there. He did not want to spend his honeymoon in Grosvenor Street with Hurst and his sisters making demands of him. I cannot say that I blame him. He invited Elizabeth to join them for the duration."

Colonel Fitzwilliam blanched. "What number?"

"I have no idea," Darcy replied. "Why does it matter? Why are you suddenly interested in Park Street?"

"Darcy," said his cousin, "have you no recollection the Harrows have also taken a house in Park Street? What if they are neighbours?"

"The Harrows? Are you certain?"

"Yes, I am certain. I have been there—to Chadwick House. It is where I was introduced to Miss Morrison."

Rubbing his forehead, Darcy looked towards the window. He felt a headache coming on. "This is...most inconvenient."

"I am inclined to agree, but perhaps it might end up working to your advantage."

"How so?" he asked, his tone doubtful. "Lady Harrow does not comprehend subtlety any more than she practises propriety. I do not like the idea of her being Miss Bennet's neighbour."

"It is highly unlikely she will deign to pay Miss Bennet a call. Attend the theatre or go for a walk in Hyde Park with Miss

Bennet on your arm and there will surely be talk. By the time calling hours are over and done with, the whole of society will know you are no longer on the marriage market. Lady Harrow will likely be so affronted by the business she may even spread the word herself. There is nothing she can do but grit her teeth and wish you joy should you have the misfortune of meeting with her."

"There is plenty she can do," Darcy said darkly. "She is spiteful and vindictive. She can disparage Miss Bennet."

"So, what if she does? Do you think Miss Bennet cannot defend herself? She is as intelligent as she is attractive and has a tongue as sharp as a rapier. For heaven's sake, she handled Lady Catherine's remarks with unmitigated grace and aplomb. Miss Bennet will be fine. I doubt she will allow some catty society mamma to best her, especially one who has set her cap at you."

"Lady Harrow did not set her cap at me," Darcy replied irritably. "She wanted me for her daughter."

Colonel Fitzwilliam laughed. "Tell yourself that if it brings you comfort, but we both know first-hand where that woman's proclivities lay. Had you indulged my mother and married Eliza Harrow, you would have found her ladyship in your bedchamber before long wearing nothing but her title, whether she was welcome there or not."

"Who is your letter from, Cousin Lizzy?"

"Emily," her mother chided, "leave Elizabeth alone. She is entitled to her privacy, however little we can afford to give her."

Emily swayed closer. "Is it from Longbourn? Is it from Cousin Jane? Is it from Mr Darcy?" she asked, batting her eyelashes innocently. "He is very handsome."

"That is enough, Emily. You have your lessons to attend to, or have you forgotten? Perhaps I should send for your father and have him remind you of the necessity of your education."

"Enjoy your letter, Cousin Lizzy," Emily called, performing a hasty curtsey before quitting the room.

Mrs Gardiner shook her head at her daughter's antics and resumed her fine work. "Who is your letter from, Lizzy?"

"Why, Aunt," Elizabeth replied with a teasing lilt, "I was under the impression I am entitled to my privacy."

"Oh, hush," said her aunt, smiling. "Is it from Mr Darcy?"

"It is from Jane. She writes to say she and Mr Bingley will come to Gracechurch Street at nine o'clock this evening to retrieve me."

"That ought to give you plenty of time to visit with Mr Darcy. I had thought to invite him to stay for supper again if he has no prior engagements. Perhaps Jane and Mr Bingley can join us as well. Why do you not write to her, and suggest the idea?"

Elizabeth had no sooner finished her missive to Jane than the Gardiners' maid announced not only Darcy's arrival, but Colonel Fitzwilliam's as well.

The gentlemen entered the room and Darcy's steady gaze settled upon her at once. Elizabeth greeted him warmly and introduced Colonel Fitzwilliam to her aunt. He had treated her with kindness and solicitation when they had met at Rosings Park last April, and she had thoroughly enjoyed his company. Her smile for him was as warm.

"It is good of you to call upon us, Colonel Fitzwilliam," Elizabeth said to him. "Seeing you is a delightful surprise."

"The pleasure is entirely mine," he told her with a wide grin as he claimed a seat beside her on a small sofa, effectively preventing Darcy from doing the same. "When Darcy told me this morning of your engagement, I insisted on accompanying him. I cannot begin to express my joy that you have accepted him. We are as close as brothers. I have always wanted a sister."

Darcy snorted. "You have a sister, Fitzwilliam."

His cousin waved his hand dismissively. "Josephine does not count." He returned his attention to Elizabeth. "She is my brother's wife, Lady Emerson, and one of the most wearisome creatures in all of England. Come to think of it, my brother is extremely tedious as well. I daresay they are well suited."

Darcy looked disapprovingly at his cousin and shook his head. "Compared to you, Fitzwilliam, everyone appears dull."

"It goes without saying that you can certainly use some liveliness, but I am well enough acquainted with our dear Miss Bennet to know that she does not. Certainly, you do not mean to say that you find your future wife dull, Darcy?"

"I implied nothing of the sort," Darcy told him exasperatedly. "You are putting words in my mouth. It is a most unfortunate habit—one I recommend breaking yourself of else Mrs Gardiner begins to regret your acquaintance."

Colonel Fitzwilliam chuckled. "Forgive me, Mrs Gardiner," he said with a winsome smile. "Where Darcy is concerned, I cannot seem to help myself. We have developed a dreadful habit of ribbing one another, as gentlemen are wont to do. In truth, his friendship is extremely dear to me, dearer than my own brother's. There is nothing I would not do for him. He is the very best of men."

Mrs Gardiner returned his smile. "I have become well acquainted with Mr Darcy, Colonel, and cannot but share your sentiments. He has become dear to us as well. There is no better man I could have wished for Elizabeth. And if he needs a bit of liveliness from time to time," she said with a mischievous glint in her eye, "he has come to the right place. I daresay my niece has enough liveliness for both. She is an excellent tease."

Elizabeth felt a blush bloom upon her countenance but smiled despite it. "Mr Darcy is no stranger to my incorrigible teasing and impertinent nature. Perhaps, if he is feeling generous, he might be so good as to impart a bit of seriousness upon my levity. I am confident we can instruct each other, for I have come to learn there is as much value to be found in gravity as there is in humour." She looked to Darcy and was gratified to see a small, private smile tugging at the corners of his mouth as he regarded her with a sincerity that made her pulse quicken.

"You are indeed an incorrigible tease, Miss Bennet," he replied, "but I consider myself most fortunate in my choice of wife. I am confident our life together will not be the least bit dull."

🌿 22 🌿

WHERE EVERYONE KNOWS, BUT NOT
EVERYONE IS HAPPY ABOUT IT.

"**C**ovent Garden," Mrs Gardiner remarked with pleasure. "That sounds wonderful, Mr Darcy. We would love to accompany you tomorrow evening."

"I hope you will also join me in my home on Brook Street for supper at six o'clock. I am looking forward to returning your hospitality, Mrs Gardiner."

There was an expression of real pleasure on Darcy's face as he continued to speak animatedly with her aunt about the theatre; it made Elizabeth smile. Darcy and Mrs Gardiner had grown close and seeing such happy evidence of their mutual regard warmed Elizabeth's heart. Mr Gardiner, too, had developed a genuine fondness for Darcy, a fondness that likely prompted him to think highly of Colonel Fitzwilliam as well. The two gentlemen had settled themselves on the far side of the drawing room with Bingley and appeared to be engaged in a lively conversation about Netherfield's fishing prospects.

Elizabeth turned towards Jane, seated beside her on her aunt's settee, and her smile faltered. From the moment Darcy had announced their engagement to Bingley at dinner, Jane had seemed out of sorts. Elizabeth knew her sister had harboured ill feelings towards Darcy before she and Bingley married, but Jane had promised to do her best to put them behind her. Until this evening, it appeared to Elizabeth that she had.

Elizabeth had no idea what to do to reconcile the situation, no idea how to improve her sister's opinion of Darcy—or even how to encourage a conversation between them. They were to be brother and sister, whether Jane liked it or not. Having the two people Elizabeth loved most in the world at odds with each other was disheartening.

If only she could have a few minutes alone with Jane to talk, then perhaps Elizabeth could make her understand how deeply she cared for Darcy; there was little opportunity in her aunt's home for privacy, especially since the gentlemen had been all too happy to forgo a separation after supper and remain with the ladies.

Jane emitted a long-suffering sigh.

Unable to maintain her silence, Elizabeth reached for her sister's hand. "You seem out of spirits tonight."

"I am by no means out of spirits. I am married to the most wonderful man in the world, and we are very happy. Indeed, I could not ask for a better husband than Charles."

"I am inclined to agree with you. Mr Bingley positively dotes on you, and you deserve every ounce of his adoration and devotion. I am exceedingly glad to be able to call Mr Bingley my brother."

Jane removed her hand from Elizabeth's, smoothed an imaginary crease on her gown, and studied the carpet. "It appears I am to have a new brother as well. I am surprised to hear you have accepted Mr Darcy. I did not think you liked him."

Elizabeth shook her head in disbelief. "You know that is not true. You know I have esteemed and admired him for many months now."

Jane frowned. "Since you were at Pemberley. I always thought you would marry for love."

"Jane, I *am* marrying for love. I love Mr Darcy with all my heart."

"Perhaps you only think you love him. Perhaps you are mistaken."

Elizabeth gaped at her, astounded that her dearest sister could entertain such a thought. "I am by no means mistaken in my regard. How can you say such a thing to me? How can you think I do not know my own heart?"

"I hardly know," Jane muttered.

In her voice Elizabeth heard real regret. "Why are you so set against me marrying him? Why can you not be happy for me?"

"We ought not speak of this now. Forgive me." She squeezed Elizabeth's hand, offered her a tight smile as she rose from the settee, and crossed the room. Bingley, Mr Gardiner, and Colonel Fitzwilliam stood as she approached and offered polite bows of acknowledgement. With a gallant wave of his hand, Bingley offered her his chair. She glanced once towards Elizabeth, then quickly away, and accepted it.

Elizabeth did not know whether she wanted to throttle her sister or dissolve into tears.

The cushioned seat of the settee dipped as Darcy joined her. "It appears your sister has abandoned you for her husband. I am sorry for your sake but gratified for my own."

Elizabeth pushed her frustration with Jane aside. "How bold of you, Mr Darcy," she teased, "to sit so close to me in front of all these people."

"I would not call it bold, Miss Bennet, so much as resolute. These people are hardly strangers. Save for Colonel Fitzwilliam, they are dear members of your family. Soon they will be mine as well."

"You appeared much at ease while conversing with my aunt. I daresay you are fond of her."

"I am. I like the Gardiners very much. In a way, they remind me of my own parents. The genuine pleasure they receive from each other's society is apparent. It has been a long time since I have had the honour of knowing a husband and wife who enjoy a marriage born of real affection instead of suffering an arrangement of convenience."

"What of Colonel Fitzwilliam?" she asked. "He is so good-natured and attentive I cannot imagine his parents do not share a similar temperament. Lord and Lady Carlisle must be quite well matched."

"Well matched indeed," said Darcy. His voice contained a distinct note of dissatisfaction. "I know of no two people more disenchanted with each other than Fitzwilliam's parents. While they share similar views regarding duty and breeding, they share little else, certainly not affection. My uncle is...difficult." Darcy huffed in annoyance. "When I say he is 'difficult' I mean he is arrogant, prejudiced, and boorish."

"Oh dear. I am sorry to hear that. I can imagine the earl is not an easy gentleman to please. He is Lady Catherine's elder brother, is he not?"

"He is, but Lord Carlisle makes Lady Catherine appear quite demure in comparison."

Elizabeth was surprised. Lady Catherine de Bourgh was not a woman whom Elizabeth would have described as demure. There was nothing her ladyship liked better than to hear herself speak and to have her way in all things, including matters that did not concern her. It was impossible to imagine any person making Darcy's cacophonous aunt appear reticent or unassuming. "Do you get along with Lord Carlisle?"

"Not," Darcy said, "without expending a great deal of effort on my part, and as of late, not at all."

"Again, I am sorry."

Darcy shook his head. "I am not."

His voice had taken on an acerbic edge, and Elizabeth suddenly understood. "You informed him of our engagement."

"I did," Darcy admitted after a brief hesitation.

"I suppose he does not approve."

"There is very little of which my uncle does approve. He would have me marry where there is no affection, no regard, so long as the lady has a large dowry, a title, and absolutely no proclivity for original thought or intelligent conversation. He does not know me, and what is more, he does not care to know me. He barely knows his own wife."

Elizabeth could hardly credit what she had heard. As mortifying as her family was at times, she could not imagine having a father or uncle who insisted she marry a shallow, simple-minded man rather than one who loved her and respected her and made her happy. If that had been the case, she would either have been disowned or living in Hunsford, married to Mr Collins.

Until that moment she had given little thought to Darcy's relations beyond their station and wealth. Yes, she had met Lady

Catherine, but Elizabeth had always believed her to be an anomaly of sorts, as eccentric as she was in her opinions and views of the world. It saddened her to learn that Darcy not only appeared to be a stranger to his uncle but undervalued by him in all the ways that mattered.

"You are very quiet." Darcy touched one finger gingerly to the back of her hand and lowered his voice. "I fear it is my fault. I should never have mentioned my uncle's disapprobation. You must know I will never allow him to treat you with disrespect. In fact, you need never even make his acquaintance."

Elizabeth shook her head. "I do not fear your uncle," she replied, her voice laced with sadness. "I was thinking of the value you place upon your family connexions. It must be hard to feel a sense of obligation to such a man. You lost your father at a young age and have carried a heavy weight of responsibility upon your shoulders ever since. From what you have said of him, I gather your father was an excellent man. Even Mr Wickham, as duplicitous as he is, had much to say of your father's honour and goodness. I cannot imagine losing the counsel, the friendship of such a beloved parent only to be thrust under the scrutiny of a dogmatic, critical man who understands so little of your nature. It grieves me to know your uncle neither sees, nor appreciates the man you truly are."

Darcy stared at her, his expression one of unmitigated tenderness. "Elizabeth," he murmured in a low voice. "You do not know how desperately I wish I could kiss you right now."

Elizabeth smiled, ever so slightly. "We are by no means alone, so there is little chance of that happening. *My* uncle, exceptional man though he is, will not look upon such a lapse of propriety with an approving eye."

"Perhaps he will be generous enough to allow you to see me to my carriage, then."

"Are you leaving, Mr Darcy?" she enquired, raising her brow archly. "And without your cousin?"

Darcy laughed. "I am embarrassed to admit I have completely forgotten about him. No doubt it has something to do with your proximity. You have a way of making me forget myself."

"So long as you do not forget *me,* sir. It would be most disloyal of you."

His countenance grew serious, and he reached for her hand.

Elizabeth, sensing his need for reassurance, surrendered hers as discreetly as possible.

A full minute passed before he spoke. When he did, his voice was hoarse, flayed by a surge of emotion that startled her. "I have *never* been able to forget you. If I am anything, I am loyal. I am constant. You need never question my faithfulness. You need never doubt my devotion. I am yours, in body and soul, for as long as I am able to draw breath."

Elizabeth did not expect such an intimate, reverent profession, not in a room full of her family. She was moved—incredibly moved—by the spontaneity of Darcy's declaration and the sincerity behind it as much as she was by the steady, fervent expression of love in his eyes as he gazed at her.

She tightened her grip on his hand and was about to reply when her sister appeared by her side.

"Lizzy," Jane said, effectively ending their private communion. Her eyes travelled from Elizabeth's flushed face to the couple's clasped hands, partially hidden by the folds of her sister's gown. "It is time for us to depart."

Darcy released her hand at once and rose from the settee. "Of course," he said sedately, averting his eyes as he quietly cleared his throat. "We should be going as well. Please permit me the pleasure of escorting you to your carriage, Miss Bennet."

This time Elizabeth extended her hand to him. "I am honoured, Mr Darcy."

⚜

Ensconced in the room Jane had given her in Park Street, Elizabeth sat upon the bed in her night shift and robe, absently plaiting her hair. She was lost in thought—thoughts of Darcy. She smiled to herself. She could not help it. She had never been happier. The only thing marring that happiness was Jane.

As if her sister had been privy to her thoughts, Elizabeth heard a knock upon the door, followed by Jane's soft voice. Elizabeth bid her enter.

"I hope you will like it here, Lizzy. Charles wanted to give you a much larger room, but that one is situated at the front of the house and overlooks the street. I thought you would prefer this one, which has a lovely view of the courtyard instead."

The room itself was beautiful, and Elizabeth could find no fault with its location, furniture, or closets. As for the view, she would have to wait until morning to see what delights it afforded. "It is a cosy, inviting space, elegant and tastefully decorated. I like it very much."

"I am glad. Thank you for agreeing to come to London, for joining me on my honeymoon. I do not know what I would have done had you decided against it."

"You and Mr Bingley would get along perfectly fine without me. I am pleased my presence still affords you comfort, but, as your husband, Mr Bingley can provide comforts I cannot. It is late. I imagine you would rather be in your own bedchamber with him than in here with me."

Jane coloured deeply and averted her eyes. "I am tired. Charles has been a most...attentive husband."

The corners of Elizabeth's mouth lifted with a smile. "Are you attentive to him as well?"

"Lizzy," Jane admonished, stifling an incredulous laugh. "How can you speak of such things?"

Elizabeth bit her lip. "Quite easily, I am afraid. I confess to feeling a certain amount of curiosity. What Mamma had to say on the subject cannot be all there is to the business. Surely there must be more."

Jane's eyes grew wide. "Lizzy, you are incorrigible! I told you all Mamma related already. Truly, there is little else to divulge."

Elizabeth cocked her head. "Mr Bingley expects nothing from you? He makes no requests? He offers no encouragement? No...inducement?"

Jane appeared truly perplexed. "I do not know what you mean. What sort of requests? What sort of inducement?"

Elizabeth's thoughts turned to Darcy and his fervent plea that she kiss him often once they were married, as well as his ardent reaction when she had inadvertently grazed the skin of his neck with her fingertips, and his adeptness at coaxing passionate responses from her with his kisses and caresses and words of love. She felt a flush of heat. "I hardly know, but there must be more. More than lying beneath the counterpane prone upon the bed until one's husband is sated. What of kissing? Of...touching? Surely, a husband desires more from his wife than what Mamma proclaimed."

Jane sat upon the bed and plucked at the counterpane. Her blush intensified. "I have done what she instructed, and Charles appears pleased. It is gratifying to be the source of such joy for my husband. I cannot imagine anything more fulfilling."

Elizabeth's smile was half-hearted at best. She could not imagine simply lying corpse-like in her marital bed, nor did she believe Darcy would want that, not if his passionate responses to her kisses and innocent caresses were any indication. "I am happy for you. You are very good. Mr Bingley is fortunate in his choice of wife."

"As I am fortunate to have such a husband," Jane told her. She straightened and clasped her hands upon her lap. "Lizzy, I would speak to you."

Elizabeth wrapped her hand around the ornate, mahogany bedpost and sighed. "If you mean to speak of my engagement to Mr Darcy, I must caution you to take care. I have no desire to quarrel with you tonight."

"You mean to have him, then."

Elizabeth laughed incredulously. "I do not 'mean to have him', as though he is a prize to be won. I am going to marry Mr Darcy because I love him. There is nothing more to say on the subject."

Jane's shoulders slumped. "I am sorry. This ought to be a happy time for you, yet I am ruining it."

"You are ruining nothing," Elizabeth said carefully, making a concerted effort to conceal her irritation, "but your dislike of Mr Darcy does complicate matters. You are displeased with my choice and that pains me. I would be dishonest if I said otherwise. While I can understand your dissatisfaction with Mr Darcy to some extent, your reasoning is not sound. You are safely married to Mr Bingley now. Mr Darcy did not prevent it from happening, nor did he wish to prevent it. He encouraged his friend and supported him even before Mr Bingley returned to Netherfield to claim your hand. He stood beside him in church. He wished you both every happiness."

"It is true. I know it is true, and try as I may, I cannot find fault with his conduct."

"Then why do you insist on holding him accountable for Mr Bingley's decision to remain in town for nearly a year?"

Jane leapt from the bed in distress. "If I absolve Mr Darcy of his role in the affair, the blame must fall solely upon Charles. I cannot bear the thought of feeling such resentment towards my husband. I cannot! I would be miserable! I would become bitter and hateful, and Charles would resent me for it."

"Did you never consider that by holding such a grudge against Mr Darcy you are risking your husband's ire in any case, despite your misguided logic? You have said yourself that Mr Darcy is Mr Bingley's oldest friend. When I marry Mr Darcy, he and Mr Bingley will become brothers. Do you think your husband will not be injured by your coldness towards a man so dear to him? Do you think witnessing your prejudice against Mr Darcy will not spark bitterness in Mr Bingley? Do you think he will not become angry with you? Do you think he will not resent your inability to let the past remain in the past?"

"I...do not know. I did not think of it in such terms."

Elizabeth rose and took her sister's hands in both her own. "You ought to think of it in precisely those terms. I do not want to see you and Mr Bingley injured by this any more than I wish to see Mr Darcy injured. You must let bygones be bygones. You have done as much with Mr Wickham, who is a scoundrel at heart, yet you continue to persecute Mr Darcy, who is in every facet of his conduct Mr Wickham's superior in essentials."

She paused for a moment to draw a calming breath. "I will speak plainly. By refusing to extend the same courtesy to Mr Darcy, you are risking more than your husband's discontentment. You are jeopardising our closeness as well. I love you, Jane, with all my heart, but I have come to love Mr Darcy as much. If you only knew what he has done—the sacrifices he has made, how truly selfless he is—then perhaps you would be better able to put aside your scorn."

Jane regarded her with furrowed brows. "What has Mr Darcy done?"

Elizabeth slowly shook her head. "I cannot tell you. I cannot betray his trust. I can only assure you of his honour and goodness. That will have to be enough."

✣ 23 ✣

WHERE MR DARCY IS SEEN WITH ELIZABETH
AT THE THEATRE, AND LADY CARLISLE IS
SEEN BY MR DARCY.

D arcy's carriage, one in a long line of countless others, rolled slowly towards the entrance to Covent Garden Royal Theatre. He drummed his fingers against the upholstered seat, his impatience to reach the front of the line at odds with his desire to remain within the obscurity and privacy of his conveyance. He glanced at Elizabeth, who was seated across from him beside her aunt, and felt his heart swell with adoration. She looked beautiful. Her hair, her complexion, her figure, her gown—Darcy could not focus on any one feature for long else he become irrevocably distracted by her loveliness. Her eyes were bright with curiosity as she absorbed every detail of her surroundings; her lips were upturned with delight. He turned aside his head with a measured exhalation. In that moment he dearly wanted to kiss her.

At last, they reached the theatre's entrance. The footman opened the door to the equipage, and the comfortable atmosphere of the conveyance turned brisk, prompting the ladies to wind their wraps more securely about their shoulders. Darcy alighted quickly and extended his hand to Elizabeth. She grasped it firmly with her gloved fingers, paying careful attention to the placement of her feet as she descended the carriage steps. Once she was standing safely on firm ground, she gave Darcy a beatific smile that made him wish they were not surrounded by a horde of people about to enter Covent Garden, but ensconced within Darcy House and much alone.

"Thank you," she said, making a slight adjustment to her wrap.

Darcy resisted the urge to kiss her tempting mouth and tucked her hand securely into the crook of his arm instead. "You are very welcome."

As Mr Gardiner alighted and assisted Mrs Gardiner, they were joined by the Bingleys, Colonel Fitzwilliam, and Mrs Lawrence, who appeared well entertained by Darcy's charismatic cousin. She wore a spectacular gown of royal blue satin, a fur cape, and a mischievous expression that immediately put Darcy on his guard. Fitzwilliam was speaking to her of God only knew what, making her laugh. Darcy hoped it was not a colourful account of his cousin's exploits in the army.

"Shall we go in, Darcy?" Bingley suggested, grinning despite the frosty bite to the air. Without waiting for a reply, he led Jane towards the entrance.

The rest of their party followed.

They entered the lobby, and though the air was decidedly warmer, Darcy felt a coldness descend upon him. The crowd assembled within was a crush. His spine stiffened and he felt his mask of composure slip into place. Beside him, Elizabeth tightened her grip upon his arm, and he instinctively drew her closer as they slowly made their way through the elegantly attired throng of theatregoers.

Conversation was impossible over the noise, but that did not stop at least a dozen acquaintances from greeting them along the way. Though the interactions were brief, Darcy noticed many of the gentlemen eyed Elizabeth appreciatively, while the ladies' looks ranged from curiosity to scrutiny. Elizabeth, Darcy was pleased to see, bore it all with her customary grace and good humour.

At long last they reached the sanctuary of Darcy's box. He saw the Gardiners and the Bingleys settled towards the front, then guided Elizabeth to a seat directly behind her sister. He claimed the seat beside her as Colonel Fitzwilliam ushered Mrs Lawrence into the seat to Darcy's left. Once all the ladies were comfortably situated, the gentlemen followed suit.

"What a lovely evening, Mr Darcy," Bingley's aunt said to him. "I must thank you again for including me in your party. It has been many years since I have been to the theatre. This is a treat I will not soon forget."

"I am pleased to have you join us, Mrs Lawrence. You are staying with the Hursts and Miss Bingley in Grosvenor Street, are you not?"

At the mention of her nieces, Mrs Lawrence emitted a long-suffering sigh. "I am grieved to discover," she said with a conspiratorial lilt to her voice, "there is not much fun to be had in Grosvenor Street. Though the neighbourhood appears quite fashionable, my relations who reside there are rather tiresome. I am considering decamping to Park Street tomorrow for the duration of my stay else I either lose my composure or die of boredom. As I have yet to see anything of London, it would be a most untimely demise."

Beside her, Colonel Fitzwilliam chuckled. "Your husband, Mrs Lawrence, must have been a most affable gentleman, and extremely fortunate in his choice of wife. You do not suffer fools gladly."

"Can one suffer a fool any other way?" she enquired with a twinkle in her eyes. She inclined her head towards Bingley. "Charles's excellent disposition notwithstanding, I have always considered it a misfortune that, while one can pick one's friends and one's neighbours, sadly, one cannot pick one's relations."

"I suppose it depends upon where one looks," the colonel replied. "You can always take another husband, madam, if you want amusement."

Bingley's aunt laughed merrily. "Goodness! You are a trouble-maker! If I were thirty years younger, I daresay I would be in some danger."

"If I were twenty years older, Mrs Lawrence," he proclaimed with a roguish wink, "the danger would be entirely mine."

She returned his wink and patted his hand fondly. "That it would, young man. That it certainly would. Do not doubt it for a moment."

Darcy leaned towards Elizabeth, who was making a valiant effort to contain her laughter. "They are incorrigible," he whispered, endeavouring to repress his own mirth. "I ought to have known better than to introduce the two of them."

"Indeed! It appears the good colonel has met his match with Mr Bingley's aunt."

"Why did you not caution me?"

"This is a fine thing, sir," she replied archly. "You can hardly expect to hold me accountable for your lapse of sound judgment! It is most unfair of you to cast blame where blame is not due. You are a man of the world. You ought to have known better."

Darcy laughed. "And you, my dear, ought to know you are entirely to blame for my lack of attention to such matters. If you were not so lovely—if you had not bewitched me so—perhaps I would have had my wits about me instead of my head in the clouds."

Elizabeth's expression softened, though her smile remained. "I believe you are the incorrigible one, Fitzwilliam. But I cannot fault you for it. I can only admire you, most ardently."

Darcy stared at her—at her blushing countenance, her artless smile, and the sincerity in her eyes—and felt a lightness, a completeness he only ever felt in her presence. A wayward curl rested upon her cheek. Boldly, he extended his hand and gently wrapped it around his finger. "I cannot imagine my life without you."

"I am very pleased to hear it," she replied tenderly, "for I feel much the same."

❧

The following morning found Darcy in his study, sitting at his desk attending to his correspondence when his butler informed him of Lady Carlisle's arrival. Glancing first at the clock upon the mantel and then at the pile of letters requiring his attention, Darcy repressed an oath. It was a most unwelcome interruption. He considered telling his butler to send his aunt away but dismissed the idea at once. Refusing to see her would only serve to offend the countess. It mattered little the purpose of her visit was likely to offend *him*. Darcy's reply to his steward would have to wait.

She swept into the room with her usual self-possession, the train of her gown swirling dramatically about her feet in what Darcy had long suspected was a practiced contrivance. Rather than claim a chair beside the fire, she took up residence before his desk and remained standing.

Darcy remained standing as well. "To what do I owe this pleasure, Lady Carlisle?" He linked his fingers behind his back and awaited her reply.

She did not answer but watched him with a steady, indecipherable expression.

Darcy grew uncomfortable under her scrutiny but maintained an air of neutrality as he studied her in turn. He had the distinct impression she was taking his measure. For what purpose he could not begin to guess.

"You were at Covent Garden last night," she said at last.

"Yes."

"I was there as well, as Lady Harrow's guest."

Darcy inclined his head. "I did not have the pleasure of seeing you there, nor did I happen to see Lady Harrow."

"No," she said briskly. "You only had eyes for the young woman seated beside you. Even when her attention shifted to the performance on stage, yours remained fixed upon her. I believe I am correct in assuming she is the one you intend to marry. What is her name? Miss Eliza..."

"Miss Bennet. Miss *Elizabeth* Bennet. Our engagement has not yet been made public, but our attendance of the performance was alluded to in the society page this morning."

"I saw that, too." Lady Carlisle walked to the hearth, ran her gloved fingers over the mantel, and examined them for signs of dust.

Darcy's tolerance for her theatrics was waning. "I trust you did not come all this way to ensure that my housekeeper is diligent in her duties."

Lady Carlisle continued to look peevish, but when she spoke her voice sounded less harsh. "She made you smile, Darcy."

It was the last thing Darcy expected his aunt to say to him.

The countess continued in the same vein. "She made you laugh. I do not remember the last time I saw you laugh, but suspect the occasion likely involved Richard and some sort of boyhood antics, not a pretty, young woman in a pale, satin gown. Tell me, do you often laugh with Miss Bennet?"

"Miss Bennet often makes me laugh, yes."

"What did she say to you last night, to make you laugh?"

Darcy stared at her in consternation. "At the moment I cannot recall. Most likely, she was teasing me."

"This young lady teases you?" Lady Carlisle enquired, seemingly surprised by such a response. "Is that why you like her so much? Because she teases you?"

"Her sense of humour is but one reason among many. Miss Bennet is warm-hearted, charismatic, artless, and intelligent. She is a great reader and plays the pianoforte. She sings. We share many of the same interests and tastes. I do not merely *like* Miss Bennet, your ladyship. I greatly admire and esteem her. I love her."

"And does she love you?"

"I believe she does."

Lady Carlisle sighed and turned back towards the hearth.

"Why are you here, Lady Carlisle?" Darcy enquired, not unkindly.

"I would like you to perform an introduction. Obviously, Miss Bennet cannot wait on me at Carlisle House. Darcy House will have to suffice."

Darcy felt myriad emotions. Most prominent among them were shock, relief, perturbation, and incredulity. He hesitated, unsure whether he ought to trust his aunt's motives. It was out of character for her to want to make the acquaintance of anyone she deemed beneath her notice. Though Elizabeth was a gentleman's daughter and possessed all the qualities and attributes Darcy professed, she was also sister to Bingley, cousin to Mr Collins, and practically undowried. He did not want the countess to say or do anything that might upset or offend her. Knowing his aunt, it was highly likely.

"I would be honoured to introduce Miss Bennet to your acquaintance," he said carefully, "but confess I am surprised you want to meet her. I was under the impression neither you nor my uncle approve of our engagement."

"Your uncle," she replied irritably. "Do not speak to me of your uncle, Nephew. I have no stomach for that man of late."

Darcy could well imagine the disgust and humiliation his aunt suffered upon learning her husband had taken several mistresses during their marriage and kept one now. He made no reply.

"The man has used me extremely ill," the countess continued, "but there is nothing to be done. He does what he wants. That is his way."

The truth of her statement raised Darcy's ire, but he held his tongue. His aunt sounded tired.

She walked to the broad leather sofa positioned before the fire and sat upon it. "It has always been Henry's way," she uttered resentfully. "Henry's way, his father's way, his grandfather's way. Your cousin Arthur is certainly no prize either. I know Richard thinks her dull and perhaps she is, but Lady Josephine ought to be nominated for sainthood for putting up with a husband such as my son.

"Then there is Richard," she said exasperatedly. "He is above thirty and appears determined to remain a bachelor. I have introduced him to countless eligible young ladies, to no avail. He finds something to criticise in each one. I have begun to despair of him ever taking a wife, but he speaks highly of your Miss Bennet. Very highly, in fact."

"They became quite friendly in Kent."

"I know." Lady Carlisle rolled her eyes. "Cousin to Catherine's parson, Darcy? Really! Are there any other unsightly connexions Miss Bennet has of which I ought to be made aware?"

Darcy pursed his lips in annoyance. Though he appreciated Fitzwilliam championing Elizabeth, he would have a few choice words for him about talking too much. "Miss Bennet," he began perfunctorily, "has two uncles in trade and her eldest sister is lately married to my friend Bingley. She has three younger sisters. The youngest is married to George Wickham, and her mother suffers frequent fits of nerves." It was better to get it all out at once, he decided, though he doubted any of what he related would be received by his aunt with any modicum of pleasure.

Lady Carlisle shut her eyes as though pained. "Wickham!" she repeated scornfully. "I cannot believe you would dare to have anything to do with that scoundrel! How can you want to marry a woman so intimately tied to him! Good Lord. No wonder the poor mother suffers nervous fits. She must be appalled by the connexion!"

Darcy remained silent. No good would come of revealing Mrs Bennet's fondness for the blackguard. There was little chance the two would meet in any case. He could not foresee his aunt travelling to Hertfordshire to wait on Elizabeth's mother, nor did he believe Mr Bennet, who had long detested London, would consent to bring his wife to town.

Lady Carlisle shook her head disgustedly. "Wickham," she muttered once more. "It is most distressing! That connexion can never be mentioned, especially to your uncle. It would only serve to further enrage him. The parson poses a problem as well, but there is little we can do in that quarter. His connexion to Rosings is already established. Poor Catherine," she lamented. "Not only are you jilting Anne, but her funny little parson will be able to claim a familial affiliation to the noble House of de Bourgh!"

Darcy sighed as he joined Lady Carlisle on the couch. "Why do you want to meet Miss Bennet? You are displeased by her lack of dowry, displeased by her connexions, and displeased that I chose her over Lady Harrow's daughter.

"While I will never acknowledge or consent to receive George Wickham, you should know I have grown extremely fond of Miss Bennet's aunt and uncle here in London. The Gardiners are very respectable people. They are genteel and fashionable. Their manners are elegant. Mrs Gardiner and Miss Bennet are close."

Lady Carlisle lifted her hand to her forehead. "And where do this aunt and uncle of hers reside in town?"

"On Gracechurch Street," Darcy replied. "Near Cheapside."

"Cheapside!" she cried. "Really! That is simply...I cannot believe you...Cheapside...and Wickham, too! Oh, your uncle...!" Lady Carlisle stood, walked to the hearth, then returned to the couch and sagged upon it. "Oh, the devil be hanged. I suppose it is to be expected with the uncle being in trade. But they *are* genteel people?"

"I have never met with pleasanter people than the Gardiners. They were among my guests at Covent Garden last night."

Her ladyship huffed. "Very well. Is there anything else you must confess? Any skeletons in closets, or whispers behind hands? Has the lady been compromised in any way that would necessitate your marrying by week's end?"

"No," he said tersely.

"Good. Her virtue is intact. Unlike yours."

"Not all men are cut from the same cloth," Darcy replied irritably. He was not a saint, but neither was he in the habit of keeping a mistress like his uncle and half of London.

Lady Carlisle laughed disdainfully. "You are nearly nine-and-twenty, Darcy. Do not *dare* tell me you have never known a woman, for I will know it to be a lie."

"I will not indulge such talk."

His aunt rolled her eyes. "Because it is not proper, no doubt."

"Because it is none of your business," he snapped. "You have yet to answer my question, Aunt. Why do you want to meet Miss Bennet? Be forewarned, should I condescend to arrange an introduction, I will not tolerate any manner of disrespect towards her. If it is your intent to abuse and disparage my future wife, you will regret it. Now, answer my question."

The corners of the countess's lips lifted an infinitesimal degree. "*That* is why."

Darcy had little patience left for cryptic replies. "Speak plainly. I do not take your meaning."

"You are the most level-headed gentleman I know. You make intelligent, well-informed decisions regarding all aspects of your life. You rarely allow your temper to get the better of you, nor is it your habit to respond to provocation.

"The other day, when you informed your uncle of your engagement, he berated and belittled you for your choice and insulted Miss Bennet. You did not bite your tongue. You did not present a passive disposition as you have on countless other occasions. You defended Miss Bennet, and you championed her with an ardency and a temerity no gentleman—including your uncle—has ever exercised on *my* behalf.

"Your passionate regard for Miss Bennet moved me and my curiosity was piqued. What sort of woman can affect such an alteration in such a cautious, conscientious man as yourself? Even within your family circle, you are the epitome of self-control and a slave to convention, yet you went against the expectations and wishes of all your relations and friends. You threw off convention, and proposed marriage to a woman of inferior birth who is practically undowried. You incurred your uncle's ire and threatened to forsake your most prominent and important ties for this young woman whom you claim to love. I ask you, Nephew, how can I not be curious, especially when she makes you laugh?"

It was decided that Darcy would inform Elizabeth of his aunt's desire for an introduction, but beyond that initial effort he could make no promises. Despite her ladyship's expectations of the meeting, the decision to wait upon her would ultimately be Elizabeth's. He could tell his aunt was not only displeased by his response, but affronted. In the end, Lady Carlisle's curiosity surrounding Elizabeth seemed to surpass her dissatisfaction with the terms and she acceded to her nephew's proposal, albeit grudgingly.

As he had various matters of business that required his attention that could not be put off, Darcy was adamant that no introduction would take place that day. He would attend to his correspondence, visit his solicitor, and call upon Elizabeth that evening. Lady Carlisle adjusted her pelisse with a haughty sniff and informed him she would return the following day at two o'clock sharp.

Once she had gone, Darcy returned to his desk, but his mind was on his aunt's visit, not on letter writing. He assumed his uncle had no idea his wife had called in Brook Street, nor that she wished to arrange an introduction to his betrothed. Should Lady Carlisle's disloyalty be discovered, the earl would be outraged. Darcy did not know if he was pleased or perturbed by the idea. Her ladyship's words were convincing, as were her sentiments, but Darcy knew her well. Like her husband, she adhered to certain convictions, opinions, and societal protocols, however misguided and prejudiced Darcy considered them.

It had long been Lord and Lady Carlisle's opinion that a fortune amassed from trade was almost as distasteful as being in trade. It was no secret the countess held Bingley in contempt. Elizabeth was now Bingley's sister. Her uncle was in trade. Would she treat her any differently? Darcy could not say. He could only hope Elizabeth would still be amenable to marrying him after Lady Carlisle's inquisition, assuming it ever actually took place.

He laid aside his pen—it needed mending anyhow—and reclined in his chair. He had made so many harsh judgments upon Elizabeth's family, many of which were undeserved. His own family's conduct was far from irreproachable. From Lady Catherine's condescension to Lord Carlisle's crassness to Lady Carlisle's snobbery to Darcy's own arrogance and presumption, the conduct of each was not only lacking, but shameful. Not for the first time did he marvel at Elizabeth's ability to overlook his offences and forgive him. He wondered what he had ever done, not only to deserve her love, but to deserve *her*. Surely, it was not insulting her before they had ever been introduced, or separating his friend from her sister, or offending and demeaning her during his first proposal, or abandoning her for weeks on end when he believed she did not return his regard.

If Elizabeth had been any other lady, Darcy would have attributed such a pardon to Pemberley and all it encompassed— in short, to his extensive wealth. But Elizabeth was unlike any other woman of his acquaintance. She was charming, unaffected, discerning, and compassionate. Her generous nature knew no bounds. Whether they argued or embraced, Darcy was enamoured. He fully suspected that he could live the rest of his life with her and still she would continue to surprise him with her insight and her grace and her passion.

Her passion.

Darcy had barely done more than kiss her, yet she was responsive in a way he had scarcely dared to dream. His wedding night could not come soon enough. There was so much he wished to show her, so much he wished to share. Would she enjoy being in his bed as much as she seemed to enjoy being in his arms? Would she crave his lips and his hands on her body? Would she kiss him often, as she had intimated, once they were man and wife? Would she allow him to see all of her, to taste her and touch her and love her in the light of day? Or would she only yield to her desire in the dark of night? Would she feel all the pleasure he was sure to feel? Would she tell him what pleased her, or would she be shy? *No,* he thought, feeling a flush of heat and the insistent stirring of desire. She might blush, but his Elizabeth would not be shy.

Darcy laid the back of his head against the supple leather of his chair and rubbed his hands over his face. Such thoughts were not conducive to attending to matters of business. Shaking his head as if to clear it, he straightened and began to mend his pen.

❧ 24 ❧

WHERE MR DARCY GOES TO PARK STREET FOR
SUPPER.

"Mr Darcy," Mrs Lawrence said with a grin as she greeted him in Bingley's drawing room. "Allow me to welcome you to Park Street."

"Thank you, Mrs Lawrence. You look very well this evening. Tell me, are you merely visiting, or have you made good on your promise to move in directly?"

"You are a tease after all," she told him delightedly. "Indeed, I have come to stay. I could not abide another minute in my niece's house. At breakfast I mentioned you had become engaged to Miss Bennet and Caroline choked on her toasted roll for a full two minutes. She is beside herself and emphatic that Miss Bennet has entrapped you. One would have thought you had met with a grievous demise. Not even on Drury Lane have I witnessed such theatrics! It was far too much moaning and fussing to endure. I ordered my trunks packed immediately, and here I am."

Darcy rubbed his brow. He could well imagine Miss Bingley's reaction to his engagement and her abuse of Elizabeth. With any luck they would not cross paths any time soon. He settled into a chair opposite hers beside the fire. "I am afraid Miss Bingley has never warmed to Miss Bennet. I would not call them friends."

Mrs Lawrence snorted indelicately. "I should say not."

Darcy disguised his laugh with a cough. He had never known anyone quite like Bingley's aunt. "Are you alone, Mrs Lawrence, or is the rest of the household in hiding?"

Bingley's aunt grinned. "You find me quite alone. My nephew took the ladies to Oxford Street this afternoon to shop for lace and they have yet to return. Would you care for a cup of tea?"

"I would enjoy a cup of tea, thank you." He was disappointed to hear Elizabeth was not at home but reasoned she must return eventually. With any hope, sooner than later as the sun was beginning to set, and the streets would soon become icy, and, also, because he missed her.

Bingley's aunt poured the tea. "Cream and sugar?"

"No thank you."

"A man after my own heart. I care not for such sweetness in my tea, but I will confess to adding a bit of brandy. Just a splash. I find it a comfort on a cold day such as this one. Would you care for some brandy in your tea? You may have as much as you like. I will be as silent as the grave."

Darcy could not suppress his smile. "Not at the moment, but perhaps I will have some after supper, if you would be so good as to join me."

"I would like nothing better," she insisted, "but I suspect Mrs Bingley might be scandalised if I remained with the men after supper. Your Miss Bennet, on the other hand, is a peach. She procured this bit for me while her sister met with the housekeeper and I daresay no one is the wiser. You should marry her as soon as may be, and I will pay you a visit the following week. Mrs Bingley is a classic beauty and a sweet girl, but Miss Bennet has spirit and a figure that is light and pleasing. I like her prodigiously."

This time Darcy laughed.

⚜

Dinner was an intimate affair with three courses and, to Mrs Lawrence's satisfaction, no separation of the sexes when the dishes were cleared away. Before Darcy could offer his arm to Elizabeth, Bingley's aunt claimed her. She linked their arms together companionably and winked at Darcy, who was relegated to follow behind them as they made their way to the drawing room. Shaking his head, he bypassed the tea things and proceeded to the sideboard, where he poured two glasses of brandy, then joined the ladies.

"Mrs Lawrence," he said, offering her one of the glasses. "I believe you had your heart set on a glass of brandy."

The elder lady's eyes sparkled with pleasure. "You remembered, Mr Darcy. That speaks well for your future as a married man. Miss Bennet is a lucky woman."

He smiled in response and turned to Elizabeth. "Miss Bennet, would you care for a glass as well?"

"I would, thank you. Will you join us?"

Darcy surrendered the other glass to her. "Thank you, yes. If I may be so bold, Miss Bennet, I would like to speak with you later, when you can spare a moment."

Mrs Lawrence, who had taken a sip of her brandy, waved them off. "You need not concern yourself with me. I will be perfectly fine for fifteen minutes without my friend here. I will enjoy my brandy and the company of my new niece." She gave Elizabeth a gentle nudge, encouraging her to rise, and called to Jane. "My dear, do come here and sit with me. I am desperate to hear about your afternoon in Oxford Street. You, too, Charles."

The Bingleys rose to attend Mrs Lawrence and Darcy offered Elizabeth his arm. There was a cosy sofa on the opposite side of the room, and they made their way over to it in companionable silence.

"Mrs Lawrence is a force to be reckoned with," Elizabeth remarked as she sat down, cradling her glass in her hands. "I feel very fortunate that she likes me. I shudder to think what would happen if one incurred her displeasure!"

Darcy settled beside her. "I can only imagine. Mrs Lawrence is quite taken with you, but it is hardly surprising since I am quite taken with you myself."

"As gallant as ever," Elizabeth replied pleasantly. "Did you mean for us to pass the rest of the evening in this delightful manner, or is there some other purpose for your luring me away?" She took a sip of brandy.

"My aunt the Countess of Carlisle paid me a visit this morning. She expressed a desire to make your acquaintance."

"You sound impenetrably grave, sir. Is there more to this visit, pray?"

"I am yet uncertain, but I do not wish to alarm you unnecessarily."

Elizabeth laughed, but it was a nervous laugh. "I am afraid it is a bit late for that. Perhaps you ought to simply say your piece. Even if what you relate is upsetting, I would rather you be honest with me."

Darcy leaned forward and propped his elbows upon his knees. "Very well. I cannot determine whether she is in earnest or whether she has an agenda. Her ladyship said very little when I informed my uncle of our engagement, but she had much to say this morning. She is not an unfeeling woman, but she has decided beliefs and opinions that accompany them. It has long been her wish that I marry the daughter of a particular friend of hers who made her debut last Season. I made it clear to both my uncle and my aunt that would never happen. We have nothing in common and I have never felt an attraction to the young woman. I cannot even say that I like her. She is nothing like you."

"It appears," Elizabeth observed with the hint of an ironic smile, "that all your aunts entertain grand hopes of you either marrying their daughters or the daughters of their friends. I am not surprised. Not only are you exceedingly handsome, but you are also in possession of an abundance of admirable qualities. Surely, someone other than I was bound to appreciate your steadfastness, your caring nature, and the intelligent turn of your mind."

Darcy snorted contemptuously. "You are the only lady of my acquaintance who has ever bothered to look beyond my pocket-book. I am viewed as a commodity, and little more."

"Surely, that is not the case."

"It matters little. There are few in town whom I consider real friends. I had not yet reached my majority when I learnt to guard myself from the machinations of the *ton*. There was little incentive to allow anyone to become more than an acquaintance, particularly those of the fairer sex."

"I cannot imagine how difficult that must have been for you. I am sorry. I fear I gave you little incentive to like me throughout the course of our acquaintance as well. It is a wonder you came to like me at all. That you love me is incredible."

He laid his hand upon her arm, a brief touch where the warmth of her skin presented a stark contrast to the coolness of his own. "No. You are different. After you have spent a Season in town you will likely understand why I found your impertinence so appealing."

Elizabeth nodded absently. Her eyes appeared incredibly dark. She bowed her head and Darcy watched her lashes brush her cheeks. She brought her glass to her lips and took a sip—longer this time, unhurried—and licked the brandy from her lips.

Darcy forced himself to concentrate on the topic at hand before he surrendered to the very ungentlemanly impulse to taste the brandy upon her mouth for himself. "Will you not say something?"

"What would you like me to say? Would you like your aunt to meet me?"

"It is more a question of whether I would like you to meet her. I have no ready answer. If Lady Carlisle were to accept you, it would likely secure your place in London's first circles. But my friends—the few I do have—will undoubtedly appreciate the value of your society and welcome you warmly, regardless of her opinion.

"If she likes you, my aunt's blessing may pave the way with my uncle as well. She is furious with him for something he has done, and he is eager to make amends. She went so far as to threaten to divorce him, though I do not believe that will come to pass. My uncle would never stand for it."

Elizabeth appeared contemplative. "If you do not mind my asking, what has the earl done to anger her to such a degree?"

Darcy shook his head. "Nothing gentlemanly."

"As I am not a gentleman, I require further clarification. I have read my father's books, Fitzwilliam. All of them, even the ones on the top shelf. Would you rather I speculate and arrive at my own conclusion?"

Of course, she would have read every damned book in her father's library. Darcy ran his hand over his eyes as he remembered the argument that they had in Mr Gardiner's study and the look of devastation upon Elizabeth's face when she believed he did not trust her.

His options were clear: he could leave Elizabeth to form her own conclusion and risk her ire, or he could simply tell her the truth. It was one thing for his own stupidity to come between them, Darcy reasoned; it was quite another matter when the stupidity must be attributed to his uncle. Lord Carlisle's indiscretion and lack of decorum had bitten him in the leg and infuriated his wife. Darcy would not permit it to cause discord with Elizabeth as well.

"My uncle keeps a mistress," he said lowly, making a concerted effort to keep his contempt from his voice. "I believe my aunt suspected as much, but he admitted to it the other day. I do not believe she has spoken to him since."

Elizabeth coloured and averted her eyes. "I can certainly understand why she would be upset."

"She is humiliated more than anything. They do not care for each other the way your aunt and uncle Gardiner do. They have very different notions regarding what makes a marriage harmonious."

"But still, Lady Carlisle must have cared for him once. She married him, after all."

"Theirs was not a love match, Elizabeth. It was a union based upon wealth and sanctioned by entitlement, nothing more."

Elizabeth shook her head. "There is always something more where a lady is concerned. They may not have loved each other, but I am certain your aunt would have wanted to be admired by your uncle, even now. It must be a very painful reality for her to discover her husband's admiration lies elsewhere and likely has for some time."

Darcy wondered how she continued to astound him so thoroughly with her perception. She had never met Lady Carlisle, yet Elizabeth was able to feel a compassion towards her person and situation even the countess's family had not.

He thought of his own parents—of their love for each other and the happiness they shared—and felt discomfited and ashamed. Because his aunt and uncle had never treated each other with the same reverence and respect, Darcy had assumed they cared little what the other thought—that they neither valued nor desired the other's admiration. If Elizabeth was correct, his aunt did in fact care what his uncle thought of her, and to learn Lord Carlisle barely thought of her at all must have been nothing short of devastating.

"You are quiet, sir. May I ask what you are thinking?"

"I am thinking how incredibly astute you are, and how utterly wretched my powers of perception have always been. I am ashamed to admit I did not consider my aunt might be heartbroken as well as humiliated. My uncle is the most demanding, condescending, miserable man I have ever known. I never understood how Lady Carlisle could bear being married to him. Perhaps she cares for him in her way. You are correct. She must at least care what he thinks of her."

"I believe I would like to meet her. My curiosity is piqued. If she is horrid, then I shall take my leave of her and go in search of you, so that you can improve my mood using whatever means you see fit."

A slow smile lifted the corners of his mouth. "I believe my means may be different than yours."

A lovely blush appeared upon Elizabeth's countenance, but she smiled despite it. "Perhaps we might compare our methods. I do not anticipate yours being so very different from mine, for in essentials, Mr Darcy, we are much the same."

෧෪ඁ

Darcy had stepped into the hall to order his carriage and was about to return to Elizabeth when Mrs Bingley approached him. He offered her a polite inclination of his head. "Thank you for an enjoyable evening, Mrs Bingley."

"The pleasure is ours," she replied softly, offering him a tentative smile. "Your friendship means the world to my husband."

"Bingley is a dear friend. There is nothing I would not do for him."

She bit her lip, seemingly in indecision. "Mr Darcy," she said hesitantly, "I owe you an apology. I have not been very kind to you, and I am sorry."

Darcy trained his eyes upon the carpet. That she had been unkind to him, he felt, was an understatement. In Hertfordshire, she had been rude, spiteful, and even cruel. But her manner had improved since she had married Bingley, and Darcy's mood had certainly improved since he had become engaged to Elizabeth.

He recalled Elizabeth's tear-stained countenance in Kent every bit as clearly as he did her anger when she berated him for ruining the happiness of her most beloved sister—the sister standing before him now. He had done much to bring pain to both sisters, but disappointing Jane's hopes by separating her from his friend was perhaps the lowest he had sunk. Darcy realised he had much to atone for as well. "I accept your apology, Mrs Bingley, and hope you will be so good as to accept mine."

"I have no idea why you would apologise, sir."

But Darcy could tell by the set of her shoulders and the tightness around her mouth that she did know. "I am sincerely regretful," he told her as he fixed her with a steady, meaningful look, "for any pain I have caused you *and* my friend. I have long been heartily ashamed of myself. It was poorly done. I should never have interfered."

"Oh!" She covered her mouth with her hand.

Darcy was alarmed to see tears in her eyes. "Mrs Bingley, are you unwell? You look very ill."

"I am not," she insisted, shaking her head emphatically. "Indeed, I am not. I am perfectly fine. For the moment I am merely overwhelmed."

They were in the hall and he led her to a small alcove at the end of it, where there was a comfortable chair. He helped her to sit down, then offered to fetch her a glass of water, a glass of wine, a glass of brandy—whatever she desired.

Again, Jane shook her head. "I thank you, Mr Darcy, but I require nothing."

"Are you certain? Will you not permit me to summon your husband? Indeed, you look very ill."

"No," she said, "please do not call for Charles. I do not want to alarm him. I am only...I did not know...that is to say, I appreciate your apology, sir. I always suspected, but I did not know for certain. Charles's going away injured me so very much, but not nearly so much as his staying away."

"I am sorry," Darcy began, "exceedingly sorry—" but she interrupted him.

"Please, do not say anything further." She closed her eyes as though pained. "Elizabeth told me his returning to Hertfordshire was your own doing. She was adamant about it, as adamant as I have ever seen her. I did not want to believe her, Mr Darcy. It would not speak well of Charles, you see, and I love him so much. It was easier, less painful, to imagine that you kept him from me—locked away in London—and that he returned to me of his own volition. In my heart, I believe I have always known that was not the case."

"I can well understand," said Darcy, "how laying blame wholly upon someone else's shoulders can make an agonising situation seem less painful. In this instance, your blame was not entirely misplaced. For the sake of our future happiness, and the happiness of those whom we love, I do hope you can find it within your heart to forgive my offence, if not now, then eventually. We are to be brother and sister. I would be most grateful if we can also be friends."

Jane dabbed at her eyes with her handkerchief and offered Darcy a watery smile. "I have tried before, but my pain was too much, my resentment too great. Now that we have spoken of it and I can see how regretful you are, sir—and how much Lizzy loves you—I believe I shall be better able to put the past behind me and move on. I thank you for your apology, and I accept it. I would like for us to be friends as well."

❧ 25 ❧

WHERE ELIZABETH VISITS DARCY HOUSE AND MUCH HAPPENS.

"What kind of cake did you say you have, Mr Darcy?" Mrs Lawrence asked.

They were in Darcy's coach, on their way to his home in Brook Street. "Rum cake, but I believe my cook mentioned there will be tarts and biscuits as well."

The elder lady's eyes brightened. "I love rum cake," she crooned. "I trust there will be brandy for the tea?"

Darcy inclined his head. "Of course. I would be terribly remiss not to have brandy on hand."

Across from him, Elizabeth grinned as she turned her head aside to look out the window. She was seated beside Bingley's aunt, who had offered herself as their chaperon for the afternoon and into the supper hour. Darcy liked Mrs Lawrence considerably but could not help wondering if he poured half the decanter of brandy into the teapot whether she would be amenable to giving them some time alone.

His carriage turned onto Brook Street and rolled to a stop in front of his house. The door was opened by his footman and Darcy alighted to assist Mrs Lawrence, then Elizabeth from the conveyance. He offered each lady one of his arms and escorted them to the door, which was promptly opened by his butler.

"Welcome home, sir. Lady Carlisle is waiting for you in the drawing room."

Darcy glanced at the Chippendale clock in the foyer and resisted the urge to utter an oath. It was not even half past one o'clock. *Blast that woman for being early when it suited her!* "Thank you, Sowersby." He assisted Mrs Lawrence with her coat, relieved Elizabeth of hers, and handed both to his butler. "Tell her I will be with her shortly."

Sowersby bowed and went off directly while Darcy ushered both ladies towards the solarium at the back of the house. It was a beautiful room with high ceilings comprised of clear glass panels, leaded glass windows, and a marble floor. There was an impressive variety of lush, exotic plants laden with bright, colourful blooms and tantalising fruits. In the centre of the space stood a table draped in crisp, white linen with an assortment of decadent desserts arranged on top of it.

Mrs Lawrence grinned. "Oh, yes. This is just the thing, Mr Darcy. You do know how to please an old woman. Go, sir, and see to your aunt. I will just help myself to some cake. I see you have a pot of tea ready, and look," she remarked with pleasure, "here is the brandy."

Darcy pulled out her chair and helped her to sit. "I am glad you approve," he told her, smiling at her enthusiasm as she reached for the crystal decanter, removed the stopper, and inhaled the brandy's spicy scent.

Mrs Lawrence closed her eyes and sighed contentedly. "Now, this is brandy, sir. My dear Harold would have approved. This is just the sort of stuff he liked. Off you go. You must not keep a countess waiting."

"As you wish. Should you require anything at all, please do not hesitate to ask. The bell pull is by the door. My staff will be most attentive to your desires."

Bingley's aunt, however, was already slicing into the rum cake, her eyes alight, likely in anticipation of its rich, buttery flavour.

Darcy doubted she had heard a word he said. He offered his arm to Elizabeth, and they left to attend Lady Carlisle in the drawing room.

"Do you think she will leave any cake for us?" Elizabeth asked, swaying closer with a diverted smile.

"I cannot say. Perhaps, if we make haste and can get rid of my aunt in good time, we may be able to share the last piece. I would not count on having any brandy, however. Mrs Lawrence is quite the connoisseur."

"Indeed," Elizabeth replied. "She is always in excellent humour, but I do not think it is owed to brandy. She is incredibly astute and wonderful company, and there is never a dull moment when she is near. I am glad she has come to stay in Park Street."

"I am glad you like her." They had nearly reached the drawing room, and Darcy slowed to a stop. He removed Elizabeth's hand from his arm and grasped it between both his own. "Elizabeth," he said. "I feel I must apologise."

"Whatever for?"

Darcy sighed. "I fear my aunt will say something to offend you. Please know you need not remain in her company if she does. We can leave at once and join Mrs Lawrence, or we can go somewhere else. Whatever you like. I will not abide her upsetting you."

"Do you really believe her intent is to be cruel to me?"

Darcy shook his head. "I do not believe so, but she is used to saying whatever is on her mind with little regard for whether or not she causes offence. Only with my uncle does she curb her tongue."

He was surprised to see the corners of her mouth lift with the hint of a smile.

"She sounds much like Lady Catherine. Perhaps it is naïve of me, but I find I am not so intimidated by the idea of Lady Carlisle as I probably ought to be. Let us not keep her waiting any longer. It will only try her patience, and perhaps prolong any unpleasantness should she decide I am entirely unsuitable to be your wife."

She turned towards the drawing room door, but Darcy remained where he was, holding tightly to her hand. "I hope you know her opinion carries no weight with me, not where you are concerned. She can say what she will. There is no lady in all of England who is better suited to me than you."

Without averting her eyes from his, Elizabeth returned to him. "I know, and I am grateful to you for telling me. I hope you know I feel the same. There is no gentleman who has ever made me feel more than you do. Anger or admiration, passion or despair, I have never felt so strongly for another person. I am convinced I never shall."

"When my aunt is gone," he told her, his voice pitched low, "I would very much like to kiss you, Elizabeth."

She closed the distance between them and raised herself on the tips of her toes. "When your aunt is gone," she said, brushing her lips against his jaw, "I believe I may let you."

Lady Carlisle was elegant, far more so than Lady Catherine de Bourgh, but where Lady Catherine's manners were condescending and shrewd, Lady Carlisle's were guarded and cool. Darcy had no sooner introduced them than his aunt took command and ordered him from the room. She would speak to Elizabeth alone.

Darcy protested and Lady Carlisle insisted until Elizabeth grew weary of their wilful banter and encouraged him to attend to Mrs Lawrence instead. He looked at her, questioning with his eyes if his leaving her was truly what she wished. With a slight inclination of her head and what she hoped was a convincing smile, Elizabeth wordlessly told him she would be fine. She could tell by the set of his shoulders and his frowning countenance he was not happy about it, but rather than argue, he bowed to his aunt and kissed Elizabeth's hand. It was a brazen gesture, as possessive as it was intimate. Lady Carlisle rolled her eyes.

Once he had gone, the countess regarded Elizabeth with an indulgent turn of her mouth. "I am gratified to see, Miss Bennet, that you bear no resemblance whatsoever to your cousin Mr Collins. Woe to you if you did, for my fastidious nephew would never have given you a second glance."

Elizabeth would not be intimidated. "I quite agree, your ladyship," she replied. "Mr Darcy barely glanced at me at all when we first met."

Lady Carlisle raised one slender brow. "Is that so?"

"It is," Elizabeth assured her.

"Where was it that you met?"

"We were at an assembly in Hertfordshire."

"Darcy detests assemblies, and most especially country dances. But I suppose, once he had a second look at you, he asked you to stand up with him and there was an end to it."

"He did no such thing. As I said, Mr Darcy barely glanced at me in the first place, so there was little chance of our dancing together."

"So, you did not dance, and he did not speak?"

"On the contrary. I did dance, and from what I saw Mr Darcy did speak to the members of his own party. We did not, however, dance and speak with each other."

"How singular!"

"Hardly, madam. As your nephew did not pay me the least bit of attention and I did not wish him to, the entire business was rather unremarkable."

Lady Carlisle narrowed her eyes. "You have a smart mouth, Miss Bennet. I suppose you inherited your impertinence from your mother."

"My impertinence is entirely my father's influence. I share little in common with my mother. It was my father who saw to my education."

"Your father! How eccentric that your father and not your mother would be bothered with educating you. Surely, he had more pressing matters to attend to than seeing to the education of daughters."

Elizabeth offered her a measured smile.

The countess continued in much the same vein. "Did your mother reject the idea of educating females altogether, or was she simply not inclined to bother?"

"My mother puts little stock in education in general. As she has five daughters and no sons, she is far more concerned with our marrying well than whether any of us had an inclination for learning. She is not fond of reading and therefore does not comprehend the benefit of improving one's circumstances by the acquisition of knowledge."

"And I suppose you disagree with her," Lady Carlisle replied coolly.

"On many counts."

"My word, but you give your opinions very freely for one so young! I suppose you write poetry, stage performances for your friends, and consider painting tables and speaking French dull."

"While I enjoy reading poetry, I neither write, nor act, nor do I claim a talent for painting. I spend much of my time out of doors. I walk and I read and, when the horses can be spared, I ride. If the weather is disagreeable, I attend to my embroidery and play the pianoforte. My father has a well-appointed library and I have always had access to it. I learned Latin when I was quite young."

"Latin!"

Elizabeth suppressed an amused smile. "I have always found Latin fascinating, and far more useful than French. Of course, should Napoleon conquer England, which I believe is implausible at present, I will likely come to regret my neglect of the modern languages. It would be most inconvenient, would it not, to be under French rule and yet unable to speak a word of French."

"Are you a bluestocking, Miss Bennet?" the countess demanded in alarm, her hand fluttering to her neck.

"No, your ladyship," Elizabeth told her, resisting the urge to laugh at the scandalised expression upon her countenance, "but

I am of the opinion that if women possess a greater capacity for sensibility, compassion, and virtue than men, surely we must also possess an aptitude for academic enlightenment."

Lady Carlisle frowned. "Were you educated at a seminary in town?"

"I was not."

"Did you have a governess?"

"I did not."

"Hmph," was all her ladyship had to say in response. She scrutinised Elizabeth for several moments, then said, "Tell me what you thought of my nephew when you first saw him."

Elizabeth raised one finely arched brow. "Not much, madam."

"Oh, come now," said the countess crisply. "Darcy is handsome and rich! Surely you were taken with him."

"Handsome though Mr Darcy may be, I can assure you that I was quite perturbed with him. Any lady would be had he proclaimed her 'not handsome enough' to tempt him."

"He said that to you!" Lady Carlisle exclaimed, and to her credit, she appeared truly horrified to have received such a shocking account of her nephew.

"Mr Darcy was speaking to his friend, but his voice carried over the din of the musicians. As I happened to be sitting nearby, I overheard his comment. I am afraid it could not be avoided."

"But that does not sound like Darcy at all! I have never heard him mention a young woman by name in public, nor openly criticise one! I trust he was mortified his comment had been overheard and apologised at once."

"He did not," Elizabeth replied. "In fact, I did not receive an apology for his remark until recently."

"Did he not slight you when you *first* knew him?"

"He did."

The countess appeared genuinely confused. "Yet he did not apologise until now?"

"That is correct."

"And you have known one another for a year at least?"

"A little longer than a year, yes."

"And in all that time, Miss Bennet," Lady Carlisle proclaimed incredulously, "my nephew did not see fit to apologise to you at all!"

"It does appear that way."

"That is very singular behaviour! Very singular indeed!"

Elizabeth could tell the countess was extremely displeased, though whether the source of her displeasure was owed to Elizabeth's frankness or Darcy's ill manners she could only speculate. She offered a polite inclination of her head. "Mr Darcy is a very singular gentleman, your ladyship."

"This business is quite distressing! But tell me, Miss Bennet. My nephew informed me that he proposed to you once before. Is that correct?"

"It is."

"He also claims you refused him, but that cannot be right."

"I assure you it is true. As you must know, Mr Darcy abhors deceit of any kind. There is nothing to be gained by his lying about my refusal of his proposal, though one might wonder why he mentioned it in the first place."

Lady Carlisle appeared thunderstruck. "Why on earth would you refuse such an offer?"

"I am afraid Mr Darcy's proposal left much to be desired."

"Left much to be desired?" she repeated dubiously. "It *was* a proposal of marriage, Miss Bennet, was it not?"

Elizabeth pursed her lips. "Yes."

"Then I fail to see the problem. Did you not comprehend the honour my nephew had bestowed upon you by asking for your hand?"

"I was not insensible of it. Quite the opposite. I assure you Mr Darcy's first proposal would have been received far more favourably had I actually liked him."

"You did not like him?" The countess's tone revealed the utmost astonishment.

"No, I did not."

Lady Carlisle stared at Elizabeth as though she had never seen anyone quite like her in the entire course of her life. "You did not like him? You did not like him at all? Not even a little bit?"

"I did not. In fact, I considered Mr Darcy the last man in the world I could ever be prevailed upon to marry."

"I find that positively shocking!"

"As you say, Lady Carlisle."

"But you like him now, Miss Bennet. You like him and want to marry him."

"Very much," Elizabeth told her warmly, unable to repress her smile. "I have found Mr Darcy improves upon further acquaintance."

Lady Carlisle shook her head as though to clear it. "How much of an acquaintance?" she demanded, and in her tone, Elizabeth not only heard a note of accusation, but a hint of smugness as well. "Darcy is very rich and owns a vast deal of property. Pemberley is one of the finest estates in all of Derbyshire. Surely, you are not ignorant of its existence. Is that what changed your mind about marrying my nephew? His estate? His wealth? The pin money and notoriety you will surely have as his wife?"

Elizabeth's smile slipped from her face. That his aunt could so easily overlook the richness of Darcy's character while championing his worldly riches pained her. For the first time during their exchange, Elizabeth felt affronted rather than entertained by the countess's manner. "I have had the pleasure of visiting Pemberley, Lady Carlisle. It is certainly not without its charm, but as I am sure *you* must know, there is far more to Mr Darcy than his estate, his income, and his handsome figure. He is warm and caring and the most honourable man I have ever known. Had I met him at Pemberley, I believe I would have loved him far sooner. Not because of his stately house or beautiful grounds, but because it was at Pemberley where I first had the pleasure of seeing him completely at ease."

"Enough." It was one word, uttered quietly but with an unmistakable air of authority.

Elizabeth felt a wave of relief. Darcy was striding towards them from across the room, his footsteps echoing upon the pristine marble floor. She was startled to see his eyes were fixed upon her, not his aunt, and that his expression was not only open, but fervent and tender.

Lady Carlisle sat a little taller in her chair. "Darcy. It appears Miss Bennet has quite a talent for putting words in your mouth. I recognised the foundation of the speech you gave the other day in hers just now. It cannot be a coincidence."

He claimed a seat beside Elizabeth, then shifted his focus to the countess. "It is no coincidence."

"She claims to know you well, Nephew."

"Except for Bingley and Fitzwilliam, there is no one who knows me better."

"I cannot pretend to know anything of Mr Bingley's powers of discernment," said Lady Carlisle to Elizabeth with a haughty air, "but my second son and Darcy have always been extremely close. Richard speaks highly of you, Miss Bennet. It should come as no surprise to hear he was quite taken with you last Easter when you met at Rosings. I daresay he admired you so much that, had he his brother's fortune, he might very well have proposed to you himself." She cast an artful glance at Darcy and folded her hands primly upon her lap.

Darcy stared at her. His shock was clearly displayed upon his countenance. Obviously, his aunt's design had been to discompose him. It appeared she had succeeded.

It was Elizabeth who responded. "While I am flattered Colonel Fitzwilliam thinks highly of me," she said, her voice a combination of archness and sweetness, "I happen to know his friendship with Mr Darcy runs deeper. He and I were not thrown together so much as your ladyship seems to believe. You have quite mistaken the matter."

Lady Carlisle offered her a small, conciliatory smile. "Perhaps I have," she replied. She looked at Elizabeth then—really looked at her—and raised her chin. "You are not at all what I expected, Miss Bennet. I will admit I was not pleased when I heard Darcy had chosen you. I thought he was acting the fool, fancying himself in love, and throwing himself away on an unknown country girl of little consequence. I did not believe you could honestly love him, and I certainly did not think it was possible he could really love you. How could he?"

"Lady Carlisle," Darcy warned, "I did not introduce you to Miss Bennet so you could disparage and insult her. Yesterday, you gave me reason to hope you were truly interested in knowing her. I see I have mistaken your intent."

"You have mistaken nothing," the countess replied. "Calm down."

Darcy glared at her. "After the inquisition Miss Bennet was subjected to just now, and the blatant insinuations you made at my expense, I do not know how to believe you. You have failed to show even an ounce of kindness to her."

"Kindness?" Lady Carlisle repeated. Both her tone and expression hardened. "You expected kindness? Do you think the society matrons who had their eyes on you for their daughters will be kind? Do you think Lady Harrow will be kind? Or your uncle? You are naïve if you think they will feel anything less than resentment towards your choice."

"I gave none of them any indication I favoured their daughters," Darcy said heatedly. "Especially Lady Harrow. I gave Lady Eliza no encouragement, paid her no notice! In fact, I never showed any lady even a modicum of preference, not once!"

Elizabeth laid her hand upon his arm. It was nothing more than a fleeting touch given with the intent to soothe Darcy's temper. While she understood his anger, she also understood the importance he had long placed on his family connexions. She saw no reason for him to be at odds with his aunt as well as his uncle if it could be avoided.

"That may be," said Lady Carlisle as she observed Elizabeth with an indecipherable expression, "but you are in London, Darcy, not Derbyshire. There is a pecking order, and there are certain expectations attached to it. Lady Harrow was not pleased to see you arrive at Covent Garden with a mysterious, beautiful young woman on your arm. While you were making love to Miss Bennet in Hertfordshire, Lady Harrow spent a vast deal of time intimating that you admired her daughter above everyone's. Our entire circle heard her insinuations, just as they saw where your admiration truly lies—quite obviously not with Eliza. Everyone is talking about it. There was mention of it in the paper. Lady Harrow is livid."

"Let her be livid, then. She is a hateful, scheming woman. It is high time she learned that just because she wants something does not mean she will have it, most especially where I am concerned. Considering my total lack of interest in her daughter's society—and hers for that matter—it should come as no surprise to either that I have chosen a wife elsewhere. Lady Harrow ought to have kept her tongue in her mouth. This situation is entirely of her own making. Whether she is mortified or furious, I care not."

"You ought to care, Nephew! Lady Harrow is not to be trifled with. She can be quite mean-spirited when she sets her mind to it. I ought to know. I have seen what she is capable of—how she thinks, how she acts."

"As have I," Darcy muttered.

Lady Carlisle looked disapprovingly at him. "However poorly Lady Harrow treats others, she has been my friend for many years. But you are my nephew, my family. Blood will always be thicker than the diaphanous bonds of friendship."

Making a show of adjusting the lace on her sleeves, her ladyship proclaimed, "I care for Eliza and want to see her well settled, but not at the expense of your own happiness and prosperity. Despite any hope I once harboured that you would marry her, I now see I would be doing you both a disservice were I to continue to promote a match between you. Miss Bennet suits you in ways dear Eliza never shall. I would rather see you married to a clever young woman who genuinely likes you and makes you happy than saddled with an immature young girl whom you cannot respect, and whose ignorance of the world will only incite your ire. Believe me when I tell you that a union without respect for one's spouse is no way to pass your life."

Lady Carlisle returned her attention to Elizabeth. She appeared to hesitate, then squared her shoulders. "I was not disposed to like you when I first learned of your existence, Miss Bennet. Then I saw you at the theatre. Darcy was smiling at you, and you said something that made him laugh. He looked into your eyes. He touched your hair. It was clear to me that he was besotted with you. It was entirely out of character for him to behave in such a forward manner in public. I was shocked, as was everyone who saw you together."

Her ladyship's gaze had grown intense, so intense that Elizabeth found herself resisting the urge to fidget. She folded her hands upon her lap instead, raised her chin, and looked Darcy's aunt in the eye.

"It was necessary to take your measure," the countess insisted. "I needed to see what you are made of, so when the naysayers do all in their power to test your mettle, you will not only know how to handle them, but you will also do so with dignity and poise. If you are to be Pemberley's new mistress, you have much to learn, though perhaps not quite so much as I had originally feared."

❧ 26 ❧

WHERE MRS LAWRENCE NAPS VERY SOUNDLY,
AND MR DARCY GIVES ELIZABETH A TOUR OF
THE HOUSE.

Lady Carlisle stayed above two hours with them, taking
tea in the solarium with Mrs Lawrence, whose sunny
disposition thawed the countess's cool demeanour
considerably within half an hour of their meeting. Her ladyship
had warmed to Elizabeth as well and was disposed towards
conversation, a rarity in Darcy's experience. She spoke of going
to Covent Garden, of the actors and the performance, as well as
Colonel Fitzwilliam's pleasure at being included in Darcy's
party and the enjoyment he received from making Mrs
Lawrence's acquaintance. Apparently, Elizabeth was not the
only lady whom Fitzwilliam had spoken of so highly.

Though it was not four o'clock, Darcy took a leaf out of Mrs
Lawrence's book and poured a bit of brandy in his tea when the
subject shifted to Rosings. As he listened to his aunt recite his
cousin's glowing commendation of Elizabeth's virtues, he
wondered whether much of what she related was calculated to
provoke a reaction from him. That Fitzwilliam not only liked,
but esteemed Elizabeth in Kent was no secret; but had he truly

entertained the idea of marrying her? The possibility made Darcy's stomach lurch unpleasantly.

Lady Carlisle glanced at him from the corner of her eye with a sly turn of her mouth and raised her teacup to her lips. Her smile, though rare, appeared identical to her second son's. *I will be damned,* Darcy thought as he shook his head at her antics, thoroughly baffled by such blithe behaviour from such a dour woman. She was teasing him, much like he knew Fitzwilliam would be if he were present. Though Darcy had always known his cousin's light-heartedness did not come from the earl, he was startled by the revelation that Fitzwilliam's uncanny ability to torment him might have come from the countess.

It was in that moment Darcy realised his jealousy was not only misplaced, but entirely unfounded. His cousin would never injure him by declaring himself to Elizabeth—not then, and certainly not now. He was the one who suggested Darcy return to Hertfordshire and follow his heart. Aside from Bingley, he was Darcy's oldest and dearest friend—his most beloved cousin and truest confidant. No one knew him better, nor was there another person he trusted more. Could he fault Fitzwilliam for being attracted to Elizabeth? Could he resent him for admiring her intelligent nature and generous heart? Darcy looked to the woman he loved and was startled to see her dark eyes gazing back at him. She raised one slender brow, a gesture Darcy interpreted as a silent enquiry as to whether he was well. He answered her with a reassuring turn of his mouth. He was fine. In fact, he had never been better.

Elizabeth ran her fingers lovingly over the polished ivory keys of the pianoforte as Darcy watched from across the room. "It is a beautiful instrument," she said softly, almost reverently.

You are beautiful, he thought with equal reverence. The words were on the tip of his tongue, but instead of allowing them to escape he kept them to himself.

"Miss Darcy is correct. You are a most generous and considerate brother."

Darcy wanted to tell her she was mistaken, that if he had truly been a considerate brother, he would have kept Georgiana with him instead of procuring an establishment for her in London, hiring an unsuitable companion for her, and allowing her to be taken to Ramsgate where she was preyed upon by Wickham. He cast his eyes upon the floor, studied the pattern of the carpet, and concentrated on keeping those words to himself as well. He would not ruin this precious time alone with Elizabeth by broaching a subject that would afford neither of them any satisfaction.

"Will you play something for me?" he asked instead. He required a distraction, and it had been far too long since he had the pleasure of hearing her play.

To his delight, Elizabeth smiled at him. "If you wish," she replied, settling herself upon the smooth, polished bench, "but I am afraid my performance will be a sad substitute for your sister's exceptional abilities, for I do not play half so well as Miss Darcy."

Darcy claimed a seat upon the couch to her left, where he could better admire her figure and the delicate profile of her face. "You undervalue your own talent. I have always thought you play remarkably well. I have never found anything lacking in your performance."

"You are too kind, sir," she said lightly, "no doubt because you are biased. But I shall accept your generous compliments in any case, if for no reason other than they gratify my vanity." She glanced at him with an impish gleam in her eyes. "Now, what would you like me to play?"

Darcy shook his head, the corners of his mouth lifting with a smile. "Anything. Whatever you wish, Elizabeth."

She chose Mozart—the twenty-first piano concerto. It was light and pleasing, so much like Elizabeth, Darcy decided. He let the music wash over him and felt himself relax in a way he had not been capable of in a very long time; not since the summer when she had been with him at Pemberley. Having Elizabeth in his home again—hearing her play his instrument so beautifully—stirred feelings and emotions that went far beyond the physical. Darcy's pleasure in having her with him this way was spiritual. It was transcendent. He closed his eyes. If he were to die right now, he would die a happy man, knowing he had everything he could possibly desire in life: Elizabeth, happy. Elizabeth, in love with him.

She played for half an hour, her fingers moving over the keys with energy and grace. When she had done, he rose from his seat and applauded.

Elizabeth blushed. "You are far too generous."

"I am nothing of the sort," he assured her, extending his hand.

She accepted it and permitted him to assist her as she rose from the bench. "You most certainly are, sir, and therefore, far too partial to mention my flaws."

"While I admit to being far too taken with you," he confessed, "I certainly cannot find it within me to repine it. You have no flaws."

She laughed. "So, I am a woman without flaws! That is unlikely. No one is without flaws, though I am exceedingly flattered you are gentlemanly enough to take it upon yourself to ignore mine."

"I stand by my opinion, but I will not quarrel with you. We must agree to disagree." He ran his thumb across the back of her hand, a slow caress, and watched her eyelids flutter. In that moment he dearly wanted to kiss her, but feared once he started, he would not be able to stop. Elizabeth had referred to his conduct as gentlemanly. He would adhere to it.

A change of venue was in order. "You have seen the solarium," he told her, "the drawing room, the dining room, and the music room, but you have yet to see the rest of the house. Allow me to show it to you before Mrs Lawrence awakens from her nap and demands more tea." He raised her hand to his lips and then, rather than place her hand upon his arm, linked their fingers together and tugged her towards the door.

Darcy led her into the main foyer, where a wide, sweeping staircase rose to the second floor. He escorted her up the carpeted steps, through a long gallery containing numerous portraits of his ancestors, and into the guest wing, where he proceeded to throw open the doors and name every room depending upon what he found inside: the blue room, the yellow room, the green room, the room with the enormous chandelier.

After what seemed to Darcy an indeterminable length of time, they entered another corridor, more secluded than the first, which contained the family's private apartments. He bypassed each one without opening any of the doors until he approached the mistress's apartment. Drawing a fortifying breath, he turned the gleaming brass handle, opened the door, and stepped aside so Elizabeth could enter.

It had been a long time since he had been in these rooms. Though they were tastefully decorated, there was no question in his mind they needed to be updated. "Once we are married, these rooms will become yours. You can do anything you like to them. You can order new furniture, window dressings, paper for the walls, anything you desire."

They were in a finely appointed sitting room with pale green and ivory papered walls, elegant but comfortable furnishings, and a well-stocked bookcase that lined the entire length of the room, save for the marble fireplace situated in its midst. Elizabeth smiled at the sight of so many books. Darcy smiled as well, both upon seeing her pleasure, and the recollection of his own enjoyment of the room. He had passed many pleasant afternoons here as a young boy, curled upon the couch as he and his mother read companionably together. He imagined Elizabeth doing the same with their children, perhaps even with him.

The double doors leading to the bedchamber were open and he noticed she had paused at the threshold. He joined her, then hesitated for a moment before he placed his hand upon the small of her back and guided her through the doorway.

The bed was large, with delicately carved spindles set between rich, burled maple posts. Elizabeth ran her hands over the intricately embroidered counterpane. "It is lovely," she said softly. "Everything is lovely." She proceeded to the window, brushed the heavy drapes and sheer lace curtains aside, and peered through the glass.

The mistress's chamber overlooked the garden, barren now that winter had tightened its hold upon the natural world. Fat drops of icy rain splattered the windows, the sides of the house, and the ground below. "In the springtime there are tulips there," Darcy said, pointing to a spot on the far side of the space, "and irises and hyacinths there. In the summer months several varieties of roses climb the trellis and lilies bloom near the fountain. The fragrance is heavenly."

"I can well imagine. Do you spend much time in town in the summer?"

"No. It is often too hot and disagreeable to remain if there is no need to do so. As lovely as this garden is when it blooms, I promise you Pemberley's gardens are ten times more beautiful."

"I remember," she said with a wistful smile. "I confess I am looking forward to seeing Pemberley again. It was stunning in summer, but I imagine it must be equally magical in winter."

"It is lonely," Darcy remarked, thinking of the endless days confined indoors with only Georgiana for company, to say nothing of the long, cold nights. "This year will be very different, though. I will have a beautiful, impertinent wife to entertain me." The corners of his mouth turned upward.

"So, you shall, and I will have a handsome husband to keep me well occupied. I imagine we shall think of many ways to pass our time most pleasantly, particularly in the evenings."

Not for the first time that afternoon did Darcy feel a powerful inclination to kiss her. Instead, he indicated a painting that hung above one of the chests of drawers in a gilded frame. It was a landscape—Pemberley at dawn—that was both expertly and beautifully executed by a local artist from Lambton.

Elizabeth recognised the prospect at once. "This is wonderful. One can almost feel the mist as it rises from the lawn, the crisp morning air of the park. That I will be so fortunate to see this prospect—both real and imagined—nearly every day as your wife brings me such joy. Thank you," she said feelingly. Standing upon the tips of her toes, she placed her hand along his jaw and pressed a kiss to his cheek. "Thank you for choosing me, for loving me, for wanting to share your life with me."

Darcy's eyes closed of their own volition. He was nearly overcome by the sweetness of her kiss. It was not a lover's kiss by any means but innocent and gentle, wrapped in a sincerity he was not used to receiving from anyone other than Georgiana.

He took a moment to steady himself. His impulse to return her kiss with one far less innocent, but no less heartfelt, warred with his determination to remain a gentleman.

Her hand slipped from his face. Beside him, he heard a door handle turn, the quiet swish of Elizabeth's gown, and then silence. Darcy opened his eyes and saw he was not only alone, but that the door to the master's chamber had been opened.

"Elizabeth," he murmured, and hastened after her.

She had not ventured far but far enough for the situation to stray from improper to wholly inappropriate. Darcy's breath caught as he beheld her, standing beside his bed as though she were temptation incarnate. He could see nothing beyond her delicate femininity in his masculine space—the utter loveliness of the pale pink muslin of her gown against the deep, midnight blue backdrop of his counterpane, his dark, richly papered walls, and the soft, luxurious pile of his Persian carpet. In fact, Elizabeth's gown perfectly matched the roses in the crystal vases his housekeeper had placed upon the bedside table, the chest of drawers, and the small mahogany table by the hearth.

Darcy's throat felt conspicuously tight. If it had been imprudent for him to accompany her into the mistress's chamber without a chaperon, being alone with her in his own bedchamber was a thousand times worse.

With a heavy exhalation he stepped forward, but advanced no more than a few paces before he forced himself to stop. The scent of roses permeated the air, hitting Darcy with the force of a thunderclap. He swallowed thickly, realising too late the scene before him was far too reminiscent of his dreams for him to remain in this room with Elizabeth and keep a level head. Agitated, he raked his hands through his hair, only to realise they were shaking. He uttered a quiet oath. He had no idea what to do.

Elizabeth had barely moved.

Like the heady, fragrant air of the room, the cravat about his neck threatened to suffocate him. "You should not be here." His voice sounded rough to his own ears. He could only imagine how it must sound to hers.

"Forgive me," she stammered. She turned to face him but did not meet his eyes. "I had no idea that door led to your private rooms, sir. If I had known I never would have presumed…"

"I am at fault, Miss Bennet." He dared not call her by her name. Not here, not now. Calling her by her name would only further enflame his ardour and give voice to his wildest, basest fantasy. He was terrified that at any minute he might throw off every ounce of gentlemanly restraint he possessed and give in to his desire to enfold her in his arms, lay her upon his bed, and taste every inch of her skin as he made passionate love to her. "I should have told you where that door leads. I should have been more attentive." Darcy hardly knew how he was capable of speech.

Without meaning to, his eyes settled upon the neckline of Elizabeth's gown. The heated blush upon her countenance had spread lower, and Darcy realised the lovely flush of colour upon her otherwise pale skin likely encompassed her entire body. It was a detail that did nothing to ease his discomfort; it only served to make his situation worse.

She raised her eyes and regarded him from beneath her lashes— so long and lovely and dark—and Darcy's equanimity slipped further. "Excuse me," he rasped, then turned abruptly on his heel and strode from the room.

❧ 27 ❧

WHERE IT RAINS VERY HARD, AND EVERYONE IS FEELING HUNGRY.

E lizabeth released her hold upon the lovely blue and white floral curtains and turned away from the bedchamber window. The stirring of cool air as they fluttered closed encouraged her to move towards the warmth of the fire. When the rain had turned to ice shortly after the supper hour, Darcy's housekeeper had prepared the blue room for her—a delightful confection of pale blue velvet, white damask, and fragrant white roses. Unlike the mistress's chamber, no bookshelves adorned its walls. For one whose animated thoughts made finding sleep impossible, it was the worst sort of inconvenience.

With a resigned sigh, Elizabeth donned her robe and wrapped a shawl around her shoulders. If there was no book within her rooms to assist her in finding repose, she would have to go in search of one. Though she had yet to see evidence of a library, Elizabeth could not imagine Darcy living without a well-established, varied collection of titles in his London residence. She determined to discover it. Borrowing a book from the mistress's chamber was out of the question.

After retrieving a candle from the bedside table, Elizabeth slipped into the hall. She had no sooner shut the door behind her when she felt a hand upon her arm.

"Good evening, Miss Bennet," said Mrs Lawrence in a hushed voice. "How wonderful it is to see you about as well—and with a candle, too! If you do not mind, I could use your assistance finding the kitchen. I have my heart set on some of that magnificent chocolate cake that was served for dessert."

The candle sputtered, then flared as Elizabeth expelled a startled breath of air. The last thing she expected at such a late hour was to meet with someone else and had nearly screamed with fright. "I did not expect you, Mrs Lawrence. You gave me quite a shock!"

"Oh, dear. I am terribly sorry to have scared you." She relieved Elizabeth of her candle, linked their arms together, and proceeded to lead her towards the sweeping staircase at the end of the hall. "This is such a beautiful house, but I find it confusing. I am all turned around, but so I always am whenever I spend the night in a home other than my own. I suppose it is all part of the adventure."

"It *is* a beautiful house," Elizabeth agreed as her racing heart slowed to a gallop.

"And it is to be your home very soon. What a fortunate young woman you are, Miss Bennet. In addition to being mistress of all this, you will have a dashing husband with whom to weather life's storms. He was especially quiet this evening, but so many young gentlemen shoulder much in the way of responsibility these days. I daresay he will speak when he is of a mind to do so. Still waters, if you will remember, my dear. Your Mr Darcy is no shallow wading pool. He is an ocean with complex currents and fathomless depths." Her eyes appeared to twinkle in the candlelight. "I certainly hope you can swim!"

The hint of a smile played at the corners of Elizabeth's mouth. It was not the first time Bingley's aunt had compared Darcy to the sea, nor the first time Elizabeth thought such an analogy was fitting. She was hard-pressed to name a more complex man than her future husband. Though he had by no means lost his penchant for seriousness, little by little Darcy's staunch reserve was dissolving, revealing a softer, more playful side he rarely showed to others. Whenever they were together—and most especially when they were alone—Darcy not only appeared much at ease, but truly happy.

Elizabeth had been happy as well, but upon entering Darcy's private apartment that afternoon, the ease and general light-heartedness that had developed between them since their engagement had been altered. Had she an inkling of what awaited her on the other side of that door Elizabeth would never have opened it in the first place. What Darcy must have thought of her brazenness! She should not have been ignorant of a husband's requisite for a private entrance to his wife's bedchamber, but it appeared she was precisely that ignorant. Darcy's admonishment had left Elizabeth mortified, but when he quit the room, she had wanted to weep. By the time she felt mistress enough of herself to follow him, Darcy was nowhere to be found. A full hour passed until she saw him again, and then only in the presence of Mrs Lawrence. Though he had gazed at Elizabeth near constantly, each time their eyes met, he quickly turned his head aside and proceeded to focus his attention on any object other than herself.

Supper had been a quiet affair. Darcy was subdued and distracted and offered little in the way of conversation besides the usual courtesies and polite observations. Fortunately, Mrs Lawrence spoke enough for all of them and managed to carry the weight of their conversation through three courses. Elizabeth contributed what she could of her share, but Darcy proved far more introspective than he was talkative. Elizabeth could not help drawing an almost identical comparison between this version of him and the sedate, brooding version she had originally known when they had first met in Hertfordshire more than a year ago. It pained her to think he was so shocked by her entering his rooms and so affronted by her intrusion upon his privacy that he could not stand to speak to her.

Elizabeth had passed the remainder of the evening in distracted conversation with Mrs Lawrence while attempting to embroider a pair of gloves but was so distressed by Darcy's withdrawal that most of her time was spent tearing out her uneven stitches. Though Darcy had joined them in the drawing room for coffee and dessert, he kept to the opposite side of the room attending to his correspondence; in actuality, Elizabeth noted he spent far more time staring into the fire than writing his letters. Not only was she confused and hurt by his continued silence and the distance he appeared intent upon putting between them, but frustrated as well. She had made an innocent mistake and, though she desperately wanted to rectify it, had no idea how to accomplish such a task without equal cooperation from Darcy. To resolve the matter, they must first speak; yet he appeared intent on avoidance.

Shaking off her melancholy ruminations, Elizabeth addressed Mrs Lawrence with an air of forced cheerfulness. "You need not concern yourself with me. I learned how to swim even before I knew how to walk. I shall keep afloat, even if my future husband's countenance was so very grave this evening."

"I suspect Mr Darcy is a man of deep feeling, but you shall succeed in teasing him out of his sombre mood before long. Keep in mind that men like to do things in their own time, and the good ones never do anything by halves. We women must simply indulge them and give them what they desire most—a safe harbour and a calm port when the weight of the world weighs too heavily upon their shoulders."

"You are very wise. I hope someday to have your good sense, as well as your keen powers of observation."

"And so, you shall, my dear. Many years of marriage to a wonderful, caring, ardent man will do wonders for a woman's powers of perception, to say nothing of the acquisition of patience! My Harold was the best thing that ever happened to me. I almost married a viscount, you know, but it was Harold I loved, and so I accepted him without a moment's hesitation. If given the chance, I would not choose to do even one thing differently. I could live a thousand lifetimes and still I would marry my dear Harold every time. Besides," she whispered conspiratorially, "he was an eager, indulgent lover, and quite accomplished in the romantic arts."

Elizabeth felt a flush of heat, though she doubted her companion noticed her blushing countenance in the dim interior of the hall. She could not help herself—she laughed. "Forgive me. I have no idea what is considered a proper response to such a bold statement."

"You need say nothing at all. I daresay you shall take my meaning in a few weeks' time." Her grin was cheeky as she held the candle aloft. "Mr Darcy," she said warmly, startling Elizabeth. "We are very glad to have found you! Miss Bennet and I are in search of some cake and have become hopelessly lost. Will you not be a dear and escort us to the kitchen?"

It seemed almost impossible that they would come upon him now, but there was no denying Darcy was in fact standing before them. He carried no candle to light his way, but Elizabeth was able to see his eyes widen almost comically by the light of theirs. His surprise at meeting with her was evident in his every feature.

"Of course," he replied after a moment of stunned silence, stepping aside so Elizabeth and Mrs Lawrence could pass. "I am glad to be of service. This way if you please."

⚜

After two pieces of cake, a pot of tea, and what equated to a glass of brandy, Mrs Lawrence was finally sated and announced her intention to return to her apartment.

At once, Darcy pushed his chair away from the table and stood to attend her.

"Oh, there is no need for all of us to go, Mr Darcy. I believe I saw a footman in the foyer above stairs who should prove quite useful in the event I lose my way. No doubt the young fellow could use a bit of employment. It will keep him on his toes. No, sir, you stay right here with Miss Bennet and finish your brandy. Have a nice little chat and we shall see each other in the morning."

Elizabeth watched, dumbstruck, as Bingley's aunt looked meaningfully in her direction, collected her candle, and bustled out of the kitchen, leaving them alone. She opened her mouth to protest, but it was too late. Mrs Lawrence had already gone.

Elizabeth glanced at Darcy and saw that he had not only reclaimed his chair but had raised his glass to his lips and was draining its contents. When he had done, he discarded his empty glass upon the table, shook his head with a rueful laugh, and cradled his head in his hands.

"Bingley's aunt is as charming as she is entertaining, but a most neglectful chaperon. Forgive me. I should have arranged for your sister to join us today as well, but I did not wish to take her from Bingley during their honeymoon. I had not even thought to ask Mrs Gardiner until this evening and by then it was too late."

Elizabeth's heart sank. "I am sorry that you feel as if I have inconvenienced you today, sir. I will importune you no more. Goodnight." Irritation was at war with her disappointment as she rose from the table and made to leave. Darcy's hand upon her arm prevented her progress.

"You mistake my meaning."

"Today, it seems I have made many mistakes," she replied stiffly, "and though I wish I could go back in time and undo them, I do not possess that power. I can only assure you what has been done was done in error, not on purpose. There was no calculated intent."

"You have done nothing wrong."

"Obviously, sir, I have. You are dissatisfied with me."

"I am not dissatisfied with you," he said exasperatedly. "I find myself in uncharted waters. I have no idea what I am doing, Elizabeth. I only know that being alone with you—here, in my house, but more particularly in my *bedchamber*—has both tempted and tested my resolve beyond what I feel I am presently capable of enduring. I cannot deny I have handled the situation poorly. I ought to have sought you out afterwards instead of avoiding you, but I did not. It was unpardonably rude of me, and I am sorry. I should not have hidden myself away."

"You are still hiding, sir. You have not looked upon me once since we entered this room."

Darcy laughed without humour. "Of course, I have not. You are wholly indecent. If I were to look upon you now, I fear my self-control would fail me utterly. It is hanging by a thread as it is."

She bowed her head and examined her appearance as well as she could, and saw she was wearing a nightshift, a robe, and a shawl. All belonged to Miss Darcy. Elizabeth was horrified. How on earth had she become so distracted as to have forgotten she was dressed for bed and not for dinner?

"So, I am," she conceded miserably as a fresh wave of mortification surfaced. She tugged her shawl more securely about her shoulders and attempted to tame the unruly mass of curls spilling down her back. "It appears I am destined to behave in the most inappropriate manner imaginable today. Again, this was not my intent."

"I know. And again, it is I—not you—who have behaved inappropriately. If you knew my innermost thoughts you would not remain a moment longer in my house, never mind in my presence."

"And what do you suggest we do to remedy that, sir, for I find myself in uncharted waters as well."

"I hardly know, but for the moment I would give anything to hear you play for me again. Perhaps I might then be able to sleep once we part for the night."

His eyes sought hers, and he sighed as though in resignation. "While it is my intent to remain a gentleman, I fear I am in no state of mind to ensure such a promise at present. You are an enchantress—an enticing nymph—and I am bewitched. As I look at you, I am reminded of Walter Scott's *The Lady of the Lake*. I have long considered you the handsomest woman of my acquaintance, but tonight you exceed my fantasies. I have longed to see your hair loose and tumbling past your shoulders almost as long as I have desired to kiss you."

Elizabeth felt a flush of heat upon her countenance and bit her lip. She desperately wanted to tell him he was welcome to kiss her, but the look in his eyes—a combination of blatant desire and self-conflagration—caused her to refrain from issuing such a forward invitation, especially after the emotional turmoil of the afternoon. They were in dangerous territory, and though a part of her craved the reassurance of Darcy's tender attentions, another part warned her to proceed with caution. Instead of provoking him, she settled for reciting several lines from Scott's poem:

> "'I ne'er before, believe me, fair,
> Have ever drawn your mountain air,
> Till on this lake's romantic strand,
> I found a fey in faerie land'."

Darcy swallowed audibly. "You know it."

"It is a favourite of mine. My father was fortunate enough to procure a copy last year for his collection and I have since read it more times than I can count."

He raised his hand and tenderly brushed a wayward curl from her cheek. "Come," he said softly, and took her hand in his, pressing a lingering kiss to her fingertips.

Hand in hand, they made their way to the music room and entered. Darcy, who had held fast to her as they moved through the darkened house, surrendered her hand and walked to the hearth to add more wood to the dying fire, coaxing the bed of glowing coals into a roaring blaze. Once the entire room was bathed in warm, burnished light, he escorted Elizabeth to the pianoforte and deposited her upon the bench.

Rather than take a seat on the couch, he walked to the door and shut it with a quiet click, then returned to Elizabeth and claimed a seat beside her.

Elizabeth shook her head at him. "This is highly improper, Mr Darcy." Her tone contained far more of a teasing lilt than any admonishment. "What will Mrs Lawrence think if she discovers us thus?"

Darcy snorted. "It is well past midnight. She has consumed an entire snifter of brandy with her tea. I doubt she will come in search of us tonight." He looked at her then, and she saw his unwavering love for her reflected in the expression of his eyes. "Play something, Elizabeth. Please, else I go distracted and do something scandalous with you in this room meant for music and polite conversation."

Any words Elizabeth thought to utter became tangled in her throat. She had no idea how he did it—how his saying something so seductive and forbidden could make her body ache in such a glorious, equally forbidden way.

She drew a fortifying breath and began to play Beethoven's *Moonlight Sonata* from memory while Darcy watched her with hooded eyes. Her heart beat erratically. She could feel the heat of his body against hers, the solid press of his thigh, and made a valiant effort to give herself over to the music; but it was difficult to focus on playing with Darcy in such proximity to her, so closely attending her every movement.

He lifted his hand to caress her hair with utmost gentleness, carefully combing his fingers through her loose curls before brushing them aside to gain access to her skin. Slowly, torturously, he traced the tip of his nose along the column of her neck, inhaling her scent. Elizabeth's breath hitched, her eyelids fluttered closed, and she felt the warmth of Darcy's breath, the insistent softness of his lips, and the velvety wetness of his tongue as he tasted her. His fingers skimmed her shoulder and Elizabeth's fingers faltered on the keys. The discordant sound of her fumbling was a stark contrast to the enticing harmony of Darcy's deft ministrations.

When both of his hands found purchase upon her waist, Elizabeth found herself complying with his unspoken request by turning towards him of her own volition. With her hands upon his shoulders, he guided her upward and over, arranging her with care upon his lap. The hem of her nightshift was raised well past what was proper, exposing her feet and her calves, her knees, and a scandalous sliver of thigh. Despite the coolness of the air against her bared flesh, Elizabeth felt a delicious, searing heat spiral outward from the base of her spine as Darcy eased her closer.

"Lizzy," he said on a breath, and claimed her mouth in an ardent kiss. His fingers tangled in her hair, anchoring her in place as he deepened his assault on her mouth.

He had never called her Lizzy before; that he had chosen to do so now, in the heat of passion, served to fuel her desire for him even more. The deep cadence of Darcy's voice, so rough yet so intimate, held an underlying desperation that was never present in her family's staid pronunciations of her name. She raised her hands to his beloved face, traced the line of his jaw with her fingertips, and slid her hands into his hair, savouring the novelty of being able to touch him so freely and intimately as she returned his fervent kisses with equal ardour.

As though he sensed her inability to formulate a coherent thought, Darcy slowed his passionate onslaught. With utmost tenderness, he trailed trembling fingers along the underside of her breast, to her ribs, and finally her waist. His kisses grew unhurried as well. They became more languorous—less demanding, but no less loving.

With one last lingering kiss to her mouth, Darcy released a shuddering breath and embraced her tightly, pressing his lips to where her shoulder met the curve of her neck. "This was not what was supposed to happen," he whispered unsteadily against her skin.

"What did you suppose would happen?" Elizabeth asked, her voice equally quiet and unsteady. Her hands sought his hair again, and she proceeded to comb her fingers through its softness, as much to soothe herself as to soothe him.

"I wanted to show you I can be a gentleman, not some indecorous churl who is constantly thinking of taking advantage of you."

Elizabeth stilled. "Do you think of taking advantage of me?" When he did not answer her, she said, "Please, talk to me. Do not hide what you are thinking or feeling from me. How will I ever know what is wrong otherwise?"

Slowly, Darcy raised his head but avoided meeting her eyes. Instead, he exhaled harshly as his fingers fidgeted with the belt of her robe. "I would be lying if I said I did not desire you the way a husband desires his wife, but no, I would never deliberately take advantage of you. Until now my resolve has served me well, but you have a way of testing my self-control to its fullest extent. Today has proved challenging in ways I had failed to foresee when I first brought you here to meet my aunt. Though it was not my intent, much has happened that exceeded the bounds of propriety, and I fear I am ill-prepared to face my shortcomings with any measure of composure. While I am by no means proud of my conduct, I find I cannot bring myself to repine it, not fully. Not in the way a gentleman ought to do."

His bitter confession caused a fresh ache of longing to bloom in Elizabeth's heart, and with it a flicker of understanding. She recalled how Darcy had sounded that afternoon when he had discovered her standing in his bedchamber—the tightness of his voice and the curtness of his words as he told her she should not be there—and felt the missing piece of a puzzle fit into place. "Do you think I do not desire you as much? Do you believe the idea of reciprocating such affection as your wife does not also cross my mind?"

Darcy groaned, low and guttural. "Saying such things to me—sitting here, looking as you do—you are not helping." Nudging her from his lap, he rose and walked to the hearth, where he propped his elbows upon the mantel and rubbed his forehead with his hands.

Elizabeth watched him intently—there was no denying the depth of his discomfiture, nor his confliction. Both emotions were apparent in the stiff, almost unyielding set of his shoulders and the harshness of his breathing. "If you will recall, sir, my own conduct has been far from prudent today, on many levels. In truth, I am overwhelmed by the depth of my feelings for you. Is this how you felt when you discovered me in your bedchamber this afternoon? Overwhelmed?"

"Yes," he rasped. "Of course, it is how I felt. What did you think? That I was devoid of all proper feeling? That seeing you standing next to my bed was distasteful to me?"

"I did not think you devoid of feeling, but regarding your reaction to my presence in your bedchamber, yes. That is precisely what I thought."

He turned to face her; incredulousness was etched upon his countenance. "How could you possibly think such a thing?"

"What was I supposed to think? Not only did you inform me I ought not to be there, Fitzwilliam, you left me there alone."

"I left you there because if I did not there was a chance you would no longer be a maiden, Elizabeth! The urge to touch you was overpowering. The entire room smelled of roses—*your scent*. Your gown was so pale it nearly matched your flesh. It did not take much for me to envision you without it. And your blush...! You can have no idea the effect your blush has upon me! Had I stayed in that room even one moment longer I could not have been held accountable for my actions."

"Did you not bother to consider that perhaps I would not hold you accountable for your actions?"

Darcy's eyes, which were by nature exceptionally dark, darkened further with a look of ardency so intense Elizabeth felt her knees grow weak. He took several purposeful steps in her direction before he appeared to recall himself, abruptly stopped, turned, and strode to the French windows on the far side of the room, where he stood as rigid as a board while his hands gripped the casement.

Elizabeth could see his anguished reflection in the glass. "You are hiding again," she told him, folding her arms.

"I am not hiding," he said tightly, "but I can hardly face you and retain my dignity when you insist on saying such provocative things to me. It is more than I am capable of for the moment."

"I am sorry."

"You have no reason to be sorry. It is I who am sorry. If I were the gentleman I claimed to be, then—" He exhaled heavily and shook his head. "What do you expect of me?"

"What I expect is for you to be honest with me. I expect you to speak to me of whatever weighs on your conscience, not avoid me and make me feel as though I have done something wrong."

"We have been over this. You have done *nothing* wrong."

"It did not feel that way today, sir! Attempting to comprehend your motives while you battle some internal demon of which I am unaware is not an experience I wish to repeat. I thought I offended you this afternoon—that by entering your bedchamber I invaded your privacy and that you were angry with me because of it. Not only did I believe I was not welcome there, but I believed you would not wish me to join you there even after we are married. You avoided being alone with me for the rest of the afternoon and avoided speaking to me most of the night." A lump had formed in her throat, and she struggled to swallow around it. Her composure had waned. "I was devastated, Fitzwilliam!"

Darcy was across the room and reaching for her in a heartbeat. *"Elizabeth!"* Embracing her tightly, he pressed his lips to her hair. "Forgive me, dearest. The last thing I meant to communicate to you is that you are not welcome in my bedchamber. *Nothing* could be farther from the truth. It is my fervent hope that when we marry, we will spend all our nights together. Whether we sleep in your bed or in my own does not signify. I love you beyond all measure." He pressed another kiss to her hair, and then her shoulder. "It pains me to be without you," he confessed. His voice was barely above a whisper.

"Once we marry," she assured him with equal emotion, "you shall never be without me again—this, I promise."

The sound of a door handle being turned prevented Darcy from offering a proper response. They separated, albeit reluctantly, and a moment later the door opened. A lone figure bustled into the room—it was Mrs Lawrence. "There you are," she said, adjusting her shawl as she approached the two lovers.

Elizabeth, feeling as though her cheeks were on fire, stood beside the pianoforte while Darcy positioned himself before the hearth and cleared his throat.

Bingley's aunt chuckled. "Oh, there is no need to look so sombre and grave, my dears. Despite the lateness of the hour, I am certain you both have behaved respectably. I have every confidence in your good judgment, else I would never have left you alone."

She patted Elizabeth's hand and addressed Darcy. "I know I have been a bit relaxed in my duties as Miss Bennet's chaperon, sir, but I would never be so remiss as to retire without seeing her safely to bed.

"Come along. It is late and we must be on our way." She regarded her charge with a discerning eye. "You appear a bit flushed, my dear. I daresay you have stayed too long by the fire. Fear not, the corridor is quite cool, and you will soon be set to rights.

"You as well, Mr Darcy," she said, casting a shrewd glance at the master of Pemberley. "Pleasant dreams, sir."

❧ 28 ❧

WHERE, DESPITE THE LATENESS OF THE
HOUR, MR DARCY CANNOT SLEEP.

Despite the lateness of the hour, Darcy found he could not sleep. Even now, as dawn was about to break over London, sleep eluded him. He rose from the upholstered chair in his bedchamber and walked to the hearth, stirred the coals, and fed several logs to the dying fire, sending bright bursts of sparks up the chimney.

His bed had been turned down by his maid hours ago but remained otherwise undisturbed. Yesterday had been a trying day—an emotional day—and Darcy could not bring himself to lay upon it, not when he burned for Elizabeth. He ran a hand across his eyes as he recalled her responsiveness to him with startling clarity. Not only had she permitted his bold ministrations but had eagerly reciprocated his passion with her own. She had allowed him liberties a gentlewoman would only ever allow her husband, and the memory of her warm, willing body embracing his own enflamed his ardour to an absurd degree.

Agitated, Darcy strode to the window, pushed aside the drapes, and leaned his forehead against the glass. While the sharp chill of the frost-covered pane soothed his fevered countenance, it brought no ease to his troubled conscience. Having Elizabeth in his house with only Mrs Lawrence for a chaperon, while wonderful, had been a mistake. He had only intended to steal a few kisses during the day; but after the shock of seeing Elizabeth in his bedchamber that afternoon and their chance meeting late that night, Darcy was overcome with desire, emotional as well as physical.

Had he not been able to stop himself, Darcy felt certain Elizabeth would likely have surrendered herself to him completely. As it was, he had claimed a good portion of her innocence last night. The thought distressed him, though apparently not enough to regret all they had done with as much vehemence as he should. One thing was certain: he could not allow such a degree of impropriety to happen again before Elizabeth became his wife. Her father, her uncle, and Bingley trusted him to do right by her. All had consigned her unto Darcy's care, and Darcy had no doubt the liberties he had claimed would shock, infuriate, and disgust them. Though he was utterly devoted to her in all ways, his conscience knew Elizabeth deserved better, far better than being seduced in the music room in the dead of night by a gentleman who claimed to love her.

Lifting his head from the window, Darcy glanced at the clock upon the mantel. It was nearly time to rise, but he had yet to retire. Exhaling heavily, he moved towards the comfort of his bed. With its beautifully carved mahogany posts and tall, stately canopy, it was an imposing piece of furniture, though no less elegant for its sheer size. He extended his hand and smoothed a crease in the pristine, white sheets. The silk felt cool to his touch, and his mind drifted again to Elizabeth, whose affectionate glances and honest, intelligent conversation had become as necessary as the air he breathed. Her beauty as she stood in his bedchamber yesterday was undeniable, but last night wearing a simple shift and robe, with her lush, chestnut curls tumbling down around her shoulders and her swollen lips, she looked exquisite.

Darcy shut his eyes and raked his hands through his hair. His arousal was almost painful. It was no use. There was no sleeping in such a state. He rang for his valet and ordered his bath.

An hour later, he was dressed for the day and seated at the desk in his study sipping a steaming cup of coffee. Before him were the settlement papers for his wedding, presently unsigned. Darcy sighed, rubbed his forehead, and ignored the dull throb of a headache as he reviewed them for what seemed the thousandth time. Unfortunately, travelling to Longbourn to gain Mr Bennet's signature would have to wait until another day as the London streets appeared to be little more than ice-laden ruts after last night's storm. There would be no travel today beyond Mayfair if at all. Hertfordshire was out of the question, but for Elizabeth's sake he hoped Park Street was not. Though the last thing he wished was to part with her, Darcy knew another night like the last would be torturous at best—his undoing at worst.

Suddenly, waiting until Christmas to marry seemed an insurmountable task. It was the second of December and already Darcy had ceded too much of his staunch self-control to his baser self. He wondered absently if he could convince Elizabeth to marry him within a week, and whether Mr Gardiner would be willing to act in Mr Bennet's stead regarding the settlement. If so, then perhaps Darcy could also obtain his consent for an expedient wedding. He had gone to Doctors' Commons and obtained a licence, then sent a letter to Longbourn stating his and Elizabeth's wish to marry at Pemberley before Christmas but had yet to receive Mr Bennet's reply.

After their passionate interlude, Darcy could not imagine waiting nearly a month to take Elizabeth as his wife. He had waited more than a year already, and where three more weeks should seem like nothing in comparison, after having her in his home responding to his ardour with equal fervour, it was painful to have to give her back.

As though thinking of her had summoned her to his side, Darcy looked up from his paperwork to see Elizabeth being ushered into his study by a footman, who bowed dutifully and promptly shut the door.

Her lips lifted with a sheepish smile as she approached him. "Forgive my intrusion. My intent was to find your library, but I encountered one of your footmen, who kindly brought me here instead."

He was on his feet at once, his gaze steady and warm. They had parted mere hours ago, but Darcy was immensely pleased to see her. As had been the case the night before, he felt a powerful inclination to take her in his arms but feared doing so would lead to kissing her, which would in turn lead to other pleasant, though far more forbidden, activities. No, Darcy would remain where he was for the moment—behind his desk with his hands neatly folded behind his back. "Good morning, my dearest. I hope you slept well."

Elizabeth regarded him from beneath her lashes. "While the room was certainly lovely, and the bed very comfortable, I found it difficult to find repose. My mind was hardly quiet after we parted."

"Nor was mine," he replied as he held her gaze with his own. "I confess I did not sleep at all. I thought only of you."

A lovely blush appeared upon her countenance as she tucked her hands behind her back and cast her eyes about the room. "I hope I am not interrupting your work."

Darcy cleared his throat, wishing he could read her better. She was wonderfully receptive last night, alluring and warm a moment ago, but now she seemed almost reserved. Or was she merely embarrassed by his allusion to their intimacy? Darcy shook his head and offered her an encouraging smile. "You are very welcome here, Elizabeth. In fact, I was reviewing the settlement papers. Would you care to see them? Your father has yet to offer his stamp of approval."

"I would be honoured."

Rather than gesture for her to sit in one of the chairs before his desk, he gathered the papers together, extended his hand, and escorted her to the couch. It was early yet, and the fire in the grate had only recently been lit, so the room was not yet as warm as it might have been had the hour been later. Once Elizabeth was settled, Darcy surrendered the documents, observing her closely as she proceeded to read through the neatly formed handwriting that covered the entirety of several sheets. He did not trust himself to sit beside her just yet, and so remained standing.

She looked as lovely as ever, her face freshly scrubbed and her dark hair piled upon her head in a simple, but elegant style. A few rebellious curls brushed her cheek and the nape of her neck, and the faint scent of rosewater sweetened the air. Darcy found himself leaning towards her, even as she seemingly ignored him, and straightened. Memories of their passionate interlude were vivid in his mind and the compulsion he felt to kiss her—to drag his tongue along the column of her throat, to remove each delicate pin that held her hair in place and lose himself utterly in the pleasures of her mouth—increased.

Elizabeth's brows furrowed, and she raised her head. "This is very generous of you, Fitzwilliam, but entirely too much. I cannot possibly accept this amount you have settled upon me. It is far too exorbitant."

It took a moment for her words to penetrate the fog of Darcy's desire, but he quickly recollected himself. "I beg to differ. It is an appropriate sum for my wife. You will have many obligations throughout the Season that will require a certain style and quality of dress and our position in society will demand that you uphold that standard.

"In the event of my death, you and any children we may have will be well provided for. You need never leave Pemberley, Elizabeth—ever. Should we have a son, our home will become his birthright, but until he reaches his majority you will have full control of the entire estate. If we have only girls the same will apply, the eldest being my heir. Should she desire to marry, Pemberley will not belong to her husband. It will pass to her eldest son upon your death and remain within the Darcy bloodline. In the event we are not blessed with a child, Pemberley will pass to Georgiana's children. Either way, Pemberley will be your home for the rest of your life. You need never fear for your future."

She bit her bottom lip and returned her attention to the settlement. "I suppose there is no point arguing with you, is there?"

Darcy extended his hand, placed his fingertip upon her lip, and eased it from between her teeth.

Elizabeth lifted her face to him, and their eyes met.

"None at all. On this matter I will not be moved. I intend to provide a generous income for you and our children and have considered every circumstance, every detail with utmost care. This is the best course. This is what I wish."

Elizabeth looked away. "I cannot think of what I have done to deserve you. You are far too forgiving, far too benevolent, and far too good. I come to you with nothing—no dowry, no title, no connexions of any true significance. You will gain nothing by marrying me, yet you offer me everything—your wealth, your love, your *birthright*, all without hesitation."

Darcy lowered himself to the couch so he could sit beside her. "I will have *you*, Elizabeth," he stated with quiet conviction as he took her hand in his own. "I will gain a wife and a friend and a lover. I will gain an intelligent, compassionate, trustworthy partner with whom to share my life. Already, you have enriched my existence and lightened my burden by looking beyond the heft of my purse and seeing the man I am. You care little for my name, or my property, or my money. You care for *me*. No other lady has ever done that in all the years since I have come of age. Not even my own family is able to see past Pemberley's material wealth with enough clarity to appreciate what the stewardship of it truly represents to those who live upon its land and rely upon its bounty for their livelihood. You are the only woman I have ever loved—*could* ever love—and you are worth far more to me than any sum printed on any sheet of paper. I can well afford to marry you. It is not marrying you I can ill afford."

There were tears in Elizabeth's eyes as she gazed at him, but she smiled despite them. "It is well then," she told him softly, but there was great feeling in her tone. She raised her hand and gently caressed his cheek. "I do love you, so very much. That you continue to love me, even after the despicable way I treated you in Kent...I cannot tell you what it means to me. With all my heart, I thank you."

He pressed a tender kiss to her lips, brief but heartfelt. "You need never thank me for what I am glad to do. It is easy to love you, as easy as breathing." It was in that moment Darcy noticed the delicate skin beneath her eyes appeared bruised from her lack of sleep the previous night. He traced the slight discolouration with his fingertip and frowned. "You are tired. You should rest."

"I am fine for the moment."

"Would you not rather be abed?"

"I would prefer to stay here. Might I remain with you for a while?"

Darcy scrutinised her for a long moment, conflicted by his desire to have her as close to him as possible and his need to protect her should his baser instincts reappear. In the end, he was forced to own that he did not want to send Elizabeth away any more than she wished to leave him. Yes, they were alone in his study, but she was clearly exhausted and there were servants about, stoking fires and polishing floors and cooking meals. What harm would it do if he agreed to let her stay for a while? Surely, she was in no danger from him when she required sleep and the entire house was awake and aware of their presence? "Very well," he conceded with a chaste kiss to her forehead. "I shall open the door."

He made to rise, but Elizabeth's hand caught his coat sleeve. Darcy regarded her curiously.

"Pray, do not. I would like for you to hold me, and you cannot do that if you open the door."

He swallowed thickly. "Elizabeth…" he said gently, reluctant to grant her such an intimate request. "I do not think that is such a good idea under the circumstances."

She averted her eyes. "Nevertheless, I would like for you to do it in any case."

"If we are discovered—"

"Then we shall marry sooner than later. And if we are not discovered, all will be well. I understand your staff is not only loyal to you, but the soul of discretion. Surely, they would prevent any mention of impropriety from becoming public knowledge."

"And what of Mrs Lawrence?"

Elizabeth shook her head. "I hardly know. Despite her abandoning us to our own devices, I believe her affection is genuine and that she sincerely wishes to see us happy. I do not think she would betray us to my family. I would hope she would not. I am sorry. I do not know what I am about this morning, or why I am suddenly so emotional and in need of such reassurance from you."

"Yesterday was an emotional day, for both of us. You are tired. We are both tired, and there is something to be said for reassurance, whether or not it is required."

"Then perhaps we may both rest for a while. It need not be for long." By firelight, her eyes were luminous and dark, as dark as Darcy had ever seen them. As always, he was caught by the intelligence and tenderness he found there. He rose, kissed her hair, and walked to the door to turn the lock, then returned and settled himself beside her once more. "Barring an unforeseen circumstance, no one will disturb us for the next hour." He opened his arms to her. "Come here, my love, and allow me to hold you."

Elizabeth slid closer, curled her legs upon the couch, and snuggled against Darcy's chest. His arms were around her in an instant, his lips caressing her hair as she placed her hand over his heart, laid her cheek upon the lapels of his coat, and tucked her feet beneath an embroidered pillow. With a contented sigh, her eyelids fluttered closed. Within a matter of minutes, she was asleep.

Two hours later, Darcy was at his desk finishing a letter to his solicitor. He signed his name, dusted the missive with sand, and waited for the ink to dry before he folded, sealed, and addressed it. He added his letter to the growing pile of correspondence ready to go out in the morning's post, then reclined in his chair with a tired exhalation, linked his hands behind his head, and shut his eyes.

A short distance away, Elizabeth slept peacefully on the couch before a blazing fire, her cheek pillowed upon her hands and her slender body draped with a soft rug. Though it was not his intent, Darcy had fallen asleep within minutes of taking her in his arms. He awakened sometime later when the mantel clock chimed half past the hour.

Taking care not to disturb her slumber, he had extricated himself from the couch and crossed the room to open the door. It was one thing to hide from the world when the sun had barely risen; it was quite another to openly flout propriety when the day was well under way and they would be missed.

Eventually, Mrs Lawrence came in search of them. "Good morning to you, Mr Darcy," she said brightly, pausing at the threshold of his study. "I trust you had pleasant dreams."

He rose at once and bowed politely, inviting her to enter the room. "Good morning, Mrs Lawrence. I fear I did not get much sleep last night. I hope that was not the case for you."

"Oh dear. How dreadful. I daresay you will be dead on your feet come noon. You really ought to get some rest, sir. I had a wonderful night's sleep."

"I am glad to hear it. Is there something I can help you with, or help you to find? Breakfast should be ready within the hour."

"I cannot seem to locate Miss Bennet this morning. I understand she is usually an early riser, and she is not to be found within her rooms. I wonder if you have seen her?"

"In fact, I have," Darcy admitted, feeling a flush of heat rise along the back of his neck. He gestured towards the couch.

Mrs Lawrence's brows rose to her hairline as she observed Elizabeth's sleeping form. "Well, well," she murmured. "I confess I did not expect this at all. How long has she been here, sir?"

"She has been sleeping soundly for several hours. I have not the heart to wake her."

Mrs Lawrence sighed. "No, nor do I. She looks exhausted, poor thing. Tell me something, Mr Darcy—did either of you sleep at all after we parted ways last night?" She regarded him shrewdly as she claimed one of the chairs before his desk.

Darcy resisted the urge to roll his eyes as he reclaimed his own chair, perturbed by her enquiry as much as he was the tartness of her tone. Bingley's aunt had essentially left them alone the day before with no thought to any consequences that might arise. Yes, she had come back in the end, but it was a bit late, all things considered. "I cannot speak for Miss Bennet," he said, taking care to maintain a steady, unaffected tone, "but I believe I already informed you I did not in fact have a restful night, Mrs Lawrence."

The elder woman stared at him for a long moment, pursing her lips as she studied his countenance. At length, she sighed. "You remind me much of my late husband, Mr Darcy. Harold was clever, industrious, and handsome, and ardently devoted to me through forty years of marriage. He was the one person I knew without question I could rely upon, and the only man I knew I would do absolutely anything for, should he only condescend to ask. We trusted one another implicitly in all matters, for ours was a union of equal respect, admiration, and esteem. From the moment we met we wanted nothing more than to be together. He was the very best of men, and my one great love."

"You were most fortunate to have had so many years with your husband, Mrs Lawrence. Hearing you speak of your relationship I would wager a good deal you were his one great love as well."

The hint of a wistful smile tugged at the corners of her mouth. "As Miss Bennet is yours," she uttered with quiet conviction, "and as you are undoubtedly hers. Take care, sir."

Darcy bowed his head. He had no idea how to respond. Mrs Lawrence saved him the trouble of forming an answer. She rose and patted his hand. "I shall see you both at breakfast, Mr Darcy. I do hope your French cook will condescend to serve some bacon. My constitution requires it."

❧ 29 ❧

WHERE ALL IS WELL IN HYDE PARK, BUT NOT
SO NICE ON PARK STREET.

That afternoon, Elizabeth and Mrs Lawrence were safely returned to Bingley's keeping.

Due to an incessant bout of rain, the three ladies residing in Park Street were forced to pass the next few days quietly at home; but by the end of the week the weather saw such a marked improvement that Darcy suggested escorting Elizabeth on a tour of Hyde Park the following day. Since the roads through town were muddy and the footpaths within the park itself were likely to be worse, he proposed riding rather than walking, a prospect that pleased Elizabeth immensely. She was rarely given the opportunity to ride in Hertfordshire; that she would be able to do so in London with Darcy felt like an indulgence.

She did not have a riding habit, but Darcy assured her it would be no trouble to secure one for her. His sister kept several at Darcy House, including two she had outgrown during the last Season. Though Miss Darcy was formed on a larger scale than Elizabeth, a few minor alterations were easily and efficiently made for her slighter build and by the end of the day Elizabeth was outfitted with a stylish winter habit and a pair of riding boots.

Since she and Darcy were both early risers, they arranged to meet shortly after sunrise the following morning, when the ever-crowded streets would be empty and London most at peace. With the rest of the household still abed, Elizabeth stood before a looking glass in the back parlour, struggling to pin her hat to her head. The veil attached to the hat was long and cumbersome, and the hat itself felt heavy and uncomfortable. Try as she might, she could not affix it to her person in any way that satisfied her.

A quick glance out the window revealed that Darcy had arrived and was walking towards the house from the stable yard. Elizabeth cast an exasperated look at her reflection and bit her lip. *Oh, hang this ridiculous thing! I shall not wear it.* She tossed the bothersome hat onto a nearby table, threw open the door, and greeted Darcy with an arch look that dared him to disapprove.

He smirked at her expression, ignored her hatless head, and placed a chaste kiss upon her gloved hand. They did not tarry, but proceeded directly into the yard, where a groom waited with the horses. Darcy had personally selected a horse from his own stable for her to ride that morning—a grey mare with an elegant form and noble bearing. She was easily sixteen hands high.

"Oh, Fitzwilliam," Elizabeth exclaimed, smiling with genuine pleasure as she lavished affection upon her horse. "She is beautiful. What is her name?"

"This is Houri. She has a calm temperament but is not so docile that you will become bored with her. With the proper encouragement, she can be quite spirited, but I have never known her to be obstinate. I believe you will be pleased with her. Her gait is one of the smoothest of any horse I have ever owned."

"I believe I shall like her very much. I must thank you for your consideration in choosing her for me. If you had given me an impertinent horse our temperaments would clash to very ill effect!"

Darcy snorted. "It is most fortunate then, that all my impertinent horses are currently stabled at Pemberley. I am your servant, Miss Bennet. Come, allow me to assist you in mounting your most civil and affable horse."

Offering his hand to Elizabeth, he attended her while she climbed onto the block and up into the saddle. When she was comfortably settled, Darcy mounted his own horse, a regal black Arabian named Pharaoh. Side by side, they headed towards Upper Brook Street and continued onto Park Lane, chatting amicably as they followed the wide avenue to the entrance at the Grosvenor Street gate. They met with no one, save for a handful of servants on errands for their masters. Mayfair's more stylish residents were likely still asleep.

The fashionable hour in which to see and be seen in Hyde Park was in the evening, not in the early light of morning. As Darcy waxed eloquent about Kensington Gardens, which lay just beyond the Serpentine, Elizabeth admired the impressive figure he cut on Pharaoh. She imagined him dressed in his finery, riding along Rotten Row with London's elite, and wrinkled her nose. She had no doubt he preferred to enjoy Hyde Park without making a spectacle of himself. The staid master of Pemberley was no dandy. There was a chill in the air that morning, but there was no one about to intrude upon his solitude or force him into superficial conversation. There were no gentlemen to make demands of him, or ladies to impose upon him. He was at leisure to be himself, and Elizabeth basked in her excellent fortune of being one of the privileged few for whom he cared, and whose society he truly welcomed.

They entered the park and Darcy fixed her with a look that clearly communicated his delight at having her with him. "Where did you learn to ride? You have a magnificent seat."

"Thank you," she replied, warmed by his look of undisguised admiration. "Riding side-saddle is hardly comfortable, though. I am far more proficient when I ride astride."

Darcy's eyes darkened with a look Elizabeth now recognised as barely restrained desire. "I should like to see that, Elizabeth, once we are at Pemberley."

Elizabeth gave him an impudent look, but her joy could not be contained, and she smiled. "On one of your impertinent horses, no doubt!"

"No doubt," Darcy agreed, returning her smile as he gently touched her cheek, then one long, curly lock. "Your hair has come down."

"It always does. I am forever losing my hairpins. It is a wonder that I bother putting it up anymore whenever I ride!" She touched her hair self-consciously and glanced around the park. Her smile slipped from her face. "Forgive me. I must look a fright."

"You are utterly charming," he told her with a quiet reverence that immediately restored a fair measure of her self-confidence, "but I confess this is a look on you that I would prefer to keep for myself alone."

She managed to find a few spare hairpins in a pocket and twisted her wild tresses into some semblance of respectability. When she had done, they continued through the park at a leisurely pace, their ride punctuated by private glances, easy smiles, and engaging but earnest conversation.

Hours passed as they trotted and cantered about the park, but the passage of time felt more like a handful of minutes to Elizabeth, who could not recall ever having enjoyed herself in the company of any gentleman so much as she had while touring the park with Darcy. It was not only his solicitation for her comfort that delighted her, but the natural flow of their conversation, his wry sense of humour, the warm looks he continuously cast in her direction, and the ease and openness of his manner—even in such a public setting. Darcy's conduct made her feel loved and cherished in a way that no one—not even her parents or the Gardiners—had ever done.

Though she was loath to leave the happy bubble in which they had immersed themselves, when the sun had risen high enough to indicate the breakfast hour would soon be upon them and Darcy suggested they return to Park Street to break their fast, Elizabeth reluctantly agreed.

They had just passed through the Grosvenor Street gate and back onto Park Lane when Darcy said to her, "You have yet to answer my question."

She regarded him with some degree of puzzlement. "For the life of me, I cannot think of what you mean. I have answered all your questions, sir, and with great energy and cleverness if I do say so myself!"

"All but one," he replied with a cryptic turn of his lips. "You never told me where you learned to ride."

Elizabeth turned her head aside to conceal her smile. "I learned to ride in Hertfordshire, of course."

"What I meant, teasing woman, is who taught you?"

She laughed. "Forgive me. I could not resist. I learned to ride with Mr Ellis when we were children."

"Mr Ellis?" he said with some surprise.

"Surely, you know enough of my father to comprehend that he approached my induction of the equestrian arts much as he approached the management of most everything concerning his daughters—by leaving it almost entirely to chance. Consigning my instruction to Mr Ellis's father, the late Colonel Ellis, cost him very little inconvenience, though the benefit to me was invaluable."

Though he glanced at her with some measure of concern, Darcy ignored the flippant tone in which her speech was delivered. He said only, "Mr Ellis's father is the one who taught you to ride astride, then."

"Oh, no. Not the colonel. He was an ordered, sectarian man and quite adamant that young ladies should ride only as God intended them to ride—using a side-saddle. I remember watching my friend race across the park at Purvis Lodge with such speed and manoeuvrability while I struggled to keep my seat on such an awkward contraption. Keeping pace with him was impossible—I hated it. Eventually, I succeeded in my endeavours, but I still wished I could ride like my friend. One day, when we were very far from Meryton, Mr Ellis took pity on me. It was he who taught me to ride astride, in secret without his father's knowledge or approbation."

"How old were you?"

"I was eleven."

"And Mr Ellis?"

"Not yet fourteen."

Darcy made no response.

A small, wistful smile tugged at Elizabeth's mouth as she recalled the pleasure of racing across the barren fields bordering their fathers' estates. "At the time, there was nothing I enjoyed more than to ride out with him. Jane was too slow, Mary too frightened, and Kitty too young. Charlotte was stubborn and disinclined to learn. So, whenever I wished to ride like a savage across the countryside, that left Mr Ellis for me."

They turned onto Upper Brook Street and Darcy acknowledged a fashionably attired gentleman who tipped his hat to them. "Your father did not disapprove of your spending so much time alone with him?"

Elizabeth shook her head. "He was amused by our adventures but did not appear overly concerned about our friendship. He certainly never withdrew his consent, even after my mother voiced her disapprobation. My mother's objection was not on the grounds of impropriety, you see, but because she detests horses. She feared I would become wild."

"Did your parents have any idea that you had learnt to ride sitting astride?"

"They knew only that I enjoyed spending time with my friend. It was Colonel Ellis who eventually discovered my secret." Elizabeth repressed a shudder. "I had never seen him so angry as I did then, on the day he caught me sitting astride one of his fastest horses. I was castigated for my audacity and ran the two miles from Purvis Lodge back to Longbourn in tears. My friend was beaten for his defiance. He had disregarded his father's wishes, which the colonel viewed as a blatant and deliberate act of insubordination. By some miracle, we were not forbidden to see one another or even to spend time alone afterwards, but it took a long while for Mr Ellis's injuries to heal."

"I would imagine Mr Ellis's most painful injuries were not merely physical ones, nor did they truly fade."

"No. His relationship with his father was never the same afterwards. Both tended to avoid one another, and they rarely spoke for the sake of conversation. The colonel assumed my friend had been properly deterred from encouraging my unladylike behaviour after such a harsh reprimand, but if anything, Mr Ellis was more determined than ever to see me excel where I otherwise should not have and doubled his efforts for the simple reason that it made me happy."

"Mr Ellis," Darcy said with quiet conviction, "must have valued your friendship—must have cared for you deeply—to risk his father's disapprobation a second time."

Houri snorted and Elizabeth took a moment to caress her neck as they turned onto Park Street. "He did. He does. Our temperaments have always been very similar, and we understand one another. We both had parents whose conduct caused us some measure of pain and drove us to seek solace in our friendship. So much the better if we were astride a horse."

"It is obvious that you care for Mr Ellis, quite sincerely. It does you credit." For a moment, Darcy appeared to hesitate, then cleared his throat and said, "Elizabeth, in Hertfordshire your mother…"

"My mother happened to have some very unfortunate ideas, none of which Mr Ellis and I have ever shared. He is a dear friend, a protector, and a surrogate elder brother, nothing more. He looks upon me as he would a sister, just as he looks upon Charlotte and Jane and Mary and Kitty and Lydia. At one time he did imagine himself much in love with Jane, but that was to be expected. What mortal man has not fancied himself in love with Jane at one time or another? But, other than that, his relationship with us has always been quite brotherly. Nothing has changed."

"Nothing?" Darcy enquired blandly. "I daresay quite a lot has changed since you were children. Do you still ride out with him?"

"Mr Ellis went away to school, attended university, and then travelled to America. He has only recently returned to England, but yes. I have ridden with him since he has come back to Hert-fordshire."

"Dare I ask if you rode with him in the same manner as you wished to ride with me this morning?"

Elizabeth's lips quirked. "You mean did I throw caution to the wind and ride like a wild tempest across my father's fields without an ounce of regard for anyone else's sensibilities or the state of my appearance?" The house Bingley had let loomed just ahead. Elizabeth found she was not ready to share Darcy with her family just yet and tugged Houri to a stop. She regarded him in silence—his beloved face, the concerned crease of his brow, the steady, slightly vulnerable expression of his eyes.

He gazed back at her, patiently awaiting her answer.

"Yes," she admitted, "though our meeting with one another was entirely by chance, not by design. Spending time with Mr Ellis is something I have always enjoyed but not in the same way I enjoy spending time with you. You are the only gentleman I have ever allowed to kiss me. You are the only gentleman I will ever wish to kiss. That will not change because I happened to ride from Netherfield to Longbourn with my childhood friend."

He bowed his head. "I did not think that it would."

"But you are worried about it."

"No. I trust you implicitly but confess to some degree of uncer-tainty regarding your friend. I barely know Mr Ellis, yet he has known you intimately for most of your life. Surely, he must realise your worth."

"I am engaged to you, not to Mr Ellis."

"And I cannot, for the life of me, figure out why."

"Why I have chosen you?" she cried feebly, growing more confused by the moment.

Darcy rubbed his forehead and sighed. "No, Elizabeth. I cannot understand why you have not chosen each other. You said yourself that your temperaments are similar. You care for each other. Clearly, you would suit."

She stared at him in shock. "Certain aspects of your temperament are much like Jane's—dutiful, reserved, and steady. Does that mean you should wish to marry her simply because you share those commonalities?"

Darcy turned aside his head. "Mr Ellis is handsome," he muttered.

Elizabeth noted the petulance of his tone and almost smiled. "So is Jane," she countered. "For that matter, so are you."

"I cannot deny your eldest sister is quite pretty, but I do not love her. I love you."

She looked pointedly at him and raised one brow in an arch manner. "'*Quite pretty?*' Everyone in Hertfordshire will tell you that Jane is far more beautiful than I, far more deserving, and the epitome of goodness! How can you not wish to marry her? How can you possibly love me instead?"

He shook his head and, with a great deal of exasperation and a hint of a smile, said, "Because you have captivated me from nearly the first moment of our acquaintance. Because you are intelligent and teasing and compassionate and ten times more handsome than any other lady I know. Because you are uniquely you, and so long as you exist in the world, I can never love another. It is well. I see your point."

"I am relieved to hear it. I could never abide marrying a man who has so little sense as to fail to see reason, and it is entirely reasonable that I should want to marry you above anyone."

He extended his hand to her, palm upward, and Elizabeth grasped it with her own. "I would have it no other way." He lifted her hand to his lips and bestowed a kiss upon it. "Should Mr Ellis ever decide he absolutely must have you, I shall take great pleasure in telling him he cannot."

With a wry turn of her lips, Elizabeth squeezed his hand. "I doubt that shall ever happen. He likes you, firstly, and secondly, I believe Mr Ellis is in love with someone else. He has not said much about it, nor do I desire to force his confidence, but he intimated he had met someone while he was at Oxford, someone special and unique. I have no idea what happened between them, only that my friend insists their relationship, as society sees it, is impossible."

For the briefest moment, Darcy's eyes widened infinitesimally. Then he cleared his throat and, with a quiet but decided note of compassion, said, "I knew men like Mr Ellis at Cambridge. Good men, of divergent interests." He appeared on the verge of saying something further when a voice—a woman's voice— called his name with some urgency.

Elizabeth felt his grip upon her hand tighten, watched the set of his shoulders grow rigid, and the lines of his mouth harden. The softened version of the gentleman she had come to love so well all but disappeared before her eyes, and in his place sat the Mr Darcy of old. He cast an apologetic look at Elizabeth, took a fortifying breath, and released her hand.

"Lady Harrow," he said evenly, guiding Pharaoh a few paces away from Houri, but remaining close. "Good morning."

"So, it really is you, Mr Darcy! For a moment I thought I had quite mistaken your figure. Whatever are you doing in the middle of Park Street at such an ungodly hour? The weather is horrid, and the sun has barely even risen!"

"You exaggerate, your ladyship. The weather is by no means unpleasant, and it is quite late by country standards. We have already been to Hyde Park."

"Hyde Park? At this hour? I cannot believe you would waste your time. I would wager there is absolutely no one about this morning." Her gaze shifted to Elizabeth and, regarding her coolly, she added, "At least no one of any consequence that I have seen. Besides, this is London, sir, not Exeter."

"Elizabeth," said Darcy, "I do not believe you know Lady Harrow. She is an old friend of Lady Carlisle's. Your ladyship, it is my honour to present Miss Elizabeth Bennet, my betrothed."

Elizabeth glanced at Darcy. Despite his professed dislike of Lady Harrow, she was surprised that he would slight his aunt's dearest friend by ignoring her superiority of rank and introducing Lady Harrow to *her*. One only had to look at the woman's piqued countenance to see Darcy had indeed angered her; but Elizabeth suspected he could have followed protocol to perfection and Lady Harrow still would have taken offence simply because he was to marry Elizabeth and not her own daughter. She decided there was little she could do at this juncture but pretend to an agreeableness she did not feel. With a polite turn of her mouth, she said, "It is a pleasure, Lady Harrow."

"I am sure," the countess replied with an insincere smile. "Allow me to congratulate you on your conquest, Miss Bennet. For over ten Seasons now, our Mr Darcy has been in high demand among the ladies of our exclusive little society. Imagine our surprise when we learnt he had been snatched up from beneath our very noses, and by you—a total stranger of no consequence! Why, half of London is scandalised, the other half desolate—my own dear daughter included. Lady Eliza admires Mr Darcy exceedingly, but then again, so do we all. I daresay we have come to think of him quite as our own."

Lady Carlisle's words about pecking order and petty, embittered society matrons resounded in Elizabeth's head, and she understood that the strength of her performance now would set the stage for establishing her own rank and position in London society as Darcy's wife. She resolved not to give this grasping woman any reason to believe she would tolerate intimidation or abuse, either by her or others of her ilk. She said confidently, "While your daughter's disappointment, and your own for that matter, is certainly pitiable, your ladyship, I cannot account for it. Mr Darcy is a man of the world. He belongs to nobody but himself. As intimate as you must be, this cannot have come as a surprise—nor should my inability to repine my own excellent fortune of having earned Mr Darcy's affection in the first place. He is the best man I have ever known, and I shall enjoy being married to him immensely."

She heard Darcy choke, then cough, but did not dare turn her eyes upon him.

"Of that I have little doubt," Lady Harrow said with barely concealed disdain. "Your dowry, I hear, is but a thousand pounds."

"It is," Darcy replied, "but I will receive consolation of far greater value with Miss Bennet as my wife. Surely, Lady Harrow, even you can comprehend the unmitigated satisfaction and unparalleled advantage of making a love match over a tepid arrangement orchestrated purely for convenience."

Though his tone was mild, his eyes shone with a quiet, tightly reined fury Elizabeth had only ever seen once before: when he had met George Wickham in Meryton over a year ago. She could not account for it, even with the pointed barbs and slights her ladyship had aimed at her.

Lady Harrow made no reply, but her mouth twisted unpleasantly, as though she had tasted something sour.

"We will not keep you," Darcy told her with the same smooth, unaffected air. "I will be sure to offer your compliments to my aunt when next I see her." He turned towards Elizabeth and said, "Shall we go, Elizabeth? Your sister is no doubt desirous for your return."

Without taking her eyes from Darcy's, she smiled—the barest curve of her lips—and said, "Yes. Good day, your ladyship," and urged Houri towards home.

❦ 30 ❧

WHERE DARCY DOES NOT LIKE LADY HARROW
AND DECIDES TO DO SOMETHING ABOUT IT.

Darcy consigned Pharaoh and Houri to Bingley's groom, then offered his arm to Elizabeth and they began walking in the direction of the house. They had not advanced more than ten feet when she subtly redirected him towards the back garden instead. Darcy pursed his lips. She likely had much to say about his mood, which had not improved since quitting Lady Harrow's presence.

He indulged her, but when they reached the garden, barren except for a bunch of brittle stalks and denuded ornamental bushes, Darcy released her, held up his hand, and said, "Elizabeth, I abhor that woman for a plethora of distasteful reasons I cannot possibly divulge. I beg of you, be satisfied with that much and do not ask me to enumerate her offences. We have yet to break our fast and I have not the stomach for it—nor do I desire to cause you undue distress."

"Very well," she said equitably. "You may keep your secrets. I shall simply imagine the worst and content myself with that instead."

Darcy scoffed. "You presume you would be able to deduce the truth of the matter. In this case, I assure you would not. In the event you did learn of it, I can guarantee you would by no means be content with your discovery. Lord knows I was properly horrified at the time."

"So, the proof of the pudding is in the eating, then," she responded dryly.

"Something to that effect," he muttered, then stalked off towards the fountain in the centre of the garden. It was empty and there were several cracks in it. Clumps of dried grass poked between the stepping-stones leading to the house. Darcy glared at the unkempt slate path, then at his mud-spattered boots. Scenes from a drunken night a week after his father had died flashed before his eyes. He was not yet three-and-twenty. It was by far one of his most repugnant memories.

He had spent the week grieving, and a good portion of that evening imbibing with Fitzwilliam and Arthur, attempting to numb the incomprehensible pain of loss. He had no idea how he had navigated the staircases, but with his cousins' assistance he managed to arrive at his bedchamber unscathed. Once there, he stripped down to his shirtsleeves and breeches, only to discover he was by no means alone. Darcy had been shocked to the point of inaction by the audacity of the woman in his bed; her nudity and coquettish smile had sobered him like nothing else.

It was Fitzwilliam who had come to his rescue, knowing that Darcy would never accept her blatant invitation—not even while in his cups—and was more likely to give offence than she was to give a damn about making a scene when Darcy refused her. Paying her the most indulgent compliments, his cousin handed her robe to her with a roguish smile and charmed her from Darcy's bed and into the viscount's, ensuring her ire was not raised and her vanity gratified. The gratification of her desire would follow.

After that night, Darcy had assumed Lady Harrow would never dare attempt such an assignation with him again, but the insufferable woman seemed to view his rejection as a perverse sort of challenge. In the future, whenever he stayed at Levens Hall, his uncle's country seat in the north, he locked his bedchamber doors, regardless of whether he was within.

He was brought back to the present by the soothing touch of Elizabeth's hand upon his arm. "What in the world is troubling you to such a degree? Your sordid history with Lady Harrow aside, what has upset you so? Is it her treatment of me? I can assure you I am not ruffled by her insinuations any more than I am by her ill manners. Has my own impertinence towards her displeased you? I know she is a peer of the realm, but I could not help it! I never could respect myself if I had allowed her to cow me in such an infuriating manner. I dearly hope your aunt will not be too displeased with me for failing to hold my tongue. It would be most inconvenient if Lady Carlisle were to decide she cannot abide me after all."

Darcy stared at her, utterly incredulous. "I cannot imagine why you would possibly care what my aunt thinks at this point."

Elizabeth appeared taken aback. "Of course, I care what she thinks. She is Colonel Fitzwilliam's mother and your relation. While she is certainly not as warm as my own dear aunt, Lady Carlisle is engaging enough, and I had begun to like her. She is important to you. There is no sense in denying it."

He shook his head and, fixing her with a pointed look, said angrily, "Lady Harrow knew the price of your dowry, Elizabeth. How? There could be but one way and one source only, and that is my aunt. She has clearly been speaking of it—speaking of *you* —and that is an act of disloyalty I cannot abide."

"Ladies' dowries are usually commonly known and therefore discussed, especially among other ladies."

"Not yours. You are yet unknown to London society."

"Does it matter?"

"It matters, Elizabeth! It matters to *me*. You were there. You heard my aunt. She spoke of blood being thicker than the bonds of friendship! She assured me, in my own home, that she desired to see me happy and believed you were the woman best suited to the task. She professed an inclination to help you find your footing in society, despite the disapprobation and jealousy of her friend. And then she does this! Her duplicity and disingenuousness will not be tolerated!"

"What can we possibly do about it at this point?"

"I intend to speak to her, of course!"

"And say what exactly?"

"Whatever I deem appropriate. Pray make my excuses to Bingley and your sister."

Elizabeth's eyes widened in disbelief. "You expect to speak with her *now?*"

"I am hardly fit for company in such a state," he replied irritably, running a hand over his mouth.

Elizabeth sighed. "I suppose not. Please do not say anything to Lady Carlisle you will regret. There may be more to this business than what you think."

The corners of his mouth lifted. "You sound suspiciously like Mrs Bingley, but you will not sway me into believing something I cannot. I will call upon you later."

"I would like that, but my sister and Mrs Lawrence are looking forward to visiting Bond Street after breakfast. Unless your visit with her ladyship is a short one, I fear I shall not see you until much later. We dine in Gracechurch Street tonight, but you know you are welcome as well. My aunt and uncle are very fond of you and will be pleased to see you."

Darcy raised her hand to his lips and quickly kissed her fingers. "Until later then." He took his leave and strode to the stable, where he re-saddled Pharaoh himself, mounted, and urged him down the drive at a purposeful trot. As he neared the street, a carriage was arriving at Chadwick House. Its crest was familiar, as familiar to him as his own name. Darcy tugged Pharaoh to a stop and watched as Lady Harrow smiled and greeted the occupant within, then climbed into the conveyance. A moment later the carriage pulled away from the kerb and proceeded down Park Street.

There is my proof, Darcy thought bitterly, surprised at how deeply his aunt's duplicity wounded him. He spurred his horse in the opposite direction, towards Grosvenor Square. Lady Carlisle would not be at home, but she would eventually return. Darcy was willing to wait.

He arrived at Carlisle House, dismounted, and handed Pharaoh's reins to one of the grooms in the stable yard. His aunt's butler eyed him distastefully as he entered the house with his mud-spattered boots but said nothing beyond the usual salutation.

"Is Colonel Fitzwilliam at home, Douglas?" Darcy enquired, handing the man his greatcoat and hat. "I should like a word with him."

"Yes, sir. He is breaking his fast with her ladyship in the breakfast parlour."

Darcy stared at him. "With Lady Carlisle? Are you certain?"

"Absolutely certain, sir. If you like, I will take you there directly."

He answered in the affirmative, then followed Douglas down the hall and into the breakfast parlour, where he did indeed find his aunt sitting at the table across from her son, buttering a piece of bread.

"Mr Darcy, your ladyship," Douglas announced, then quit the room.

"Darcy," she said pleasantly, "what a delightful surprise." Her eyes alighted on his boots and her demeanour changed considerably. "Your boots are covered in mud! Really, you ought to know better than to come traipsing through the house in such a state. My carpets will have to be washed as well as the floors!"

"I beg your pardon. I have been riding this morning with Miss Bennet."

"I see." She gave him a sly smile and reached for her teacup. "I suppose I shall overlook your indiscretion this once, then. How is your clever Miss Bennet? Is she also covered in mud?"

"She is well," he replied stiffly, "but I require a word, your ladyship. Now, if you please."

Fitzwilliam discarded his toast and addressed Darcy with some concern. "I hope all is well, Cousin."

"All is not well but that is a matter that concerns your mother and me."

His aunt frowned. "You are dissatisfied, that much is clear, but I can think of no reason why your dissatisfaction originates with me. Come, Darcy. You must sit down. I insist."

"However insincere you choose to be, you will not find me so. It has come to my attention that you have been speaking of Miss

Bennet to none other than Lady Harrow. More particularly, of her dowry. What I cannot understand is why."

Lady Carlisle regarded him with an expression of some surprise. "I have said nothing of Miss Bennet to Lady Harrow! In fact, I have neither seen nor heard from my friend since our evening at Covent Garden last week. It is unusual, I grant you, but she has been out each time I have called. In truth, she was most displeased when she saw you with your Miss Bennet at the theatre. It is entirely likely she blames me for your choice. You know how she can be when she is vexed about something and has not gotten her way."

Darcy shook his head slowly. "If you have seen nothing of Lady Harrow since then, nor spoken to her, how is it possible that I witnessed her climbing into your carriage this morning not half an hour ago on Park Street? Surely, she cannot summon your conveyance without your express permission, madam!"

"That is impossible," Lady Carlisle insisted, setting her teacup upon its saucer with some distress. "My carriage is being repaired as we speak—at your uncle's insistence, no less, though I discerned nothing amiss with it myself. He took it in any case, with no expectation of a timely return. I have not had use of it in over a week!"

Colonel Fitzwilliam, who had been silent throughout their exchange thus far, cleared his throat. "Darcy, a word, if you please." He indicated the hall with a tilt of his head.

Lady Carlisle would have none of it, however, and rolled her eyes sardonically. "Richard, I am not an infirm nincompoop! Whatever you must confide to Darcy you will also relate to me or I shall lose my patience with you entirely. I will not abide your whispering to each other in the hall like a pair of ill-bred, gossiping schoolgirls. Out with it!"

Darcy yanked a chair away from the table and sat upon it. "You heard your mother," he said crisply. "Out with it."

"Surely, you recall that my mother is not the only member of this household privy to Miss Bennet's worth."

"Fitzwilliam," he said darkly, "if you are trying to tell me that you—once again—are the one with loose lips, I will not be amused."

"Of course, I am not! You know my father was by no means happy with your choice, nor with you for that matter, especially after you threatened to sever ties with him. Do you not think that must account for something?"

"And so, he ran off to his club and complained to his friends like a gossiping woman," Darcy muttered in annoyance. "Where is he?"

Fitzwilliam looked pointedly at Darcy and said with utmost gravity, "He is neither at home, nor at his club. He has not been seen there all week, nor here for that matter. He has not visited any of his other haunts either. I have made enquiries."

Darcy stared at him with purpose. He could not very well mention his uncle's mistress in the presence of his aunt, but that is where his mind travelled without delay.

Apparently, Lady Carlisle harboured no such compunction. "Surely, your unscrupulous father," she said disdainfully, "has more than one loose woman at his disposal, Richard. Either you know who they are, or you do not. But if Darcy wishes to speak with his worthless uncle, you had best find out. He once mentioned Drury Lane and King's Place, but surely, there must be other dens of iniquity where London's so-called gentlemen scurry off to meet their mistresses while their wives sit at home keeping their houses and raising their heirs."

Darcy grimaced. His aunt had an excellent memory, but in such a case as this a good memory could be unpardonable, for it obviously afforded the countess much pain. It was unfortunate his uncle did not share that same attribute. Had Lord Carlisle been able to remember the date of their wedding, perhaps he would also have recalled the vows he had made to his wife in church and taken them seriously instead of merely taking a succession of mistresses.

Suddenly, Darcy recalled something himself. "Lady Carlisle, from where does Miss Bennet hail?"

She looked at him as though he had lost his mind. "Darcy, surely, you have not forgotten! Oh, this does not bode well for your future as a married man if you cannot even recall that the woman you love is from Hertfordshire! Really, Nephew..." She shot him a look of utmost exasperation.

He glanced meaningfully at his cousin. "When I spoke with her this morning, Lady Harrow said 'Exeter', not 'Hertfordshire'."

Colonel Fitzwilliam shrugged. "So, what if she did? Obviously, she was mistaken and—"

"She is not the only one who was mistaken."

"My father?"

Darcy nodded. He glanced at the countess, who appeared remarkably composed considering the implications at hand. "Pray accept my apology, Lady Carlisle, for my abhorrent suppositions."

"You, Nephew," she said briskly, "I can forgive. Your uncle, and *his* abhorrence, is another matter altogether! He has made his bed and now must lay in it—my so-called friend as well. Let *her* console him from now on, along with his string of other mistresses! Let them console each other! They are both the most undeserving, disloyal people of my acquaintance, and I no longer wish to know either of them! In fact, from this day forward I shall not."

She rose from the table with an alacrity that startled both gentlemen, and they quickly followed suit. The countess raised one hand to her forehead, shut her eyes, and sighed. "I believe I would like a divorce, Darcy, as expediently as possible. I trust you to help me obtain one."

"I will assist you in whatever way I can. But are you certain? A divorce—"

"I am aware of the repercussions of such a measure, and of the scandal that will ensue once it becomes public knowledge. I am sorry for any difficulties it may cause you and Georgiana, but I can no longer abide being married to such a man. I am three-and-fifty. I cannot spend the rest of my life living miserably in his shadow.

"Richard, you will help me to pack my things. I cannot bear to stay in this house a moment longer. Once we have done, I will go to Darcy House, where I will reside until I can make other arrangements. And Darcy," she said, "I would like to see my future niece and her new aunt once I am settled. I am feeling extremely dull this morning. I daresay they will do an admirable job of raising my spirits."

Lady Carlisle fidgeted with the handles of her reticule as Darcy's carriage made its way through the cobbled streets of Mayfair towards Cheapside. "Are you quite certain these relations of Miss Bennet's—this Mr and Mrs Gardiner—will not be put out by my coming?"

"Not at all," Darcy replied. "They are expecting you, and they are pleased by your coming. And before you speculate upon the source of their pleasure, let it be understood that it is in no way connected to your rank. Mr and Mrs Gardiner are easily two of the most agreeable people I have ever known. They take immense enjoyment in their family. Once I marry Miss Bennet, you will become their family. All is well."

She opened her mouth to speak, but Darcy knew her well, and before she could utter a word, he interrupted her to reiterate his point. "The Gardiners, and Miss Bennet for that matter, could not care a whit if you were a duchess or a milkmaid so long as you are gracious."

Lady Carlisle huffed. "Oh, very well. I cannot believe I will soon be dining in Cheapside, of all places. And they will become your relations—not that you have much in the way of relations to boast of on the Fitzwilliam side, of course, save for Richard and Georgiana, and poor Anne. Josephine, I fear, will eventually be driven to despair over Arthur, for he is as unscrupulous and wicked as his father."

Darcy felt it best not to comment and so remained silent. It was nothing short of a miracle that he was able to convince the countess to accompany him to Gracechurch Street. He had desperately wanted to see Elizabeth but did not want to abandon his aunt to her own devices on her first night in his home, nor did the countess wish to be idle. This seemed an acceptable solution.

She emitted a long-suffering sigh and looked out the window. "You are lucky your Miss Bennet is a clever, sensible young woman. I doubt she will ascribe any of our failings onto you, regardless of the situation or intent. Tell me. Did she really put Lady Harrow in her place this morning, and in the middle of Park Street no less?"

Darcy inclined his head. "She did. With consummate grace and diplomacy, as per your guidance, but I expected no less from Miss Bennet."

Lady Carlisle's lips lifted with a smile. "Of course, she would say what needed to be said and not permit herself to be insulted and abused. She will do fine with the rest of them, then, if she can stand up to Lady Harrow without so much as batting an eye. Your Miss Bennet was an ideal choice, Nephew."

"Miss Bennet was the only choice. I never could have been happy with another. There are no pretences between us, no concealment, no deception. She is privy to all my deficiencies and loves me despite them. Look," he said, and pointed towards the window, where a line of neat, well-kept row houses lined one side of the street. They appeared charming, despite their barren flower boxes and their proximity to the warehouses just beyond. "We are nearly there. Gracechurch Street is just around the corner. The Gardiners' house is somewhat larger than these homes and is elegant and tastefully decorated. Mrs Gardiner has a discerning eye and excellent taste. There is a park in the neighbourhood, though not nearly as grand as Hyde Park. The children often play there when the weather is fair. I have been there myself."

Lady Carlisle glanced at him sharply. "You like it here," she said in astonishment. "You, who live in the most exclusive part of London, cannot possibly prefer Cheapside to Mayfair!"

Darcy shook his head. "While I cannot deny that I enjoy spending time in Gracechurch Street, it is not the neighbourhood per se, but the people who reside here that I like. I have told you before I am fond of the Gardiners. They are among the few people I know who have no expectations of me, but whose esteem I will always strive to deserve."

"I shall endeavour to like them, then," his aunt replied with improved civility. "I confess I am curious to meet Mr Gardiner. You tend to speak very differently of Miss Bennet's uncle than you do of your own."

"Mr Gardiner," Darcy said succinctly, "is nothing at all like the earl. Therein lies the difference. Deference for one's rank is given. Respect for one's character must be earned. They are hardly one and the same."

A moment later they arrived at the house, and Darcy assisted his aunt from the carriage. At the door, she paused to straighten her gown. Pressing her hand to her stomach, she took a fortifying breath, then nodded to her nephew, who knocked upon the door with a firm hand.

They were admitted by a harried-looking maid, who showed them into the drawing room, then hurried off and promptly shut the door. No one was about except Mrs Lawrence, who greeted them with a curtsey and a wry turn of her mouth. "I am afraid there is much excitement to be had on Gracechurch Street this evening, Mr Darcy. Mrs Wickham arrived not twenty minutes ago in a fit of pique. Apparently, she has lost her husband."

Darcy's brows rose to his hairline. "Lost him?" he repeated. "As in he has expired?"

"I hardly know, sir. The way Mrs Wickham tells the story, it sounds as though her husband has simply misplaced himself somewhere. She is insistent that he has lost his way. He has not been home now for three days, not even to sleep, but Mrs Wickham has apparently thought nothing of it until now. She plans on attending an assembly this evening, you see, and requires an escort so she will have someone to dance the first set with her. She is quite put out."

"Goodness," said Lady Carlisle with some distress. "The scoundrel has most likely run off and left her!"

Mrs Lawrence agreed. "Are you at all acquainted with Mr Wickham, Lady Carlisle?"

"Certainly not, Mrs Lawrence," she said with a haughty sniff, "though I am quite familiar with his dissolute habits from his youth. He was positively wild during his formative years and caused Darcy much trouble throughout their time at university as well. I can hardly believe he was permitted to marry one of Miss Bennet's sisters, nor can I imagine any lady of sense accepting him!"

Mrs Lawrence grinned. "Then you are clearly not acquainted with Mrs Wickham either. While Miss Bennet is the epitome of good sense, Mrs Wickham revolts against the very idea of its existence. Two more different sisters you will never meet."

Darcy rubbed his forehead with his hand. "Perhaps we should go. I would not wish to importune the Gardiners at such a time."

"Really, Nephew," Lady Carlisle exclaimed. "Surely, you are not thinking of abandoning your future family at such a time. I daresay they would appreciate your assistance in the matter. If anyone can find Mrs Wickham's worthless husband, it would be you. Go, find your Miss Bennet, and offer your assistance to her poor sister. I shall remain here with Mrs Lawrence in the meantime, and we shall call for some tea. If I remember correctly, Mrs Lawrence, you prefer a spot of brandy in yours, do you not?"

"Oh, yes! That is just the thing, your ladyship. Mr Darcy, do be a dear and order a pot of tea, will you? We would be indebted to you."

Though he would have preferred to remove his aunt from the house altogether—more for the Gardiners' sake than for hers—Lady Carlisle appeared entirely disinclined to oblige him. He found it ironic that a woman who had turned her nose up at the very idea of visiting Cheapside was now adamant about remaining. "Of course," he said equitably. "I am your servant, madam."

"And some brandy, Nephew," she added. "Do not forget the brandy!"

"Certainly not," he muttered. "I shall in all likelihood have need of some myself."

As he made his way towards the door, he heard Mrs Lawrence say confidentially to his aunt, "I do hope Mrs Wickham does not have to get a divorce."

"I am getting a divorce," said Lady Carlisle matter-of-factly. "My husband is a philanderer and keeps enough mistresses to fill a stable."

Darcy exhaled heavily and shut his eyes.

✵ 31 ✵

WHERE GRACECHURCH STREET IS IN AN UPROAR, AND MRS WICKHAM DOES NOT GET TO DANCE THE FIRST SET.

Elizabeth had been locked away upstairs with her sisters and aunt for thirty minutes, but it felt more like hours. It was one thing to know that Darcy had paid to bring about Lydia's sham of a marriage; it was quite another to watch the irrefutable evidence of its hypocrisy unfold before her eyes. Clearly, her youngest sister cared more for dancing than she did the welfare of her absent husband, just as Mr Wickham cared more for himself than for his silly wife. They were far better matched than Elizabeth had originally thought, but it brought her no comfort, only disgust.

When someone knocked upon the door, Elizabeth literally leapt at the opportunity to answer it, praying she would find Hannah waiting just beyond the threshold, poised to announce Darcy's arrival—or better yet, Darcy himself come to claim her. Elizabeth had no patience for Lydia's petulant complaints, her aunt's wearisome lectures, and Jane's useless reassurances. She wished to be anywhere else—all the better if she could find respite from the mayhem in a quiet corner in another part of the house with

Darcy. She opened the door and nearly sighed with relief when she saw Hannah.

"Begging your pardon, miss, but Mr Darcy is downstairs with a fine-looking lady."

"Mr Darcy!" Lydia cried. "Finally, someone who can be of use to me, for none of you have done anything at all to find out where Wickham has gone. Of course, I shall go to the assembly in any case, but if he is not to be found I shall be very angry with him, I daresay!"

She made to push past Elizabeth, but Elizabeth had more than her fill of Lydia's self-professed entitlement for one evening; she would not allow her to accost Darcy, especially in front of his aunt. She took her firmly by the arm and said, "You will stay here Lydia and you will stop arguing with Aunt Gardiner at once. *I* will speak to Mr Darcy."

"La, Lizzy! Why should you do it? Wickham is *my* husband, after all."

Somehow, Elizabeth resisted the urge to shake her. "And Mr Darcy is soon to be mine. You will remain in this room and be silent or I will send Mr Darcy out of this house without a word to him about your troubles. Lady Carlisle does not need to know of your misfortunes. Indeed, I am tired of hearing of them myself." With an apologetic look at her Aunt Gardiner, Elizabeth quit the room, amazed that she had retained enough self-possession not to have raised her voice or put her spoiled sister over her knee.

She all but ran down the stairs. She was halfway to the drawing room when the door was thrown open and Darcy stepped into the hall, shutting it firmly behind him. Her heart sank as she observed his countenance—he appeared vexed. Upon seeing Elizabeth, however, his demeanour softened.

"Sir," she said with more composure than she felt, "please forgive me for failing to welcome you and Lady Carlisle upon your arrival. I have been otherwise engaged."

Darcy shook his head and went to her. "I am the one who is sorry. Mrs Lawrence informed us of Mrs Wickham's situation—in detail."

Elizabeth covered her eyes with her hands. "Mrs Lawrence's knowledge of it is embarrassing enough. That your aunt should be privy to our troubles is absolutely mortifying."

To her utter shock, Darcy snorted, removed her hands from her face, and raised them to his lips. "In all likelihood, she thinks nothing of it at this point. Her ladyship has had an eventful day herself and, while she is certainly concerned for your family and what *you* likely suffer, I believe she is almost relieved to have something other than her own misfortunes to occupy her conscience. She appears quite happy to visit with Mrs Lawrence. I have been dispatched to fetch tea."

Elizabeth regarded him with some scepticism. "That is a relief, I suppose, though I am sorry to hear that your aunt has suffered any sort of misfortune. I hope nothing serious has occurred."

"It is quite serious, I am afraid, but nothing to concern yourself with for the moment. I am certain you will hear the sordid details later, and likely from Lady Carlisle's own mouth. One would think my proper aunt would desire privacy and discretion, but it seems that is not the case. She readily revealed all to Bingley's aunt with little prompting." He paused, then frowned, and drew her farther away from the drawing room, towards the back of the house where they would have more privacy. "How are you?" he asked, tenderly touching her cheek. "How is Mrs Wickham?"

Elizabeth stepped closer to him, close enough that their bodies touched, and laid her head against his shoulder. In the next moment she found herself enfolded in his arms. "She is as unrepentant and selfish as ever and speaks only of dancing," she replied, wrapping her arms around Darcy's waist. "It is clear to me Lydia cares as little for Mr Wickham as he does for her. I can hardly credit that I am related to such an unfeeling, self-centred creature."

"Nor can I," he said, placing a kiss upon her head, "but she is your sister, in any case."

Elizabeth received no consolation from this statement, only more dissatisfaction. *"My sister,"* she said in annoyance, "expects that you will go out of this house at once and find her husband for her—that you will drop everything and see that it is done. She is determined she will dance the first set at some ridiculous assembly this evening. Should Mr Wickham fail to oblige her by being found, I would not put it past her to demand you escort her in his stead."

"That, I will never do. While I take great pleasure in dancing with *you,* I have no desire to attend an assembly with your youngest sister. I need to attend my wayward aunt instead, as she is now my houseguest until further arrangements can be made. I will write to Colonel Fitzwilliam, however, and inform him of Wickham's absence."

"You need do nothing of the sort."

"As I said, she is your sister. Do you not want Wickham to be found and held accountable for abandoning her in the middle of London?"

"I want only to be rid of him!" She was dangerously close to losing her composure. "He has done nothing but cause misery of the acutest kind, and I do not refer to the fresh misery his truancy has caused today. I refer to his lies and his deceit and the general malaise and devastation he leaves in his wake wherever he goes.

"Had I never met Mr Wickham, I would not have heard his abhorrent tales about you and believed them. I would have gotten to know you without his hateful interference, despite your initial comment about my looks. I despise and loathe him! At this point, I care nothing for his return to my ungrateful sister. She cares little for him beyond what her vanity allows. There is little point in any of us exerting ourselves on their behalf, for neither of them shall ever appreciate our efforts. They cannot even appreciate each other."

Darcy's hold tightened, and he sighed as he laid his chin upon the top of her head. "Where is your uncle?"

Elizabeth lifted her head from his shoulder and willed herself not to cry. "He is in his study with Mr Bingley. They have been in conference there since shortly after Lydia's arrival."

"Then I will go to them now. I will only be a moment, then I will return to you. I do not wish to burden the Gardiners with additional guests when they are already dealing with Lydia's calamity. I will bring my aunt and Bingley's to Darcy House, and you as well should you desire to leave Gracechurch Street, though I must warn you that both ladies are more likely to be engaged with each other than in overseeing our respectability."

Elizabeth touched the shining brass buttons upon his coat, then laid her hand over his heart. Its steady cadence calmed her and allowed her to better compose her disjointed thoughts. At that moment, there was nothing in the world she wanted more than to leave her uncle's house to be with Darcy. Darcy House, Pemberley, Scotland, even a ship bound for Australia; accompanying this man whom she loved to the end of the earth was preferable to remaining under the same roof as Lydia. "While I would be willing to go to the moon with you," she told him, her lips lifting in a melancholy smile, "I cannot leave Jane. She is on her honeymoon. She should not have to deal with Lydia's wretched behaviour any more than I should, or my dear aunt and uncle for that matter. To abandon her to bear the weight of it would be unfair."

Darcy pressed a lingering kiss to her forehead. "I will speak with your uncle and send word to Colonel Fitzwilliam. Wait for me here. I will not have you distressing yourself further." He turned towards the direction of Mr Gardiner's study, but a sharp knock sounded upon the front door, and he paused.

Hannah appeared out of thin air, brushing past them in the narrow hall. A moment later voices could be heard in the vestibule, Colonel Fitzwilliam's among them.

Elizabeth's eyes widened as she looked to Darcy, and together they hastened down the hall. They arrived in the foyer just as Mrs Wickham came running down the stairs. Mrs Gardiner and Jane, each wearing an exasperated expression, followed closely on her heels.

"Lord!" Lydia cried, wrinkling her nose at the colonel's presence. "*You* are not my Wickham. Why is everyone standing about in such a stupid manner?" She stomped her foot on the stairs. "I want to go to the assembly!"

Colonel Fitzwilliam ignored her. "Darcy," he said, "I have been all over for you." Behind him, crowded into the tiny vestibule, stood a half dozen uniformed officers with grim countenances, grasping the hilts of their swords. "Not only has our friend deserted his post in the north, but he has left several debts of honour in his wake. I have been charged with returning him to his regiment."

Elizabeth's hand flew to her mouth. Mr Wickham may have been unscrupulous and dissolute, but in her worst dreams she had not expected he would become a deserter, an offence that was punishable by hanging; at the very least he would be painfully and publicly flogged for insubordination and dishonourable behaviour.

Darcy offered his cousin a curt inclination of his head, then turned to Lydia, whose countenance exhibited only sullenness rather than any degree of concern. "Mrs Wickham," he said, "you are in luck. These fine gentlemen have come to assist you in locating your husband."

⁂

It was nearly ten o'clock at night, and Elizabeth was seated at Darcy's pianoforte, endeavouring to distract herself from the chaos of Gracechurch Street by teaching herself to play a concerto by Haydn. Darcy lounged upon the couch, watching her with an intensity that made more than her countenance flush with warmth.

Mrs Lawrence was there as well. She and Lady Carlisle had claimed another set of sofas on the far side of the room, where they appeared wholly engrossed in conversation. The two had been as thick as thieves since they departed Cheapside nearly six hours ago and their delight with one another's society showed no sign of waning. Their joint consumption of two pots of tea, a snifter of brandy, and several plates of chocolate biscuits after supper had cemented their newfound friendship. At one point they had put their heads together and giggled like schoolgirls until the countess had lost her composure entirely and expelled tea from her nose. Darcy had gawked at their antics, but Elizabeth had hidden her smile behind her hand. The ladies exuded cheerfulness—an emotion she had come to understand Lady Carlisle had not experienced for many years.

Elizabeth hit a discordant note, huffed her displeasure, and ceased playing. She was too distracted to master the more complex chords and was growing irritated with her inability to execute even the more basic fingering of the piece with any sort of proficiency.

Darcy made his way to her side and lowered himself onto the bench, sitting so close to her that his coat sleeve brushed her arm. Without comment, he offered her a glass of madeira, which she accepted with a grateful turn of her mouth.

His fingertips lingered longer than necessary on the glass, purposely grazing her own. That he would dare to behave so brazenly in front of his aunt and Bingley's both surprised and amused her. He relinquished the glass to her, and she took a slow, measured sip of wine as the corners of her mouth lifted in the hint of a teasing smile. She took another sip, then offered the rest to Darcy, who promptly set the glass atop the pianoforte. "I believe a change of scenery is called for," he informed her. "Perhaps a walk through the solarium. It will do both of us a world of good. You have been sitting too long in one attitude."

Elizabeth glanced at the two ladies whispering together across the room and shook her head, marvelling at their complete disregard for their charges. "And what of our chaperons?" she enquired archly. "Though they appear oblivious to our existence for the moment, at some point they will have exhausted every topic of conversation and realise we are missing."

Darcy chuckled. "They really are awful chaperons." He extended his hand to her and rose from the bench. "Come. Let us test our theory, Miss Bennet."

Elizabeth slipped her hand into his and stood. "And what theory is that, Mr Darcy?"

"The theory that both aunts are so engrossed with each other that they will not even notice our leaving the room."

As it turned out, Lady Carlisle and Mrs Lawrence did notice their leaving the room and called out to them just as the couple set foot in the hall. Darcy froze, but Elizabeth pushed him in the direction of the solarium with a giddiness she could not contain. He grabbed her hand and they sprinted down the hall, only slowing their pace once they were inside the enclosed glass room.

Because it was night-time, there were no candles lit, but a low fire crackled in the grate of a large marble fireplace set against one of the interior walls, providing an additional heat source for the abundance of flowering plants and fruit trees within. With a small, private smile, Darcy guided Elizabeth deeper into the room and away from the door. His strides were even and sure, despite having to navigate the dimly lit interior.

They moved through a maze of mysterious, animated shadows cast by the myriad of exotic plants housed within. Their object was an upholstered chaise piled with pillows and thick rugs along the far wall. Darcy settled himself upon it and tugged Elizabeth onto his lap with a playful grin.

She was startled, but by no means disconcerted by his boldness. She felt only a sense of warmth and contentment, and a lovely ache blooming in the pit of her stomach—the desire their ever-increasing familiarity never failed to arouse in her whenever they touched. Sighing, Elizabeth wrapped her arms around his neck, pressed a tender kiss to his jaw, and laid her head upon his shoulder. "How dearly I love you," she told him softly as her fingers toyed with the artful arrangement of knots on his cravat.

"As I love you." His voice was pitched low, but she could hear the adoration in his tone as he spoke the words, and an under-lying note of satisfaction.

She smiled and nudged his chin with her nose.

He responded by tilting his face towards hers and capturing her lips in a kiss as sweet as the scent of the flowers filling the room. She answered him in kind, and Darcy gradually deepened their kiss. Memories of their sensual interlude in the music room intruded, and Elizabeth felt a sudden rush of emotion for this man who not only loved her so deeply, but constantly and without reserve.

To her surprise, Darcy's hands did not roam her body as they had the other night while they kissed; instead, his thumbs drew slow, lazy circles upon her back and her thigh as he held her. The sensation was heavenly, but the exquisite gentleness of his ministrations ignited a spark within Elizabeth that was gradually fanned to a fire. Desperate to experience the same delicious intensity of pleasure she had felt with Darcy days before, she shifted in his lap.

Immediately, Elizabeth sensed a shift in their dynamic. Darcy's careful, well-honed control ebbed. His hands travelled to her waist, then her ribs as his fingers sought purchase within the folds of her gown, urging her closer. His breath hitched as she complied; but her skirts were voluminous and multi-layered— far more so than the simple nightshift and robe she had worn in the music room at Darcy House—and she soon found her legs hopelessly tangled in a mass of sprigged muslin. It was frustrating and ridiculous and not at all what she had intended. Elizabeth could not help herself—she started to laugh.

With a rueful laugh of his own, Darcy withdrew from their kiss, laid his forehead upon her shoulder, and exhaled heavily as his hands came to rest upon her hips. "It is just as well. Her ladyship and Mrs Lawrence are bound to come in search of us sooner than later. All things considered they have been surprisingly generous in their allowances."

"They have," Elizabeth agreed, running her fingers through his hair, "and it would not do to repay their generosity by shocking them unnecessarily."

Darcy lifted his head and hummed contentedly, approving of her attentions. "Indeed." His hands caressed her hips, then slid to her waist. "You are lovely," he murmured, "and too tempting for your own good." His hands drifted higher.

"And you, sir," she said with undisguised affection, "are incorrigible."

However much Elizabeth wished they could continue in this delightful manner indefinitely, the likelihood of being discovered was too great. Should they be caught in such a scandalous embrace, Elizabeth felt certain she would die of mortification. Rather than tempt fate, she kissed Darcy chastely, untangled her skirts, and rose from his lap.

He did not permit her to go far. He stood, enfolded her in his arms, and repaid her kiss with another—a slow, sensuous press of his lips that served to undermine Elizabeth's resolve to be good. "Thank you," he said as her hands returned to his hair, seemingly of their own volition. His eyes were hooded, glossy, and dark and entirely focused upon her with a tightly reined ardency she desperately wished she could feel the full effect of, for better or worse.

"For what?" she enquired, trailing one finger along the contour of his ear.

Darcy's eyelids drifted closed. He expelled an erratic breath and said with some effort, "For permitting me to pretend you are already my wife, and for trusting me enough to remember to stop because you are not."

"I do trust you," she all but whispered, "I trust you with my heart, and I appreciate your determination to remain a gentleman and treat me with care. But I long for the day when you will cast aside your gentlemanly restraint and your proper behaviour and will not stop."

He exhaled harshly and rested his forehead against hers, taking a moment to compose himself. The scent of his breath was sweet, like the wine they had consumed in the music room. "I wish to God I did not have to return you to Bingley tonight."

"Then take me to Pemberley tomorrow," she said against his lips, "and make me your wife in three days' time."

"*Elizabeth.*" His pronunciation of her name was reverent, as was the kiss that followed. With unexampled tenderness, he caressed the curve of her cheek, the column of her neck, and the hollow at the base of her throat. His fingertips drifted along her collar bone—back and forth, over and over. They continued thus until the sharp staccato of approaching footsteps intruded, penetrating the haze of their ardour with an acuteness that sent a ripple of panic through Elizabeth's heart.

With an unintelligible oath, Darcy quickly strode several paces away, increasing the distance between them to one infinitely more proper.

Lady Carlisle entered the room a moment later. Elizabeth felt almost dizzy. She glanced at Darcy in alarm, but he was barely attending as he raked his fingers through his hair, attempting to coax it into some semblance of respectability, then tugged roughly at his coat. His back was turned.

Elizabeth quickly smoothed her skirts with slightly unsteady hands and breathed deeply, willing her flaming cheeks to cool as Darcy's fastidious aunt crossed the room in good time. Their eyes met, but instead of flagrant chastisement, Elizabeth was shocked to perceive a hint of diversion in the countess's expression. She did not know what to make of it and, while she felt some small measure of relief, her embarrassment at having been discovered by Lady Carlisle and the awkwardness attendant upon it was too severe to ignore.

Likely sensing her discomfort, Darcy returned to her and placed his hand on the small of her back for the briefest moment, a gesture likely meant to reassure her. "All will be well," he murmured in her ear.

Lady Carlisle raised one perfectly sculpted brow and pursed her lips. "Fitzwilliam George Darcy," she said crisply. "I expected far better behaviour from you, of all people. You should consider yourself most fortunate that I and not Mr Bingley have come to retrieve poor Miss Bennet, or you would find yourself in an even more disadvantageous position, and quite possibly on the wrong end of a pistol!

"Now, set yourselves to rights and come to the music room directly. Miss Bennet's sister and brother have arrived to collect her, and Richard is here as well. He wishes to speak with you regarding a matter of some urgency." The countess clapped her hands together in rapid succession and both Darcy and Elizabeth flinched. "Come, Darcy. Make haste. I really do not relish having to explain Miss Bennet's absence to her relations."

❦ 32 ❦

WHERE MR WICKHAM HAS MUCH TO SAY AND
PUTS IT IN A LETTER.

Darcy,

I write to you not to demand money, nor obtain forgiveness, but to inform you that I am leaving England with no intent of ever returning. Dependent upon the number of days that pass until this letter finds its way into your hands, I am unlikely to be on English soil but bound for a new continent with new prospects. So much the better for me. By now you must have learnt of my desertion and the debts of honour that prompted it, several of which I confess are rather more serious than my usual scrapes. I am not proud of myself by any means, but such has become my lot in life. While I endeavoured to be a good husband to my wife and to give the appearance that our marriage is respectable, you, more than anyone, ought to know that opportunity aided by circumstance often poses too great a temptation for me. In short, I have not remained faithful to my wife and for that I do feel some small degree of remorse, as I believe Lydia cares for me quite sincerely. Whether you believe it or not, I have grown fond of her as well— as fond as I can be of an affectionate, impulsive, silly girl I neither intended nor wished to marry in the first place.

But I digress. When my circumstances in the north became extremely dire, I knew I must either desert my post or face certain retribution from which I would never recover. My course was easily decided. I could not possibly bring Mrs Wickham with me. While the journey itself shall likely be arduous and of some duration, you must have surmised I do not have sufficiently ample funds to purchase suitable accommodations for myself and safe passage for my wife. It only stands to reason I must have something to live on when I reach my destination; the two-thousand pounds I have recently acquired should provide adequate support until I can make my fortune elsewhere. You understand my character intimately enough to guess that my owning to already having a wife at this point would render my scheme impossible. Do not think me too cold-hearted, however, as I did try to return Mrs Wickham to Longbourn last month. Had she not insisted on accompanying me to town she would now be safe within the bosom of her family and none the wiser.

As it was at your insistence that I married her to begin with, it will now fall to you to see that no harm comes to her. I hereby consign her unto your protection, and that of my dear sister Elizabeth, who I have come to understand has recently agreed to marry you. Please extend to her my best wishes for her health and happiness. I have no doubt she will find ample consolation as the new mistress of Pemberley, if not in the honour of being your wife.

Yours, etc.,
George Wickham

Darcy glared at the letter in furious disbelief, his ire escalating with each fresh reading of it. He was ensconced in his study with Bingley and Fitzwilliam, who had discovered a letter bearing Darcy's name within the lodgings the Wickhams had taken in a marginally disreputable part of town. It was late and the ladies—Lady Carlisle, Mrs

Lawrence, Elizabeth, and Jane—awaited them in the music room.

"Well," said Colonel Fitzwilliam impatiently, "what does it say?"

Disgusted, Darcy thrust the letter at him. "Wickham has left England. He does not intend to return."

Bingley appeared incredulous. "Never?"

Darcy scowled at the leather blotter upon his desk. "So, he says."

"What of Lydia? Surely, he cannot simply abandon his wife!"

"Not only has he abandoned her, but he consigned her unto my protection."

"That is absurd," Bingley stammered. "Wickham's wife is hardly *your* responsibility."

"It appears she must become someone's," Darcy said irritably, "as he intends to make his fortune in America by taking a new one."

"A new wife?" Bingley gaped at him. "But he already has a wife!"

Darcy rolled his eyes. "Thank you, Bingley, for pointing out the obvious."

The colonel looked up from Wickham's letter, his countenance dark. "You believe the blackguard is headed for America? I have seen no mention of it here."

"While he failed to mention his destination by name, Wickham is lazy. He is not heading to Australia or Canada. They are too rough for him, and the European Continent is too close and therefore too widely known. He has not the stomach for India— it is far too hot and dusty. It would take him six months or longer simply to reach it in any case, and Wickham is too spoilt to forgo the comforts of civilised society for half a year to travel there in the first place."

"Not to mention," the colonel added ruefully, "he would likely fall out of favour with whomever he managed to swindle while onboard the ship and more than likely find himself thrown headlong over the side of it. No, I believe you are correct. He must be bound for America."

Bingley slumped against Darcy's desk. "Whatever are we to tell Jane and Elizabeth? Or Lydia for that matter?"

"We tell them the truth," said Darcy. "They deserve to know what Wickham has done."

Bingley shook his head. "I cannot see the point. Lydia will never believe you in any case. You heard her at the Gardiners'. She was positively unreasonable, and hell-bent upon attending that blasted assembly, even after Colonel Fitzwilliam explained the severity of the situation to her. The way she went on about her new gown and dancing the waltz while her husband was to be court-martialed was astonishing! And her tomfoolery did not cease there. She complained of the unfairness of being made to stay at home for a full two hours! Why, I almost consented to escort her to the damned dance myself simply to shut her up!"

Darcy reclined in his chair, rested his head against the back of it, and rubbed his forehead with his hands. "I am sorry for abandoning you, Bingley. I ought to have been there as well."

Bingley waved his hand dismissively. "It is perfectly all right. Once Mr Gardiner finally lost his temper, she stormed up the stairs and locked herself in one of the bedrooms. It was far more civilised after that, despite the occasional bout of crying and stomping around we heard coming from upstairs."

"And this is the way you and Mrs Bingley must spend your honeymoon," Darcy muttered.

"Bingley may be newly married," said his cousin, "but you and Miss Bennet have only recently become engaged yourselves. You have had no courtship to speak of, only a week or so of betrothal and a history riddled with misunderstandings and regret."

"Too true," Bingley agreed. "Jane and I had two wonderful months of engagement and are now happily married. There was nothing you could have done that Mr Gardiner and I did not do. You were right to take Elizabeth away. No one bears you any ill will for doing what you believed best for her. The Gardiners certainly do not, and Jane and I agree. And it was very good of you to include my Aunt Lawrence in your party. She has enjoyed herself a vast deal more here than she would have while suffering Mrs Wickham's tantrums in Gracechurch Street."

"So would we all," Colonel Fitzwilliam commented dryly, rising from his chair. "I am afraid I must be going, gentlemen. Though I can do nothing further tonight, I will visit the docks tomorrow morning and see if there were any ships bound for America within the last three days. If Wickham was on one of them, all the better for England I suppose. If not, I will find the reprobate eventually."

"You will keep me posted?" Darcy asked.

"I shall be in touch tomorrow as soon as I have something to relate. Bingley, it was good to see you as always. I must say I am rather jealous. You are as fortunate in your choice of wife as my discriminating cousin here. It is a pity there is no beautiful Miss Bennet for me," he said with a roguish smile.

Bingley grinned good-naturedly; Darcy pursed his lips. "Off with you," he said, "or I will not be held responsible for my actions."

The colonel laughed at him and took his leave.

୧୨୨

The following morning saw Darcy breaking his fast with Elizabeth and the Bingleys in Park Street, where he and Bingley discussed calling upon Mr Gardiner without delay. While the gentlemen had intended to go alone, Elizabeth begged Darcy to take her along as well, and insisted she would not take no for an answer. Bingley observed their exchange with an expression of consternation upon his face, especially when Darcy did not assert his authority over his future wife but merely pressed her hand in an affectionate manner and acquiesced to her demand without batting an eye.

Though Elizabeth had wanted to speak with him the previous night before she departed Brook Street, there had been no time for Darcy to relate anything of his meeting with Bingley and Colonel Fitzwilliam to her; Jane was eager to return to the comfort of her own home, and both Lady Carlisle and Mrs Lawrence were present. He had assumed Bingley would have at least informed his wife of the particulars once they gained the privacy of their own apartment, but Elizabeth had told him Bingley had not done so, nor had he spoken so much as one word on the subject to either of them that morning.

Darcy recalled Bingley's comment about seeing no point in sharing the contents of Wickham's letter with the ladies, the bewildered look on his face at the breakfast table when Darcy had told Elizabeth she could accompany them to Gracechurch Street, and the speech he had made at Netherfield about desiring a compliant wife and shook his head. He suspected that once they reached Gracechurch Street his friend would likely be opposed to allowing Elizabeth to join them in her uncle's study. Darcy wondered whether Mr Gardiner would oppose her presence as well.

Mr Gardiner did not, and despite the look of dismay Bingley wore, Darcy was glad. Once behind closed doors, he retrieved Wickham's letter from his coat pocket and presented it to Elizabeth's uncle, whose countenance grew more indignant the farther he progressed down the page. When he had done, he laid it upon his desk and Elizabeth reached for it, but Bingley was faster. He carefully folded the letter and handed it directly to Darcy. Rolling his eyes, Darcy plucked it from Bingley's hand and surrendered it to Elizabeth, who thanked him and proceeded to devour every word. As she read, her expression wavered between blatant disbelief and alarm.

"Darcy," Bingley muttered while Mr Gardiner looked on. "I hardly think allowing a lady to read such an unprincipled missive is appropriate."

"You are entitled to your opinion, just as you are entitled to either share or conceal whatever information you see fit from your wife. It is no concern of mine, nor will I interfere with your prerogative. However, I expect you to extend the same courtesy to me regarding my own wife. I see nothing wrong with Elizabeth reading the contents of this letter, nor does Mr Gardiner appear to object."

"Lizzy is hardly your wife at the moment. She *is* my sister, however, and her father has charged me with her protection."

Darcy stared blankly at him. "Are you insinuating Elizabeth needs protection from the contents of a letter or from me, Bingley?"

Bingley appeared appalled by his suggestion. "Of course not," he cried. "Surely, you cannot think I do not trust you, especially after all we have been through together. I meant only that the contents of Wickham's letter are most shocking and written in a corruptness of spirit I have rarely witnessed myself. Elizabeth is an unmarried gentlewoman and as such her sensibilities are hardly suited to such vile, wholly inappropriate topics."

Having finished reading the letter, Elizabeth relinquished it to Darcy and fixed her brother-in-law with a look so caustic Bingley took a step in the opposite direction. "There is nothing the matter with my sensibilities, Mr Bingley, nor my intellect, nor with my being a woman for that matter." She looked as though she intended to say far more, but her uncle intervened.

"Mr Bingley," said Mr Gardiner diplomatically, "while I appreciate my niece is currently a guest in your household, she is still my niece and currently visiting in my home. I have known her far longer than you have, sir, and can vouch for her sensibilities, as well as her constitution. In this case, Mr Darcy and I are of one mind. No harm will come of Elizabeth reading the letter. However, a better understanding of her sister's circumstances and Mr Wickham's motive and plan will surely be gained."

"Yes, well, perhaps you are right, Mr Gardiner. Forgive me, Lizzy. I spoke out of turn."

Darcy thought that was a bit of an understatement, especially as Bingley had dared to imply Elizabeth was not the strong, determined, intelligent woman she was, but insensible and weak.

She exhaled a measured breath. "All is forgotten, Charles. We are all on edge, I fear. While I am by no means in danger of succumbing to a fit of nerves, I cannot but agree with you on one count—Mr Wickham is the vilest, most unprincipled man I have *ever* known. His audacity alone is inconceivable! And yet the proof of it is clearly written by his own hand."

"Yes," her uncle agreed soberly. "This is quite a serious turn of events. As Mr Wickham claims he has fled the kingdom, the question of what to do about Lydia remains. She cannot be trusted on her own and so must stay here for the time being, preferably under lock and key. In the meantime, I will write to your father, Lizzy. He ought to come to London at once. If he receives my express this afternoon, he may be here by tomorrow morning."

"Thank you, Uncle."

Mr Gardiner reached over to pat her hand. "There, now. All will be well. We have made it through a similar hardship before and everything worked out in the end. If the good Lord is willing, we will get through this spot of trouble as well." He turned his attention to Darcy. "What say you, sir, to this business? Do you believe the scoundrel has truly left England?"

"Knowing Wickham, it is entirely likely, but Colonel Fitzwilliam is looking into the matter as we speak. We suspect he is headed for America. No one will know him there and pursuing him across an entire ocean would be too expensive and pose too much of an inconvenience to us, as well as to his regiment. He believes he will be safe."

Mr Gardiner frowned as he drummed his fingers upon his desk. "This is a very disagreeable business. Would that it never happened in the first place! I do not know who is more to blame —Lydia or her worthless husband."

Darcy glared at the carpet. Though both Lydia and Wickham were certainly culpable, he knew the truth—his previous failings had yielded yet another scandalous bout of misfortune for the Bennets. "You well know the blame falls to me, Mr Gardiner, the same as it did the last time. Had I revealed any of my prior dealings with him to your family when he first appeared in Hertfordshire, Mrs Wickham would still bear the name of Bennet. Now her situation has been made worse."

"It has been made worse," said Elizabeth, "by Lydia's own hand and Mr Wickham's. Not by yours."

"Elizabeth, you know as well as I that is not the case."

"I know of no such thing. Lydia flirted outrageously with half the regiment in Hertfordshire. I can only imagine how she behaved in Brighton, and Mr Wickham, the profligate opportunist that he is, acted accordingly. The fault lies with them, *not* with you, sir."

Darcy gave her a meaningful look he felt she could not possibly misinterpret. "Their marriage would never have come about otherwise."

She answered him with a quiet ferocity he had not expected. "Your entire *life*, Fitzwilliam, you have made amends for that man's treachery, and you have paid dearly for your benevolence in the process. The guilt you bear for the havoc his moral deficiencies have wreaked upon society is not only misplaced, but insupportable! I for one am glad to be rid of him. I love my sister dearly, but whatever his abandoning Lydia costs her is entirely inconsequential to me at this point, so long as *you* shall no longer suffer by his design."

She came to him then, and in front of Bingley and her uncle—against all that society considered proper—laid her hand upon his chest, directly over his heart. Her fingers trembled as she pressed them against his coat.

Darcy was troubled to see tears shining in her eyes.

"You are dear to me," she proclaimed with feeling, "and your heart is filled with such goodness! I cannot tolerate seeing you harmed by Mr Wickham's disregard any longer."

He reached for her, but Elizabeth withdrew her hand and quit the room.

Darcy stood in the middle of Mr Gardiner's study, silent and stoic, struggling to retain his composure. He did not have to look at Mr Gardiner and Bingley to know they must be staring at him. Elizabeth's speech, the fervency behind it, and the fact she had made it in the first place had deeply moved him. He did not dare glance at Bingley. Darcy needed only to see a flicker of disapproval on his friend's face to prompt him to say something truly regrettable. He inhaled a slow, steady breath instead. *Let Bingley enjoy his easy, compliant wife. I would not trade Elizabeth and her impassioned spirit for all the world!*

Behind him, Mr Gardiner cleared his throat. "Go ahead, Mr Darcy," he said gently. "Our business will keep for the moment."

Without uttering a word, Darcy went in search of Elizabeth.

彩 33 彩

WHERE MR BENNET IS INCONVENIENCED BY
HIS MOST WORTHLESS SON-IN-LAW AND
THEREFORE DISINCLINED TO OBLIGE
ANYONE.

Three days passed before Mr Bennet came to London. It had taken him that long to commit to making a journey that took no more than four hours by carriage when the weather was agreeable. It had been clear and dry for the past several days, with no clouds in sight. Elizabeth loved her father, but she had little patience left for his tardiness and neglect, not when something needed to be done about Lydia.

Her youngest sister had been troublesome to her aunt, disrespectful to her uncle, and as petulant and self-centred as ever. Mrs Wickham wanted to go out, was angry she was forced to remain in the house, and was perturbed about having missed the assembly she had wanted so badly to attend. Even though her husband had not returned from wherever it was she imagined him to be, she flatly refused to believe her 'dear Wickham' had abandoned her forever. Surely, he had just gone off to see to some important matter of business somewhere and would soon come back again. If he had lost his way, then Darcy ought to go out and find him. Short of showing Lydia the letter Wickham had written, which Jane and Bingley insisted would be an unkindness, there was no proof anyone could possibly present to Mrs Wickham to convince her she had been abandoned by her husband.

Colonel Fitzwilliam, astounded by her stubbornness and incomprehension, had offered to throw her over his shoulder and carry her to the docks himself. Surely, hearing a first-hand account of a gentleman fitting Wickham's description boarding a ship bound for America from five dock workers, three merchants, nine naval officers, and one Bow Street runner would make her see reason—but Elizabeth knew better. The king himself could announce the news at St James's Court, but that did not mean Lydia would ever believe him.

It was eventually decided that Mrs Wickham must return to Longbourn, despite her father cheerfully suggesting she remain in town with Jane and Bingley until they returned to Netherfield the following month. Bingley appeared horrified by the suggestion; Jane blushed and averted her eyes. Elizabeth was disappointed that he would joke about consigning Lydia to Jane's care while she was on her honeymoon. It was in poor taste, but her father just laughed at what he perceived as his own cleverness, opened a thick tome, and waved them off as he engrossed himself in Shakespeare's *Othello*.

As Mr Bennet ignored his family in favour of his book, Elizabeth noticed Darcy studying him from across the room. His countenance revealed nothing of his inner thoughts, but Elizabeth could tell by the rigidity of his posture he was not amused by her father's flippancy, or his dismissal, or the excess of time it took his future father-in-law to come to town and claim responsibility for his youngest daughter. That Mr Bennet had failed to reply to the letter Darcy had sent regarding their desire to marry at Pemberley likely added to his annoyance. Her father's complacent behaviour raised Elizabeth's ire as well.

Two days passed and, aside from attending a dinner at Darcy's home and spending an afternoon at a local bookseller's, Mr Bennet remained at leisure within the walls of his brother-in-law's residence and did not venture out. When Lydia's insistent speeches about being a married woman and therefore entitled to do whatever she wished became too tiresome for him, he retreated to the peace and quiet of Mr Gardiner's study. Elizabeth watched all with a heavy heart. Her sister's presence in Gracechurch Street was a burden on the Gardiners in more ways than one, yet her father appeared content to let her aunt—and even Jane and Elizabeth—handle the situation in whatever way she saw fit.

Darcy had attempted to broach the subject of a Christmas wedding at Pemberley on several occasions, but Mr Bennet smoothly changed the topic to books, horses, husbandry, and on one occasion the state of the roads. Elizabeth could see Darcy's patience waning and knew if she wished to avoid the issue coming to a head between them, she must speak to her father herself.

The following morning dawned sunny and mild, and Mrs Gardiner and the Bingleys had taken the children to visit the park at the end of the street. Even Lydia had been permitted to accompany them, though she made it clear she had no interest in seeing a bunch of noisy geese in a dried-up field when she could be enjoying herself in Bond Street. Mr Gardiner was at his office, but Mr Bennet had cloistered himself in his brother-in-law's study after breakfast. Though Elizabeth would have preferred to have visited the park with the others, she stayed behind to speak with him.

"Come in, Lizzy," he said when she appeared at the door.

She took a seat upon an upholstered chair near the fire. Her father had claimed the other. He was reading the London newspaper, and a pot of tea and a plate of biscuits had been set beside him on a pretty, painted table. Elizabeth thought he looked as much at home here, in her uncle's study, as he did at Longbourn in his own.

Without looking up from his newspaper, he said, "Has your sister's silliness driven you to seek solace in the only room where two words of sense are still spoken together, or do you finally desire a reprieve from Mr Darcy's incessant attentions? He appears uncommonly solicitous of you. What a difference from when you first knew him, eh, Lizzy! I believe he only thought you merely tolerable then."

Elizabeth felt a flush of heat rise along the back of her neck. "My aunt," she said sanguinely, choosing to ignore his comments about Darcy, "has taken the children to the park, and Jane and Lydia have gone as well. Mr Darcy has business this morning and will not be able to call until later. Save for the servants, we are quite alone."

"A rarity indeed!" He licked his fingertip and turned the page. "Are you come to keep me company, or is there something particular you require of me?"

"I would like to speak with you, sir, if I may."

"Go ahead then, child. You may say your piece and then leave me to mine."

It was a typical response, one Elizabeth had heard a thousand times from him over the years, but for some reason it sounded very different to her today. She knew her father loved her and even enjoyed her company. He had always treated her with a marked preference and a consideration he rarely showed to any of her sisters; but at that moment she did not feel favoured— she felt placated and dismissed. "I understand that Mr Darcy has acquainted you with our desire to marry in the chapel at Pemberley before Christmas. I would like to hear your opinion on the subject."

Mr Bennet shook his head. "Finding husbands and planning weddings is your mother's business. I have no opinion whatsoever on the subject, aside from advising you that marrying anywhere other than Longbourn will never do for your mother."

"Since it is not my mother's wedding but my own, I fail to see how my marrying at Pemberley should affect her to such a degree. Surely, it is my own satisfaction and Mr Darcy's that matters most on the occasion. Mamma can have no objections. Mr Darcy's home is warm and elegant, the grounds are beautiful, and Mr Darcy's aunt, the Countess of Carlisle, has graciously offered to arrange the wedding breakfast."

Her father lowered his newspaper. "Gracious and willing though Mr Darcy's aunt may be, your mother has been chattering non-stop about gowns and gloves and flowers and all manner of useless frippery for the past fortnight. Do not get me started on the breakfast—the courses, the cake, the seating arrangements!" He rolled his eyes. "In any case, her heart is set on having this event at Longbourn, where she can show you and Mr Darcy off to our friends and neighbours like a pair of lions at the London Tower. She will no doubt consider herself extremely ill-used if she were denied the pleasure. I would not attempt it if I were you." Likely considering the topic closed, he returned his attention to his reading.

Elizabeth, however, would not be dismissed. "Papa, Mr Darcy has his heart set on marrying me at his home, in his family chapel upon Pemberley's grounds. I see no reason why we cannot oblige him."

"And I see no reason why we should have to oblige Mr Darcy by going all the way to Pemberley when our home is at Longbourn." He turned to the next page of his paper, shook out the creases, and recrossed his legs.

Elizabeth did not think it possible for her tolerance for her father's complacence to deteriorate further, yet it did. Somehow, she managed to keep the tone of her voice equitable. "It is Mr Darcy's dearest wish to marry me from his beloved home. It is the least we can do considering all he has done."

"And what pray has Mr Darcy done that merits our running all over England to accommodate him? He is certainly rich and therefore used to having his way, but that is hardly reason enough for us to submit to his whims. No, Lizzy. Let him come to us."

"I do not wish to make Mr Darcy come to us," she said as the last vestige of her patience waned. "We are indebted to him."

Her father stared at her in confusion. "Indebted to him? How are we indebted to him? In what way?"

"In *every* way, sir!" she cried in frustration. "Mr Darcy happened upon me last summer in Lambton after I had read Jane's letter —the very letter that bore the most wretched news from home. My uncle took me to Longbourn, but Mr Darcy took it upon himself to leave Derbyshire—to leave his guests and his own sister to go to London to search for mine.

"It was Mr Darcy who canvassed the most disreputable neighbourhoods and discovered them. It was Mr Darcy who met with them repeatedly, worked on Mr Wickham, and ultimately paid him an exorbitant price to marry Lydia. He attended their wedding! You yourself professed that Mr Wickham would have been a fool to take her for less than ten thousand pounds. That is Mr Darcy's income for an entire year, yet he spent such a sum upon an impulsive, thoughtless, ridiculous girl he can neither esteem nor respect, and whose behaviour has not altered since! Had it not been for Mr Darcy, sir, we all would have been ruined! Jane would not be married to Mr Bingley, and Mr Darcy certainly could never have proposed to me."

Mr Bennet stared at her in shock. "Is *this* the reason you agreed to marry him, Lizzy?" he said with some distress. "Is *this* why you accepted him? Because we owe him a debt we cannot possibly repay? Did he press you into this marriage?"

Her father's accusations pained and angered her, and Elizabeth struggled to rein in her temper. "Of course, not," she told him tersely. "Mr Darcy would never press me to do anything I did not desire myself, nor does he expect so much as a shilling in compensation for his troubles. I had no idea of his involvement when I accepted his proposal. He neither intended nor wished for me to ever learn of it and was very upset to discover that I had."

Unable to sit still a moment longer, she rose and paced to the window, to the hearth, and back again. She *would* remain mistress of herself. She would not lose her temper. Drawing a fortifying breath, Elizabeth smoothed her skirts and reclaimed her chair. As composedly as possible, she told her father, "I accepted Mr Darcy based upon what I have come to know of his excellent character, his honourable nature, and his kindness. I accepted him because I have come to *love* him. There is no other gentleman of my acquaintance whom I respect and esteem more highly. He has no improper pride and is perfectly suited to me in understanding, taste, and temperament. Truly, Mr Darcy is the only gentleman I could ever be prevailed upon to marry."

Mr Bennet ran a hand across his mouth.

Though he was clearly agitated, Elizabeth was gratified to see he also appeared contrite; but his contrition did little to assuage her disappointment in him, nor ease the distress induced by his words.

He reached for her hand and clasped it tightly.

Elizabeth turned her head aside, determined not to give way to tears.

"I am sorry, Lizzy—exceedingly sorry," said her father solemnly as he pressed her hand. "I did not mean to imply your Mr Darcy is not a good man. I knew he was honourable when he came to me to ask for my blessing. I would not have given it otherwise. Nor did I mean to imply you accepted him out of duty. It appears I have become a jaded old man who knows not what he says."

A lump had formed in her throat. She swallowed it with some effort and said, "You accused Mr Darcy of having his way in all things. I can assure you, he does not. He has suffered the loss of both parents, assumed the responsibility of raising a sister more than ten years his junior, and has undertaken the management of a vast estate, all before the age of three-and-twenty. He has known disappointment. You did him a disservice when you implied otherwise, and you pained me by speaking of him in such terms."

"That was not my intent, Lizzy, truly."

Elizabeth made no reply, and after a moment of stilted silence Mr Bennet sighed. "So, your heart is set on going to Pemberley, then."

"It is, and before you enquire whether I am merely placating Mr Darcy, I am not. Pemberley is more than a fine estate with picturesque grounds. It is to be my home. It is where Mr Darcy and I came to have a better understanding of each other. It is where I first saw evidence of the man he truly is, not the man I had so unjustly perceived him to be in Hertfordshire. At Pemberley, we became friends. It is only fitting for us to become husband and wife there as well."

"You need say nothing more. I am convinced. If Pemberley is where you wish to marry your Mr Darcy, then to Pemberley we shall go. I would not like to see you unhappy, my dear. I will write to your mother this morning and break the news to her.

Until some other gentlemen come for Mary and Kitty, she will have to be satisfied with Jane."

Elizabeth's smile, though slight, was genuine. She squeezed his hand, rose from her chair, and kissed his cheek. "Thank you, Papa."

When Darcy arrived in Gracechurch Street that evening Elizabeth met him at the door with a small, private turn of her mouth. Before he could so much as bid her hello, she placed her finger upon his lips, took him by the hand, and led him to a secluded little parlour at the back of the house.

"I do not believe I have ever been in this room," he told her, pleased that she had thought to steal him away before her family learned of his arrival. The parlour was sparsely furnished, dimly lit, and colder than the rest of the house, despite the soft glow of coals in the grate; but Darcy had no complaints, not when she was looking at him with such warmth.

"It is rarely used," Elizabeth replied, cradling his hand in hers.

"Even so, I am glad of its existence, since it enables me to have a few minutes alone with you."

With measured deliberation, she traced her fingertips along his palm, from the base of his wrist to the tips of his fingers. One lone curl had slipped free of its pins to caress the side of her face and her lashes rested upon her cheeks—two smudges of inky black against her ivory skin. Darcy felt his heart constrict. She was utterly beautiful, and she was his.

Neither spoke as Elizabeth repeated her ministrations again and again. With each pass of her fingertips along his hand her featherlight touch became lighter, more languorous, and more tantalising. Eventually, Darcy's eyelids drifted closed. The urge to take her in his arms and kiss her senseless was currently at war with his determination to remain a gentleman. He reminded himself they were in her uncle's house, surrounded by countless members of her family. Surely, her father would not look kindly upon him if he were to catch them in an amorous embrace. While most fathers would likely demand an expedient marriage in the event of such impropriety, Mr Bennet was not like most fathers. Darcy suspected Longbourn's master would not only suggest a longer engagement but would receive immeasurable amusement in seeing his future son-in-law suffer.

"Hello, Mr Darcy," said Elizabeth.

Her voice was pitched low, and, in her tone, Darcy could hear evidence of her smile. His lips turned upward in response as he opened his eyes. Sure enough, Elizabeth regarded him with a teasing curve of her mouth and eyes that sparkled with mischief. She appeared inordinately pleased with herself.

Closing the distance between them, he captured her hands and brought first one, and then the other to his lips. He turned them over and pressed a series of soft, lingering kisses along each palm. "Hello, Miss Bennet," he murmured, moving his mouth to her wrist, brazenly tasting the salt of her skin and something sweeter; something that was uniquely her.

Her eyes darkened, her breath quickened, and Darcy's heart swelled with satisfaction. That his Elizabeth was so responsive to him was a gift he would cherish until the day he died. Every ardent look, every intimate caress of hands, every sound of encouragement from her lips; nothing was sweeter than knowing she not only loved him but desired him as her lover.

Beyond the parlour, the reality of the outside world intruded—the sounds of servants going about their respective tasks, relations engaged in conversation, and children giddy with laughter. The door to the parlour was wide open, and Darcy sighed his frustration. It was neither the time nor the place for such intimacy. Realising he and Elizabeth would likely have no time alone together once they left the room, he laid his forehead against hers for a moment, then gently kissed her lips, and straightened. "How was your day, my dearest?"

Her voice sounded endearingly uneven as she said, "My morning was surprisingly productive. I went shopping with Jane and Aunt Gardiner. I also spoke with my father."

"I trust your conversation was a pleasant one?"

"Not all of it, not initially. But in the end, I was appeased."

Darcy regarded her curiously. "I do not have the pleasure of understanding you."

She bit her lip, and Darcy could see she was holding back a smile. "My father would like to know when you desire to leave for Derbyshire so that he might make the proper arrangements to follow us with the rest of my family."

Darcy stared at her, too surprised to credit what he had heard. "Your father approves? He is in favour of our marrying at Pemberley?"

"Not at first, but he was soon persuaded to see reason and has since written to my mother. His letter was sent this morning by express."

A slow smile brightened his countenance. "Is tomorrow too soon?"

Elizabeth laughed. "Certainly not for me, but I believe we must take into consideration that we are not the only ones travelling to Derbyshire, sir. While I could happily make do with wearing sackcloth at this point, I fear my sisters and our aunts would appreciate at least a few days' advance notice to prepare for the journey."

"Perhaps by the end of the week, then."

"Perhaps," she said archly.

He rewarded her with a kiss—a tender press of lips, deliberate, lingering, and warm—and grinned.

Comprehending his pleasure, Elizabeth laughed and kissed him again.

❦

After they had dined and the gentlemen had separated from the ladies, Darcy approached Mr Bennet. "I wish to thank you, sir, for consenting to come to Derbyshire. It means very much to both Elizabeth and me to be able to marry at Pemberley."

"Think nothing of it," his future father-in-law said, taking a sip of port. "My daughter was quite adamant about the event taking place at your home. There was nothing for it but to give the scheme my blessing. She has had enough distress of late. Lydia's foibles have done nothing but bring misery upon us, and to Elizabeth and Jane in particular." Mr Bennet bowed his head. "I understand," he said quietly, "that my family and I owe you a debt of gratitude. I would like to pay you back if I may."

Darcy felt a flush of heat rise along the back of his neck. *So, this was how Elizabeth convinced her father to oblige us.*

"Do not blame Elizabeth," said her father. "It was only after I had antagonised her quite thoroughly that she revealed your involvement to me in a fit of temper. I believe she would have remained as silent as the grave otherwise."

Darcy raised his glass to his lips. "That is not necessary. I did not do it to garner your approbation, nor your thanks, but to right a wrong. Had I but revealed my knowledge of Wickham's habits to the world in the first place, many good people would have been spared much anguish and hardship, your family included. You owe me nothing, not even your thanks."

"Even so, sir, you have it all the same."

They stood in silence for several moments, until Mr Bennet enquired when Darcy anticipated leaving for Derbyshire.

"As soon as Elizabeth informs me that she is ready to depart. Perhaps by the end of the week or the beginning of the next if the weather allows for the journey." A thought occurred to him. "I understand you intend to return to Longbourn to travel to Derbyshire with the rest of your family, but I would like to propose a slightly different arrangement, if you would be so good as to hear it."

The elder man raised his brows. "Speak on, Mr Darcy. Any suggestion you have to offer on the subject of sparing me a three-day journey confined to a coach with my wife, her nerves, and my three silliest daughters will be most welcome."

Darcy pursed his lips. The man could be truly awful regarding his family, but Elizabeth loved him, and her father's good opinion was important to her. It was for her sake he ignored Mr Bennet's flippancy and said, "This is what I am thinking..."

❄ 34 ❄

WHERE DARCY HOUSE RECEIVES AN
UNEXPECTED VISITOR WHO, IN SUCH
CIRCUMSTANCES, BELIEVES FRANKNESS IS
BEST.

D arcy was sitting with Lady Carlisle in the drawing room of his Brook Street residence, staring out the window while she talked of idle nothings. In just a handful of days he would be travelling to Pemberley with Elizabeth. The journey would take them three full days if the weather cooperated, and they would be joined in holy matrimony the second morning after their arrival. He could not repress his smile. In little more than a week she would be his wife.

"…exactly like your mother's, Darcy," said her ladyship, startling Darcy from his musings. "Lady Anne had such elegant taste. Her table linens were of the highest quality, and her china was exquisitely painted in one of the loveliest patterns I have ever seen." She handed him a cup and saucer.

"Was it?" he asked staidly, ignoring the pang of guilt he felt for not attending. He offered her a hasty smile as he accepted the proffered teacup, took a sip of tea, and grimaced. Darcy had never cared for green tea, but the countess enjoyed singlo, so he put up with it. For *years* he had put up with it. Shaking his head, he recalled his conversation with Mr Gardiner weeks before about the sacrifices he was in the habit of making to avoid disappointing those for whom he cared. When was it to stop? This was his house, not his aunt's. He should have oolong if he wished it, or black tea, or coffee for that matter. He laid his cup aside and rang for a servant.

A footman appeared promptly, bowed, and awaited Darcy's instruction.

"I would like a pot of oolong tea, Smith, and some chocolate tarts. That will be all."

"Oolong, Darcy?" his aunt enquired, frowning as Smith the footman quit the room. "When have you ever preferred oolong to singlo? Singlo is your favourite!"

"It is not my favourite. It is Arthur's favourite, and yours. I like many kinds of tea but singlo is not one of them."

She appeared confounded. "Really! You have never refused it before—quite the opposite in fact. You were always glad to accept a cup from me whenever you called at Carlisle House."

Darcy shifted in his chair and crossed his legs. "I have never cared for singlo tea, nor any variety of green tea. I have tolerated it for your sake because I did not want to inconvenience you. If my drinking singlo pleased you, it was no great sacrifice on my part."

"Why did you never say anything? I would have served you something you did like!"

"Would you have?" Darcy remarked dryly. "I recall mentioning my preference to you on several occasions, to little effect. Refusing a cup of tea from you, Lady Carlisle, was much like refusing an invitation to an evening party. You would thrust it at me and smile when I accepted and browbeat me whenever I did not. It was easier to simply suffer it in silence."

"You allude to more than tea, Nephew," said the countess, raising her teacup to her lips.

Darcy bowed his head. "Perhaps. It is done, however. I am to marry Miss Bennet in seven days." Even as he said the words, he could not repress his smile.

Lady Carlisle laughed at him. "You are a hopeless case. Would that I had known of your Miss Bennet sooner! Perhaps I would have abandoned my efforts to find you a wife long ago, especially after seeing how you both admire one another."

"I doubt it. There was a time when Miss Bennet did not admire me, and you are nothing if not tenacious, madam. My one consolation was that you appeared entirely disinclined to encourage me to marry Anne."

The countess rolled her eyes. "Of course, I could not support such a scheme. You are far too exacting for our Anne. She needs someone with more liveliness, someone to draw her out of her shell, much like Miss Bennet has done for you. I daresay the idea of marrying you has likely terrified her! I have no doubt Anne will be relieved to hear you have chosen Miss Bennet instead and is now blessedly free of you."

Darcy scoffed. "If ever Anne manages to extract herself from beneath her mother's thumb long enough to meet a gentleman she wants to marry, I will support her and wish her every happiness. Until then, Lady Catherine will not relent."

"Have you written to Catherine, Darcy?"

"I have not. I considered notifying her of my engagement several times, but as I cannot guarantee she will remain quietly at Rosings for the duration of it, I decided to forgo antagonising a sleeping tiger. It will be more prudent to present my marriage to Miss Bennet as a fait accompli rather than risk Lady Catherine paying me a visit to voice her disapprobation, or worse—paying Miss Bennet a visit and haranguing her in front of her family."

"No," Lady Carlisle agreed with an air of superiority and just a hint of satisfaction, "that would never do at all. I feel quite honoured, Darcy. So far, I am the only relation of yours to whom you have granted leave to harangue your future wife. I have no desire to share such an exalted distinction with the likes of Lady Catherine de Bourgh, I assure you."

"Indeed," Darcy quipped as a maid entered the room bearing a tray with a pot of tea and several chocolate tarts. "Thank you, Martha."

Martha arranged everything on the table, curtseyed, and returned to the kitchen as Darcy reached for the teapot and poured himself a steaming cup of oolong. The toasty, slightly chocolatey notes imbued his senses with a rich, full flavour, and he sighed contentedly as he raised his cup and took an appreciative sip.

His contentment, however, was not to last as Colonel Fitzwilliam was shown into the room twenty minutes later with none other than Anne de Bourgh attached to his arm. Dismayed, Darcy discarded his chocolate tart and stood to greet them.

"Anne!" his aunt cried with equal surprise. "We were just speaking of you not half an hour ago, my dear! I must say you look remarkably well. Whatever are you doing in London?"

Fitzwilliam saw Anne settled comfortably beside his mother on the sofa, then claimed a chair near Darcy's. "Anne has some news," he said, looking pointedly at Darcy with a flicker of amusement in his eyes.

"It is good to see you, your ladyship," Anne replied with her usual gravity. Though she was still thinner than most other ladies of his acquaintance, Darcy observed a brightness in her eyes, and a hint of warmth in her sallow complexion.

Anne turned her full attention to him then, and her lips lifted with a gentle, deliberate smile as she offered him her hand. "Cousin," she said softly, "I trust I find you well today."

Darcy accepted her hand, bowing politely before relinquishing it. He was shocked to see her. It was highly unusual for Lady Catherine to come to London, but even more so for Anne to make the journey, as her delicate constitution usually prevented her travelling beyond Kent. In fact, he could not recall Anne ever being in London since her presentation at court eleven years prior, nor looking so well when she had. Try as he may, he could not account for her presence, and the starry-eyed expression she wore as she looked at him did not make him want to enquire. Realising he had been silent too long, he said, "I am very well, thank you, Anne. I hope your journey to town was a pleasant one and not too taxing."

"I am extremely well, Cousin, I thank you. The carriage ride was rather long, but not the least bit unpleasant. As you can see my health is much improved since the spring and I am gratified to have been able to make such a journey. From what I recall of London, it is an exciting place. I am looking forward to seeing more of it in the coming weeks."

It was the longest speech Darcy could ever remember hearing her make. "Yes," he said succinctly, growing increasingly uncomfortable under her attentive gaze. "Would you care for some tea? We have oolong or singlo. You are welcome to either."

"Darcy does not care for singlo, you know," the countess remarked dryly.

Anne pursed her lips. "No, he does not. My mother has spoken of oolong being Darcy's favourite for years. Though it suits him,

I have always found it too severe for my liking, at least the way Darcy takes it. A nice, mild cup of green tea is far more to my tastes."

Lady Carlisle's lips quirked. She cast her nephew a self-satisfied look from over the top of her teacup and raised one pert brow.

Darcy made a valiant effort to ignore her and proceeded to pour a cup of singlo for Anne. "I believe Fitzwilliam mentioned you have some news."

The colonel snorted. "Does she ever."

Darcy glanced sharply at him, but the colonel merely shook his head and endeavoured to hide a smirk behind his hand.

Anne accepted her tea and promptly placed it upon the table. "I believe in such circumstances that frankness is best." She smiled demurely at Darcy and said, "Cousin, I have recently learnt that I am to become a married woman."

Darcy, who had just taken a sip of tea, began to choke. "Good God," he stammered, frantically wiping tea from his coat with a linen napkin. He could not decide whether he was more horrified that news of his engagement had reached Rosings—and therefore his aunt—or that Anne seemed to suffer from the delusion that she was the lady he wished to take as his wife. He tossed his napkin upon the table with the tea things and said incoherently, "Anne, I am not at liberty...I am entirely besotted with...that is to say that I cannot possibly—or rather, *we* cannot possibly—"

To his utter consternation, Colonel Fitzwilliam, who had been quietly snickering through Darcy's attempt to correct Anne's misapprehension, lost his composure completely and laughed outright.

"Richard!" Lady Carlisle admonished. "That is quite enough out of you!"

Unlike her cousin, Anne appeared distressed. "Oh, dear," she cried, blushing profusely. "Oh, no, Darcy. No, I do not mean I am to marry *you*. I refer to my engagement to Mr Joseph Sutherland."

Darcy gaped at her in astonishment. "Mr Sutherland? You are engaged to marry your physician?"

Anne coloured more deeply, but the happiness radiating from her countenance could not be denied. "We are to be married next month."

"But your mother!" he blurted ineloquently. "Lady Catherine cannot possibly support your being engaged to your physician! Forgive me, Anne. Excellent man though he is, you must admit Mr Sutherland's position in society is hardly equal to her aspirations for you."

The smile slipped from Anne's face. "You mean his standing in society is very different from your own. I mean no disrespect, but Mr Sutherland suits me—nay, he complements me—in ways that you never have, nor ever will. Though I care for you, Cousin, I never desired to be your wife. That was my mother's dearest wish, not mine. While she spoke of nothing but her anticipation of our betrothal, I spent most of my life dreading it. It was not until April last, when I saw how you looked at Miss Bennet with such admiration and yearning, that I finally understood I was safe from ever receiving your addresses. When news of your engagement reached Rosings two days ago, I gathered my courage and revealed my heart to my mother. As you can imagine, it did not go well."

"No," Darcy muttered sheepishly. "I would imagine it did not. I am sorry, Anne—exceedingly sorry—that you ever believed I would appease your mother in such a fashion. We ought to have spoken of it long ago. Lady Catherine must have been livid."

"She was," Anne admitted with no little emotion. "She abused poor Mr Sutherland abominably, and she blames Miss Bennet for the entire business for having distracted you from your duty. I attempted to impress upon her the utter futility of her forwarding a match between us, but she refused to hear a word I uttered. She intends to remind Miss Bennet of the inferiority of her station and her circumstances in life and convince her to break her engagement to you. Mother is confident she will carry her point. Once you are free of Miss Bennet you will come to see the error of your ways and seek consolation with me. I will, of course, miraculously forget Mr Sutherland ever existed, and you and I will do our familial duty and wed, thereby uniting Rosings and Pemberley under one name."

"That is utterly absurd," Darcy declared, agitated and alarmed. "Even Lady Catherine cannot influence what is in a person's heart!"

"She underestimates us," said Anne with a stringent verity that startled all in the room. "She underestimates Miss Bennet as well. She is a clever young woman and has far too much self-respect to permit herself to be worked on in such a manner. You have long been your own master, Darcy, and can well afford to marry whomever you choose. I am nine-and-twenty and the heiress to Rosings Park. I have the means to seek my own independence and marry whomever I desire as well. I intend to do exactly that, regardless of my mother's opinion on the subject."

In all the time he had known Anne, Darcy had never heard her oppose her mother, or even so much as voice a difference of opinion. He was stunned by her mettle, impressed by her speech, and in awe of her determination. She would make a wonderful mistress of Rosings, if she and Mr Sutherland could only manage to banish Lady Catherine to the dower house.

"Well said, Anne," Lady Carlisle told her with a mixture of haughtiness and pride. "While I cannot deny I would have preferred to see you marry a wealthy heir to a large estate, a physician is hardly the worst you could do. Bring your Mr Sutherland to dine and I shall be pleased to make his acquaintance. Darcy will not object, will you, Nephew?"

"Mr Sutherland," said Darcy, "is an excellent man and I welcome the opportunity to know him better. I assume from what you have related that Lady Catherine has not accompanied you to town, Anne. But dare I ask if Mr Sutherland escorted you?"

Anne flushed scarlet. "Mr Sutherland would not hear of me travelling with only a footman for protection, and Mrs Jenkinson was kind enough to accompany us. His sister and brother-in-law have a fine home in Curzon Street, where we plan to reside until our wedding. Mr Sutherland has left his practice in the hands of his associate, Mr Walker, for the time being. We will be married from Curzon Street at the end of January and then return to Rosings shortly thereafter."

"And Lady Catherine remains at Rosings?"

"Oh," she said dolefully, "that is the other matter I wished to mention. I am so sorry, but I am afraid my mother has already gone to Hertfordshire."

Darcy paled. "To Hertfordshire? She would not dare!" But one look at Anne's sympathetic countenance told him that Lady Catherine most certainly had dared to do just that and more. He strode to the window, slammed his hand upon the casement, and uttered an oath.

"Her efforts will amount to nothing," said Fitzwilliam with far more confidence than Darcy felt. "As Miss Bennet is currently in London, she will never even see Lady Catherine until after she becomes Mrs Darcy. All will be well."

"All will not be well, Fitzwilliam," Darcy said in frustration. "Elizabeth's mother and two of her sisters are still at Longbourn. Mrs Bennet is as stubborn and irrational as Lady Catherine! Despite her initial awe of our aunt's affluence and position in society, the two will certainly end up arguing and there will be no one of any sense there to intervene."

"Oh, surely, it will not be so bad as all that," said Lady Carlisle.

He gave his aunt a pointed look and said grimly, "You have met Mrs Wickham. She does not take after her father."

"Goodness," muttered the countess, frowning into her teacup. "I had not given that a thought. How unfortunate. Your poor Miss Bennet, to have such interesting relations. We shall have to do something to improve upon their manners once you are married, her youngest sister especially."

Darcy snorted. "I give you leave to do whatever you can to instil an ounce of sense into Mrs Wickham and wish you the very best of luck in your endeavour."

❧

Darcy breathed a sigh of relief as his hands encircled Elizabeth's waist. They were blessedly alone for the moment, but were by no means alone in actuality, a fact Darcy had difficulty recollecting as Elizabeth's fingers traced light, intricate patterns upon his waistcoat. The hour was late—well after midnight—and they had been granted a few moments of privacy to say goodnight before Darcy departed for Brook Street. Elizabeth had pulled Darcy into a little parlour at the front of the house her sister favoured during the day, where a bed of dying coals provided a warm, intimate setting.

All the way from the drawing room, Darcy could hear Caroline Bingley proclaiming her fatigue to the Hursts. He shut his eyes and repressed an urge to utter a sarcastic retort under his breath. The woman had done nothing but make herself disagreeable that evening, complaining about everything from the neighbourhood, to the house and its furnishings, to the number of courses, to Jane serving beef instead of fish for supper. The new Mrs Bingley had borne it all with equanimity and grace, but Bingley had shot his sister a series of caustic looks throughout the night that did little to quell the flow of her commentary. Even the Hursts appeared annoyed and embarrassed by her remarks—a first in Darcy's experience.

Though he had been friends with Bingley for many years, and therefore thrown into company with his family for nearly as long, he was hard-pressed to recall a more unpleasant evening spent with Bingley's youngest sister. If not for Elizabeth's presence, Darcy would have made his excuses and departed far sooner. Now, it had grown so late he had little choice in the matter. The thought of parting with Elizabeth pained him.

"Come home with me," he whispered, enfolding her in his arms. "I will secret you away in my greatcoat pocket. Bingley will be none the wiser."

She laughed at his silliness and slipped her arms around his neck. "As tempting as your offer sounds, I believe propriety demands that I decline. Even if Charles did fail to notice my absence, which I highly doubt, you know my sister will not. No, sir, you must choose again, and choose well. 'Like as the waves make towards the pebbl'd shore, so do our minutes hasten to their end'."

"'Then give me one kiss'," he replied feelingly, "'and I will give it thee again, and one for interest, if thou wilt have twain'."

With utmost tenderness, Elizabeth whispered, "'Touch but thy lips with those fair lips of thine'." Before Darcy could oblige her, she stood on the tips of her toes and bestowed a soft, sensual kiss upon his lips that warmed him like a flame from within. He met her with equal feeling as she stroked the side of his face and wound her fingers through his hair, deepening their kiss of her own volition.

With a surety that threatened to overwhelm him, Elizabeth traced Darcy's ear with her fingertip, the line of his jaw, and the edge of his shirt collar. She was not wearing gloves, and the moment her fingers dipped beneath the fabric and grazed the sensitive skin of his neck, Darcy found himself struggling to retain what little remained of his self-control.

He kissed her with an ever-increasing hunger while his hands explored her slender form with as much gentleness as he could bring to bear—her back, her shoulders, her waist. When his fingers teased the supple flesh along the neckline of her gown, then followed the column of her neck and sought the clutch of rich curls at her nape, Elizabeth gasped and moved to embrace him more fully.

Darcy stifled a groan as a shower of hairpins fell to the floor and several long, dark tresses tumbled free to brush against his hand. He worked his fingers into her hair, pressing her against the wall as he kissed her with abandon. With a ragged breath, he pulled her body flush against his, dragged his mouth along the curve of her neck, the smooth dip of her shoulder, and tasted the sweet, salty flavour of her pulse.

Somehow—Darcy hardly knew how—the sound of the Hursts and Miss Bingley bidding their hosts a good night in the drawing room registered in his lust-fuelled brain. With a herculean effort, he removed his hands from Elizabeth's body and his lips from her throat and tore himself away. "Forgive me," he rasped, reaching out a hand to steady her as she faltered, then righted herself against the wall. He drank in her flushed countenance, her dishevelled hair, and the glazed look in her eyes as they both struggled to catch their breath.

Mrs Hurst's bird-like laughter floated into the hall, prompting Darcy to act. "I must go. It is the last thing I want to do, but I am not fit to be seen and neither are you. Once again, my behaviour has been reproachable. I am so sorry."

"*Our* behaviour," Elizabeth whispered in earnest, blushing more deeply as she caught his hand and raised it to her lips. "I promise you I feel no regret, nor will I once you have gone. I love you so dearly."

Her sincerity moved him as much as her proclamation of love, so much so that a lump formed in Darcy's throat. With difficulty, he swallowed it and said, "And I you. In six days, I shall show you how much." He heard footsteps in the hall, and Bingley's genial voice. In no state to meet with Miss Bingley and the Hursts, or to engage in benign pleasantries with his hosts, he quickly pressed a kiss to Elizabeth's lips, strode from the room, threw open the front door, and quit the house. He dearly hoped she would be able to extract herself from the parlour before anyone saw her hair in such a state of dishabille. If not, Bingley would likely be paying him a call in the morning that had nothing to do with being sociable.

❧ 35 ❧

WHERE DARCY IS TIRED AND NOT AT ALL
PLEASED UPON RETURNING TO BROOK
STREET.

T
he carriage ride to Brook Street from Park Street was blessedly uneventful, and for that Darcy was thankful. His ardent farewell with Elizabeth was fresh in his mind, as fresh as the flavour of her skin on his lips. Darcy rested his head against the back of the carriage seat and closed his eyes as he relived every kiss, every caress, every sigh, and quickened breath.

Before he knew it, he was home, and his footman had opened the door to his carriage. As Darcy alighted and made his way to the front door, his thoughts remained fixed upon Elizabeth. She had believed he was teasing her when he suggested she come home with him, but there was a part of him that had been entirely serious. His words about tucking her away in his coat pocket may have been in jest, but his desire for her society was sincere and heartfelt. How much warmer his home would be if she had responded with a 'yes' instead of laughter—how much warmer his bed! *Two more days until we leave London,* Darcy thought happily as he entered the house. *Six more days until I may call Elizabeth my wife!*

In the foyer, he shrugged off his greatcoat and handed it to his butler. "Goodnight, Sowersby."

"Goodnight, sir. If you please, your aunt, Lady Catherine de Bourgh, is in the drawing room with Lady Carlisle."

Darcy stared at him. Surely, he had misheard. "What was that you said?"

"Lady Catherine, sir. She has been here since six o'clock this evening. I had every intention of sending a note to Park Street with one of the footmen, but Lady Carlisle insisted it was not necessary and that she would entertain her ladyship until your return. I am sorry to report neither she nor Lady Catherine appear well pleased with one another's society."

Good God, those two women! All he wanted was to go directly to his bedchamber, climb between his sheets, and fall into oblivion as he dreamed of Elizabeth. Now he had Lady Catherine to deal with instead.

And Lady Carlisle.

Damnation.

Darcy ran his hand over his mouth in agitation as he weighed his options. He could simply slip away, but no, that would never do. Lady Carlisle would never forgive him, and Lady Catherine was far too stubborn to leave him alone until the morning. He doubted she would even leave his house. He swore under his breath as he imagined her pounding on his bedchamber door, or worse, barging into the room itself and verbally accosting him while he slept in his bed.

No, there was nothing for it except to allow her to say her piece and hopefully usher her from the house as expediently as possible. "I will see to her, Sowersby. There is no need for you to wait up."

"Very good, sir."

Hardly, Darcy thought resentfully as he headed towards the drawing room with a grim countenance. He could hear Lady Catherine's cacophonous voice within and paused to collect himself before nodding to the footman stationed in the hall. The footman opened the door and stepped aside so his master could enter.

"Darcy," Lady Catherine cried at once, her face pinched with anger. "Where have you been! I have been waiting all night for your return. It is most ungenerous of you to keep me waiting at all, but nearly eight hours together is unforgiveable. I am not accustomed to such infamous treatment!"

"Of course, you are not, Catherine," Lady Carlisle said as though she were placating a fractious child. She reached for her teacup, raised it to her lips, and looked pointedly at Darcy, the corners of her mouth lifting in a sardonic smile. "I cannot imagine what happened to prevent our nephew from rushing home to attend you. I spoke with his butler hours ago."

Darcy rolled his eyes at her. "Lady Catherine," he said dryly, "to what do I owe the unexpected pleasure of your company?"

"There is no pleasure in such a visit," said his aunt, "at least none so far as I can see! A report of a most alarming nature reached me two days ago and I have come to insist upon having it universally contradicted."

"If you refer to my engagement to Miss Bennet, I am afraid you have travelled a great distance only to suffer disappointment. I cannot contradict such a report, nor do I have any wish to deny its existence. Miss Bennet and I are to be married within a matter of days."

"And what of *my* daughter!" Lady Catherine cried in outrage. "What of Anne! Is she to suffer such a humiliation, such a degradation and disappointment? It is not to be borne!"

Any hope Darcy entertained of getting rid of his aunt in a timely fashion dissipated with each shrill syllable she uttered. *Bloody hell.* As if her presence was not bad enough, he felt a headache coming on. "Lady Catherine, having already discussed the matter with Anne, I can say with absolute certainty my cousin shows as much disinclination to marry me as I feel to marry her. The disappointment and humiliation, madam, appears to be all on your side. You may go on about arranged marriages, familial duty, and Anne and I being formed for one another all you like, but all your arguments can have no merit. All your wishes amount to nothing if neither Anne nor I desire such a union. Since we do not, I suggest you desist. Anne has given her heart to Mr Sutherland, and Miss Bennet has long been in possession of mine. It is too late. Nothing can be done."

Lady Catherine leapt from her chair, waving her cane in the air as she advanced upon Darcy. "You and Anne and your accursed hearts! You have been drawn in, the two of you! Of course, something can be done! There is always something that can be done, some way a person of low morals, who cares only for what they can get, can be worked on! Where is Miss Bennet? I know she is in London. That woman who claimed to be her mother told me as much. I will speak to her at once and I will make her see reason, even if you will not!"

"You will do nothing of the sort," Darcy replied in furious indignation. "Low morals indeed, madam! I will not have you forcing your insulting vitriol or your misguided notions upon Miss Bennet's sensibilities and compassionate heart! She deserves no such treatment, nor does she owe you any such courtesy."

"She owes me every courtesy for my attentions to her last April! If it were not for my generosity, she would never have been thrown into company with you at Rosings for countless weeks! She would never have been noticed by you at all!"

"Oh, do not be ridiculous, Catherine," Lady Carlisle interjected, rolling her eyes heavenward. "That is the most unfounded drivel I have ever heard! Darcy met Miss Bennet months earlier in Hertfordshire and was already well on his way to being in love with her. You and your precious Rosings had nothing to do with any of it, unless you count the excellent opportunity you provided Darcy for comparison between you—for Miss Bennet's manners are inarguably superior to yours, and her conversation far more amusing."

"Who asked for your opinion?" Lady Catherine demanded, turning on her sister-in-law with barely contained contempt. "No one, as usual! You ought to have learnt to hold your tongue by now, Virginia! You ought to know without doubt where your loyalties lie! You are the wife of an earl! You are a member of the noble Fitzwilliam family!"

The countess laid her teacup upon the table with a clatter, rose from her chair, and marched over to Lady Catherine. "With any luck, I will not be much longer!"

"That is enough!" said Darcy sternly, fixing both ladies with a look of utmost dissatisfaction as he stepped between them. "I have no intention of listening to your bickering. Lady Carlisle, if you wish to remain under my roof, I suggest you retire to your rooms at once. Lady Catherine, I do not appreciate being lorded over and badgered in my own home! While I care for Anne, I have never wanted to marry her, never intended to marry her, nor shall I ever oblige you by marrying her."

Lady Catherine made to speak, but Darcy held up his hand. "No more, madam! It is late, I have had an eventful day, and I wish to retire else I lose my temper entirely. You may stay the night in your usual room, but if you do not cease your pettiness and arguing and leave me be, I will have you thrown from my house, regardless of the hour.

"Lady Carlisle," he said stonily. "I will see you in my study at ten o'clock in the morning. It is high time we have a little talk." Having said his piece, Darcy fixed both of his aunts with an icy glare, turned on his heel, and left them to their own devices.

❦

"She is driving me out of my mind," Darcy muttered the following morning as he sat behind his desk in his study. He reached for his teacup and raised it to his lips, but paused when he detected a mild, slightly fruity aroma instead of the familiar, toastier notes he preferred. *Deuced singlo!* Scowling, he returned his cup to its saucer with a clatter and shoved it aside.

Across from him, Colonel Fitzwilliam scratched his brow. "I am afraid I require some clarification if I am to commiserate with you in the appropriate manner. Both Lady Catherine and my mother are a handful on the best of days. To which do you refer?"

Darcy gave him a withering look. "I refer to your mother. She has taken it upon herself to interfere with the running of my household. Singlo tea at every turn, mutton for dinner, instructing my servants not to notify me when disgruntled relations suddenly show up on my doorstep! While I can live quite happily without any knowledge of Lady Catherine's comings and goings, I cannot abide having mutton at my table."

The colonel's lips twitched. "A serious offence indeed, but hardly the worst-case scenario. Take comfort that she has restrained herself from sending out invitations for one of her evening parties. There is no telling what sort of indignities you would be made to suffer on such an occasion."

Darcy stared at him, horrified by the idea of Lady Carlisle hosting dinners and evening parties in his home for her insipid friends and their daughters. "She would not dare," he whispered, but even as he uttered the words, he could see soup and roast pheasant and mutton and puddings and cakes, card tables and cucumber sandwiches and custards and punch and ladies seated upon his drawing room sofas preening and gossiping and tittering as clear as day.

He shut his eyes and dropped his head into his hands. "This arrangement is not working, Fitzwilliam. You must find a way to lure her back to Carlisle House before I lose my sanity. We leave for Pemberley in two days. Last night, instead of a restful sleep, I suffered a series of nightmares in which Lady Catherine attempted to drown me in a vat of singlo tea while your mother nibbled chocolate biscuits and insisted that I would learn to like it. The look in her eyes was maniacal."

Fitzwilliam barked a laugh. "Let us hope it does not come to that." He reached for his teacup and shook his head. "You may be interested to know I have finally spoken to my father. He was furious, by the way, when he returned home to find my mother and most of her gowns and jewellery gone. I have told him very little beyond the *who, what, why,* and *when* of the business, but have said nothing about her staying here with you. It is only a matter of time before he discerns her whereabouts. That said, I doubt I can persuade my mother to return to Carlisle House willingly. The last time I spoke with her about it, she asked whether pigs had sprouted wings yet."

"You are a great strategic mind and a credit to His Majesty's army. The Major General cannot make do without you. Surely, you can think of something that will appease everyone in this scenario."

"I would rather deal with Bonaparte than my parents at this point. Bony is a tenacious devil, but my parents are utterly impossible. I can make no promises regarding my father, but I will do all I can to persuade my mother to behave herself." He rubbed his chin thoughtfully, then frowned. "Though I cannot say I favour such a resolution, what of a divorce? Is it even possible?"

"It is not. I spoke with my solicitor and several of his associates at length, as well as the bishop. Her ladyship has no recourse. There are three ways for their marriage to be dissolved, and none of them are applicable to her situation. The first option would be for your mother to take a lover, rendering your father the injured party, whereupon he could petition to divorce her based on grounds of her unfaithfulness. The second would be to have a physician declare your father deluded, necessitating a dissolution of their marriage based on reasons of insanity. The third involves impotency, which is hardly relevant in the earl's case." Darcy shook his head with a look of manifest disgust. "I have learned that any man in England could cheerfully beat his wife within an inch of her life and still the lady would be bound to him by law unless the worthless blackguard decided otherwise."

"Thank goodness that is not the issue in this case, although my father would have answered to me long ago if he were prone to violence rather than lustfulness and infidelity. Have you broken the news to my mother yet?"

"No. Not yet. I do not relish telling her she must remain married to your father when she is dead set against it. And angry. Perhaps they can yet reconcile…"

"Darcy," said the colonel tiredly, "they have spent most of their married life reconciling. At one point my mother was even reconciled to the fact that my father would do as he pleased, regardless of whether it pained her or not. Perhaps they could have continued as they were, but you became engaged to Miss Bennet, championed her intelligence and her candour, and ignored her lack of dowry because you love her. In my father's eyes, you are a fool. He would have you take Miss Bennet as your mistress and marry some rich harridan instead—something we both know you would never do, regardless of your morality. He does not understand your heart. Case in point, his alluding to taking a mistress in front of his wife. It raised my mother's ire something dreadful. How could it not? It is no great secret that my father married her for her thirty thousand pounds and her noble lineage. Not for the turn of her mind, not for her wit, and certainly not for love.

"Then," the colonel continued, "there is the matter of Lady Harrow. However truly debase that woman is at heart, she was my mother's friend for a long time. You are the spitting image of my father when he was your age. You know Lady Harrow set her sights on him simply to scratch an itch, and if she was able to twist the knife in my mother's back a bit for failing to persuade you to marry Lady Eliza, all the better."

Darcy sighed. "So, no reconciliation."

The colonel laughed without humour. "It appears unlikely."

❧ 36 ☙

WHERE THE STORM WILL COME BEFORE THE
CALM...OR RATHER THE WEDDING.

Elizabeth wrapped her hands around Darcy's arm as they made their way along Piccadilly Street in St James's. They had separated from the rest of their party, which consisted of the Bingleys, the Hursts, and Mrs Lawrence. The weather was chilly, but they moved at a leisurely pace towards a local book shop Darcy frequented without fail whenever he was in London.

The exterior of the shop was unassuming but tasteful, while the interior was expansive, open, and inviting. What must easily have been tens of thousands of books filled every available square inch of shelf space from the floor to the ceiling. Except for London's circulating library, Elizabeth had never seen so many books in one place. The sight of their smooth, leather bindings and lovely gilded spines pleased her beyond measure.

They passed more than an hour browsing the shelves. Darcy stayed close to Elizabeth as she wandered the aisles, listening with an indulgent turn of his mouth as she reminisced about countless rainy days spent in her father's library devouring works by Homer, Chaucer, and Shakespeare. While she skimmed her fingertips along a seemingly endless collection of poetry, noting each title and author as she went, he caught her hand and pulled a book of sonnets from one of the higher shelves.

The collection happened to be a favourite of hers, and Elizabeth could not refrain from voicing her pleasure that Darcy had chosen it. He guided her to a quiet, secluded corner at the back of the shop, where he settled her in a comfortable chair, opened the book, and proceeded to read aloud to her. As she listened to him recite such poignant words of love and longing, of affection lost and later found, Elizabeth felt an undeniable sense of warmth and an overwhelming gratitude. The soft timbre of Darcy's voice, the pleasant curve of his mouth, the devotion in his eyes, all served to endear him to her even more. Impulsively, she reached for his hand and pressed a lingering, heartfelt kiss to his knuckles.

Darcy's voice faltered. Without taking his eyes from her, he closed the book and placed it on a nearby shelf. "Are you well, Elizabeth?" he enquired gently.

She nodded and rose from her chair to stand before him. "I am happy," she told him. "You make me so happy, Fitzwilliam."

It was early yet, and there was no one else in that section of the shop; they were quite alone. Darcy urged her closer, bowed his head, and caressed her cheek with the briefest brush of his fingertips. They remained thus until the sound of voices at the front, beyond the maze of aisles and countless rows of books, reminded them that they were in public and their behaviour was far from appropriate. Darcy withdrew his hand, but before he could step away Elizabeth reclaimed it and bestowed one last kiss.

"Thank you," she said.

With unexampled affection, Darcy asked, "For what are you thanking me?"

"For knowing me so well. For understanding what I enjoy—what brings me pleasure."

"We marry in five days. I look forward to a lifetime of being able to bring you pleasure."

Elizabeth felt a flush of heat at the double entendre of his words.

A slow smile spread across Darcy's countenance, and Elizabeth laughed.

The sound of a throat being cleared interrupted their clandestine moment.

Startled, Elizabeth shifted her gaze to a tall, imposing gentleman who looked to be about sixty years standing a dozen or so feet away. His resemblance to her future husband was so uncanny she could not prevent herself from openly staring at him.

"Lord Carlisle," Darcy said with the barest modicum of civility as he squeezed Elizabeth's hand, then released it. "To what do I owe this honour?"

The earl's voice was gruff, but his penetrating gaze was not levelled at Darcy; it was focused on Elizabeth. "I suppose this is the girl you intend to wed in—what did you say, Nephew—five days?"

"This is Miss Elizabeth Bennet, my betrothed. Miss Bennet, my uncle, Lord Carlisle."

Elizabeth curtseyed. "My lord." She was surprised when the earl acknowledged her with a slight bow. It was very slight, but it was far more than she had expected after hearing such disagreeable accounts of him from Darcy and Lady Carlisle.

"Miss Bennet," he muttered brusquely as he scrutinised her appearance from her bonnet to her half-boots with a brazenness that disconcerted her. "Very handsome, but then again, I expected nothing less from you in that quarter, Darcy. You always did have a discerning eye when it came to women."

Elizabeth stiffened. That Darcy's uncle had just appraised her in much the same manner that a farmer might appraise a horse did nothing to improve her opinion of him, but she positively bristled at his implication about Darcy. She was mortified by this man's crassness, but soon recalled he spent most of his time with his mistresses instead of his wife. Rather than take him to task for his vulgarity, Elizabeth bit her tongue in the figurative sense. She had no desire to make an unpleasant situation worse.

Darcy appeared to have no such compunction. "Unacceptable," he said tersely. Turning his back to his uncle, he snatched the book of sonnets from the shelf and pressed it into Elizabeth's hands, then closed the distance between himself and the earl in three long strides. "I have warned you," he said in a low, furious voice. "I will not tolerate your disrespect, nor your insinuations, nor your insults. Miss Bennet does not deserve them, and neither do I. Apologise to my future wife, or from this day forward I shall not know you."

"Come, Darcy," said the earl with a flippant wave of his hand. "Do not be ludicrous! All this damned nonsense over a woman. We are men. We are family—"

"Miss Bennet will become my wife in five days. She will be the mistress of Pemberley—the mother of my children. *She* will be my family."

The sound of coquettish giggling was heard and a woman's voice calling, "Henry? Wherever are you hiding yourself among all these awful books?" A moment later Lady Harrow appeared wearing a catlike grin and a gown better suited to an evening at the opera than a morning in a book shop. Her smile was wiped from her face when she saw Darcy standing toe to toe with Lord Carlisle. Without speaking so much as one word, she averted her eyes and disappeared the way she had come.

Darcy fixed his uncle with a look of loathing so intense his lordship took a step backwards. "You dare to appear in public with that woman!"

"Listen here, Darcy—"

"You dare to insult your *wife*," he whispered harshly, "to injure your *wife*—in so complete and reprehensible a fashion as to flaunt your affair with a woman whose proclivities are so debase and immoral that countless respectable gentlemen refuse to admit her to their homes?"

"Hold your tongue, Nephew," Lord Carlisle warned. "We are friends, Lady Harrow and I—of course, we may be seen together. It means nothing! You can prove nothing!"

"She called you by your Christian name! Last week I watched you collect her in Park Street at an hour far too early for a respectable call! Do you comprehend the damage you have done —the injury you have inflicted upon my aunt? The irreparable harm you have done to your marriage?"

Lord Carlisle's eyes darted around the shop. His mouth was set in a grim line. His colour was heightened. By all appearances, he was incensed. "This is no place to conduct such a conversation. We will send the ladies on their way and reconvene at Carlisle House in half an hour. I would speak to you of your aunt."

"No," said Darcy coldly. "Until you apologise, and until Miss Bennet accepts your apology, you will not find me at leisure to discuss any such topic. I am no longer at your disposal. I am not one of your dogs. I shall not come when you call."

Turning his back to his irate uncle, he extended his hand to Elizabeth. "I apologise, Miss Bennet, for losing my temper."

Elizabeth silently accepted it, lifting her chin as Darcy placed her hand upon his arm and ushered her past Lord Carlisle without so much as a glance.

At the front of the shop, Darcy paid for the book of sonnets and they left. His mien was serious and his anger at his uncle was barely contained, but Elizabeth was at a loss as to what, if anything, she ought to do or say. He pulled her along the crowded street in silence for some time. His long strides made it difficult for her to keep pace with him. It was cold and she was feeling tense as well as tired. When she spied a coffee house looming ahead with a crowd of fashionably attired couples spilling from its entrance, she tugged on his arm. "Come inside, sir. Let us warm ourselves with some chocolate. This pace you are keeping is too brisk, even for me."

After softening his demeanour and uttering an apology, he acquiesced and allowed her to lead him inside the coffee house to a secluded corner of the room, where they claimed a cosy table draped with a crisp, white cloth. There, they would have some privacy, if not necessarily peace. Among the constant buzz of the other patrons, they ordered chocolate and marzipan and cake.

"I am sorry," said Darcy, reaching for her hand beneath the table and giving it a gentle squeeze. "I should never have spoken so candidly to my uncle. I should never have lost my temper. He manages to infuriate me more each time I see him. Today I could barely look at him without my stomach turning. As my uncle, he is owed the lion's share of deference and respect, but I find it increasingly difficult to grant. Despite his position in society, he had no right to say what he did, any of it."

"So, you do not agree with his opinion that I am handsome, then?" she replied, attempting to tease him out of his black mood. She lifted her chocolate to her lips and took a long, satisfying sip as she regarded him over the rim of her cup. It was rich and thick and tasted heavenly. Elizabeth licked her lips.

Darcy smirked at her. "If you are yet unaware of the fact that I consider you to be very beautiful, there is either something greatly remiss with my lovemaking, or I have been sadly misled and you are in actuality a simpleton and not the intelligent, discerning woman I believed you to be."

Elizabeth arched her brow. She had not expected him to tease her, not in such a crowded venue, and certainly not at that moment. "A simpleton, sir?" she repeated indignantly, then laughed, unable to help herself.

Darcy laughed as well. "Forgive me. I could not resist. As handsome as you are, there is far more to you than your physical beauty. While I appreciate that you are so lovely on the outside, it is your inner beauty—your spirit, your compassion, and the intelligent turn of your mind—that made me fall in love with you." He shook his head and frowned. "To my uncle, those qualities are of little significance. What he implied was simply...He is vulgar and crass and void of any sort of gentlemanly principles. I was perfectly serious when I said I will not speak to him unless he delivers an apology to you—one that you see fit to accept. Perhaps not even then."

"That, sir, is entirely up to you," she said gently. "In the meantime, we should speak of pleasanter things than the earl. We were having a delightful time before we met with him and I would like to continue doing so. It is our last day in London. I refuse to give such a wretched, disappointed man the power to ruin it, especially when we have been granted this rare time to spend alone together."

"Pray, forgive me," he said again, reaching for his cup of chocolate. "Of course, I would rather speak to you of pleasanter things. Since we are not in a ballroom, Miss Bennet, I believe we may speak of books. How did you find Mr Hatchard's shop?"

Turning her attention to her plate, Elizabeth smiled. "Very well indeed. Thank you for purchasing the collection of poems. It is a beautiful volume. I could not have asked for a more perfect gift."

"I am gratified to be the one to have purchased it for you, then. Giving you something you desire is a pleasure I plan on repeating many times over the course of our life together."

For the next hour they sipped chocolate and spoke of books. They would eventually have to re-join the Bingleys, the Hursts, and Mrs Lawrence, but for now they were content to pass their last afternoon in London quite pleasantly, if not quite alone.

❧ 37 ❧

WHERE ALL IS WELL, THEN NOT SO WELL AT ALL, BUT THE LAST BIT IS PERFECT.

"How do you like Pemberley, Lizzy?"

Elizabeth linked her arm companionably with her friend's as they followed a manicured gravel path adjacent to the lake. A thin sheet of ice had formed on the lake's surface at the shoreline, where the vast, rolling front lawn met the water. Without warning, a stiff winter gust blew in from the north, buffeted Elizabeth's gown against her legs, and tangled her skirts about her ankles. Startled, she emitted a peal of laughter and held tightly to Mr Ellis's arm until it had passed, then released him to untwist her gown. "I believe I like Pemberley every bit as much as I did the first time I visited, perhaps even more so now that I shall never have to leave." She smiled cheerfully as she reclaimed his arm. "Now you must tell me your impression of my new home, Mr Ellis. Does Pemberley and its beautiful grounds meet with your approval?"

Mr Ellis grinned at her as they resumed their walk along the lake. "I imagine there are very few who would not approve. In all my travels, I cannot recall ever seeing a house so happily situated. Pemberley is truly one of the finest estates I have ever had the pleasure of visiting. I am eager to see more of it. Your Mr Darcy is a man of considerable consequence, far more so than I had initially surmised."

"Now that you have taken his measure," she replied blithely, "I suppose you must wonder what he sees in an impertinent country miss like me?"

"Not at all. Anyone with eyes can see how sincerely he loves you. You are impertinent, yes, but I would wager your frankness must have been a breath of fresh air after passing years in a stale room full of sycophants. No, your staid Mr Darcy is far more pleased by your country manners than he ever was by flattery and flirtation from the first set."

Elizabeth smiled. She had often thought so herself and said, "He is not so staid as you might think, but I do believe you are correct."

"As I often am," he teased. "It is good of him to allow me to walk out with you alone this morning. I had thought he would guard you more closely, especially as you have yet to exchange your vows."

She wrinkled her nose at such a pronouncement. "Mr Darcy is to be my husband, not my keeper. Nor does he begrudge me wanting to spend time with you."

"He is generous."

"He is that, but he is also considerate. He is compassionate and understanding."

Mr Ellis raised an inquisitive brow. "And what pray, does Mr Darcy understand about us?"

"He is not ignorant of our history. He knows he has nothing to fear."

Frowning, Mr Ellis slowed and their leisurely progress along the lake came to a halt. "What did you tell him, Lizzy?"

Biting her lip, she let go of his arm. "I told him how you taught me to ride. I told him about your father." Deciding her confession could use some levity, she admitted, "I told him how you once thought yourself madly, hopelessly in love with Jane."

Mr Ellis rolled his eyes at her silliness. "For shame, Elizabeth Bennet. Should Bingley call me out before supper, I shall know precisely who is to blame."

"You do not know the first thing about it," she insisted with a smile. "Mr Darcy is far too honourable to mention such a thing to his friend. Your secret is safe."

"So is Jane," he replied with a rueful twist of his mouth as he reclaimed her hand and placed it upon his arm. Tugging her forward, they resumed their walk. "Dear Jane. It has been a long time since I have thought of her in such a regard."

Elizabeth looked off towards the lake, where a flock of geese had gathered to primp and preen. "Mr Darcy knows your heart belongs to another. Pray do not be angry with me for telling him. I only wished to ease his mind, to make him understand he has nothing to fear from you. It is my dearest wish that you and he will be friends."

Mr Ellis pressed her hand. "I would like that as well. The Gardiners are especially fond of him, and Bingley and Jane also think highly of him. I understand he intends to settle three thousand pounds on Mary and Kitty."

The lightness Elizabeth felt moments before was replaced by exasperation as she recalled not only Darcy's generosity to Mary and Kitty, but more specifically her mother's insistence that Lydia ought to have something, too. "Mr Darcy is the very best of men, but sometimes he is too good."

Mr Ellis looked at her askance, and she sighed. "While I cannot object to his wanting to improve Mary's and Kitty's prospects, I fail to see how any good would come of his giving Lydia money. Lydia cannot manage it. She cannot even manage to conduct herself as a respectable, married woman! Her husband has abandoned her and left her penniless, yet she has grand ideas of being established in town, with a fine carriage and more pin money than Longbourn's coffers see in a year."

"Despite such aspirations, it sounds as though Mr Darcy has no intention of giving Mrs Wickham three shillings, never mind three thousand pounds. She will go to Longbourn instead and reside there, much as she did before."

"That may be what Mr Darcy, my brother, and my father have agreed to, but my mother does not favour such prudence. She has even gone so far as to recommend that Lydia make her home with us, at Pemberley." The moment the words had left her mother's mouth, Elizabeth had completely lost her composure. She had been appalled by her suggestion; the prospect of Lydia living in the same house with Georgiana absolutely horrified her! She hardly knew how Darcy had kept his temper in check.

Mr Ellis chuckled. "That is not likely to happen. Your Mr Darcy has made it clear he has no intention of keeping her, especially since you are so opposed to the scheme. All will be well, Lizzy. Mrs Wickham will return to Longbourn and the charity and protection of your father, and that will be an end of it. You need not even have her to visit."

"Thank goodness for small favours," she replied dryly.

They walked on for some minutes in companionable silence, slowly making their way back to the manor house. When they were within a hundred feet or so of the family's private entrance, Elizabeth looked up and noticed her mother framed charmingly in a second-storey window, wearing her best morning frock and a frown. Elizabeth forced a cheerful smile to her face and waved.

Mrs Bennet raised her handkerchief and waved it about in an abrupt manner, but instead of returning Elizabeth's smile, her expression became more severe.

A pang of unease settled in Elizabeth's breast. "Mamma does not appear well-pleased. I wonder what could have happened now. It is not yet breakfast."

Rather than commiserate with her, Mr Ellis snorted. "Fear not. She is likely bracing herself for an attack of nerves."

"Dear Mamma," Elizabeth mused. "Whatever shall she do when she has no more daughters to marry off to eligible gentlemen?"

"I daresay she shall go distracted," said her friend. "You are not yet a married woman, though. Until you promise to obey your husband in church, there is still every chance you will abandon propriety and run wild through Derbyshire at my behest, likely sitting astride a hateful horse. Your mother will, of course, conceal the scandal as best she can, but Mr Darcy's servants are not only efficient, but loyal. He will be informed without delay, regret choosing a wilful, impudent girl for his bride, and call off the wedding before your poor mother can call for her salts. After that, I suspect it will be pistols at dawn."

"Certainly not!" she cried with an incredulous laugh. "I refuse to believe that is the case! While I readily admit my mother's fear that I shall run wild through Pemberley's grounds and risk scandalising the servants with my improper comportment is not entirely without merit, she cannot possibly be worried Mr Darcy will refuse to marry me because of it. The marriage articles have been signed. My gown has been pressed. There is nothing more to do but exchange our vows in church."

"Which will happen first thing *tomorrow*. A rational person would take all those things into consideration and arrive at the obvious conclusion, but this is your dear mother we are speaking of, Lizzy. Surely, you must have noticed her unprecedented silence last night when we first arrived."

"I did notice," she confessed, "but I soon arrived at the conclusion that to look a gift horse in the mouth would do no one any favours. My father did not appear to disagree. He was nearly as silent as my mother, though he did not appear to be the least bit cowed by Pemberley's splendour."

"No, but your father never was one for pomp and circumstance. His silence likely has to do with losing you, his favourite child. As for your mother, she certainly overcame her awe quickly enough. If nothing else, you may take comfort in this—she can think of nothing so fitting as a rich gentleman wanting to marry one of her daughters, even if that daughter is you."

Elizabeth swatted his arm and he endeavoured to duck out of reach, laughing all the while. "Goose," she muttered, pretending to be cross. Her quirking lips soon gave way to laughter.

"Consider yourself fortunate. Though your mother mortified you quite thoroughly last night, you were at least spared the indignity of travelling with her. For three days she complained about your father going to London without her, Lydia's misfortunes, Lady Carlisle hosting the wedding breakfast, Lady Catherine haranguing her in her own home. Then there was the usual talk of hems and lace and nerves and countless other nonsense too numerous to name."

Elizabeth could well imagine the severity of her mother's agitation. That her father had gone to London and left her at home would have vexed her mother to no end, but his remaining in town for weeks and enlisting Mr Ellis to escort her and two of their daughters to Pemberley in his stead only increased her vexation. Lady Catherine's visit had made everything worse, but from what Elizabeth understood from Mary and Kitty, her mother had given her ladyship a piece of her own mind as well.

"Was it truly awful?"

"Lizzy, I thought I would run mad. Then we arrived at Pemberley with its long drive and picturesque park and ponds and streams and woods. The farther we advanced into the park, the less your mother had to say. By the time we arrived at the manor house, her eyes had become as round as saucers and she had stopped speaking entirely. Mary felt inclined to remind her to breathe."

"Oh dear," Elizabeth said with a laugh.

Mr Ellis shook his head. "We all knew Mr Darcy was rich, but I believe none of us, aside from you and Bingley and the Gardiners, had any idea he was quite so rich. The reality is staggering. I do believe Pemberley and all its grandeur stripped your poor mother of her previously held opinions." His lips quirked. "And her ability to speak—at least temporarily."

"Let us hope," Elizabeth remarked, "that Mamma shall remember precisely how rich my soon-to-be husband is and say no more on the subject of Mrs Wickham."

From the upstairs window, Mrs Bennet pressed her nose to the glass and attempted to lecture her daughter through it, with little effect.

"Yes," Mr Ellis agreed, laughing as she raised her fist over her head and shook it. "Let us hope."

"Begging your pardon, sir."

Darcy looked up from the pile of correspondence scattered across his desk to acknowledge his butler, then resumed his perusal of the letter in his hand. "Yes, White, what is it?"

"The Earl of Carlisle's carriage has arrived."

Dumbfounded, Darcy raised his head. It was the last thing he expected to hear. "His lordship's carriage is here, at Pemberley?"

"Yes, sir. Lord Carlisle should be ascending the front steps as we speak."

As if on cue, the earl's gruff voice was heard in the foyer. It echoed off the walls and the marble floor as he advanced through the house. "You there," he barked. "Where is my nephew? And do not tell me he is not at home to callers! I will see him now or I will see you dismissed!"

White brought his hands behind his back. "Shall I have the earl's usual rooms prepared, sir?"

Darcy tossed the letter he had been reading onto his desk and ran his hand over his mouth in annoyance. That his uncle had come all the way to Pemberley to speak with him the day before his wedding did not bode well for his equanimity. "No. No. Show him in straight away, else he takes to abusing the staff. If he intends to stay the night, I will inform you."

"As you wish, sir." With a deferential bow, White quit the room. Not ten seconds later he reappeared and announced, "Lord Carlisle to see you, sir."

Pushing his way past White, his lordship entered with a scowl upon his face. "I am not accustomed to chasing anyone across England," he snapped, forgoing the usual pleasantries, "especially my own flesh and blood. What is the meaning of leaving town without so much as a by-your-leave? You and I have unfinished business, or have you forgotten what is owed to me as the head of this family?"

Across the room, the door was shut with a quiet click.

Rather than rising and greeting his uncle properly, Darcy remained seated behind his desk. Steeling himself for the unpleasant conversation that was sure to follow, he looked the earl in the eye and said, "Welcome to Pemberley, Uncle. To what do I owe the unexpected pleasure of your company?"

"My wife," said Lord Carlisle impatiently as he made a vague gesture that encompassed the entire room. "I suppose she is here somewhere, and Richard as well. I should teach him a lesson once and for all and reward his disloyalty with disinheritance, but you would likely take it upon yourself to finance his first circle habits to spite me. Were it not for me, your cousin would be in the poor house begging for his supper, not riding around town in a fancy curricle."

Darcy reclined in his chair.

The earl uttered an expletive under his breath and paced to the window, then back to Darcy's desk, where he glared at the inkwell and the letter-strewn blotter.

"Is there something particular you require of me?" Darcy asked. "I have a letter pertaining to an investment in Manchester that requires my attention and ought not to be put off."

The earl shifted his glare to Darcy. "Despite what you think of my interference in your affairs, I do not want to see you get the short end of the stick in life. I certainly do not want to see you lose half your fortune over some frivolous act of descension. Your father would never forgive me."

Darcy made no reply.

The earl narrowed his eyes with a contemptuous snort. "And now I am to get the silent treatment, for I dare not hope you have seen the error of your ways and are attempting to pay me my due!" He pursed his lips and resumed his pacing between the desk and the window. Suddenly, he stopped. "Speaking of my due, my wife *is* here. You may as well admit it. I have already checked everywhere else."

"She is," Darcy replied after a moment. "Unless Lady Carlisle indicates otherwise, she will continue to be my guest for the foreseeable future. Regardless of your ire, I shall not turn her out."

He had expected his uncle to become angrier after his admission, but Lord Carlisle merely grunted non-committally, waved a dismissive hand, and claimed a tufted leather chair before Darcy's desk. "I am not concerned about your aunt. She may stay at Pemberley for as long as she likes. She will come home eventually, either to London or to Levens Hall. She knows Lady Harrow is like all the others—a distraction, a way for me to amuse myself for a time, nothing more. Virginia is simply cross over her friend's betrayal, just as Lady Harrow is cross with her for failing to promote her daughter. They shall both get over it, and sooner than later. Women always do whenever they are offered something else that they want." He paused and levelled Darcy with a severe look that could not be misinterpreted. "You must know you are about to make the biggest mistake of your life."

"By mistake, I take it you mean marrying Miss Bennet. I have already told you I intend to make her my wife. Nothing has changed. The marriage articles have been signed. Her family is at Pemberley. We marry tomorrow. There is no undoing what has already been done. It is too late for that now."

"Nonsense!" the earl insisted. "There is nothing that money cannot fix. A clever girl like Miss Bennet cannot be insensible of the way the world operates. You had your fun with her, but now you must be prudent! You must choose a woman of your own station, from your own sphere! A woman so far beneath you will only damage Georgiana's prospects. If you marry her, she will never be fully accepted by your friends. Even your wealth and consequence cannot buy her admittance to Almack's."

Darcy refrained from mentioning that he could not care less about Almack's. If Elizabeth felt inclined to dance, he had friends enough in Bingley's set and a few at his club who would welcome them, regardless of his voucher being revoked by Lady Sefton. As for Georgiana, she had expressed nothing but joy for his choice.

"Where will you go?" demanded the earl. "Who will you see? No one of consequence, that is for certain."

"As I have mentioned on prior occasions, your ideas of who and what constitutes good company are not in accord with my own."

"Given time," said the earl with a disagreeable twist of his mouth, "that will change. I doubt it shall take long, perhaps a year or two before you come to resent the girl. You have known superior society all your life, but Miss Bennet and her inferior relations will force you lower. She will spend your money, flirt with your friends, and give no thought to the indignities you must suffer for the sake of having her. The chit will punish you for her own inferiority! When the children come, she will lose her figure and her allure. You will seek your pleasure elsewhere and she will grow bitter. Her pretty face will become as ugly as her temperament! I have seen it before. If you elevate this upstart, you will live to regret it."

Darcy struggled to rein in his temper. "What I regret," he said in a low, furious voice, "is paying you the courtesy of informing you of my intentions regarding Miss Bennet. What I regret," he continued, rising from his chair and splaying his hands firmly upon his desk, "is paying you the deference and respect I was taught to believe you were owed as my mother's brother."

Lord Carlisle's hand came down heavily upon the desk. "I am a damned earl, boy, and you would do well to remember what I am owed! I am owed your deference! I am owed your respect! I am owed your loyalty and obedience and you damn well better start paying me my due!"

"What you are owed and what you deserve, are by no means one and the same. You are a member of the peerage—deference must be given with regard for your station. As for respect, I am no longer of the opinion that you deserve it. Respect is not something you are born with. Respect must be earned. It must be deserved. You have done nothing to deserve mine, and even less to earn it."

"You have become an insolent, ungrateful whelp," Lord Carlisle hissed as he rose from his chair in a rage. "If your father could see you now, he would drag you behind the stable and take a horse whip to you!"

"My father," Darcy replied as furiously, "would recognise I am a grown man and not some errant schoolboy! He would respect my choice! He would welcome Miss Bennet to his family and embrace her as his daughter and see you thrown from his house!"

"George Darcy would do nothing of the sort! I became his brother when he married your mother! I have had admittance to Pemberley before you were even a glimmer in your father's eye!"

"As of today, you shall no longer have that privilege." Darcy stalked to the bell pull and gave it a savage tug. "I am Pemberley's master. Miss Bennet will soon become its mistress. You have persisted in disparaging and insulting us both and interfering with my personal affairs to a reprehensible degree. I will not tolerate your disrespect, either at Pemberley or in town. Should we meet again, I shall not acknowledge you.

"I strongly suggest you also rethink your philosophy regarding women and their worth. No woman enjoys being belittled, dismissed, and ignored. No woman enjoys knowing her husband has sought the favours of other women. She enjoys it even less when those women are her friends."

The earl's countenance turned an alarming shade of crimson. "You dare presume to lecture me on how to handle women? How many have you known in your lifetime? How many have you bedded!"

Disgusted, Darcy strode to the door. He yanked it open to find his man White flanked by a veritable army of liveried footmen.

Darcy was too angry to be impressed by his foresight. "See to it that his lordship is escorted to his carriage without delay. He has pressing business that will prevent him from returning to Pemberley for the foreseeable future."

"Very good, sir. This way if you please, my lord."

Surrounded by no less than a dozen men, the earl glared at his nephew. "There will come a day when you shall regret disregarding my counsel, Darcy. There will come a day when you shall regret your choice!"

"Speaking it will not make it true." He nodded to White, who in turn signalled the two largest footmen.

Lord Carlisle appeared close to suffering an apoplectic fit. "Lay so much as a finger on me," he threatened, "and I will see you hanged from the gallows!" He spun on his heels and stalked from the room, slamming the door behind him.

"What a shame," murmured the countess that evening as she sat beside Darcy in the music room examining the lace on her gloves. "To think Henry came all the way from London and I missed him! Perhaps next time he will think before he speaks... or travels three days in a carriage on a fool's errand. Then again, he is an old dog. To think he can learn to behave any better at this point would go against the laws of nature." Smiling affectionately, she patted Darcy's arm. "I am glad you are getting married tomorrow, Nephew. Unlike your uncle, you show all the promise of being a good husband. Trust me, your wife shall thank you for it, and thank you well."

Beside her, Mrs Lawrence concurred. She uttered some nonsense about lovemaking and sea bathing to Lady Carlisle and both ladies erupted into girlish laughter.

Darcy rolled his eyes and turned his attention to Elizabeth and Georgiana, charmingly situated at the pianoforte playing a duet. Tomorrow the two would become sisters. The thought of Elizabeth, whom he had loved for so long, becoming his wife filled Darcy with such anticipation he could barely sit still. To distract himself, he looked around the room, where he saw Bennets and Bingleys and Gardiners and Fitzwilliams seated upon his couches and chairs. There were smiles on their faces, and laughter on their lips. There were murmured conversations, and the delighted voices of Robert and Emily Gardiner, who had been granted the rare treat of remaining with the rest of the family past their bedtime. Filling Pemberley with children—Elizabeth's children—was Darcy's dearest wish after marrying her in Pemberley's chapel.

His eyes, as they often did, returned to her. She looked lovely; she always looked lovely. Darcy ached to go to her, to touch her and kiss her and tell her how very happy she had made him by agreeing to become his wife.

As though she had discerned his thoughts, Elizabeth chose that moment to look up from the pianoforte, where her fingers were moving with a practiced ease along the keys. Their eyes met, and they shared a private moment from across the room, one of many they would undoubtedly share over the course of their life together.

Darcy's heart swelled with love for her.

Tomorrow could not come soon enough.

⚜

"Have I told you," Darcy murmured in her ear, "how beautiful you look this evening, Mrs Darcy?" They were man and wife and had been so for most of the day. Darcy could barely contain his smile.

"You are off to a fine start," said his wife as her fingers toyed with his impeccably tied cravat. "I do not believe I have ever received so many compliments from you before. Take care, Mr Darcy, or my vanity shall soon grow accustomed to it."

"Elizabeth," he said, drawing a tremulous breath as her fingertips grazed his jaw, then his ear. "You are driving me mad. Please let me kiss you."

They were ensconced in a curtained alcove not ten feet from the dining room, where their relations—fifteen in total, save for the children—were enjoying a repast of cold meats, seasonal fruits, cheeses, pies, and cakes. Laughter spilled from the room and carried through the hall—Georgiana's and Anne's as boisterous and merry as any of the Bennets'.

Elizabeth wound her arms around Darcy's neck and stood on the tips of her toes. "You need not ask my permission, Husband. After all, I did promise just this morning to obey you."

Darcy's eyelids fluttered closed as she pressed a soft, teasing kiss to the corner of his mouth, his jaw, and his ear. His hands slid from her waist to the swell of her hips. Her body, so perfectly situated against his own, warmed him in ways he dared not consider at present. "You are quite right," he murmured. "From now on, I shall employ my time much better."

This kiss was not their first as man and wife, but it was by far their most passionate. All day long they had snuck off to out-of-the-way places—deserted halls and unused rooms. Darcy was growing frustrated with having to steal kisses from his wife in his own house. What he wanted was to sweep her into his arms, carry her upstairs, and take her to bed.

The Chippendale clock in the foyer struck nine o'clock.

"Come with me," he whispered hoarsely against her lips. He grasped her hand tightly and tugged her towards the staircase in a haze of desire.

Elizabeth glanced self-consciously around the foyer as they crossed it with alacrity. "Fitzwilliam, we have guests."

He raised her hand to his lips and kissed it. "They will still be here tomorrow when we break our fast."

"Surely, we cannot abandon them," she said with an incredulous laugh. "Whatever will they think?"

At the foot of the grand staircase, he stopped and turned to look at her. Wrapped in dove-grey silk and adorned with pearls, she took his breath away. In the candlelight, her skin looked almost luminous. Her eyes sparkled. Her hair was arranged in an elaborate style his fingers itched to take down. Darcy had never seen her looking more beautiful. Unlike their clandestine meeting in the back hall of the Meryton assembly rooms nearly two months ago, there was no pang of desperation within him; there was no uncertainty. Now he felt all the satisfaction of knowing Elizabeth was finally *his*.

So many prejudices, misconceptions, and misunderstandings had come between them in the last twelve months, but one fateful April day had set them on a new course. It had been the catalyst they needed to understand one another better. Darcy's affection, unswerving, faithful, and true, had been there almost from the beginning; it had taken much longer for Elizabeth's dislike of him to take a more proper form and blossom into love.

Nearly overwhelmed by his love for her, Darcy closed the distance between them and gently, tenderly touched his forehead to hers. "They will think," he told her with considerable emotion, "that I am ardently, passionately in love with my wife and never wish to be parted from her."

Darcy heard Elizabeth's breath catch and felt the gentle pressure of her hand upon his chest, just over his heart. He felt the warmth of her body and inhaled her sweet, heady scent. She was so close that not even a hairsbreadth remained between them. If they were in his bedchamber, hidden away behind a locked door, he would peel her gown from her body and kiss her senseless. He would touch her and taste her and worship her in every way a husband who is passionately, violently in love with his wife is wont to do.

A lump formed in his throat.

Elizabeth clasped his hand more tightly. One slender finger traced the gleaming gold band on the third finger of his left hand. "It is well, then," she whispered feelingly, and encouraged him up the staircase with a kiss.

The End

The author and Quills & Quartos Publishing thank you for your purchase of this book. We hope you will consider leaving a review.

Subscribers to the Quills & Quartos newsletter receive advance notice of sales as well as bonus excerpts, deleted scenes, and other exclusive content. You can sign up on our web site at www.QuillsandQuartos.com. Thank you!

ACKNOWLEDGMENTS

I began writing this story so many years ago that I lost count, at a time when the world felt normal. This year, Zoom meetings, home schooling, and online grocery shopping were made far more bearable by having this story to tell; but *Misunderstandings & Ardent Love* would never have come to fruition without the dedication and persistence of my wonderful editors at Quills & Quartos.

My heartfelt thanks to Jan Ashton, who was merciless but kind when it came to chopping this story down from over 145,000 words to something more manageable and realistic, and to Kristi Rawley, who obsessed over semicolons and sentence structure, and did not hold back when I nearly 'daresay-ed' her to death! Because of you, everything is tied up very prettily (and properly) with a big, satin bow.

Thank you also to Amy D'Orazio, whose supportive words and warm persona always shine through, even in her emails. You lit a fire under me, and told me to design the cover, and I appreciate those things more than I can say.

Finally, thank you to my family, from my husband and daughter, who put up with late suppers and my mantra of 'Wait—I need ten more minutes...', to my in-laws, who still have no idea who Elizabeth Bennet is, but who have never failed to stand behind me and offer their support.

ABOUT THE AUTHOR

When she was five, Susan Adriani wanted to be an opera singer, but changed her mind when she realised she would have to perform in front of an audience instead of her bedroom mirror. She attended art school instead and became a graphic designer who spends more time writing stories and researching the social niceties of Regency England than she does cleaning her house. She has a teenage daughter who dearly loves to laugh, and a handsome husband who is not the least bit intimidated by Mr Darcy. She makes her home in New England, and cannot imagine a world without books, Google maps, copious amounts of tea, or Jane Austen.

ALSO BY SUSAN ADRIANI

The Truth About Mr Darcy

A sexy, compelling *Pride & Prejudice* 'what if'—perfect for fans of *Death Comes to Pemberley*.

The truth always has consequences...

Mr Darcy has a dilemma. Should he tell the truth about his old nemesis George Wickham in order to protect the good citizens of Meryton from Wickham's lies and deceits? Doing so will force Darcy to reveal family secrets that he'd prefer never come to light. The alternative is keeping the man's criminal nature to himself and hoping he leaves the area before doing significant harm.

But as Wickham's attentions to Elizabeth increase, Darcy knows if he's to win the one woman he's set his heart on, he's going to have to make one of the most difficult decisions of his life. And what he ultimately does sets in motion a shocking train of events neither he nor Elizabeth could possibly have predicted.

Made in the USA
Middletown, DE
10 September 2022

10053659R00281